MELDED

Melded

JENNIE ELAINE

Ink & Quill Press

For more excellent works of fiction, visit Inkandquillpress.com

Dedications

Dedicated to Jan, my partner in crime from the first drafts to the
bitter, revised end.
This book is as much my success as it is yours. Thank you for all your
editing, care, and dedication.
To Hillary, who begged me to write Gen and Simon's story from the
beginning.
May this decision forever haunt you.
To my husband, Dakota, for his overwhelming support and sacrifices.
Thank you for everything you do.
To my grandmother, for her lifelong investments in my interests and
well-being.
Lastly, to every reader who takes part in this journey.
Melded was for me, but *Merged* will be for you.

Ippum del Haliz Fundir
"Island of Haliz Fundir"
Gen says Asterell is based on a name. meaning "To Arms"
Asterell
DO NOT GO HERE!!!
No humans allowed in north
Western Woods
Eastern Woods
Entrell Jor
Lit. "The Eastern Hold"
Torrel Del Tor
Torrel
Lit. "The Center"
The center of the center
New Caramel
Lit. "Ocean Touched"
Ét Sporrel
FARM! FARM FARM
Southern territory human-friendly. good soil for farming calmer seas, good for fishing
FISH FISH FISH
Gen was here

Day One

Chapter One

Jorel, Chelsea's Labs

The wind was whispering down the mountain the night
I sold Jask to his death. It followed alongside the darkened
path our entire journey, a fourth soul heading towards the
abyss. There was no coming back from this the same. Not for
me, not for Jask, and not for the island we called home.

The wind slipped through the leaves, caressed my skin,
and breathed a promise into my ears.

Tomorrow, it said, *tomorrow changes everything.*

Tonight, though, I had a payment come due.

We couldn't risk riding out on deer, so we'd made the
trek on foot. It hadn't been easy following the lesser-traveled
footpaths down the hillside, but it was necessary. Leaving the
city in the dead of night in black cloaks and no lantern was
suspicious enough, returning with three deer and one less
rider too much so.

I may have set out to sell a man's life, but there was
no reason to sacrifice a perfectly fine deer in the process. So
we'd walked.

Vaga had yet to speak to me the entire journey. Her
silence was familiar, if not a little heavier than usual. Her large,
imposing form was absent of footfall or sound, and it was only
the hollow outline of her scarred face in the moonlight that

reminded me she was even there. I kept my own steps silent as well, avoiding the worst of the branches and blending with the wind. I had been hunting in the Torrelian woods since I was a child, and we had both found our place in the battles up north. The forest was as familiar to us as our own skin.

Jask crashed through the underbrush like a child. If there was a root to catch, his foot found it. If there was a stone to kick he met it. If there was a drop to avoid he stepped blindly into it and went tumbling in a tangle of uncoordinated limbs. He'd fallen more times than he'd taken a successful step. If we'd had any need for complete silence on our journey, he'd long blown our cover.

Not even the wild animals came this close to the labs, though. We were as good as alone in the world.

The building loomed before us like a tomb. It was three stories high, and in the darkness the tan bricks and single pane windows became silver mirrors on a black, inky canvas. It was a boxy human thing, more for function than form. Their architecture was always lacking, but this place especially so. No lights were on in the upper floors, telling me the doctor was haunting the basement. The dilapidated fence around the property was more a formality, and we slipped through a large gap with no troubles. Even Jask managed it without hitting himself on anything.

Before us a painted metal door loomed against the stone siding. A sour taste filled my mouth. We were here, but it was anywhere else I wanted to be.

All three of us seemed to pause, no one moving forward. The heavy, silent air of the labs weighed on us like mist.

"Jask," I said in our own tongue, "let the good doctor know we're here."

At my order Jask's head was bobbing up and down so violently I was expecting his chin to smack his chest. It was all he could do to turn and scramble over himself to the door, pressing a silent buzzer in four short, timed notes.

Vaga waited until he was out of earshot, the wind carrying our voices away from him.

"Why would that witch accept him as payment?" She asked. It was the first thing she'd said all night.

I couldn't help a snort of laughter.

"You've been begging me to let you kill him for months," I mused, "Why wouldn't anyone else want the honors?"

Her good eye narrowed.

"You know what I'm asking. For everything she has given you, what value does he hold to her? I don't trust this. His life doesn't ring a fair price. He's *useless*."

"He's devout." I said.

He is *useless,* I thought. *She might have a point.* Not that I hadn't already considered this.

Vaga let me continue.

"Does it matter why she agreed? She asked for his life as payment, and we need her work. His death at her hands will be invaluable for the cause."

"You assume she aims to kill him."

I kept my face even. Forced my arms to my sides instead of crossing my chest protectively. I had never seen an animal kill for fun, only survival. But I had witnessed the doctor pull creatures into states worse than death for no reason other than the sake of her ability to do so. Of course, she had justifications, but they were paper thin and she hardly believed them herself.

Ashley Chelsea existed only to push the boundaries of her own cruelty.

It sickened me.

It enraptured me.

"His life is a fair price to pay," I said evenly, "for what her work affords us."

"It's too fair a price to pay. You never should have done dealings with her." Vaga argued.

"It's too late for that now."

"Humans cannot be trusted," she hissed, "this one especially so."

"There are worse things than humans threatening us," I said firmly, turning to face her full on. "Or have you forgotten, Vaga?"

Her scar shone silver in the moonlight. I saw her jaw tense, the muscles moving strangely against the torn flesh from her oldest and worst wound.

"No, Reid Jorel." She said at last.

"All the same," I said, turning back in time to see the metal door open from the inside, "They will also be dealt with accordingly."

If I survive the night, I silently added to myself.

Vaga said nothing at first, then turned away from the labs.

"I won't enter her space." She said.

"I won't ask you to. Vaga," I added, "if I don't return, carry on without me tomorrow."

Her eye narrowed again, a thousand arguments boiling to the surface, and then she took a few steps away towards the woods. She was an excellent second. Capable, willing to be my foil and counter my thoughts, but in the end she knew her place and would follow me to the bloody, bitter end.

We both knew there was no point in saying it. We needed my knowledge of Haliz and the work of the doctor *both*. Without one or the other, everything would fall apart. The lives of thousands rested on the whim of the only human I had the sense to fear.

We also knew that giving orders grounded me, so she'd let me say it. If I didn't come back up those stairs, anyway, it wouldn't be my problem if she followed those orders or not.

From the dark stairway beyond, Dr. Ashley Chelsea emerged. The wind seemed to still in her presence. The moonlight disappeared behind a cloud. My island shrunk away from her like prey back into its burrow.

Humans were not incapable of higher thought, I'd found, but they rarely seemed to use it in any useful capacity. At best, they were an annoyance. At worst, they were a parasite. An unfortunate addition to the ecosystem of our lives. Annoying, but nothing of major concern.

And then there was this one.

Her hair was a short but wild tangle of color the humans called red. She was tiny, even by human standards, with a girlish look that hid her age. I had never once seen her out of a lab coat.

Her eyes were as pale and sharp as any predator I had faced on the island.

The larger the animal, the more dangerous the hunt. Wisdom my father gave me on our first hunting trip.

Standing before the demure Doctor Chelsea, those words had never been so wrong. I could feel her presence like a knife to the base of my spine. It took every ounce of my will to fight my survival instinct and keep from running into the night.

I dwarfed her in size and muscle, and I had years of practice in the north taking a variety of opponents in a fight. Instinct told me none of it mattered. If this woman decided to attack me, I knew she would win.

She looked around Jask with a soft, pleasant smile. We stared each other down. Every pass of her eyes was emotionless, absorbent.

Dr. Ashley Chelsea took you in like a book; she observed you, witnessed you, read through your pages and made her own notes in the margins. She had never employed empathy in her short, miserable life. She lacked the very thing humans called *humanity*. She held a passionate, measured desire for consumption and destruction. Her core was built upon an animalistic need to tear apart the world with hands and teeth held dutifully in check by a simple, feminine facade.

I feared her. I feared her almost as much as I feared Sol, or the truth my mother refused to see.

Chelsea less so *feared* me than recognized the numbers and weight of the devout in my employ. Through that came something between us thicker than understanding but thinner than respect. Moreso it was a mutual nod towards the benefits gained from cooperation. She was, as anyone was, a tool in my employ; however, she was one tool with a mind of its own and wickedly sharp teeth.

I hoped it was enough to force her into keeping her word, and letting me leave with her work and my life.

"*You're late,*" She said sweetly, speaking in her native human tongue. "*It's unlike you to be this messy, Jorel. Nervous about tomorrow?*"

I didn't take her bait.

"*Traveling with Jask is never a linear path.*"

Jask looked between us, unable to understand our words but hearing his name like a pet. A twig fell from behind his ear. Chelsea laughed, a sound that was far too cheery and sweet to come from her. She stepped to the side, letting Jask through.

"*Step into my office?*"

She invited us in, moving her hand in a way that gave me a clear view of the long black stick in it. Jask was already hurrying down the steps, taking them two at a time in his haste to finish our business with her. I shouldn't have been surprised that she was already armed.

"*Ladies first.*"

Her face twisted into a sickening, gleeful grin.

"What a gentleman," she said, granting me the favor of going down the dark cement steps first and allowing me the high ground.

As the door swung shut behind me, I could almost feel Vaga's stare on my back. It felt every bit like walking willingly into the den of a predator.

A flashing memory of my father, the late hunter, passed my mind. I pushed it away with prejudice.

The first room off the stairs was alight and waiting for us. Jask hadn't opened the heavy door far enough, leading to the knob scraping his stomach while he tried to side-step through. His tail nearly caught as it closed behind him. Chelsea pushed it open with ease.

I stepped into the room behind her. The stench of fear permeated the lab we stood in, having sunk deep into the walls and floor from her years of work. The room was bleak enough without it. Cracked green tiles. Yellow electric lights. Smooth, organized counters and cabinetry, all of human design. A tension so thick it pulsed like an artery. I'd only felt this feeling once before, facing down the very cave my father lost his life in.

A predator lived here, and she'd taken many, many lives.

Jask had slipped further into the room, pressing his back to a counter and trying to keep his eyes on Chelsea. The electric lighting did nothing for his looks. He was a sorry sight of a kriest, lean and gangly with ears just too long and eyes just too wide. His tail was a threadbare bony thing that never stilled. His whole body was a perpetual twitch of nerves. He would have been tall, but he seemed eternally caved into him-self, granting a far shorter stature. When he spoke, it was a miracle if he got anything out without his teeth clacking.

He was in dark leggings that didn't quite fit so as to hang in odd folds and the crimson tunic wrappings of a butcher's apprentice. He had hung a meek black cloak from his shoulders, held in place with a pin of the city guard I suspected he had stolen. The pin was dull and tarnished, nearly unrecognizable as the motif of the great bear, another unkempt trinket from a helplessly unkempt man. Stray leaf bits and dark woodland dirt clung to his entire outfit in wiped-back patches.

He eyed Chelsea like a cornered animal. I guess these last two months working under her employ hadn't warmed him up to her any.

She reveled in the silence, and then her painted red lips split in a wide, unassuming smile.

"I'm surprised you brought him here yourself," she addressed me. Her boots clicked against the tile while she circled slowly around me. The long black stick she held remained relaxed at her side. I set my back to a wall. *"I didn't think you'd risk your own well being so close to the finish line."*

"Usually your threats are better veiled, Chelsea."

"It's more an observation of how dangerous the woods can be at night," she waved her empty hand, giving me another smile. Her voice came out a conspiratory whisper. *"I heard there's* bears *on the island."*

"There's plenty of monsters on the island."

From her laugh, I knew she understood I meant her as well.

"I admire your wit, Jorel. I'm going to miss our little talks, now that this transaction is coming to an end."

I detested our little talks.

"I don't rightfully care what you admire about me."

"I admire how many lives you have *and* will *take in the name of* the greater good. *Your mind is a fascinating place."*

"No great leader is without sacrifice." I said, slipping into the same moral debate she always put me in. It was almost

ironic, as I didn't believe the woman to have morals, that she always wanted to explore mine.

She smiled disarmingly at Jask, now huddled against the wall beside me. He visibly shrank at her gaze, but made no move to leave.

"As a leader," she asked, her voice low and decidedly less chipper, *"how are you feeling about this one?"*

"It is the only decided path to our continued survival."

"The only decided path, or the only path you've decided?"

My patience grew thin at her toying.

"What do you care? You're getting paid either way."

"Can't I enjoy this one last conversation with a friend?" She asked me, pouting like a child. It was her carefully curated mask slipping back into place. She almost looked normal for a moment.

Almost.

"We aren't friends."

"If not friends after all these months, then what?"

I wanted out of there. I wanted to be done with this whole sordid, bloody transaction. Some small and long forgotten part of me was begging for me to turn around and forget this whole mess. It argued that things could change without revolution and bloodshed. That I could buy into my mother's words and believe in peace and negotiation.

But it was just the wish of a child, desperate to continue clinging to his mother's skirts. The world had changed me, hardened me to fantasy and opened my eyes to the true threats my people faced. Threats my mother refused to act against. Threats *anyone* refused to act against.

"What are we doing here tonight, Reid Jorel?"

In my silence after Chelsea's question, Jask had quietly slipped his own in.

His wide, sunken eyes stared up into mine. A lifetime of complacency stood before me, and it steeled my resolve. I'd done my damndest to ensure he knew it was a high honor to accompany me tonight. His eyes had been so wide, so enraptured. Jask ate every pile of shit I fed him by the sickening, silver spoonful. He was, in that way, my favorite disciple. He'd never had an original thought in his useless, vapid head. He was nothing but a puppet begging for strings. It made him loyal, but it also made him weak.

I would never be weak again. Someone needed to step up and change things. We couldn't afford to wait for anyone else to do it. It had to be me, and it had to be decided here, tonight, in this very room. It was bloody. Almost unforgivable. But it needed to be done.

I would do it.

I turned to him, covering his meek shoulder with my hand. I swear I saw stars dance behind his eyes at the honor.

"The most important thing you've ever done in your life," I answered. "Our very goal, everything you and I and the rest of the Kor have worked for these last months, it all comes down to this. I've asked the impossible of you so many times, Jask. Yet you've always delivered. Now, I'm out of the impossible, and all I can ask of you is one final job."

I steadied my eyes to his, leaning forward and lowering my voice.

"Are you prepared?"

A sense of purpose, reverie, and wonder overtook his dusty green eyes. It was not deserved.

"Anything for you, Reid Jorel."

Then it is anything I will ask, I thought, squeezing his shoulder.

I stepped back, motioning to the far door in the room. He had to step past Chelsea to enter the space, towards the dark horrors of her labs beyond, and that was a journey he would make alone.

"Lead us forward, Jask."

Almost frozen by the request, he took one step. Another. Turned his back to me and strode with uncoordinated limbs and an inflated sense of purpose to the door's archway. I even saw his back straighten a bit. He turned to face me once more.

"S-Sanra, Reid Jorel," he stuttered, practically falling over himself to give a hasty bow in my direction. His ass jutted at an awkward angle when he bent forward, hitting the not-quite closed door on its edge and bouncing himself forward a half step. His face flushed red, and then he turned away, to the darkness beyond.

To his death.

Jask made it one step into the next room when Chelsea turned. In less than a heartbeat she raised the long black stick, pulling a lever at the end. It emitted a high, horrible sound, filling the room in an electrical shriek. Before Jask could even register the noise Chelsea advanced and jabbed the business end straight into the small of his back.

His entire gangly frame straightened, jerked, and dropped to the ground. Chelsea's electric weapon followed him down, digging into his flesh. Electricity coursed through him in a way I had never before witnessed. The room filled with the high pitched whine of the machine and a shrieking so guttural and animalistic I didn't recognize it as Jask at first. It was uncontrollable spasms of his lungs that produced the sounds that escaped. Piss flowed into his leggings and spotted the floor. Pain was etched on his face as it contorted tightly from the attack. His eyes were squeezed shut, his teeth bared, and then suddenly there was nothing.

His body still jerked from the current but it didn't fight the attack. Chelsea pressed down for a moment longer than necessary before turning off the weapon. Jask lay fully limp, rendered unconscious. The smell of burnt flesh came off his back.

I'd made myself watch. I had put him there. And for that decision, I hadn't turned away.

Actions have consequences, and this was now my burden to bear. This and so, so many others.

Chelsea stood watching him as well. I couldn't see her face as her back was still turned to me, but there was something in the tilt of her head that felt unnatural. Predatory. Satiated. It sickened me. It didn't bear further thought.

"*Tomorrow,*" I said into the silent room, "*Will you have everything in place?*"

"*I already do,*" she replied smoothly, satisfaction in her voice. She turned to face me. The weapon didn't leave her hand, but her finger was off the trigger. "*I take pride in my work,* Priest Jorel."

I narrowed my eyes at the wording.

"Priest *is not a translation of the station I will become. I will become* Reid. *A man who speaks your religious texts is a far cry from one who holds the power of* Haliz Fundir."

She shrugged.

"*Fitting enough for a man who thinks himself a god.*"

"*Charming, coming from a woman who thinks herself above one.*"

"*There is no God,*" she said, "*not here, not in this world.*"

"*So you just waltzed into the vacancy?*"

Her eyes flashed, then her teeth. A smile.

"*Should I thank you for the opportunity?*"

"*You would be* nothing *without the research I have offered you.*"

She snorted.

"*You* are *nothing without the results I have delivered to you.*"

"Then see that they are delivered." I cut her off, moving away from the wall.

Jask's body lay still in an uncoordinated heap beneath her feet. His lungs drew in small, shallow breaths.

Alive, then. For now.

"Do you ever feel remorse for what you've given me?" She suddenly asked, as casually as someone might say *do you think it's going to rain?* We both knew she wasn't just talking just about Jask. *"Are you ever kept awake at night, haunted by the work you've funded?"*

"No," I said, halfway to honesty.

"No?"

"No." I repeated, turning to face her full on.

She was not intimidated. She sneered in glee at my reaction.

"Because you always do what needs to be done?"

I stared in her eyes, strengthened by my renewed purpose in my plan.

"Because after tomorrow, I will have done what everyone else was too afraid to do, and succeeded.*"*

She watched my face, let loose a surprised bark of laughter, shook her head, then turned away. She stepped over Jask's prone body and into the next room, breaking the tense spell between us.

Casually, she called back to me.

"Your beasts will be ready on time, as promised. I await the word. Goodbye, Reid *Jorel."*

The room swallowed her in darkness, and with an effort I saw Jask's body lift and his legs be dragged in after her. The door swung slowly, slowly closed.

I left without a backwards glance, knowing my final gambit in tomorrow's plan was finally paid and secure. Everything was laid out before me in a perfect line. All that was left to gather was Gen.

Fortunately for me, he was nothing if not predictable.

The wind greeted me again when I left. The island was no more changed from Jask's fate than a river cared for a stone taken from its banks.

Vaga didn't ask. Perhaps the truth of what happened in that room was on my face. Or perhaps she was happy to let it stay a mystery. She watched me approach, and then turned to follow me, her silence a familiar friend.

"Tomorrow," I said, "await my word on the bridge. Have the twins in place. Everything is aligned."

"Sanra, Reid Jorel." She said, and nothing more.

A hollow, empty ringing filled my ears where Jask's screams had resided. It would be the first scream of many to haunt me, soon enough. I settled the weight of my choices on my shoulders and began the dark journey home. Tomorrow night, it would all be worth it.

I would do what needed to be done.

Chapter Two

Gen, Torrel Del Tor

It would have been easier for her to just admit I was a hopeless failure from the start. Instead, Mael held on to the delusion that I was someone better. That I wasn't a coward.

It made moments like these so much worse.

I was frozen in place, my hands gripping the windowsill, ready to propel me out of the room. I'd nearly been clear, but the unmistakable noise of Mael clearing her throat stopped me short. I could have ignored her, but I was never so bold.

Our eyes met over my shoulder. If I had expected to see disapproval, or even exasperation, in her face, I was let down. Reid Mael *never* looked down on others. Sometimes that was far, far worse.

She stared at me. I stared back.

It was too dark to see the rest of my room, the sparse furniture turning into undefined shadows and shapes between us, but the low blue light from the window illuminated her perfectly. It caught the wild mass of whitening curls she had yet to tame that day, followed the low line of her ears and traced the cross of her arms. I could still clearly make out the angle of her hips, propped against the door frame, settling her into the space.

Her eyebrows raised. A silent challenge.

I should have left earlier. It was one thing if she had caught me halfway down my five story climb. It was another entirely to be caught before the point of no return.

I prayed this could be one of those times where she just admonished me wordlessly. Mael had always been able to speak volumes in simple silence. I prayed for it today.

"Gen," she said, crushing my last hope of escape, "I could use your hands with the dough this morning."

I squirmed inside. My whole body ached to run. I've been doing that for nearly a year now. It was so tempting to fall away into the morning air and flee from Mael, the temple, everything again. Just like yesterday. Just like tomorrow.

I couldn't do that. Not now. I may be a coward, but I'd never had the courage to say no to her face. It was hard enough to step around her in silence, it was impossible to do it with words. To her I was never a disappointment, only a student who was failing as part of some grander lesson.

And I was so tired of learning.

"....Just the dough?" I asked, not moving from my position. She clicked her tongue and motioned to me in one fell swoop.

"In that outfit? I can hardly have you help with the blessings in that, can I?"

I was wearing my running clothes, the light shirt wrapping that exposed my stomach, the scarf tied twice over and under my ears to push my hair away from my face, the leggings that allowed for freedom of movement.

"What blasphemy. The congregation would think I've gone mad."

"They already think you've gone mad." She snorted. "If only they knew the half of it."

Ache flickered in my chest. There she was, watching my latest attempt to flee every responsibility of my life, *again*, and she'd just fallen right back into the way she'd always spoken to me. It was comfortable, playful, even. She had never been anything but honest with me without any grandeur or show.

"Gen," she said softly, "It's a ceremony day. Come help with the rolls? I won't ask for more."

I couldn't help a glance at my hand. It looked almost blue in the light, but there was nothing special to see. My skin was smooth, unbroken. The ring of scars just below my elbows were almost indistinguishable now. Most days, I could almost pretend nothing had ever happened.

Mael had given me my time and space. The least I could do was give her this. I slipped back into the room.

"I can spare time to help with the rolls," I conceded, and earned myself a smile on her familiar face. It wasn't a smile of victory, but of almost relief.

"I'll have you out in time for your run," she promised, "You need your time to breathe."

The temple needs me more, I kicked myself, falling in step behind her. *I'm sorry I can't be here for it.*

The familiar halls of the temple unfolded before us, illuminated by already lit lanterns along the wall. They cast their glow on the gray stone and threw shadows behind the rich tapestries hung between the windows. We walked past temple history and island lore embroidered on the fabrics. A two headed Kreist to symbolize the meld. Haliz Fundir in full bloom with its white bark and indigo leaves. Blood flowers tracing funerary displays, and battle scenes from the old war.

It was easier to focus on them than to think of any-thing to say.

Mael had no problem finding words between us.

"There is a perfectly fine set of stairs coming up ahead. I'm not sure that you remember how to use them anymore, so be careful not to trip."

I could feel my face heat up in embarrassment.

"I prefer the climb, it keeps me in shape."

"You spend hours every day racing around the city," she countered, "you are plenty in shape. Something your human seems to enjoy... greatly?"

My face didn't cool down any.

"His name is Simon, and it's not like that."

"Oh?" she faked confusion, "So he prefers to keep his eyes on less attractive men?"

My face was going to melt away if it got any hotter.

"He prefers *books*, especially ours."

"So his language lessons have been sticking?"

"You would think." My hand ran over the wall instinctively, the stone under my fingers worn smooth from lifetimes of hands tracing the same path. "Honestly, if it's possible, I think his kriest has just gotten worse. I've had to reteach him our letters twice now."

"Such a shame," she said, not looking at me. "Then I suppose your job as an interpreter might run longer than you'd expected?"

I gave her a sideways glance.

"Mael," I asked carefully, "did you make me a translator to keep me busy here?"

"Oh no, no." she waved a hand dismissively. "I simply needed someone who was quick with the human language, proficient in reading and writing and had both the clearance to use the archives and the free time to do it."

"So, me."

"Well," she added, putting her hands behind her back like a mischievous child, "As my apprentice, I was aware you met all the requirements."

"Mael." I said. "And as someone who sneaks out their window and goes running around the city all day, I knew you had the free time."

"Mael."

"Yes?" She replied.

"You created this position."

"Yes."

"You're the one who agreed to let a human ambassador in for this translation job."

"Mm-hmm."

"You're the one who *chose* which ambassador you'd let in the archives."

"Mm. Also yes."

"You chose the one who can't learn the language."

"Gen," she admonished, "Are you insinuating that I fabricated an entire translation job knowing it would run long and you'd have to stay at the temple more often?"

I gave her a wry look.

"Not in so many words."

"Well, you're right," she tilted her head to meet my eyes, a smile playing on one side of her lips. "But you've known that all along, haven't you?"

I didn't say anything. It was far too early in the morning for her to buy me off with little truths. She wasn't wrong, though. Some part of me *had* known. I'd still gone along with it, anyway.

Mael got to the first floor landing before me. Before I could catch up with her she turned and put her arm out like a barricade across the stone archway.

"Gen?" Her eyes met mine, a weighted seriousness washing over her. "You don't need to scale down the walls to leave. I don't want you to fall. Use the stairs more?"

I heard what she really meant. She knew I climbed out my window and down the walls to avoid her. She knew why. Mael had always been the closest thing I've had to a mother, and my first friend. I might be a let down, but it wasn't a lack of respect towards her that caused it.

Just my own inability to not fold under any amount of responsibility.

So I nodded.

"I've never fallen," I started, but when she made no motion to move, I added "... but I'll use the stairs more."

She studied my face for a long moment before relaxing, dropping her arm.

"You're too much like me for your own good," she shook her head. "That quick wit of yours will get you in trouble one day."

"Speaking from experience?"

She didn't answer, but something sparkled in her eyes.

The main hall snaked directly to the temple kitchens. The corridors were practically a maze, but the twists and turns off this main path would get you anywhere you needed to go. Despite the insanely early hour, there was plenty of traffic.

Acolytes of the temple scurried about, all set to their chores for the morning. I found myself falling in line behind Mael to make room for others to pass.

Younger teens raced by with linens headed for the washing rooms. A few began whispering when they saw us, offering a quick greeting and bow without stopping. There weren't usually many guards about at this hour, but I saw plenty posted at the doors now, upright and awake. A young boy, not quite in the double digits of age and who had yet to grow into his ears, stood on tiptoes to light the wall lanterns. He wore one shoe and had the other hooked to a belt, gripping the stone wall better with his bare toes. Older acolytes were following each other in a line with arms full of candle boxes, or lantern oil, or dried blood flower leaves. They walked with purpose, their heads held high. Their burgundy skirts and sashes flashed behind them like muted flames.

Every person who passed greeted us with the same saying.

"Sanra, Reid Mael."

It filled the hall in a wave as we passed, and with each greeting to Mael came a hidden glance at me. Some looked at my presence behind Mael with curiosity. Others, relief. A few more with disapproval.

It made me wish I really had climbed out the window. Or, maybe, thrown myself from it. Simon told me once there was a similar saying to *sanra* in his human language, *carry on.*

Even if it wasn't a perfect fit, it was the best I could explain it. *Sanra* meant *all is well, carry forward.* It could be a greeting, but it was also a formality. Different from the human saying there was a secondary nuance of reverence, sort of like 'all is well due to you, and all you do.' It was recognition that she was a pillar holding up the world. *Sanra, Reid Mael.*

If only they knew the true purpose of a reid's position.

"Gen," Mael teased as we got closer, "I can hear your stomach growling from here."

"I heard yours halfway down the hall." She lightly bumped me with her shoulder. "Don't speak to your Reid that way."

"You started it."

We continued on to the oversized wooden doors of the kitchens. Judging by the rich aromas coming from within, the ceremonial baking was well underway. Acolytes had spent most of a week pulling ground grains from storage by the cart-load. The flour was mixed in different stations into multiple doughs by skilled hands. The assembly stations then handled, formed, baked and decorated each loaf differently.

The treats were sold to local merchants to raise funds for the temple or gifted to the community after a ceremonial blessing. *This has got to be the silliest tradition,* Mael had told me once years ago, *praying over bread.*

The process of making them in bulk was long and la-borious on a good day, and insanely time consuming on a cere-monial day, so any and all hands were welcome to the work.

However, as we approached the doors we found the exception standing toe to toe with a solid guard.

"What do mean cannot enter?"

A familiar human woman stood with a hand on her hip and fire in her eyes. Her Kriest wasn't perfect, and heavily accented, but it was better than some. She sounded frustrated and a bit bewildered. Her long red hair was broken by incoming silver streaks, and today she had pushed it back with a kriest's headband and a human braiding style.

"I am baker, I am baker every morning! I get up, I come here, I bake bread. Now you say I am not make bread? Am I no baker now? I am baker last morning, I am baker morning before?" she motioned to her apron shawl.

It was a Kriest style, kind of a widened sash that crossed your chest and tied at the waist with another length of dyed cloth. Hers even had embroidered buns and grains on it, a touch she had undoubtedly earned.

"I am no time for this. I am have work to do. Bread to bake. As a *baker.*"

The guard's hand was up in a helpless, halting gesture.

"I *understand* you're a baker, that isn't the point."

"Then why?"

"Human hands on a ceremony day?" The guard sneered, "You'll spoil the offerings!"

The human's face turned a lovely red to rival her hair. Her Kriest wasn't great, but it was good enough to get she was being insulted.

"*Oh you are lucky you are gorgeous,*" she growled in Human, leaning in close. "*Otherwise I would have half a mind to take that shoulder piece of yours and use it to bash your nose flat for saying that to me! I would NEVER—*"

The guard opened her mouth with a rebuttal, and Mael took the chance to clear her throat.

The guard looked up and nearly jumped out of her skin.

"S-Sanra Reid Mael!" she called just a little too loudly, straightening instantly.

"Sanra, young guard," she replied in turn, her voice perfectly calm and even as always. That faint, ever-present smile on her lips never faltered. "What is all this?"

"She wants to be in the kitchens." the guard said, as if that explained it all perfectly fine.

The baker stood there, arms crossed, holding her temper in check.

"Faral," She chastised the guard like a mother scolding her child. "There's no need for that, not today! There's plenty of work to go around."

The human had stepped to the side enough for Mael to reach out and gently squeeze the guard's arm. Mael would never see such a familiar gesture beneath her station.

"Speaking of, could you do a lap the way we came? There is a young boy struggling to reach the lanterns to light them, and I just know he would be grateful for your assistance."

"But—" She started, and Mael cut her off.

"Haliz blesses us *all* with purpose, Faral." She said, lowering her voice. "Even if we cannot understand it."

The guard's ears lowered downwards, her face heating up.

"Of course, Reid Mael. Thank you."

"No," Mael said, "Thank you for picking up this extra shift today, and so early in the morning at that. I'll take it from here."

The guard looked surprised that Mael had noted her extra work. I was used to things like this by now. She'd always had a way with memorizing tiny, inconsequential details about everyone and using them just right. It was her ability to watch people, to listen to them, in ways most people don't or can't. I'd picked up that same skill long ago, but she'd always been better at using that information. She used it to control any room. I'd only used it for survival.

With a quick and respected nod of her head, the guard turned and jogged down the hall, her metal shoulder pauldrons glinting in the lamp light.

Then, with the same deft hand she had used on the guard, I watched her turn to the baker. She smiled in a much more familiar way with her, crossing her arms and giving her a devilish smile.

"*Elizabeth,*" she chided in Human, "*how thankful should I be that this guard met your aesthetic requirements to keep their nose intact?*"

Elizabeth let out a pent up sigh.

"*I'm sorry, Reid Mael. I just…. She said I was going to poison the bread!*"

"*A translation error, I can promise you. That poor girl has never excelled in her human courses, but she's got a way with wrangling the kids and keeping them out of the kitchens I know you appreciate.*"

"*Well, I'm not some child who's going to stick their entire muddy arm in the deer roast, now am I?*"

They shared a look, and I wondered if that was an anecdote from some cooking adventure I had recently missed. I clearly didn't come around the kitchens enough anymore. Then her smile slipped, and she crossed her arms over her stomach in a defensive manner.

"*Really, Mael, what gives?*"

If Mael was bothered by the informal way she said her name, she didn't let on.

"*Oh, Elizabeth. I really should have warned you about this sooner.*"

"*Is this about the ceremony tonight? Or about me being human?*"

"*Yes,*" she answered honestly to both. Mael always wielded the truth when she needed to.

"*I thought we were past this,*" Elizabeth said. "*I've worked in support of the temple for years, I helped bridge the distance between our cities and keep everyone's mouth fed, earn my way into these very kitchens, and for what? Five months of playing house only to get kicked to the curb the first holiday that shows up?*"

"*I can't say that you're wrong.*" Mael nodded, "*People—humans and kriest alike— are so messy. Everyone's so desperate to find any excuse to push our differences away.*"

"*So I'm out of the kitchens, is that it?*"

"*No,*" Mael held the truth in her palm and clasped her friend's hands between hers. Their eyes met in an intense stare "*I'm not going to let anyone push you away after all you've done for us. It's the night of.... melding, I believe your language translates, and even if I have to scold a hundred 'beautiful' guards, I'll remind them what that means.*"

Elizabeth blushed a bit. "*You heard that part, huh?*"

"*Oh yes.*" She grinned, pulling her towards the door. "*Now, we get in the kitchens! There's a lot of work to do before the grand ceremony! I can't spend the whole day out here with you.*"

Elizabeth sighed. "*Are you sure?*"

"*I'm always sure of everything that I say,*" Mael teased. "*I am a very sure woman! I am sure of everything, everywhere, all the time!*"

Elizabeth laughed. "*What does that even mean?*"

"*It means let's go! We've got work to do!*"

Mael flashed me a quick glance to make sure I hadn't left before striding forward to push open the doors. The wide, chaotic room beyond greeted us with a waft of heat and noise. Scents of the large brick ovens, fueled by charcoal and heated stone, fought the rich smell of bread to reach us from the exterior wall. Rows of long stone countertops with a corridor between stretched out on both sides of the room. About thirty kriest were filling the stations to keep the assembly line going. The oven workers faced the heat to keep a continuous flow of dough rolling in and finished breads rolling out. Cooling breads filled the shelves just inside a set of open exterior doors. I saw there was already a line of merchants arriving early outside to buy up what they could.

"See?" Mael said, leaning towards me. "We really needed you here today."

The room seemed to look up and notice her all at once, standing between myself and Liz.

There was a breath's worth of time where everything seemed to pause. It was as if no one could decide which was more shocking a sight - a human in the kitchens on a ceremony day, or me actually in the temple working my duties again.

Mael clapped her hands together with force.

"Sanra, everyone!" she called out, her voice filling the room. "Let's get working!"

As if a spell was broken, rounds of 'Sanra, Reid Mael!' rose from the acolytes. The room pushed into motion again, and with Mael ushering me to my usual dough station I could almost relax. With five simple words, Mael had made everyone okay with a human in our midst.

How could she ever see me and think I could someday fill her shoes?

We worked together in familiar silence for a long while. It felt good to work with my hands, to get some of that loose energy I always seemed to have out of my system. It wasn't as effective as a good run would have been, but feeling the pull of my muscles as I put my whole weight into kneading, rotating, and kneading the dough again felt right. Easy.

"It really feels like old times, doesn't it?" Mael spoke, her hands rolling out a long snake of dough before folding it and snapping it into a spiral with practice. "Do you remember the first year you'd come here? You were so small, nearly frail, I was terrified you would fall into the baskets and get swallowed by the dough."

"Was it really the right thing to do, letting Elizabeth in?" I changed the subject. I wanted to talk about my childhood even less than she really wanted to talk to me about bread.

Mael stared at her hands. Rolling, folding, snapping. Pushing the formed roll to the side and cutting another ball off with a wooden blade.

"I don't know," she answered honestly.

"It could raise the tension between the guards and the humans."

"It could also change their perception, give them a new sense of normal." I shoved more dough her way. She caught it. Set it aside. "There is a constant truth in the world, Gen. You can never know for sure how someone will react to anything. But sometimes, it's best to try."

"Sometimes," I say before I can stop myself, "You'll only be let down."

She ignored our history laid bare in those words. "I want humans to be included in our lives in every way. It's been nearly five years since they arrived here, we've had long enough to get used to them and get over ourselves."

"Pushing it could really stir up trouble, Mael."

"Not all of us can just avoid the future as we please, Gen."

It's worked out well enough for me, I wanted to argue. Kneading dough had not magically changed me from the coward I was, though, so I said nothing. In my silence she lowered her voice and continued.

"I want more than a new normal for all of us, Gen. I want *understanding*. We'll never get there by keeping to the lines we've drawn so tightly. I feel humans have more than proven they can have a place at the table. They've helped us produce food, they've shared their technology, medicine, *and* history. I want to keep inviting them in, and I happen to be in a position of authority where I *can*. People can get used to changes. It takes time, but it won't happen at all if, well, nothing ever happens. So yes, tensions could peak up a bit from Elizabeth being allowed here on the day of melding. You know what else could occur? *Understanding*. And for a chance at that,

I'm willing to shake things up."

The whole time I had been listening, I had been kneading my body of dough, hard. I moved to push it towards her and she caught my hand, held it there between hers and the dough.

I looked up. Her eyes bore into mine with a fire behind her deep amber stare.

"Gen," she said, trapping me between her stare and the dough under our hands, "I want this for everyone. But I also want this for you."

"Mael..." I began, but her grip tightened.

"Tonight, at the ceremony, I want a human to enter and witness the proceedings."

My lungs forgot how to inflate. Blood that had previously rushed through my body turned deathly still. I felt immobile, frozen in place at what she was going to do. "Mael," I tried to say again, but she wouldn't let me.

"I want that honor to go to Simon Holiday."

I sucked in a breath like needles down my throat. In nine simple words, she'd placed a large, immovable object in my lungs.

The melding ceremony carried secrets. Secrets hidden in plain sight behind rituals and traditions so that no one save a fully realized Reid would ever understand. Mael held these secrets like a metal weight around her neck. I held these secrets as well, and I ran from them every day.

What a human would bring into the ceremony, beyond the breach of sanctimony, was *perspective*. Perspective from outside the fabricated veil of misleading tradition, stories and ceremony. Someone with the potential to undo the last century and a half of careful crafting by seeing straight through the bullshit. Plainly put, we kept secrets and wielded the truth, and letting a human in to watch the display of lies we told could be the undoing of us all.

Unless, my thoughts whispered to me, *they saw the need*. Unless they became a bridge to teach the humans the lies, to pull the veil over their eyes. To establish that context correctly. Unless we offered them privilege or prestige for the work. I could practically see the logic reflected in Mael's eyes.

We didn't lie out of malice, but necessity. Would exposure be seen as a betrayal of trust, or the protection it truly is?

If there was anyone at all who could learn the ceremony with care and respect, and help teach the other humans the stories and history regarding our temple that we would want to teach them, it would be Simon Holiday.

And it would mean so, so much to him.

My chest ached at the thought of Simon's face if I offered that he be the first human to witness our most sacred of rituals. I could already feel the excitement that would fill his blue eyes, see the way he would pace back and forth, giddy at it all. At the *honor*. I could imagine what it would be like to see him there, in the central chamber, witnessing what to the humans would truly be magic.

"...you planned this," I said, letting Mael's carefully crafted pieces fall into place. "You want me to go to the ceremony, and you knew if you framed it in a way that Simon was involved, I wouldn't say no."

Mael nodded. Unashamed.

"....I can't," I said, still frozen in place. My voice barely came out as a whisper. "I can't do the ceremony, Mael. I can't....not after what happened."

The scars on my arms burned white hot with memory. I clenched my fist to keep them at bay.

"Then don't participate," she said, "Just be there. If not as my apprentice, then as Simon's guide."

My hands felt numb. My throat felt dry. A phantom memory of pain ran down the length of my forearms and scaled my bones. Then she put me right where she wanted me.

"He's the one thing you've never run from, Gen. Don't take this opportunity from him out of your own fear. Please, if not for me, then for him."

It was dirty. It was underhanded. It hurt me in ways I couldn't put to words and scared me in ways I could. The weight of what she asked me wrapped around my neck, choked me, made me want to turn and flee as far and as fast as my legs would allow.

But then, I thought of his soft blue eyes, his excited, nervous smile, and the wonder in which he saw my world. I thought of his insatiable desire to learn. I thought of his quiet admittance to be a part of anything bigger than himself.

I closed my eyes.

Just when I felt like falling apart, Mael pulled away. She took the dough from me, moved it to her station and picked up the wooden blade again.

"You have time to think about it." she said. "The ceremony isn't until tonight. Let's not fall behind on the bread."

My hands moved automatically to the next ball of dough. I didn't need to think about it.

I just had no idea if I could stick to my decision come tonight.

Chapter Three

Simon, New Caramel

"Wait!" She cried, scrambling up the hill like mad, arm extended as if she could stop the leaving cart by sheer will alone. "*Etor! Etor!* Wait! Wait! Dangit! *Desi,* please!"

I got up from my seat, grabbing for a corner post awkwardly and nearly throwing myself off.

"Hurry, Dora!" I leaned way out of the back, thankful for once for my long reaching arms. "It's the last carriage until dawn!"

She let out a mournful cry, a bit like a sob and a bit like resignation, but she kept running for the cart. Her bag clanged against her hip, one second a breath away from throwing the dozens of scroll tubes out and the next being engulfed by her endlessly folding skirts. The straight dark hair she tied back from her face was coming loose from her braid, flying everywhere. I reached for her, she reached for me, and in one last bid of desperation she leaped up from the ground, pushing away from stone with less than half the grace of a newborn giraffe.

Her hand clasped my arm. Mine clasped hers. One foot landed with a padded *thwack* against the wooden floor, and the other arm and leg swung out over open, moving road and air. Her eyes widened, her lips parted, and all she could manage was a terrified, awkward '*Whoop!!*' noise.

"Hold on, Dora!"

I strained, bracing my feet against the hay threshold to pull her in. My arms screamed in uselessness. Hers did as well. Finally, she stumbled both feet into the cart, and we landed back in a messy pile, me on my ass, a spread of arms and legs like a startled spider, and her on her knees, perfectly folded with her arms out to steady her balance. Hay fluffed up around us, coating our clothes and hair. Together, we gasped for breath.

"Your glasses," I said, pointing to her large wire frames, halfway across the passenger cart floor. She reached for them, fumbled, then grabbed them up. They were strange square things nearly the size of her palm, something she'd found in the dredges of her humanities research. She checked them for cracks before pushing them up her nose. They made her gray eyes appear huge.

"Oh, thank you, Simon!" She panted, still catching her breath. "I don't think I've had to run that fast in years!"

"You do this every day!"

"Not every day!" she gasped, clutching her chest and trying to gain control of her breathing.

"Is this really any better than being stuck at the inn again?" I offered my hand again to help her into a seat. She took it graciously.

"I spent my pay on a new ink stick." she admitted.

"The plight of academics, huh?"

She laughed fully at that, wheezing every few seconds.

"No one told me this information exchange program would be so physical!"

"It wouldn't be if you'd make the cart on time!"

She pulled a few stray bits of hay from her hair, falling into a fit of giggles all over again.

"I know, I know, but I had someone to see."

"You have no sense of time."

"At least I have better taste in men," she teased.

"Don't you start."

"Are you still pretending to be bad at our language to keep that translator around?"

I groaned.

"We both know I'm not pretending. Languages just aren't my strong suit."

"You're lucky they are for me, otherwise we'd never have become friends. Who would tease you about your love life?"

"Not much of a love life." I sighed. "Lucky for you, otherwise you'd be walking back to Torrel every night."

"Touche."

Human was— unfairly— a language Dora spoke with academic quality and perfection in line with her own and— again unfairly— the only language I could manage correctly on any given day. Through this conversation with Dora came easy. We'd both signed on as a kind of historian about a year back, and I'd found myself a friend. We both knew it was only thanks to one very excellent and dedicated translator I'd managed to hold my spot at all.

Well, and Dora's occasional help.

Was it sad to say she was one of my only friends? Probably. You could argue the definition of the word enough to claim I had three, and two of them weren't even human. I had to get better at socializing.

The hands of familiar trees enclosed us when we ascended into the woods, giving us one last, final look down the mountainside at New Caramel below.

The world we lived in was not the world I was born into. Although, through five years of effort on both our and the native's sides, it had become a new kind of home. The once unfamiliar landscapes of the volcanic island had become my everyday setting. I'd grown accustomed to the sea air wafting up from the bays, learned the cries of birds and the different small mammals that lived in the trees.

Caramel had, in the past, been a quaint New England college town. It was charming, and dreadfully *historic,* a note that had been especially played up around the Caramel University campus back in the day.

Now, looking down at the shelves of land the city rested in, all the charming brick did was manage to stand out in stark brown squares against the fertile volcanic soil. Seeing it from the road and a few elevation levels up it was almost as if some mad painter had dipped his brush in the city and smeared it across the fields. Some roads ended sharply at the end of this brush stroke, and whole houses or blocks had not made the transition here. Smatterings of ruinous buildings scattered into the eastern woods, or at least their foundations had the materials been repurposed. Halves of houses dotted the dark tree line, ghostly shells of the historic homes that now fell vacant.

The kriest kept to the upper hills and woods, for the most part. There was no hard boundary line between our main city and theirs so much as a polite and unspoken rule to keep like with like. Both sides preferred it, even if we did mix on a daily basis for commerce or work, at the end of the night we all went back home to our own kind. The humans to the valley, and the kriest to the cliffs.

There were, of course, a few exceptions to every unspoken rule, and I suppose I was one of them. While I still stayed in New Caramel as a home base, I traveled to the central city and temple many times a week and often stayed overnight. Traveling the forest paths at night was dangerous, especially for a human. I preferred to stay up late researching anyway. It kept my mind off the things I've been so desperately trying to leave behind.

"Dora," I asked finally, having let her discussion run its natural course, "Do you know any details on the actual ceremony itself?"

"On the proper etiquette to make a phone call?"

"What— oh, sorry, no, I was bringing the conversation back to the melding ceremony."

"Oh!" She smiled apologetically. "Sorry, I just get so caught up in my research... I'm sorry to say that I don't. I've never been to one, and I don't work with the temple. I got my job through the merchant council."

"But you have to have grown up with stories?"

"Well sure," she answered honestly, "But stories are vastly different from written records, history, and proof. I know it's a way to bring together great minds of our community to better our lives and city, but as far as what the actual ceremony holds, you'd be better asking your translator. I've heard he grew up in the temple?"

I sighed through my nose.

"Yes, but part of his job is also to regulate the information given. I never get the fun details."

"You think he's in the reid's debt or something?"

I shrugged.

"It seems a bit more complicated than that."

"For someone you're so close to, you don't really know a lot about him, do you?"

She wasn't wrong.

The carcass came into view when we rounded the next bend. On the side of the wood, pulled back from the road by some earlier traveler, was the stilled remains of a young deer. The deer here always reminded me of a mix between a white tail and a reindeer from back home. They had wide, muscular forms, light colorings, slim faces, and impressively large antlers on the males.

This one had been a juvenile male, judging from the little sprout of antler growing from its head. It lay unnaturally still, its legs fallen over itself in a heap. As if that wasn't enough of an indicator of death, dozens of vining blood flowers roped it to the ground and grew from its hide.

"Poor thing," Dora said, her hands in her lap. "To be so young...I wonder if it was a wild dog attack?"

"Not seen many dogs around here recently," another traveler said, a young Kriest with a bag of obsidian tools between his legs. He wore the plain wrappings of an apprentice and looked a few years younger than me. His Human was halting, but passable. "My father thinks dogs went deeper into woods."

"For the best," Dora said, her voice heavy with the absent disdain all Kriest had for dogs. "They're nothing but trouble."

"Surprised no one's stopped to get the *akai* for the dye makers," the apprentice said . "They'd make a penny."

He slapped the wooden side of the cart and hollered something in kriest—I caught the words for *asking* and *stop*—but the driver waved him off dismissively. We had other places to be.

I took in the deer as we passed. The blood flowers— *akai* as the Kriest called them— always reminded me of the poinsettias my mother flooded our house with every holiday season. The petals were long and pointed, each budding from a bulbous white center. The blooms were the size of a dinner plate fully grown and had a soft, powdery feel, like dandelions.

They grew together in clusters, vining along the ground or up any nearby walls and trees. Their colors ranged from a deep indigo to blood red and mixed to many different purple ranges in between. The flowers and plants held no nutritional value, and I had heard tasted quite awful.

They always grew where blood was spilled on the ground. Humans treated them as a macabre sort of weed. To the kriest, however, they held a lot of cultural significance, a symbol of death and the cycle beyond.

I didn't want to think about death that night. Or weeds. I'd had enough of both topics to last a lifetime. I turned away from the corpse, happy to get to the rest of my evening with Gen.

The journey was slow going around the curving uphill path. Still, it beat walking the darkening forest trails on foot, dodging carts or thieves and the occasional wild dog. Dora and I settled into our usual discussions of our work.

Well, Dora did. I was more than willing to let her talk the rest of the way.

We were maybe ten minutes out from Torrel— and halfway through one of Dora's monologues comparing food across our cultures— when it happened.

A shadow fell from the dark canopy above. The cart shook violently when it landed, and the driver pulled us to a quick stop.

I registered what was happening a second after the driver did. We'd been boarded. It was an ambush.

None of us had noticed until it was too late.

The deer pulling us screamed in displeasure from the jolt. I jumped back in fear, slamming recklessly into Dora. She let out a startled yelp, and we both stumbled back, falling over each other.

We became a tangle of limbs and swearing that was all but defenseless to the figure now rising to their feet beside us. In the darkness, I couldn't make out a face, only the long, slender ears of the Kriest and a dark, flickering tail. The others in the cart had also fallen back in surprise, and now they also gawked at the form in our midst. Only a mere second or two had passed.

It was clear none of us were armed or prepared. I wasn't sure any of us could have done anything even if we had been. My chest went icy cold.

Dora and I fought against each other to stand. My foot had caught in her skirt fabrics, her bag in the hay. My mind began to race.

Who is that? Are we under some kind of attack? Raiders? No, they prefer the convoys closer to the bay. Asterel? No, the North never sent their warriors this far south below Torrel—

A laugh, wild and familiar, filled the air. It froze me in place in a rush of relief.

"*Gen?*" I asked, as the figure covered his mouth against a fit of uncontrollable giggles.

"Oh, by *Haliz*, Simon!" Gen gasped out through his laughter, "You look ridiculous!"

I sure fucking did. Dora had resorted to pulling herself out from my frozen form like a refugee from an earthquake. I could hear her swearing colorfully in both languages. Hay had kicked up from our fall, coating us both. I blew some off my face with a sideways huff of air. I hoped it looked as indignant as I felt.

"What....*why*...?"

Gen shrugged.

"It seemed easier than trying to climb in from the ground."

I stared at him. Or, what little I could make of him. His sleek, muscular form was partially obscured by shadows, but now that I knew what to look for, the familiar angles and lines of his body came into focus.

"That's not a good enough answer," I told him, sitting flat against the cart bench as Dora worked to extradite my foot from her skirts.

Instead of replying to me he turned away to address the worried driver in Kriest. I couldn't make out the words, but the tone was familiar and friendly. Gen quickly explained something, offered coin for passage, and clapped the driver on the shoulder. The driver seemed just as exasperated as I was, but allowed him a spot. The rest of the cart settled as Dora pulled away and came to sit beside me.

"Your translator?" she grumbled.

"The very one." I sighed.

We both turned towards the front of the cart to stare at his back. He was still speaking to the driver, quietly nodding along with whatever admonishing he was being given. I caught the words for *raider* and *idiot*.

"Looks like we've got to get in line to yell at him for this," I mumbled, earning a snort from Dora.

"Is this how you treat all your friends? With lectures?"

Friends.

The word struck something low and meaningful in my chest. It hollowed out just as quickly. I offered her a smile I hoped looked believable in the shadows.

"It's just my nature, I guess."

"The driver is also chewing him out."

"I figured as much." Dora seemed to lean in, trying to make out their words. I watched her ears flick forward.

"Anything interesting?" I asked.

"Nothing you're not going to tell him yourself in a minute," she said and then froze. Her ears twitched. Once. Twice.

"Simon," she asked carefully, "What did you say his name was?"

The cart turned a corner and the forest began to thin. The setting sun had turned the trees around us a deep, hazy red. The sky I could see was a low pink, and the light that filtered through the leaves grew into a gorgeous golden-red glow. As the cart turned into the light it spread over Gen like flames, illuminating his profile in all his full glory.

He was an athlete, through and through. He had the toned, solid form of a gymnast and the curved calves of a runner. His arms looked deceptively leaner than his legs, but I'd seen his strength in climbing or pulling his own body weight. He was in one of those light running outfits he favored, and it did nothing to hide any cut line of his body.

His wild dark hair seemed to exist as a kind of afterthought; it was too long to be practical, but he was too stubborn or forgetful to trim it, so it was usually pushed back with some kind of scarf. The one he wore wasn't doing its job very well. Stray locks fell away to frame his face in a messy halo, tracing his cheeks and deep almond-shaped eyes. He had a lean, defined face with strong brows and a beautiful smile.

He had the kind of smile that men would go to war over, and women would leave their families for. It could fill a space and change your life. It was a wicked kind of magic, and one I was not immune to.

The sun painted him in warm reds and deep purples, his long black tail blending into the deepening shadows. His ears, fawn-like and as long as my hand, raised ever so slightly to hear what the driver was saying better before he launched into a laugh that lit up his entire face.

He looked unworldly. He looked *beautiful*.

Dora's eyes trained on my face—noticing far more than I had meant to share—and I realized she was waiting for something.

Oh, right. I had been asked a question. His name.

"Gen," I answered her, "why?"

"What?" Gen cut in, having stepped to the back of the cart with us. He sat next to me in the corner, throwing his legs over mine like a lounger. I scowled.

"I wasn't talking to you."

"You said my name?"

"I was—" I started, then waved a hand over his stretching legs. "Do I look like furniture to you?"

"Aren't all humans?"

"Gen!"

"Well, if you believe in the Kor mentality—"

I groaned.

"Please tell me you haven't gone all this way just to list off all the factions that want to kill me for existing?"

He snorted, stretching his arms up way above his head. His shirt slipped just a bit to expose his cut abdominal muscles. I pointedly looked anywhere else.

"That was a lot of large words to throw at me, Simon! I have been running all around the city today," he griped, "let me rest."

"Courier work?" I asked.

He shrugged.

"Not a lot of packages to deliver today. Just a good day for a run."

"Was it also a good day for a cart ambush?"

He grinned. "*Coolest* thing I have done today."

I thought of the various feats of casual acrobatics I had witnessed since knowing him. Gen had a habit of scaling buildings for fun, doing full cartwheels to pick up items that he dropped, and walking across thin stone walls with more grace than I had flat-footed on the ground. Dropping from a tree seemed like child's play compared to those.

"I somehow doubt that."

He clearly took that as a compliment. "Coolest thing I have done *so far* today."

I lightly pushed his legs, displacing them.

"I regret teaching you the meaning of the word *cool*."

"It is because I am *cooler* than you."

"Are not."

"Are yes."

"Gen, right?" Dora suddenly asked, an odd, awkward smile on her face. "From *Del Tor*?"

Gen looked at her, seeming to size her up. "Yes?"

"You're translating texts with Simon?"

He hesitated, something I wasn't used to seeing him do. Dora spoke my language far better than he did, though, so he may have been stumbling over her wording.

"Yes?"

She pointed to his chest with both her hands.

"You?"

"Mm-hmm."

"With him?"

"Mm."

"Every time?"

"Since the beginning," Gen said, shifting a bit.

"You are his only translator?"

"I do my best."

"Reid Mael assigned you to work with him?"

At this, Gen paused again. Not for the first time since I had met him, I watched him choose his words carefully.

"She approved the work, yes." He answered at last. I got the distinct impression something was being said behind his words that I couldn't understand.

In my own language.

Right in front of me.

"Why does it matter?" I asked her. Gen shifted forward, clearly wondering the same. Dora looked between us, her face unreadable. She bit her lip, kicked her legs a bit, and then a wall of words exploded from her.

"Simon told me he had a pretty translator, but I had no *idea* he was this pretty! Are all boys from the temple cut like you? Ooh, no, wait, are the *women*? I've only seen a few of the guards at Del Tor and they look mighty amazing, are you one of the temple guards? Do you have to be a temple devout to enter? My father goes all the time but I am usually working and he keeps trying to push marriage on me and is always suggesting someone from the temple but I'm not ready to be tied down! I prefer my work. Do you know what it's like to be married to your work? It's exhausting!"

Something in Gen seemed to relax the further on she rambled.. Another one of his world-shattering smiles came up on his face.

"He says I am pretty?"

"I do not!"

"Oh yes," Dora contradicted me, "all the time."

"*Dora*, please!"

"Dora, *please!*" Gen copied, "Continue! Tell me all about how pretty I am. How pretty he thinks I am."

"Your abs have abs!" I said, groaning. "It's not a compliment, it's an observation!"

A wide, wild grin spread his lips.

"I am very becompliment."

"*Complemented*," Dora corrected.

"*Neither!*" I said, turning back to Gen and hoping the red light would hide my growing blush. "Why are you here?"

He leaned forward in his seat, the picture of smugness. His eyes seemed to sparkle. I had the sense that I was in danger of falling into those eyes.

"I wanted to see your face when you saw."

"Saw what?"

He stood up, taking my arm to pull me with him and turn me towards the approaching stone arches that marked the beginning of Torrel's market district.

"My city, alive." He said in answer, and as the cart entered the lower marketplace streets I forgot all about my embarrassment.

The city *had* come to life. Festivities dressed the streets in full.

Torrel was a spread of volcanic stone and dark clay buildings wound tightly together along the mountainside. The lower marketplace was no exception. Thin the mountainside. The lower marketplace was no exception. Thin reedy alleys slipped between the homes, barely wide enough to walk through without brushing your shoulders. Buildings were rarely above three stories down here, with bottom floors being solid businesses and the top floors made into living quarters.

The market road was only as wide as a stall and a cart could allow. Merchants would line the south side of the road with their tents from early in the morning to late sundown, peddling everything from fabrics to food to art. The larger, more established storefronts settled into the northern buildings, filled with delis, cobblers, even courier runners or smoking dens.

This was the market of the working folk, far from the upper city crust, and it always had a sort of chaotic, practical charm.

Tonight it was a vibrant tapestry of celebration.

Small lanterns were hung overhead next to dried strands of *akai* petals and strings of sea glass and beads. Each stall had hung charms and decorative cloth banners full of embroidered trees, flowers and vines. Someone had taken the time to stain the road with white ash paint in murals of swirling branches and roots. The crowd moved through the design, becoming a living, intertwined part of the art.

People had paid top dollar for luxury yellow dyes to decorate sashes, or skirts, or small cloth jewelry bits. The color flashed all around me, impossible to ignore. The dye was hard to come by, almost as revered as gold, but I caught small bits of that here and there, too. It occurred to me that even Gen was wearing yellow tonight in his headband. I didn't want to think of the cost of even that little dyed fabric.

Children ran through the crowd, holding up small kites made of paper and more dried akai flowers. The air was rich with the scents of baked breads, and spiced meats, and rich, earthy incense. Even more than usual. Despite the lengthening shadows of dusk many stall owners seemed to have no plans to close, putting up lanterns with sea glass charms to catch the light and illuminate their shops.

It was magical. I could taste the excitement in the air. It coursed through me, pulling me into its ebb and flow. I turned to look at Gen and Dora, a novel's worth of questions on my mind.

Gen was watching me, smiling in delight, but it didn't quite meet his eyes. There was a tinge of something more morose there, a kind of sadness I couldn't reason or grasp. Dora, on the other hand, had been watching Gen. A curious, nervous look played on her face and worried her lip, and again I felt like I was being left out of something right in front of me.

No matter how I tried, though, I couldn't piece it together.

So, instead, I asked my first of a hundred questions.

"What is all this for? Some kind of holiday?"

"*Del Tor* is holding a melding ceremony," Dora explained to me, something to which Gen seemed grateful. "The whole city stays up to celebrate."

"Is that why the last cart left so early?"

She nodded. "And why not many humans were allowed passage into Torrel today."

"Glad to be among one of the few," I said, not actually sure how to feel.

"Reid Mael aims to change that." Gen cut in. "It's a part of why she started this program."

"Is it?" Dora said, tilting her head in thought. "I didn't know that."

"Gen lives at Del Tor," I said, "I'm sure he gets all the good gossip."

Not that he ever tells me. Not that I was upset about that, no matter what Tess expected from me.

"Oh!" Dora exclaimed, "You're an accolade, then?"

"I was, years ago." Gen answered, giving her the same curt response he always gave me when I asked.

"How did you end up working as a translator?"

"I had the free time and the skill."

"That's pretty much how I got the job, too." I added. Gen and Dora both gave me matching looks. Gen started.

"Simon, you are terrible at Kriest."

"He can't conjugate to save his life."

"His handwriting is terrible, too. He can never remember the letters."

"It's a miracle at all that he got this spot."

"I'm *right here!*"

"Which is why we are still speaking in human," Dora explained, "otherwise you'd never understand us."

I felt my face heat up again.

"I regret letting you two meet."

"Hey," Dora laughed, "what are friends for?"

"Not this."

"Sure they are." Gen said, knocking his leg against mine playfully. "We are almost to the bridge. You ready?"

"Will the ceremony disrupt our translations?"

Gen paused, another unreadable look passing over him.

"Sure," he admitted, "but I have a feeling you'll enjoy it."

"I have no idea what that means."

"Our stop!" Gen announced, standing up suddenly and half pulling me with. I turned to give Dora an apologetic look and found her studying Gen again, and I just knew the next time we saw each other I was going to be getting some full, honest opinions about the man I'd been spending all my working time with.

But, hey, what were friends for?

The long road came to another northward curve, leading up the slant to the next elevation of the city, and slowed just enough for us to disembark by the great bridge. The sound of river water was barely audible over the thick crowds of people at the end of the market, and Gen had to raise his voice to be heard.

"Watch your step— nice to meet you, Dora!" he shouted, helping me fumble out of the cart and onto the cobbled streets below.

"Take care, Simon!" She shouted. "Enjoy your evening with the pretty man!"

"Dora!" I shouted, but her laughter and the cart both were already being swallowed by the sea of kriest. Off in the distance, lined with lanterns and swimming with bodies, I saw the great stone bridge heading towards the temple of Del Tor.

"Come on," Gen said, taking my arm to nudge me in the right direction. "Before we get lost in the crowd."

"Gen?" I asked, following his lead. A line of kids with more of those paper kites ran by, giggling and weaving around us.

"Mm?"

"*Are* we going to be translating more of the sea scrolls tonight?"

Something was still not adding up. He was distracted tonight, unusually wound up. And I hadn't gotten a straight answer. His laughter had hidden it well, but now that I was looking I could see the slight tension in his stance, the nervous way the end of his tail flicked back and forth.

"Where were we with those?"

"We're almost done, the mainlanders sailed over to the island for refuge from the great war."

"Should make quick work of them."

"So we *are* working on those tonight?" I pushed, not letting up. "You never gave me a straight answer."

Gen turned with fluid grace, dancing around both another kid and my question yet again.

"*All good things come to those who wait,* is that not one of your sayings?"

"*Gen.*"

"Just," he stopped, turning back to face me, forcing a few people to go around us. "No questions, just trust me?"

I looked into his deep, dark eyes. The waves of people and laughter and music and energy washed over me, and it was all so unworldly. His hand on my arm felt so solid and alive. But so did my doubts.

He wasn't telling me something. He wasn't telling me a *lot* of somethings— but against it all, I trusted him. Gen was solid, and flighty, and far too energetic, but he'd never done wrong by me.

Whatever had him on edge tonight, and whatever that meant for our work, I trusted that he'd let me know when the time was right. I trusted *him.*

Even if he shouldn't trust me.

"Fine." I said, moving to pull him forward instead. "Let's just get off the streets, people keep stepping on my feet."

He laughed, hopping up on the stone guardrail along the side of the bridge with cat-like grace. His bare feet gripped the stone with practice, and he made it look entirely too easy.

"That's *not* what I meant!" I laughed, and for a moment, it all felt so normal. I was off to work in a new world, translating kriest stories and history in a trusting, honest exchange of information between cultures.

What an honor. What a life.

The more time I spent with Gen, the closer I came to believing it. In moments like this, I wished I really could just be Simon the translator. Not Simon the informant.

Not Simon the spy.

Excitement mixed with guilt, and it was all I could do to shove it down and follow Gen into the heart of Del Tor, praying tonight wouldn't yield anything worth reporting back home about.

I just wanted to keep pretending as long as I could.

Chapter Four

Gen, Torrel

Dora had definitely known who I was.

Her face had been familiar too, though it didn't click until we were off the cart. Simon's friend was the daughter of one of the high merchants on the council—Merchant Zorren, if I remembered correctly— which didn't grant me any points in the friend-making department. Zorren was a shrewd and devout man who favored Mael only as much as he needed to— and favored me even less.

I could remember him coming to the temple regularly since I was brought there as a child, but he'd made it clear a long time ago that Mael was no chosen reid of his. Moreso, I bet he was just pissed she could never be bought off.

He'd been even less favorable of me when she'd announced my apprenticeship, and he'd let any interactions with me slip to near hostility since I'd— well, since I'd stepped down from my training. He hated Mael for never breaking. He loathed me for breaking too easily.

His daughter was best friends with Simon.

At least she hadn't spilled all the sordid truths of my position and failings to him. Who knew how long that would last, though, or what she'd want for it. Merchants always wanted something in the end.

I hated keeping so many secrets from him. It came with being a Reid, and a runaway, and a coward. Turns out I was successfully two of those at any given time.

I held my arms and tail out for balance on the stone wall. Simon reached up to touch my tail, and I flicked it away with ease. His laughter filled what space it could on the crowded bridge, and a soft, warm glow cut through the guilt swirling in my stomach. He was so vibrant tonight, lost in the world around us.

It was hard not to watch him. Simon was in his mid twenties, maybe a year or two younger than me, with a soul far older than his years. He stood eye to eye with me in height, and his light stormy eyes seemed to take in everything around him at all times. He was perceptive, almost dangerously so. He saw the world around him in wonder, even if he never saw himself the same.

Seeing his face when we'd entered the marketplace had made me almost believe in magic again. That this world could be full of wondrous things. I so wanted to feel that again.

That night he was dressed in a plain shirt of kriest-made material designed into a button up, straight leg pants and an old pair of boots he favored. He gripped his satchel like the notes inside were made of gold. Maybe they were, *Haliz* knows I couldn't make them out with his handwriting. The light wind from the river teased his short blonde hair and pushed his bangs over his metal rimmed glasses. He reached up absently to push them away, and I turned before he caught me staring again.

It didn't matter. I had every angle of his face long memorized. I still wasn't sure how I felt about this setup Mael had pushed me into but... I was grateful I'd gotten to meet him.

I'd never had the opportunity to make friends at Del Tor. I'd been absorbed by my training and work, and not many kids wanted to be near me. The ones who'd tried hadn't stuck around for long. Jorel had seen to that.

Simon had been my first chance in a long time to know somebody deeper than a surface or working connection. And the more I'd found, the deeper I'd wanted to dive.

The feelings I held for him were going to be the death of me, someday.

I could feel his eyes still on me. He'd accepted my request to fall into silence and trust my plans for the evening, but I could tell it wasn't really enough. I was frozen in fear of putting those plans to words, of manifesting them and making them real. Mael's request had been playing in my mind all day, and the more I thought it through the more I saw the wisdom in her decision.

We needed to open up to the humans more, before they drew their own conclusions.

Simon was the best one for the job. He was trustworthy, and so damned smart. He cared about us and our culture more than he seemed to his own. We needed to take control of the narrative before outside eyes became a risk to all we worked towards in the reidship.

I may be a coward, but I wasn't disloyal to Mael and the cause.

I just couldn't bear the weight of it myself.

"Are you okay?" Simon's voice broke my thoughts, and I realized I must have dropped my careful smile.

A lamp pillar came up at the halfway point of the bridge, and I hopped down to stand beside him.

"It has been a long day," I offered, "I have just got a lot on my mind."

"Like what?"

I concentrated on his face, wondering where or how to even start. He stared back at me, eyes inviting and taking me in. I could do this, I told myself. I need to do this.

I felt the hair on the nape of my neck rise at an unseen danger. Two forms suddenly loomed over us, blocking our way.

One man spoke, his voice low and gruff.

"Well, well, if it isn't little reidling Gen. Out on a stroll, avoiding the temple tonight, eh?"

"Taking his pet for a walk," The second one jeered, and they both dissolved into dark and disgusting laughter.

I turned to face them, my senses screaming in warning, and the purple sash donned across either of their chests gave me all I needed to know.

Kor soldiers.

The second one piped up again, elbowing the first in the ribs like he was in on some big joke. From their visual similarities, they had to be brothers, maybe even twins.

"Ain't you heard, brother, he's on a break, yeah?"

This threw them into fits again. I flexed my hands into fists and looked for a way out of whatever this was. I didn't know why they had singled us out, or how they knew so much about me, but I wasn't keen on sticking around to find out.

The Kor guarded the city and fought the line with Asterel in the north. They were a separate force from the city or temple guards, and were filled with the desperate or unwanted who couldn't thrive in higher classed organizations. We owed our peace to them, and they all knew it. They were inclusive, and brutish, and always a problem when they came back to town.

Simon stepped instinctively behind me, and I couldn't blame him. Not all of the Kor had it out for humans, but it seemed in the last few years more and more carried their prejudice on their sleeves. Since Jorel's placement in their ranks, they all seemed to have a specific bone to pick with me, too. I looked up to face the brothers head on.

"If you're looking for Jorel," I answered coldly in Kriest, *"You should know he isn't around on ceremony nights."*

They were built like warriors, and armed like ones as well. One carried a set of hatchets across his hips, and the other slung a traditional spear across his back. They both obscured their tawny hair in purple sashes that matched their belts, and one's tail had been chopped at nearly half its length. It flickered out behind him, and I finally recognized who they were.

Dimi and Herris, the two wonder idiots who reported directly to Jorel. They'd grown up as street kids and had been no shortage of trouble for the merchants in the area all their lives.

Stealing, damaging property— if you could name it, they'd done it. Then someone had gone ahead with the bright idea of putting weapons in their hands and training them how to fight.

Dimi had lost half of a tail in the process. Rumor was Herris was the one who'd done it, and he'd earned the notched ear he wore in return. They were problematic, loud, and full of themselves. Perfect underlings for Jorel's grab at power in Kor exile.

He'd always needed to be in control

Herris's eyes turned to Simon while I squared off with Dimi, his ears dipping down to a displeased angle.

"You're awfully bold, bringing a human here tonight." Herris said.

"He's a guest of Reid Mael," I answered. My legs tightened, ready to run if I needed to. It would be so easy to duck around them along the wall and bolt for the safety of the temple grounds. The Kor may favor Jorel, but the temple guards were all fiercely loyal to Mael and Del Tor. It would be nothing at all to race there and hide behind the safety of their arms.

But what about Simon?

"And mine." I added. *"Move, please. We've got work to attend to."*

Dimi took a step forward, but Herris's hand flicked out to catch him. They looked at each other in silent conversation. I all but held my breath.

Herris must have won whatever debate they'd had, because with a snort they parted in synchronized movements to let us through.

I stared at them both, not moving yet. It couldn't be this easy. Nothing was ever this easy.

"Well?" Herris sneered, *"Off you go."*

I took a step forward. Then another. Simon followed me, keeping his shoulders squared as we walked through their space unbothered. We'd made it two steps further before Dimi's voice called out.

"You want us to give your father yer regards, traitor?"

An old fire rose along my spine. For a moment, reason abandoned me. That moment was all I needed to turn back and face them.

"What did you say?"

"Oh, sorry," Dimi sneered, *"touchy subject?"*

Herris continued for his brother, his short tail flicking behind him.

"I wonder how long it would take him to march down here himself if he knew his traitor son was spending his nights with a human?*"*

"A disappointment to Daddy and the Reidship."

"We'll be sure to let him know." Herris waived, as if excusing me from their presence.

I knew these words. I knew these *exact* words. I'd heard them all before from someone else's lips. Anger, against my better judgment, rose up the nape of my neck. If Jorel expected to torment and intimidate me through his lackeys, he'd clearly forgotten where I'd come from. I wasn't a stranger to this brand of bullying. I knew from hard experience what would happen if I rose to the challenge.

My muscles screamed to run. Unfortunately for me, it *had* been a touchy subject. One I wasn't prepared to walk away from after the long day I'd encountered. *Especially* not in front of Simon, when I wasn't sure how much of this he was following along with. My mouth opened on its own.

"What you tell my father over pillowtalk isn't any of my business." I shrugged, switching to Human. "I will be sure to give your mother the same regards."

The twins couldn't speak Human. Simon understood me perfectly fine though, and let out a snort of laughter. I grinned in the moment.

It was short lived.

At the reality of being laughed at by a human, the twins began to square up, advancing towards us with hands on their weapons. Simon swore colorfully, his voice pitched a bit high in panic. The crowd moved away on instinct.

I knew that was the wrong move to make. Any satisfaction at my upper hand was cut short by the gleam of their weapons being drawn. *This is why,* I scolded myself, *it's always better to just run.*

Two large, scarred hands appeared behind them and yanked the twins back by their tails.

They stumbled in surprise, and I took a step back into Simon's frozen chest. Those hands came and grabbed their shoulders, locking them firmly in place.

"You absolute idiots," Second Commander Vaga snarled. *"You'd raise arms against the reid in training before temple grounds? Tonight of all nights?"*

Vaga was an intimidating woman. She stood a head taller than either of them, but she kept her face down when looking at me. It was both a sign of respect and a way to hide the nasty scar that bisected her face. She kept her bangs longer than was considered in style for that very purpose, but wore the rest of her brown strands in a tight braided crown.

She'd earned that scar, and many others, fighting along the northern border with Asterel. She was renowned for her fighting skills and her iron-clad demeanor. Beside her— a true warrior— the twins looked like meek bullies.

"But—" Dimi started, and she leaned in close and snarled something I couldn't hear. His face grew stormy, but both he and his brother put their weapons away. She let them go with a shove.

"Forgive their words," She requested, but the amicable tone of her voice didn't reach her eyes. *"They have no respect for anything."*

I looked at her, then the twins, and finally, Simon. He was watching this whole interaction with uncertainty, his hands shaking. He didn't turn away from Vaga and the twins. My anger swelled again. I turned back to her.

"Humans use leads to keep their dogs in check," I said, feeling bolder than I had any right to. *"You might want to invest in some."*

Her face didn't move. Her voice came out just a bit harder.

"Best get to your scrollwork, Gen. Haliz has a plan for us all this evening."

It was a dismissal if I had ever heard one. The tension of the moment snapped away. All the anger left me, and exhaustion remained. I hadn't picked a fight like that in years. Then again, no one had both threatened Simon and brought up my father in the same breath before.

I was getting real tired of Jorel sharing my business over the whole island.

Especially his brutish Kor lackeys.

"Sure." I said, turning again and dragging Simon away by the arm.

He let me pull him, grateful to get away from the Kor. I felt the three's eyes on us the rest of the walk until the crowd filled in behind us.

We got out of sight of the bridge and well into the compound before I stopped to take a breath and listen to Simon's many attempts to ask what had happened.

"Are you okay? Are *we* okay? What was *that*?"

I took a breath.

"The usual Kor antics. I shouldn't have riled them up."

He crossed his arms.

"It didn't look like that was all." I couldn't meet his eyes. He continued. "The Kor *never* come this close to the temple. Why are they here? What did they say?"

"Nothing important."

"*Gen.*"

I'd lost track of how many times he had said my name in that same tone of voice that night.

"They were being assholes. Be grateful that you cannot speak the language."

He waited for more. I didn't offer it.

"*Gen.*"

"If you worked harder on your language studies," I chided, hoping this would change the topic, "You could have figured it out for yourself."

He looked at me in bewilderment.

"Are you *seriously* turning this back on me?"

"Yes."

He threw his hands up. "How are you this obtuse?"

"What is *obtuse?*"

"*You!*" he said, rubbing his face. "*You* are obtuse. You haven't answered a single question of mine point blank, you almost got into a *fight* with the Kor, and I still don't know where we're going or what we're doing tonight."

A disappointment to Daddy and *the Reidship.*

That weariness came back. I didn't want to deal with this. I didn't want to think about Jorel and his Kor, I didn't want to think of my father, or my duties I'd run from, and most of all I didn't want Simon to be upset with me.

I'd been on edge all day. I should have been with Mael, preparing for the very ceremony this city lauded. Instead, I was disappointing my only friend, running from my duties and picking fights with the Kor.

The ringed scars on my arms served to remind me of my constant ineptitude. The festivals reminded me it was more than just Mael I was letting down. I could hold my own against all of that, though. I had done it countless times before.

Looking into Simon's bright blue eyes, and the frustration he had behind them, I realized I couldn't disappoint *him*.

When did I begin to fold so easily for this man?

Across the sprawling roadways leading to the temple and the buildings before it, I saw a lone house alight in vibrant gold lantern glow. Mael's home. *Shouldn't she be in the temple by now?*

She's probably waiting for me, I realized, *she's expecting us to come by before the ceremony.*

After the strangeness that was the Kor on the bridge, I had a feeling I had more to discuss with her than just Simon. Something was off with their behavior, and Mael couldn't afford distractions while holding a melding ceremony. I shuddered at the thought of what could happen if one went wrong.

I owed Simon a better night. And I owed Mael a lot more.

Simon was still waiting. I took in a breath. Let it out.

"Come on," I said, "I'll show you."

Simon opened his mouth like he was going to object, thought about it for a minute, then closed his mouth and began to follow. Apparently this was good enough to settle on.

I wasn't great with words. This would have to do.

I took him down the main stone path. The crowd had begun to thin as everyone hurried off to celebrations or temple duties or the main sanctuary itself, if they'd been invited. The sky was almost entirely purple with only a soft haze of blue light coming from the horizon. Lanterns and more colorful glass lights decorated the walk paths, lighting the way.

I ached for an evening sitting in the library, the walls lined with shelves of scrolls and old tomes, pens scattered on the table in front of us as we fought over definitions and the impossible barrier of language between us. I thought of how peaceful it would be, how that side of the temple would be almost entirely empty save for our little corner tonight.

I knew that longing was for something I would never have again. Introducing Simon to the melding ceremony was going to change everything. It scared me, made my mind race in fear, but my thinking had already done enough damage tonight. So I put my faith in Mael's decision and kept my eyes down the paths ahead.

The temple loomed before us, surrounded by scatterings of buildings and houses and far
off trees.

Torrel Del Tor, *The center of Central City.* The temple was truly the heart of the island, with Haliz Fundir at its core. The original builders who came here escaping the wars of the mainland built the temple around it, a tall, cylindrical structure with an open top to allow rain to enter. A square building with arched ceilings served as the original temple housing and the main way in or out of the central chamber. Over the years the temple had been added to, with many buildings and walk paths jutting from the original, growing as the role of the compound changed. It was almost a small city in and of itself, sprawling over the large flat clearing the river split around. Housing and storage facilities, even a small school, had been added separate from the temple in an inclusive neighborhood.

We veered off the main path and into this area, heading up a small incline towards the largest house of the bunch. Many were dark and empty for the night, and it shone like a beacon.

Simon stepped closer to me, taking in everything around us. He'd never been taken to this part of the grounds before. Honestly, he may be one of the first humans to walk this road.

I wish I could have shown it to him in the daylight. He would have loved all the details the shadows of twilight now hid.

Mael's house was a shrine dedicated to the deft hands of every artisan in the city. Every surface, from shutters to the tall wooden doors and even the roof, carried small details, carvings or handiwork from dozens of hands over. They showed our history, motifs of our home and tiny secrets hidden in plain sight. It was gorgeous, a sprawling single floor home with treasures in every corner.

I would have loved to watch his face as he drank it all in, scoured every surface and nook and cranny like a treasure hunt to find all the hidden details. Maybe tomorrow I would bring him back.

My stomach twisted again at the thought, and I couldn't decide if it was a good feeling.

The door and windows were all open to the evening air, and I stepped over the threshold.

Simon stopped at the doorway.

"Should I wait here?"

I understood his hesitation. But if I let him hesitate, I was going to hesitate. I reached out and took his arm, pulling him inside.

"Too late," I shrugged, beginning my search for Mael. After a moment, Simon followed.

We were standing in the main living area. Wooden beams ran the length of the ceiling, some holding ceramic statues or decor and baubles. The walls were covered in hanging textiles, all vibrant and art in their own right. some from well known artisans and masters of the craft, and others still from beginners who had worked at the temple whom she'd offered support. Colorful patterns of the night sky, local folklore, and even one or two erotic tales danced through rugs, blankets, and hung shawls.

Every possible shelf space was filled with scrolls, art or collected bits of functional dinner wares that had suited her fancy. Letters from those she'd helped, thankful gifts from the community, and more were all organized and placed with care. The rooms all ran into each other, wide arches with hung tapestry dividers swept to the side beckoning you into the next space. She liked to keep low-sitting tables with comfortable cushions around them instead of taller seats to create a sense of informality and comfort.

I took us deeper into the familiar space. The kitchen was just to our left, and while Mael had been far too busy to cook today, the ever present aroma of spice lingered. The ceramics were all stacked neatly on shelves and the large cooking pot sat empty over the brick stove. The kitchen was one of the few rooms devoid of rugs, but the tiled floor was no less decorative in its place.

She'd told me over the course of many years the stories of each and every corner of her home, gifted to her by her late husband. *The tiles show the night sky the day we married,* she'd said.

And the flowers? I'd asked, one of the first things I'd ever said to her.

She'd jumped in surprise at my voice, and then settled into a soft, melancholy smile. *I used those flowers in my crown on our wedding night.*

They're almost sad, now that he's gone, she'd added, *but that is the truth of living, isn't it? Everything has a bit of sadness woven through.*

Especially for those with lives like ours.

"Whose house is this?" Simon finally asked, breaking me from the memory.

No point in delaying it.

"This is Mael's home," I answered. I saw his eyes widen in disbelief, then narrow just as quickly. His voice came out in a hiss.

"You brought me to *Reid Mael's* house?

"Into." I corrected him, and he looked at me like I was being *obtuse* again.

"You can't just waltz into the reid's home!"

"No," I corrected him, "*You* cannot. Not without an invitation. Which I gave you."

If his eyes went any wider, they were going to fall out.

"What makes you so special?" I was saved from answering by the sound of rising voices. Voices I knew all too well.

One I was far less than thrilled to hear.

"Wait here." He didn't need to get in the middle of one of their arguments. I went into the hall and towards the back of the estate, not waiting to see if he listened. His objections followed me loudly away.

Further beyond the kitchen was a small courtyard space, just large enough for a herb garden and a bit of nature. I crossed through it to the other side. The bedrooms lay beyond, as did the bathing room and the furthest sitting room. I entered the hallway, following the voices.

I shouldn't have been surprised to hear him there, but I hadn't expected it. I wouldn't have brought Simon along if I had.

Steeling myself, I stepped through the doorway.

"I am not going to discuss this again," Mael said sharply, pulling a stack of plates down to make room for some new set. There was no hostility in her voice, but there was a distinct note of finality.

His response was measured, spoken in a tight, low tone.

"Tonight, more than ever, I need you to hear what I'm saying."

"Jorel," Mael started again, but he stepped closer and put a hand on the plate she meant to grab.

"Mael," he said, "listen to me."

Something heavy filled the air. Mael was dwarfed by Jorel's massive form. His shoulders alone were twice as broad as her, and he towered above us both in height. I'd heard that Mael's late husband had been built just the same, but with a soft, quiet disposition.

Clearly that virtue hadn't passed to the physical embodiment of intimidation before me.

Jorel's sienna tail swayed like a snake behind him, the same color his mother's was before the gray settled in.. His deep chestnut hair was cropped to keep it out of his eyes, far shorter than most styles at the temple. It curled at its longest, trying to spiral out of control like Mael's wild mop. His jaw was tense, pushing his defined cheekbones out. His skin was far more tan than the last time I had seen him, a testament to his work outdoors. He was handsome in a commanding, masculine way that rolled my stomach. I'd never been one for male figures of authority, and everything about him commanded it. His looks, his stance, his arrogance.

Like my running outfit, his clothing hugged him tightly across the chest and legs, showing off his large musculature. The fabric was a deep blue, almost black in low light, made from a wide sash that first sat across the shoulders and back then wrapped twice around his torso and tied off at his pants. A purple belt hung around his waist, a few metal buttons and pins displayed in a show of his status. Each was a recognition of his achievements in the Kor. Over the base wraps he wore a leather armor piece for his shoulders. The leather was embroidered with the familiar design of a bear over a spear and hatchet; an emblem every guard position in the city wore with only a few differences. The spear and hatchet defined the Kor insignia.

He'd hung more leather at his hips, one side longer to cover his off leg nearly to the knee. His leggings were the same deep blue as his top, but it was a thicker material that disappeared into his sturdy leather boots. His arms were bare and very tan from days working outdoors, save for the few metal cuffs on either arm for protection or decor. I noticed he'd abided by his mother's rules of the house and left his spear outside

Neither noticed me at first, their matching green hazel eyes locked on each other. I was fine with being overlooked.

Things had once been simple between Jorel and I. Well, *simpler.* We were never meant to stand on good terms. Jorel was the only son of Mael— and fiercely obstinate towards anything she cared for— while I was the flighty little pupil she would never let alone. He questioned everything, and never acted without deep, extensive calculations. I'd never had the energy to gather my thoughts and ran on instinct alone.

We'd gotten on like oil and water.

Most of my early temple memories involved sitting motionless in whatever corner I could find of their open-aired home while mother and son debated. It was about anything and everything, in the beginning. Time together meant arguing laws and the construction of our society in a very meta sense. Every memory was permeated by the sounds of their debates, the sharp gleam of their wit reflecting one another.

I saw that same fire present now, but things had changed. Mael's glare had dulled with age and weariness, like a stone smoothed with the tides of life. Jorel's had sharpened into a wicked blade. When they spoke to each other, it wasn't lighthearted anymore.

Jorel had always unnerved me. But these last few years especially so.

"Sol's patrols have gotten far more bold," he reported while pacing in slow, even steps. "They have pushed their markers forward past the wood plates, one at a time, testing us. If we do not respond in kind, he will take our inaction as the weakness he's been looking for. His hunters are already taking more from the eastern trails than last year.. Something must be done."

"As I've said, that 'something' will be handled by the Kor, not Del Tor. No matter the setbacks, the Kor have always held off his fits of power grabbing. Not to mention," she added, "they have quite a capable new captain at their helm."

She patted the metal band on his bicep, a symbol of a hard earned promotion.

"If the powers that be on the counsel are not willing to step up and aid you, then convince them. If anyone could, it's you. You've always understood what drives people, use that to your advantage."

"The merchant counsel has made it annoyingly clear they won't grace us with funding if we step out of their plan of action. Of *inaction*," he corrected. "Trade with Asterel is too lucrative for them to see past their wallets. It's the same as always, and with Hen presiding over the counsel we aren't getting a majority vote."

"Color me shocked that the merchant counsel is putting money before sense," she muttered. "Then work *within* their plans, the same as always. It's all posturing with Sol, you know this. He's flexing his arms to remind us the muscles are there and nothing more. Come winter he'll have let us take back the markers to their rightful place. It's a dance we've survived a life-time."

"That's just it, isn't it?" He stopped pacing, standing with his hands behind his back and his boots pointed directly at her.

He practically towered over her, twice her width in sheer muscles and broadness alone. Mael never shrank away.

"It's a *dance* because no one is willing to step on his toes. It's a *dance* because we play along."

He leaned forward, that sharpness a wicked glint in his eyes.

"If we flex back, show off the true strength and capability of Torrel, he'll stop bothering us. He'll stop playing the ever present shadow and threat. We won't count the lives lost on the border as wasted sacrifices. We need to set an example, to be proactive instead of cowering behind excuses of—"

"Enough, Jorel!" She threw her hands up in long tired exasperation, hoping to cut off a very old fight before it even began.

"I no longer have the time or energy to keep arguing this point with you!"

"Mael," He said, his voice a low, even rumble. I didn't know when he'd stopped calling her mother, but it was long before he was kicked out.

"You don't leave the temple. You don't know the people of the city. Del Tor holds so much sway and strength, more than Sol or a few merchants could ever understand. We cannot keep wasting lives to keep a few merchants happy. People are tired, and scared. Sol knows this, and he holds that fear over us like a sword above our beds. He may never drop it, but he could, and every night he doesn't pushes the city into more panic. They know it's coming, it's not a matter of if but when."

"It's far more complicated than that," she started. Jorel kept talking over her.

"Sol holds all the power over us. There is nothing we can do if he decides to take us by surprise. Our city, this temple, we will fold beneath him. We need to even the playing field. We need to strike first."

His eyes were lost in his own convictions. I could taste the words he was about to say before he even said them. They were the same words that drove his mother to revoke his apprenticeship and banish him from Del Tor. Now they rose in him like a familiar hunger, a dark fixation he could never seem to let go.

"We can do that with *Haliz Fundir*. With the melding. The old texts tell us how, if you would just listen and see that it's the only way to end this dance for good—"

"*Enough!*" Mael raised her voice. Her bright amber eyes met her son's, and they flashed with the weight every reid carries. There was something more there, too; a pain edged with anger that welled from deep within her. It was the pain only a mother could hold for a child they had lost to the world. Tonight it burned.

"I will never hand over Haliz Fundir to you. Your passion for consequences you cannot begin to understand will end in the decimation of our people. Wielding Haliz against anyone, and especially Sol, would guarantee a war you refuse to see as losable because you can never look past your own nose. Take this dance. Be grateful that every life lost in this unending and miserable cold war is not the hundreds that would fall in a real one. Inaction against Asterel *is* protecting our people, something you have so boldly refused to see in your lust for blood."

Mael's voice had raised with every sentence until it filled the room, and then all at once it dropped. Her tone was no less firm, but all that fire and anger bled from her until only bone deep exhaustion remained.

"Your intentions are noble, Jorel, but where you lost your touch with reality I will never know. A failure on my part, for sure."

Something settled between them. Neither moved. Jorel studied her for a long second before accepting this resolution.

"So be it, then. If you won't work with me, I'll find a way without you. I always have."

He turned to go, stopping when he saw me. His lip twisted up in a sneer.

"I'll assure the city they can sleep easy knowing the greatest strength of our world is in the capable hands of two sniveling cowards."

Mael's gaze followed his to mine. It was clear she hadn't noticed me slip in.

"Oh! Gen," she said, before turning to her son. "Jorel, don't you dare start this with him tonight—"

"It's not a lie. He dropped his training by his own accord. He's a coward and a failure by every definition of the words."

I met his gaze. Anger from the scene on the bridge rose within me again.

"Better than being kicked out for being an insufferable warmonger."

"Boys!" Mael scolded, "Enough!"

Her tone cut through us like a knife.

"Gen has his path to follow," she told Jorel, "as do you. And it is not here trying out the same tiring argument only to turn in on Gen when things do not go your way."

She stepped forward, but there was less anger in her movement, less bite in her words. Just the tired scorn of a mother long weary of her sons' fighting.

"He is not your fallback, nor your scapegoat. Your shortcomings are your own. I beg for you to understand the reality of what you demand, before it is too late."

She waited for his reply. Jorel said nothing. Her shoulders sagged, a long, drawn out sigh escaping her.

"Good night, son. Have a safe journey home."

Jorel steadied his shoulders with finality.

"...So be it."

He paused on his way out, his eyes looking down at me. I didn't shy away.

"I would call you worthless, but that's not quite right, is it? Even a dead tree has its worth to the worms."

I met his eyes.

"Even assholes have purpose. Glad you've found yours, Jorel."

He stared me down, but I held firm. The moment ran long, then was cut with the snapped turn of his head.

"I'll be seeing you around," his words followed him, his shadow pulling across the door. *I sure fucking hope not.*

I turned back to Mael, solemn and lost in her own thoughts. She was back to clearing off her desk, lost in her silence. She shook as she picked up the same stack of plates.

Our hands met when I came to help, and she finally looked up at me. I gave her my best look of understanding. I earned a weak smile and a breathy sigh.

"I'm sorry," I said. "I know you hate when we fight."

"I knew from the day I brought you home it was inevitable. You two couldn't be more different," She looked lost in a memory.

"I'm hardly the size of three grown men all on my own."

She laughed at that, genuinely.

"I don't know where he got it from. I fed you both the same and his father was never *that* broad."

"You used to say it was from the stress he put on his shoulders," I offered. "Remember?"

"I do. I also quite clearly remember you correcting me that he *was overly bloated with his own ego.*"

"Well," I offered, "You did raise me to deal in little truths."

I earned a choked snort and a playfully admonishing slap on my arm.

"Gen," she scolded, but I knew I was in no real trouble. It had been so long since we'd found comfort in each other's presence, spent time together or spoken like this. Seeing Jorel again had given us common footing to face each other.

Guess Jorel's special brand of asshole was good for something, after all.

"The truth.... someday he'll come to it, I'm sure. He's just still too young, so full of energy and ready to change the world." She shook her head. "Senseless lives lost...I would rather spend a thousand years dancing back and forth with Sol's gameplay than a single day in the true carnage an arms race would beget."

"He doesn't know Sol like we do," I said softly. "Or understand the truth of *Haliz.*"

It took something out of me to bring that up. Mael noticed. She reached up and touched my cheek.

"You are far stronger than he'll ever be, for being able to shoulder this. No matter where you are now. Know that those words are true."

Her hand caressed my cheek. Fondness mixed with loss as we both remembered the final rights of reid training. It was the last big truth that Jorel had been denied. It was the truth I had crumpled under. It was the day Mael lost us both.

Another apology came to my lips, but she shook her head.

"What brought you here?"

I thought of the altercation on the bridge. I'd come here to warn her about the Kor causing trouble, and Jorel's possible hand in it. Considering Jorel himself had been here, and what he'd had to say, I didn't think it was worth telling her the rest.

"I was thinking of rescheduling our translations." I started carefully.

She paused, and her mouth turned into a slow grin.

"*Mmm.* The translations are important work, Gen. Are you sure you can skip them?"

"I was thinking of changing it to more of a cultural lesson."

"Yeah?"

The argument she'd endured with Jorel fresh on my mind, I nodded. Someone needed to not let her down tonight. Guess that would have to be me.

"Yeah," I agreed. "With one caveat."

Her lips twitched up in a grin.

"Oh? And what demands does my translator have?"

"I'd like to use a window," I said, "instead of the front door."

Chapter Five

Simon, Mael's home

I'd been left alone. I stood in the middle of the large kitchen, not daring to move. I was trapped somewhere between duty and regret, unable to ignore the call of my work but desperately wanting to.

Gen, I cursed silently, *why did you have to bring me here?*

Simon, A voice whispered in my thoughts, sounding exactly like Tess, *this is a once in a lifetime opportunity. This is what we sent you for! Stop standing around and do your damned job.*

I'm only going to ask once.

I shivered. I hated the work I did for Tess, but it was the only choice I had. Protection from Chelsea had to be paid in servitude. That was our agreement from the very beginning.

My life was only worth what information I could squirrel back to her.

I'd traded one demon for another.

I began moving around the room, careful not to touch anything yet. Guilt wracked me as I traced the lines of the cookware into my mind, and memorized the location and purpose of every chair, table, window and wall. I didn't know how long Gen would be gone, and I hoped if I could bring back schematics, at least, Tess would be understanding.

Three windows, three interior archways. Part of the floor by the stove was sunken, and the hand tiling looked like the night sky. Against the far interior wall I found a tapestry depicting seven women in the throes of ecstasy with each other, their bodies entwined with countless swords, vines, and flowers. My face heated up. *I wonder if the reid's taste in pornographic art is the kind of thing Tess wants to know.*

If she found it useful enough to overlook all the secrets I keep hidden from her about Gen, then so be it. I would trade away knowledge of his people, his home, his culture and Ried Mael herself, but never once have I told Tess any of the strange things that never added up with him.

Selfishly, I wanted to keep him safe and all to myself. A deep, guilty ache ran through my chest again. *Did I even have the right?*

"A human in the kitchen," a low voice rumbled to the side of me.

I whirled in a panic to find an absolute unit of a kriest engulfing the archway Gen had gone through. I had never met this one before. His eyes narrowed at me, not in disgust, but in a kind of rapt contemplation. I felt a shiver go through me, and for a single instant I wondered if he could have heard my thoughts. I felt exposed before his gaze in a way I had never been before. He looked between me and the tapestry, then settled on me again.

"Mael's still bringing home stray animals, it seems."

I opened my mouth, meaning to defend myself, but the words died on my tongue. My eyes had landed on the purple sash and the pins he wore. *Kor.* Judging by the arm bands, he was high ranking, at that.

His eyes remained intensely on mine. *Would Gen get here in time, if I yelled? Could he even do anything against someone like this?*

My shoulder hit the wall, and I realized I had taken a step back. I was cornered, in more ways than one.

"Your men are waiting for you on the bridge." I found myself saying. "We passed them on the way here."

He seemed interested in this.

"Oh? You met with the twins, and they let you pass?"

"I had Gen with me." I answered, wondering if his name would hold any weight. His eyes turned cold, calculating. Something in his jaw tightened. He leaned his weight on one hip, shifting. Thinking. I regretted it immediately.

"So you're the translator Mael has been pandering to." He observed.

"More like putting up with," I laughed weakly, hoping to lighten the mood.

It didn't.

He opened his mouth again, and this time he spoke fully in Kriest. My brain scrambled to keep up, but all I could make of his apparent question was *do you...think...really?*

I tried not to look stupid. I probably failed. The kriest took another step in, tilting his head.

"A translator who cannot even speak our language," he said in perfect Human. "Left alone to waltz about in the unguarded home of the current reid."

"I'm not alone," I said hastily, "Gen is here with me."

Jorel looked around the room slowly. To the left, to the right, up into the rafters, curiously, then back to me.

"In spirit, then?"

"Your language skills are flawless."

"And yours," he said, "should have been the first warning sign."

I wanted to ask what he meant by that, but I knew. I dreadfully, dreadfully knew. Somehow in only a few sentences this man had seen completely through me, and I was hopeless to stop him. I opened my mouth to play dumb, when his ear twitched and he turned back down the hall the way Gen had disappeared a few minutes before. Then he turned back to me, and I forgot how to speak under that intense gaze.

"I wonder," he said, "how this night will end for you."

"I wonder if you sound as egotistical to yourself as you do to everyone else."

I hadn't meant to be sarcastic, but it earned me a huff of breath, almost a laugh from the man. He pushed his frame away from the door and stepped into the hall, throwing one last word in as he went toward the front entrance.

"I wonder if you really are as clever as you delude yourself into believing."

And with that, he was gone.

The room settled around me, as if the house had been holding its breath in his presence. *Prick*, I thought quietly, turning back to the art I had been taking in earlier to get my mind off the interaction.

"Did he say anything to you?" a familiar voice asked just behind me, and my heart leapt at the sound. I turned to see Gen standing in the opposite doorway, his arms crossed.

"Nothing particularly awful, if that's what you're asking."

"*Mmm.*"

I met the deep gaze of his nearly black eyes. They had the deep roundness of a hazel, but lost in his own thoughts they seemed darker. His eyelashes were dark and long, enough that I had contemplated and scrapped the thought he might wear a kind of mascara at least a hundred times, and his eyebrows were crisp cut and thickly furrowed on his face. They pinched in the middle now while he stared at the space the other kriest had been.

He clenched and unclenched his jaw. Each motion pushed his cheekbones forward into stark contrast. His tail twitched at the tip like an angry cat. I'd rarely seen him this contemplative and bothered.

"Everything okay?" I asked him.

"Fine," he sighed, but one of his dark fawn-like ears twitched. They were about as long as my hand from palm to fingertips and were the deep color of midnight. I discovered to an almost disappointing level that most Kriest were not very expressive with their ears as, say, a cat would be, and he was no exception. His ears were usually cast back and down to be out of the way, and they blended well in his unruly raven curls.

So something truly was bothering him about the kriest who had left. Maybe there was history there? They didn't look related...maybe an old lover?

I didn't like the way my stomach tightened at the thought.

"Alright then. Did you get your question answered, at least?"

"Hmm?" he asked, then remembered why we had come there. His eyes met mine and in a very strange and human turn of emotion he quirked the side of his mouth and his eyebrows up just slightly. The tip of his tail flicked again, but this time in amusement.

"Yeah," he said, "You, my dear human, are about to make history."

"What?"

"Would you like to see?"

I blinked. Once. Twice. "See what?"

"The ceremony."

"Wait," I asked, "*The* ceremony?"

"That is what I just said."

"Yeah, but I didn't believe it. I still don't." Something churned in my stomach again, but this time it wasn't jealousy. It was guilt. "Why would I get invited?"

"Mael wants to change the world, to open up our ceremonies and stories to the humans."

"Isn't that what we've been working on?" I asked, "You translating old texts and me bringing them back to our education committee?"

Isn't that enough? Why would you want me to learn more? Don't you know why I'm really here?

Of course he didn't, though. I'd never told him. That was the point.

"She wants you to be welcomed and involved. And she thinks tonight is a great way to open that door." He reached over to a shelf, picked up a small glass bauble in the shape of a leaf, and rolled it over and over in his hands. Sometimes, when he got restless, he just needed to move. "She wants you to be the first human to see a melding. I want you to, as well."

My brain did that fuzzy thing again, seeing his hand extended to me, and my stomach tightened even further with guilt. More than that came an excitement I had no right to have.

I could be the very first human to ever witness the single most sacred ceremony of the temple. It was an honored invitation from the highest kriest in the temple, one who helped personally drive forward the relationship and survival of my kind since we'd arrived. And out of everyone on the island, she'd extended *me* the honor.

I wasn't worthy. I truly wasn't. But I wanted to be.

"....Okay," I breathed, words failing me.

"Okay," he said back, then got a thoughtful look on his face. "....how good are you at climbing?"

Chapter Six

Gen, Torrel Del Tor Rooftops

It turns out the answer to my question was *not well*.

The temple proper had not been built with certain securities in mind. It was designed to close off *Haliz Fudir* from the larger fold of the woods and create a platform for ceremonies. The original architect had not designed against wily preteens determined to scale the walls and explore every nook and cranny. Most of my youth had been spent familiarizing myself with every portion of the ancient walls, and now as an adult the pathways I had learned had become second nature to me.

When Mael had taken me in as her apprentice, I had been eleven years old and in a constant state of what Simon called *fight or flight mode*. I had never been much of a fighter, even if my childhood had called for it, so I'd leaned heavily into flight. It turns out, most people were fine with a lateral chase, but rarely did anyone ever want to follow you *up*. Vertical climbing was not a skill many adults, nor kids, possessed.

With that said, Simon was truly a disaster at it.

"Stop looking down," I told him, reaching for him from the next highest roof.

Even I had trouble making the long climb from ground level, so I'd opted for an easier route to my window of choice. It had taken us up a few buildings and across roofs and walkway covers, and with my human dragging behind what should have been a five minute journey at a walking pace was now dragging to thrice that length, and we *weren't even to the main temple wall yet.*

Fuck—I'd just thought of him as *my human* again.

"It's hard not to," he'd hissed back, finally pulling his eyes back up to my outstretched hand. "I've never climbed a building this high before."

"You're been in plenty of two story buildings."

"Yes," he took my hand, and with a grunt of effort let me help pull him up the small wall to the next level. "But I was *on the inside* of the buildings."

"There really is not much of a difference," I said, patting his back once he was up.

"That is a bold faced lie and you know it."

"Stop fussing, we're almost there."

"You know, being a distinguished guest and all it sure seems like we're doing anything *but* walking through the front door right now."

"I am giving you the best view in the temple," I said, and caught the look he gave me as we walked along another roof. "What? It is the truth. Stop fussing."

"I am not *fussing.*"

"Well you are not *not* fussing." He groaned, "I never should have taught you the concept of a double negative."

"That still sounds like fussing."

He swatted the air towards me playfully, and I dodged with ease, not losing my footing on the slight incline. He scowled more, motioning to what I had just done.

"Not all of us have the athleticism of a cat, Gen."

"What is a *cat?*"

He blinked, as if I had just asked a truly strange question, then blinked again in consideration.

"...An old world animal, known for its agility," he answered, then looked past me. "Is this it?"

The wall of the main temple loomed before us, connecting directly with the building we'd walked on top of. The temple wall had many smaller windows this high up, mostly to allow light in during the day, and they were the perfect size for a grown adult to slip through.

Luckily, the window I was aiming for wasn't too far up from the roof. I turned to Simon.

"Stay here," I said, taking a few steps back. He watched me intensely. I tried not to enjoy the feeling of his eyes on me.

I failed.

After a distance I steadied my feet and launched forward. My feet came down once, twice, a third time and I was pushing off, leaping to grab onto the ledge above and catching it with the ease of practice. I swung one leg up and used my foot to pull my lower body up and sideways into the arched window, coming to sit straddling the ledge with one leg in the darker alcove and the other back out in the evening air. Simon looked pale, even from up there.

"Absolutely not," he said, shaking his head. "You're going to get me killed."

"It's easier than it looks," I tried, but he only shook his head more adamantly. I rolled my eyes, pretending I hadn't fully expected this.

"It looks *impossible*."

"It's not."

"You're a hopeless showoff, you know that?"

I cracked a smile. "Only to those who appreciate it," I called down. The light was too dim to see his face, and I hope it hid the way my own warmed up.

"Relax," I finally conceded, "You don't need to jump up."

"I cannot stand you sometimes."

"It will be worth it." I found the foothold I had been looking for, up and to the side in a way I could press my knee against the stone windowsill and reach down for him with both hands, using my legs to anchor my weight firm. "Grab my hands and walk up the wall, I'll pull you in."

I paused for a second.

"Oh, and take off your shoes."

"Why?"

"It is easier barefooted."

"This doesn't look any easier."

"You can do it," I said, although I didn't feel so sure about that.

"You don't sound very sure about that."

"You're fussing again."

He groaned, wiping his face with his hand and taking a step back. He eyed the wall, then me, before steeling himself. He came to stand beneath me, reaching up to test the space and then let out a long, held breath.

"Okay," he mumbled, more to himself than me. "Okay."

Simon didn't take long to undo the laces of his short boots. They were discarded neatly beside him, facing forward with care. He stood, took a half step back, braced himself and jumped up to meet me. Despite his lessened athleticism he made the distance, and my hands clasped around his wrists perfectly. He gripped mine back, and caught himself on the wall with his toes.

He took in a hiss of breath.

"Oww," he said, but I was already pulling him in.

"Fuck," he swore, struggling to walk up like I'd told him. I didn't waver, holding tight to his wrist and pulling back with all of my core and leg muscles.

"Almost there," I consoled him, and he looked up at me desperately.

"I can't hold on much longer," he gasped, panic in his eyes.

"I can."

I pulled him in fully, catching him against my chest as he scrambled over the ledge with his knees, shins, and finally feet. We collapsed against each other on the long stone platform, the shadows of the alcove covering us entirely.

He pushed himself up and away, embarrassment written on his face. I watched him take in the small area we sat in with those curious eyes of his.

"What is this place?" he asked, "The main temple of Del Tor," I answered, "Home to *Haliz Fundir*."

"I figured that," he said, "I meant this little, uh, alcove thing? It's not big enough to be a room."

Ah.

"Once, statues were stored in these... alcoves. Over time the art's weight was making issues with the, uh, building walls." I didn't know his words for *structural integrity.* "They took them all out but left the alcoves."

The look of abject horror on his face was wonderful.

"This *wasn't* the long way in?" his eyes turned to the glow of the temple beyond my shoulder. I moved to the side so he would have room to see.

"Don't look down," I warned him again, however it wasn't *down* he was looking, but *out.*

"*Astounding*," he breathed, and I knew what he saw. We were about three stories up at this point, closer to four, and barely halfway up the height of *Haliz Fundir*'s massive form, just above the lowest branches.

The main temple chamber was a large round room surrounding the centralized trunk of the massive tree, with a single walkway emerging from large wooden doors to the main platform about fifteen feet above the roots. The bottom story was solid, without doors or windows, and during the rainy seasons it would flood up to the walkway like a lake.

The water level was low enough tonight to gather in the white roots and reflect the spectacle of a room above it. The walking path was made of dark woods, ancient and weathered but withstanding the test of time. On the central point of the room, around the tree, there was a circular platform that went directly up to the trunk, wide enough to be a large stage with room for an audience to kneel or stand.

No one ever approached the trunk itself. . It was forbidden to touch it, considered a sacred rite of the reids. *It will be fine if anyone touches it,* Mael's voice came to me in a memory, a cold chill of fear coming with it. *Forbidding it just means any rule breakers will stop with a touch. It takes more than that, as we both know, to start a meld.*

My scars ached. I closed my eyes, took a steadying breath, and tried to focus on Simon when I opened them again.

Tonight, as with any ceremony night, the central stage was decorated in evenly spaced candles, lanterns and decor. Strings of glass beads wound around the railings, broken with occasional charms or strung flowers. The strong scent of ceremonial spices wafted up in a sweet, almost earthen tone from large bowls of aromatics. The central platform had a large decorative rug against the tree, and surrounding it were baskets of breads and meats. Lights led to this central staging area, washing the floor in warm golden tones that shone against the time-polished floors.

And the tree, oh, *Haliz Fundir* itself. From the very first time I had laid eyes on *Haliz,* something haunting and mesmerizing had held me captive. The sheer size was awe inducing, nearly nine stories tall, all of it a haunting beauty. Unlike traditional dark wood trees, the trunk, roots and branches of *Haliz Fundir* were a cold white, flecked in divots and grooves of deep indigo and red tones that matched its leaves. The body was less one solid mass than hundreds of thick, coiling vine-like structures that had wound tightly together all the way to the sky. It was as hard and cool as stone. The leaves were large and flat, bigger than my head and always in vibrant arrays of reds and indigos regardless of the season.

It was ethereal. It was beautiful. It was unworldly.

It haunted my flesh and bones.

Where awe had once filled me at its sight, terror now settled deep within me. Being in the temple again made my scars sing, so I tried to focus on Simon and let myself feel his initial emotions. The wonder and awe of the life form before him. The beauty and elegance. His eyes widened in rapture.

The temple was almost empty, just a few attendants setting up for the ceremony, and no one had noticed us yet. I let Simon have his initial moment of wonder before reaching out and gently touching his arm.

"It's a lot," I said, honestly. "At first."

He turned, blinking at me. I could see a hundred thoughts racing in his mind. I yearned to hear them, even if I couldn't always understand them. I adored how he took in the world, how his thoughts could swirl in from a thousand places at once and yet come back up in organized, well-derived lines. I admired that ability. I yearned for it myself.

I pulled him down to sit with me on the statue platform. This one, at least, was still sound.

"What's that?" He asked, his voice still a tad breathy as he pointed to a nearby wall..

"An old doorway," I replied. There was enough room to sit with your back to the wall and either pull your legs up on the ledge or dangle them off. "There was a small tower next to it once, back when the collection of leaves was a more integral part of the ceremonies. The staircase and walkway have long since fallen into ruin, and instead of rebuilding it the tower was removed and the door walled off. The temple changes with each reid."

"Is that why the leaves are no longer collected?" He asked, sitting next to me with his back to the wall. I had my back against the far edge, turning my legs inwards towards him. I kept one bent at the knee, and the other hanging freely out over the space. From here, we could easily look down over the main ceremony. A low hanging branch helped obscure us from the light, and no one ever looked up on this side. We'd be decently obscured unless anyone knew where to look.

I pushed my foot against him lightly.

"You sure ask a lot of questions."

"That isn't an answer, Gen."

Because someone figured out something they shouldn't have.

"It was a change made long ago," I said in response, and that seemed to placate him. He rested his back against the wall, relaxing with his legs pulled up off the side.

"The view is astounding," He conceded, reaching out towards the closest leaf and finding it just a bit too far.

"It's perfect to see the ceremony in full, and not have to worry about the crowd."

"You've come up here often, then?"

"Often enough."

He gave me a strange look. Studying me. It was the look he gave his notes when he was trying to puzzle something out, and couldn't.

"There's so much about you that never adds up," he said, clearly. Evenly. This was something he'd thought about for a long time. "You live in the temple, but you work in the city. You're a volunteer translator, but you have access to the most hidden texts in the archive, and a knowledge of them. You claim you do not practice the temple's beliefs—don't give me that look, I didn't call it a *religion* this time—but you are intimately familiar with them, and clearly *have* participated at some point."

"That's—"

"You had me take off my shoes before we entered."

"It really does help with the jump," I started, but he cut me off.

"It's also considered a sacred practice to enter the main temple bare footed, a sentiment that's extended to many of the most inner devout where they won't wear shoes at all on Del Tor grounds."

"I never taught you that."

"It's my job to learn these things, Gen. You aren't the only kriest I've ever interacted with." he let out a slight huff of air, knowing he was right. Then he motioned to me. "Is it wrong to assume that's why you never wear shoes?"

It was not, in fact, wrong. He must have seen the answer on my face, because he reached out and touched my bare shin gently beside him.

Casually.

"Someday," he said, and there was something in his voice. He couldn't meet my eyes anymore. "I might ask to know more about you. About all of you, and all your mysteries. To get inside your head a bit."

"Someday," I answered, surprising myself, "I might let you."

Those words spoken between us felt like a shift. It was so slight, I barely noticed it at all. I felt it there nonetheless, settling across my skin like an errant cobweb.

I stared into his bright, unwavering eyes. He stared back into mine. I could hear my pulse racing in my ears, and for once I wasn't filled with the desire to run away. I swallowed.

The main doors opened down below, and a chime of music began to fill the space. It interrupted the silence between us, and not a moment too soon. I could still taste something close to the truth on the tip of my tongue, weakened and ready by those foreign gray eyes.

Who I was, what I'd meant to be, and the coward I had become. Or, at least, the basic beginning of it.

Mael believed in little truths, but it was hard to find any small or easy in my mountain of deep, hidden secrets. I was full of them. Secrets I had inherited, secrets I had come into, and secrets I had created all on my own.

My smallest secret was my desire to fall into the arms of this human man, *my* human, and the very thought scared me endlessly.

Or, maybe, that feeling was excitement. Love, however, was too dangerous. I couldn't risk it all for him. Not yet. I was close, though.

So instead, I readily turned to the beginning of the ceremony, forgot all about being *Gen, secret keeper and hopeless coward*, and settled once more into becoming *Gen, personal translator to Simon Holiday on all things kriest.*

With the door open, the walkway began to fill with spectators. Some were from the city, dressed in full indigo and fanning out along the main circular platform by the tree. Temple workers in white wraps and yellow sashes, began to line the hall. I wore my own sash as a headband now. They carried in baskets of offerings, setting them beside where they kneeled: flowers, herbs, aromatics, lanterns, and folded cloth rolls began to line the walkways. A few of the more elevated temple devotees carried in large woven barrels of the same breads the kitchen had worked on all day, strapped to their backs like a bag.

The crowd of acolytes wasn't many, perhaps about thirty, with another fifteen esteemed members of society who had been honored by the invite. They stood clearly to the side or along the central walkway around the tree, humming softly an old sacred tune I'd long known by heart. I didn't hum along with them, and neither did Mael. I didn't have to be next to her to see that. It was considered a job of the people, not the Reid.

"It smells delicious," Simon said, "does everyone get to eat them after the ceremony?"

"Yes," I said, and at his abject look of sadness, added "I'll get us some later. We can eat with Mael."

"You know," he said, "I've never heard anyone call her by just her first name. It seems... informal. You do it all the time, though"

I was slowly beginning to lose the glow of whatever moment we'd had before, and was coming to resent being in the light of his inquisitive nature.

"Maybe someday you will as well."

"Why do you, though?"

I didn't try to hide my avoidance of the topic.

"Do you want to have the ceremony translated, or would you rather keep asking me about myself?"

"Fine, fine."

"The main procession is starting," I pointed to the doors.

Mael in ceremony regalia was stunning. She was in full reid mode, playing the part with a grace and elegance I'd never hoped to master.

She walked in slowly, with the air of purpose of the highest person in the room, a true reid. She wore long, layered skirts of brilliant gold that followed her as she walked. Dyed and embroidered symbols of entwining branches, hands, and leaves emerged in brilliance when she took her spot at the dais, kneeling to allow the fabric to lay around her in a pool of the finest artisan's works. Her top was a simple loose shawl of a deep indigo, beaded through with polished glass and custom charms of the many Reids before her.

Each reid got a symbol they carried in official wear and passed on to the next. For Mael, it was a brilliant white bear, asleep under the stars. She wore it as a large pin holding her shawl in place. Her hair was loose, with occasional strands of fabric braided in, and a crown of white, stone-like wood haloing her hair. It gave her loose whitening curls a mystical glow as whisps brushed the ancient circlet.

"The crown was made just after the settlers arrived," I told Simon, "when they discovered *Haliz Fundir* and used its power for the first time."

"That had to be, what, almost two hundred years ago?"

"About."

"How has it not rotted away?"

"I do not know," I answered honestly. "The wood of *Haliz Fundir* has never behaved like normal wood should."

"What does it feel like?"

"Cold," I said from memory, "and hard like stone."

"Could I touch it after the ceremony?"

"It is forbidden," I said simply, and he eyed me.

"But you have?" "It is forbidden for *you*." He sniffed indignantly.

More chimes came, and the sound of small, high-toned drums. Mael took her place at the center of the stage, kneeling and allowing her skirts and ceremonial items to be arranged by two assistants who quickly moved back to the crowd. With the slow beat two kriest entered from the door, the last before the guards outside pushed them shut behind, sealing the chamber. It was two women, and ones I recognized.

"The elder woman's name is Kreel," I explained to Simon, leaning forward to be heard clearer. "She is the head of the fishing towns in the southern bay. She has led them through many years of rough fishing conditions, and was the daughter of another fishing leader before."

"And the younger woman?"

"Her daughter's daughter."

"*Granddaughter.*"

"Granddaughter. Her daughter passed away in the summer floods, and now she is passing on the family knowledge to her."

"That's sad..." he said, looking at the girl. She was barely a woman herself, probably not even twenty.

"It is tradition for the heads of their family to pass their knowledge on," I continued, "and where her daughter's knowledge is now lost, some of it lives on in Kreel, and will be passed to her daughter's dau—*granddaughter.*"

"How do they pass it along?"

"The melding." I answered simply.

Simon turned to face me again. "I keep hearing that word, but what *is* it?"

I didn't trust myself to tell him anything less than the truth when he looked at me like that. And it wasn't a truth I could give away. Instead, I said *"Watch."*

They were both dressed in fine gold wrappings and long, simple skirts. Neither wore any adornments or jewelry, but in each's hand they held a shallow obsidian bowl. "Why are their outfits so simple?" Simon asked.

"To create an easier melding. The fiber is made from parts of Haliz Fundir."

"I don't understand that sentence."

"You will." I said, and he looked no less confused. Below, the two came to their spots at the main platform, kneeling on the edge of the carpet before Mael. Even from this distance, I could see the steadfast set in the grandmother's shoulders, and the slight shake in her granddaughter's.

They set the bowls down before Mael, and the humming and drums faded away with one raised motion of her hand. She looked over the crowd, meeting the eyes of everyone in the room one by one, then turned her full attention to the two directly before her.

When she spoke, her voice was clear, and her words smooth with practice. Her voice carried enough for all to hear, but she did not shout. It was commanding, but not lording. As she spoke, I leaned in and translated for Simon.

"Kreel," she acknowledged, *"The favored elder of Kreator, the glorious city of our fishermen, the masters of the bay. Kreel, the namesake of the most hearty of fish, and the daughter of the blood of our founding families. Kreel, who has lost her daughter, who sat before me fifteen years prior at this very moment for this very ceremony. We revere you, Kreel. Tonight, we will walk into the blessing of Haliz Fundir together."*

"Kreel," The room repeated, and I added "To acknowledge the person as they are now, before the meld. Names are important for that."

Simon nodded, but didn't turn his face from the ceremony.

She did the same for Palium, the granddaughter. She spoke of the loss of her mother, her long lineage, and the future she has ahead.

"Palium," Simon said with the group, and I couldn't help but smile. He was trying it, tasting the word, settling in as an honored guest and attempting to experience this firsthand. Perhaps Mael wasn't wrong to choose him to be here tonight.

He wanted to be part of all of this, and he'd always tried it with a bit of respect. I had a

lot of honor for him in that regard.

"Tonight is the first night of many," she continued, somewhat off script. *"Tonight, we witness the melding of generations, to bring knowledge of the past forward into a newer, brighter tomorrow."* Her eyes glanced up, towards where we were. I met her gaze for a moment, and then she turned her eyes to Simon with a slight smile. *"Tonight, we all play our part in that tomorrow."*

I felt him stiffen, breathless, unsure what to do with the recognition or weight. "It is the truth," I found myself saying. "Mael always speaks in truths."

Wordlessly, he nodded. No one else turned to look up here, and with that Mael turned back to the two, picking up a large ceramic pitcher from beside her.

"*From two–*" she recited, holding the pitcher high and pouring a perfect amount of deep red resin into the first bowl, a slow, deliberate motion. It was too thick to be blood, and too thin to be sap. Stone bracelets met along her arms, ringing out in a strange, hollow sound. "*–to one.*

Together, we accept the gift of Haliz Fundir into ourselves."

Both of them said the line with her, and raised their filled bowls to their lips. Mael held their wrists gently, following the motion up as they drank the viscous sap. Palium couldn't help a face at the bitter taste, but Kreel maintained perfect composure.

I could remember my first practice ceremony years before. Mael's warm hands had held my shoulders from behind as I poured the sap into the ceremonial bowls just as she'd shown me: from up high, and with little splashing or effect. I had been kneeling in the same spot she now sat.

"*People like the lies, Gen.*" She'd told me, approvingly, as I filled one and moved to the other. "*They like to be told the lie is the truth just as much as we need them to believe the lie.*

They like the show we give, they find comfort in acting.

"*Through that, we can hide even the most horrible truths in plain sight, because no one wants to dig any deeper once they feel satisfied*"

The bowls had felt unbearably warm between my fingers as I'd picked them up, holding them out to Jorel, who had kneeled across for me and patiently awaited his own turn practicing the rites.

"So when you're lying, give it with nothing less than absolute sincerity. None of the showmanship is real, boys. None of the rituals, the rites, the traditions do anything but keep the followers happy. It keeps them out of the way."

"So why do it?" I'd asked, and she'd touched my face from the side, turning me to look at her.

"Because sometimes people do terrible things with the truth, Gen. Not everyone can face a truth as large as Haliz and stand strong. As a Reid, it is our job to make sure the Haliz Fundir remains palatable for everyone else. For our people, for our community.

"Now," she'd added, pouring the sap back into the ceremonial pitcher and resetting the bowls, *"Put on the show they need."*

In the present Mael, still holding their wrists, pushed their hands together and began the meld.

Chapter Seven

Simon, Haliz Fundir

There were no words that could have prepared me for what I witnessed in that moment.

I witnessed the unimaginable. I saw *magic*. An impossibility by every known law of the world, mine or this one.

Grandmother and granddaughter, prompted by Mael, touched their hands together. Instead of stopping when the skin came in contact, they just... *kept going.*

It was almost like their arms overlapped, but instead of hard lines the skin just flowed together seamlessly. Their bones seemed to meet and shift around each other, before settling for the next round. Their bodies swirled together as if in a dance, nearly turning them fully around from the reid. It was like watching two different liquids hit each other and then mix perfectly, but instead of having twice the liquid in volume what was left was someone no more the size of one person by themselves, if not a little taller.

The meld took mere seconds, barely that, and then in place of the elder and her heir kneeled a woman of middle age, swimming in the folds of the ceremonial skirts they'd worn. She was leaning forward, holding herself up from the ground with ram-rod straight arms, her ears back in a sign of emotion and distress. Her tail slunk out from under the cloth, barely visible in the folds. Her hair was a perfect blend in length and color of the gray curls of the elder, and the long wavy style of the girl. Her body heaved in breaths, unsure and almost scared.

Somewhere within that fear, though, was familiarity.

Mael leaned forward, touching this new person's shoulder. "It is alright," came Gen's voice, low and very close by. "Breathe, while the room sings."

Was he still translating Reid Mael's words, despite not hearing them at this distance? Her voice had been only for the melded to hear. I wondered if he had already known what she was going to say, like a script, but then again... he could have been speaking to me directly. I had not

taken a single breath since the meld began.

So, as the room began to fill with singing, I did. In, and out. I watched the woman below do the same, her shoulders moving up and down. Slowing with each breath. Finding equilibrium, while the haunting echo of the spectating choir rose around us.

"This," Gen's voice came again, "Is what the temple is for."

"For....singing?"

"To protect the sacred art of melding." I turned to find him leaning forward towards me on both hands, his shoulders hunched up as he supported his weight. His eyes were very serious, and they wandered my face with a solemn intent. "...and to use it to better the island."

"What is it like?" I asked, and he nodded back towards the melded below. Mael was helping the melded woman to her feet, her movements a mixture of unsure swaying and familiar certainty that felt very odd to see.

"Two minds in the same body," he answered, "they can think together, communicate in ways that...." he paused, searching for words.

"...that forgo any language barrier?" I finished for him. He frowned, but I felt understanding creep in. I thought out loud. "Sharing a mind— It's probably more convenient than speaking, and it's got to be faster, right? Large amounts of information passing between you... and do you just... understand it?"

"In a sense." he said. I chewed on this some more, watching Mael lead her down a set of stairs to the roots below, all while the choral song rose up to the leaves above.

"That's...very powerful."

"Yes," he said, watching my face still. Memories from our

"Yes," he said, watching my face still.

Memories from outranslating sessions came up, information buried deep in scrolls and tomes and stories. I turned back to meet his eyes.

"You said the first settlers came here by sea, that they turned to Haliz and used its powers to win the war with their homeland."

"Yes."

"This... this is how they did it, isn't it?"

Gen could only nod. My mind felt wobbly, full of everything all at once. I turned back to the room below.

"I...what are they doing now?"

Mael was helping her lay in the crook of the roots, the low puddles of water seeping up their flowing skirts. The melded lay back her head and closed her eyes, and Mael held her hand and spoke to her, something neither of us could see nor hear. Gen didn't offer a translation this time.

"She's guiding the meld. Giving them time to have the discussions they need, to learn memories and how to move, stories and conversations from lifetimes. Kreel has practice, but Palium is new. She is doing a longer melding than usual to help."

"How long do they normally last?"

"Only as long as they need."

"...what happens if it goes longer?"

He looked away at this.

"Nothing good."

I got another flash of intuition that he was hiding something from me, but I didn't push. I would have to talk to Mael myself at the end of this.

In all the awe, I had forgotten the horrible person I was and suddenly fell fully into the lie that I was Simon, the translator, and honored guest. I knew in that moment nothing I saw this evening would ever reach Tess's ears.

I would have hell to pay for it, though.

"Thank you," I said. "Thank you for...for bringing me here. For letting me see this. I can't believe I'm the first human....I have so many questions."

"I know," he said simply, bumping my leg lightly with his foot. "You are always full of them."

"It's my job."

"It is your nature," he countered, tilting his head to watch me.

"What's yours?"

This caught us both off guard. He seemed to freeze in place, unsure what to do or say.

Some answer was there, and I could feel him tense with it. I wasn't expecting any real sort of answer, but I got one. Under the rising tune of the choir, and the overhead winds that crested the temple walls, and the own sound of my heart in my ears.

"To run."

The main door exploded inwards, and a wind erupted into the space. Lanterns flickered wildly, if not dying outright, and the baskets of herbs and gatherings scattered their top layers into the air. A shocked cry cut into the song like a wave, starting closest to the door and rolling outwards through the procession. Some shrunk away, as if the wind moved them, too. Others held firm, blinking in the sudden intrusion. One or two continued singing longer than the rest, lost in their own reverie.

Mael's face turned like a whip from the trance-induced melded, whose own eyes were wide with surprise. Mael's, even from this distance I could see them so clearly, were narrowed. Surprised, wary, but not caught off guard. She was still as sharpened and on edge as any of the other times I had witnessed her.

From the door, four bodies came in, and then more, and then more. All were dressed in the full garb of the Kor, their black and purple wrappings and armor a foil to the whites and gold of the congregation.

Nearly thirty Kor came in and scattered, pushing through the crowds and along the walking path with spears or hatchets drawn. They pushed the devout back, holding them in place but not attacking. A path was made, at the end emerged a single kriest man of imposing stature.

I'd recognize him anywhere. It was the man I had met only an hour earlier in Reid Mael's home. Behind him flanked the scarred woman from the bridge, a surprisingly large battle ax in her hands. The twins were nowhere to be found.

He walked with a practiced purpose, one hand at his side, and the other holding a long, oversized obsidian spear. It glinted a wicked black in the light, the handle inlaid with golden metal bands like a wasp. Behind him the doors closed with a hand signal, two men outside sealing the room once again.

It wasn't silent, but it was far quieter than the ceremony had been. Jorel surveyed the room, sweeping the space his warriors fanned out to occupy, until he seemed satisfied that everything was in place.

Then his eyes found Reid Mael, and the woman she now shielded with her body in *Haliz*'s roots, and he spoke.

Chapter Eight

Jorel, Haliz Fundir

"I gave you a chance, Mael." I said, allowing the familiar stone walls to amplify my voice for all to hear. I addressed her, but my eyes and hand swept the room, speaking for everyone inside.

Haliz stood as always in the center, and despite their orders to keep their eyes on the ceremony patrons and keep them out of the way, I could see plenty of my devout glancing at its majesty. Still, their weapons did not waver.

"Your willingness to sacrifice the lives of Torrellian citizens for your own comfort is coming to an end. I am here to set the wrongs of our bloodline right, and to ensure the future of us all."

Confused murmurs arose from the temple devotees, but none dared move. I did. I strode with purpose across the walkway, my bare feet feeling the familiarity of the worn wood. I had instructed all of my Kor to remove their shoes in respect of *Haliz*. The reverberations of dozens of moving bodies echoing through the slats grounded me as I strode for the grand central stage around the trunk.

"Accolades of this great temple!" I shouted, watching them all. "See me! Know me! I am Jorel, son of Mael and Rengik, rightful heir to the Reidship and trainee under the ways of Reid. I have grown with you, walked with you, and in my time as a Kor warrior I have protected you. I stand before you here and now as that warrior. Asterel grows bolder with every day, their lord Sol pushing us to our limits again and again. They have always threatened us, scorned us, and killed us when they could. And so often, they can."

I turned to a woman in the crowd. Her face was shrouded in the guest's wrappings, but her eyes peered up at me regardless.

"They have taken so much from us, have they not, Madam Seller?"

Then I found another, an old man.

"They have taken our sons, wandered too far when foraging."

Then, a young woman I knew all too well. She had short cropped hair and something dark shadowing her face, once lovely with youth.

"They have taken our lovers, our friends, our brothers and sisters and fathers and sons in the warriors. They take and take from us, mocking us with each and every life. Maybe Mael has sheltered you here, maybe you haven't heard the death count from this summer alone fighting the toying whims of Sol. He is growing bolder, pushing our boundaries in and encroaching on our forests, our city, and our lives. It is only a matter of time before he comes to burn this temple to the ground, and all the people in it. He will be sure to lay Torrel to waste for standing in his path. He's made his prejudice against *Haliz* and all who stand in its great shadow clear from the beginning."

"Sol wouldn't dare set foot on temple grounds," a strong voice called out. Marus, an old crone of the temple and high accolade of my mother's, and her mother before her, dared speak against me. If it was going to be anyone, it was going to be her.

"He knows his place. Peace is beneficial to us both, it holds him in the North."

That was, at first glance, a fair and reasonable point. I saw the wavering of the crowd, torn from their rapt at my words. It did not shake me.

I had expected it.

"Marus is right. Sol has never come through to the temple, never made good on his threats to eliminate us. Why do you believe that to be true? What has held him at bay? Mael's charm and negotiations?"

I said this with a sneer.

"No," I answered myself, turning to face them once more, holding up my hands to the brilliant life behind me. "No, it is because Sol knows the possibilities *Haliz* holds, the possibilities and power my mother has withheld from you all this time. He knows that if we were to use the power here for what it really is, he could never win against us. We hold the power of *Haliz Fundir* in our hands, and all its possibilities and wonder, and he *fears* that. He *fears* the very gifted weapon my mother cowers at!"

I slammed my hands down, booming.

"She would rather see our children and brothers killed in unwarranted border skirmishes than stand up and do what needs done! She would rather trick you all into thinking this force of the world is only good for petty parlor tricks and transferring fishmonger family secrets than the true power it brings. She would rather pyre a thousand of our people than stand up to one lowly man on a throne with the strength *she readily wastes.*"

"Stop this," my mother called from below, but her voice was not pleading. It was furious, darkly so. Demanding. I paid it no heed.

"They have a right to the truth!" I lied, sweeping my hand to the people for her to see.

"They have a right to know the past of our people, the ways our ancestors used *Haliz* to end a war and save us all. The ways you refuse to offer them."

"You are not offering them the truth," she countered, "You are only offering them death."

"I am offering them a chance. A chance you never gave them."

She was right. I wasn't offering them the truth. Not in full, anyway. It was by her own design. I had been raised that not everyone could handle the realities of the world in full. That they would crumple under the weight of honesty if their images of life were shattered. It was clear to me now that she was one of those who had fallen. The worst one of all.

I moved my hand to *Haliz*, spoke to the crowd, but my eyes never left hers.

"When our ancestors arrived on this island, trying to flee the oppressors of the mainland, they found not a tool to only meld minds but also *bodies*. Can you comprehend the power that brings? Captured agents of the North could have the secrets of Asterel 's stronghold pulled from their very minds. The greatest warriors of all time could be melded together again and again, passing through their knowledge and strength. We still hold that power! Information, strength, unimaginable possibility and might. *Haliz's* gift can eliminate Sol and stop his reign in its tracks!"

"*Jorel!*" my mother called, and it was delicious timing. If she expected me to grant her any more mercy than she had ever given my father, however, I disappointed her.

"He knows this. The threat of *Haliz* held him at bay for decades, but he's gotten bolder. We've had it this whole time. Our refusal to call upon it, no, *Mael's* refusal to call upon it, and her insistence on keeping you in the dark, has given him all the excuses he's needed.

"Her complacency has cost us lives," I boomed, "her complacency comes from solidarity towards Sol, she has forgotten one of the most important and original duties of the reidship, to protect our home at all costs. She is working with him, and has been for a long time!"

The room spoke at once, incredulous, disbelieving. At first. Then, tiny flashes of her own words and actions spread. Memories they all held turned against her one by one. My mother may not truly be working with Sol. I didn't care. All that mattered was that they perceived it so.

The moment I had spoken my first word in this room, I had won.

All in here had bore witness to the possibility of a melding tonight, something my mother had done for me all on her own. They felt the fear of Sol's forces within them. Her hands off philosophy in backing the Kor's plea for aid from the merchant's counsel was also well known by now. I had seen that enough of our disagreements were public over the last few months to ensure
that.

I watched it all settle, and so did Mael. Anger, deeper and more volatile than she ever let show, sat clearly on her face. It was all I could do to hold back a smile.

"You have disgraced our family and our people," she said, trying up the stairs, only to be met with a warning flick of my spear towards her neck.

She stopped cold, eyeing the obsidian point, while two other Kor surrounded us on the sides of the stairs and pointed their spears at the melded behind her.

"You are a traitor." I said again. "You have let the north threaten us for a lifetime. You have let the humans crawl over this land like the wretched pests they are, consuming our resources and soiling the land they squat in. You have built yourself an image of a great leader, but you are a coward. A useless, weak-willed fool."

At this she glared at me, but said nothing. I couldn't decide at that moment if it was better or worse for me that she did not speak. While the people around me heard my words, they also had nothing of hers to base their reactions on. I needed to convert at least a few of the closest devotees against her, speak to their fear of Asterel and weariness of the humans. Even if they did not look so lowly upon them as my most devout warriors did, the distaste was there in one level or another. It was something palpable within them, something I could speak to and mold to my own use. It didn't matter why they followed me, be it against the humans, my mother, or Sol.

Only that they did.

At my mother's silence, it seemed many began to.

"Your reign is over, Mael. Release their hold," I commanded, putting on a show for everyone there. "I will not touch a meld of the false Reid."

My mother's eyes narrowed. She knew I couldn't release a meld, it was the one point of power she might have had over me, but she was too much of a bleeding heart to let the fishing women suffer. She did as I asked. She held the shoulders of the melded before her, and with a practiced force of her will the two women came apart, falling beside each other against the roots.

"These women are invaluable assets to our community," I said to the room, turning to address one of my men. "Take them home, see no harm comes to them tonight. They are innocents, and have been no less touched by Haliz Fundir."

"*Sanra, Reid Jorel,*" a guard to my right spoke, coming forward to collect the two women with firm but not rough hands. My mother's eyes lit ablaze, something coming to life within them I had not seen in a long, long time. *Rage.*

"*Reid* Jorel?" she asked, and what should have barely been a hiss sounded like a shout.

"You are no Reid, and you are no son of mine. You are disgraced, a man forsaken by the ways of *Haliz Fundir*."

"I am a man forsaken by *you*," I spoke, "and to be forsaken by a traitor is to live honorably."

"How could you go against everything I have taught you?"

she tightened her hands into fists. Tears of anger welled in her eyes and she blinked them away. If only I could care for her opinions of me.

"I have told my devout of your lies. I have told them of the power and awe *Haliz* is capable of, of the height of our strength. I have let them judge for themselves how low that secret has sunk us down by your hands."

"You have broken the sanctimony of your heritage and training—"

"I have done what needed to be done to keep us all safe!" I shouted, true anger boiling over. "I have exposed your lies and shown you for who you truly are, Mael. You would let a thousand of our people die before you used the power we already have to stop Sol!"

"There are things in this world worse than Sol," she began, but I cut her off.

"He is one of the greatest threats to us all. Just as the humans are to our culture and livelihoods."

At that moment, I saw her get it. I saw her figure out what I was doing here in this conversation, what I was willing to sell to take this power from her that she'd long since abused. She saw I would do anything, *anything* to secure that safety. Even hand over the lives of the humans to the kriest scared enough to demand them.

"I will never recognize you as a reid," she said, her normally unshaken voice dripping with vitriol and heartbreak.

It almost pained me. Almost. The time for feelings was long past, no matter how deep the wound had been to begin with. "You are a disgrace."

"Funny," I responded, "I do not recognize you as a reid, either."

Something sharp flashed in her eyes. Something similar to the old silver-tongued mother I had once known came forward.

"Gen is the only pupil I have trained who carries the constitution and lessons needed to navigate a melding. You will never learn the rituals, and you can never understand the monster you covet—"

"Perhaps not," I admitted, "not on my own. That is why I will meld with him. And I will overcome him, rip those very lessons from his mind and leave him shattered. I will tear his very existence from this world, and then I will be complete."

Horror finally cracked through her anger. I saw her pristine features twist in anguish, in rage, in the acceptance of the grotesque loophole I had discovered.

"You are a failure, Jorel. A failure to every standard I have worked to hold you to."

"You will understand someday that you are only in my way."

A look came across her face as if I had slapped her, her final words to my father thrown back at her.

Violence can be instantaneous.

With little effort at all I raised my spear and thrust it forward with both hands, piercing her chest. It was a final note I had known would come for months, but there really was no preparing you for the day you take your own mother's life. Perhaps the authority of selling Jask's life was practice for this very moment. To see what I could shoulder for the greater good of us all. It was just one more sin I would need to carry forward.

Her eyes flew open wide in shock, not comprehending what happened to her. I heard voices rise up all around us, gasps and cries at the sin I had committed. It didn't matter. Letting her live would have been a mercy, but worse it would have been a mistake.

With the same practiced motion I pulled the spear out, tossing it to the side and stepping towards her falling form.

Blood, unbearably hot and flowing in sudden excess, slicked my hands as I caught her, laying her down gently to the roots below. Her broken chest heaved in jerks as she tried to breathe, but all that filled her lungs was more blood. She choked on it, and if her mouth had tried to form anything more of a word, It was lost in the spray of blood that splashed my face and chest.

"I will keep them safe," I told her, my final words to the woman who gave me life only to take away everything I held dear. My father. My position. My trust in her. "I will do right by all of them."

Her sternum jumped, trying so desperately to speak, to say *something*, but it was lost in the carnage. Arterial blood pumped from her chest, maybe even directly from her heart, and then, like a flame dying in the wind she began to extinguish.

It takes far longer than you'd expect for someone to die, even when it is a quick bleed like this. I didn't wait for her to fall fully from life, turning away to the people sharing this moment with me. Many were remorseful, or afraid, but many more still were... reserved. They understood. Just as I knew they would.

"Set the lights!" I ordered my devout, the flames of dozens of lanterns illuminating the murder on my hands when I let her body still on the roots below. The lights glowed hot and orange, a signal to the teams outside watching the windows that this part was done, and they were to come alert me with their own signal when the temple was secured.

"Round the devout who will follow and separate any who still stand by Mael's old ways. Keep them separate, but alive. Some changes take time to settle. Tonight, we turn the tide for Torrel!"

"Sanra, Reid Jorel!" Came the unanimous cry, and taps of blades and staffs and feet greeted me.

"Sanra, my warriors!" I called to them all, knowing it was only a matter of time before my men brought to me the final piece of my success. They would collect and bring me Gen, dispose of the human who had been with him by whatever means they pleased, and when I melded with him and overtook his mind the final secrets of *Haliz* would come to my hands, and I would be the true Reid my people needed.

The true Reid my mother denied me.

The Reid to save us all.

Out of an old, long forgotten memory my eyes turned to an alcove far on high, one I had expected to be empty, but familiar in the old haunting of my adopted brother. Instead, I met the dark, grieving eyes of the very kriest who had gotten everything and failed it all.

Gen was not on his way to me from the archives, in the chains he had always needed to hold him still. He was here, witness to my final usurpation of Mael's reign. And he was not alone.

He had a *human* with him. The same one from Mael's kitchen.

In unwinding rage and terror, I saw what he was about to do seconds before he did it. And for the first moment in years, I felt truly and utterly powerless to stop what was coming. In that helplessness I found something wild and old and nasty.

Hate.

Chapter Nine

Gen, Haliz Fundir

I didn't think. Thoughts were too slow, too drawn out. If I had taken the time to think, I don't suspect I could have ever managed what needed done. My body just...moved, driving me blindly forward. Everything I had ever learned under Mael—*Mael was dead, she was really, truly dead, killed by Jorel's hands and limp on the floor*—flooded my blood like an old, unwanted guest. In less than a second I had slammed my shoulder into Simon's, bracing for the impact of flesh on flesh, my weight and force driving him to the ground—

But it didn't come.

I saw only a flash of wide, pale eyes, and then I was falling *into* him. Flesh met flesh then kept going, pushing, warping, moving my body together with this human, pulling us together as one body, one mind, an entirely new form. The familiar ache of the meld overwhelmed me, like a long, satisfying stretch of muscles that pulled my whole body and kept going, going, roaring in my ears and blinding me in its heat. I was movement and pain, and rippling screaming roaring and then...

Then, I wasn't anything anymore. I was something new. Something more.

Together, we opened our eyes.

Chapter Ten

Simon, Melded, Haliz Fundir

I didn't understand at first, but Gen did.

Jorel's face contorted in rage at the sight of Gen and I, at what we had become. His lips pulled back over his teeth as a snarl ripped from him. His bellowing shriek of loathing sent those around him back in fear.

And together, we *felt* fear. Primal, instinctual, needing no translation. A predator stared us down, hungry and mad enough to rip us to shreds without a second thought—to rip me to shreds, specifically. I felt this fact from Gen, his thoughts coming in as more emotions and absolutions than long strings of words or clear pictures. He wanted Gen for something, and I was only in the way. An instinct to flee kicked in, and before I could think of it we were moving, darting off of the statue ledge with an agility I had never known, and leaping for the nearest branch of the *Haliz Fundir*. I could feel every sensation, every pull of breath and scrape of skin against the tree, but I felt like a passenger in my own body. If this even counted as my own body anymore. Where Palium had been given time to adjust we couldn't afford the luxury, and Gen pushed my mind out of the way to do what needed done.

I struggled to form thoughts while Gen drove us forward, unsure of his footing on the unfamiliar branches but propelled by only a single thought— *The window, the window, the southern end's window—*

Something lodged itself firmly into the tree before us, a long, wicked arrow. *They had an archer?* I thought, at the same time Gen's this hissed a panicked *he brought obsidian tips into the sanctuary?!* I wanted to understand that thought, feel it out, pull in more, but Gen was too quick to think. He only reacted, allowing our body to carry us down the branch to the trunk, the words fading away.

We slid barefooted on the bark. Gen had been right; the tree felt like no living plant I had ever touched; it was as smooth as a river stone, cold as one too, and barely moved under our weight, like it was carved from marble. But from where the arrow had hit more of that deep sap had begun to flow. I had never seen a stone bleed, either.

"Asterelian spy!" Jorel yelled—no, roared, the loudest and most unhinged shout we had ever heard of him in our— that Gen had ever heard him emit in his life. *"Betrayer! Blasphemer of Haliz!*

"Bring Gen to me alive," he ordered his men, and where I could not understand his words Gen clearly did, and I heard their meaning faintly in our head. *"I don't care what you do to get them!"*

The warriors below ran after us, none attempting to climb the trunk but all aiming for our body as we scrambled through the tangle of limbs. Our escape was less a graceful one and more a desperate dance of slipping, catching ourselves, running forward between limbs and under impossibly sized leaves before beginning again with a slip. We made it through the worst of the trunk, along to the other end of the branches and to the far wall, escaping the barrage of bolts and arrows by mere margins or sheer luck. At one point, a branch we'd landed on angled down far sharper than we had anticipated and our feet had flown out from us. A thick branch caught us on the back and we slid down it at the same moment a bolt had sailed through the space our stomach had been. We'd rode the branch down before landing hard against the trunk, and we'd barely managed to pull ourselves upright and move away before another two bolts followed.

I saw our next move just as we tensed to make it. "It's too far," our mouth said, seeing the far window above our height and an impossible distance from the end of our branch.

Our teeth gritted. "No," we said, and before I could react our legs turned, pushing us along the full length of the branch in long, even strides. A startled shout mixed with a cry of effort as we leapt forward, stretching, reaching out...

We hit the wall. Hard. The shock of a stone wall at full speed slammed through us, knocking me blank for a moment. Knocking us both blank for a moment, but luckily for us Gen had never run on thoughts alone. Our arms caught the ledge, holding us there desperately.

Muscles rippled under our chest and arms, tightening and pulling our body up with a strain of effort. Our right leg— long, I noticed, with the athletic curve Gen's always had and the muscles to match—reached out sideways with a swing of our core to catch the ledge as well. Our toes gripped the textured surface to give us a third point of contact and enough leverage to roll over the sill. We paused, straddling the window, half in and half out, unsure of something.

I could feel Gen's thoughts in bursts, wild calculations of memories and feelings of what would happen if we leapt, slid, missed whatever surface he'd hoped for us to escape to from this window. There was no convenient building to catch us, only a dark distance down to the ground far below. Interrupting this, something pinged metallic and deadly to our right. A thrown rock?

Or maybe more bolts. *No, not bolts,* I thought, it had sounded heavier, more impactful. *A spear?*

We're wide open! My thoughts broke through in a panic, and that seemed to settle something with Gen. With only a second's glance back—at the tree, the blood, Mael's body broken on the roots and Jorel and his Kor all racing towards us—we swung over our last leg and dropped down and away from the window.

"Ah!" I cried, our body feeling almost weightless for the second I was sure we would fall to our death. Instead, Gen pulled our hands to grab the ledge we'd just jumped from, swinging our legs down to an uneven stone protruding from the wall. It was a hard maneuver, but we managed with practice. Our shoulders and arms pulled. Our knee hurt like hell where it hit, bone deep pain reverberating through our leg.

He kept us moving, hand below hand as we descended the wall, running on sheer memory alone where visuals failed. The moon couldn't catch this side of the tower yet, and outside of the light spilling from the window we were in full darkness.

Yet, we were *doing* it. In the dark, blind and panicked, we made it along the wall and down its length. He didn't even think about it, just trusted our hands and feet to move us along.

Our fingers screamed from the effort. Our toes were scraped and bleeding.

The part of us that Gen occupied kept us going. Shouts came from around the building, and I knew that more of Jorel's warriors were making their way outside to find us. *Just how many followers does he have?!*

I wanted to urge us on faster, but I was terrified both in losing our grip and breaking Gen's concentration with an errant thought.

We dropped the last few feet to the ground. We bent with the impact, absorbing it easily enough, but it was still a rough landing. Piles of emptied storage crates littered this side of the tower, to be cleaned up and used for winter.

I.... wasn't sure how I knew that. I wasn't even sure what —or who—I was. Or what was happening to us. *Why had Jorel killed Mael? What he had said to the crowd to placate them?*

Why was he chasing us and trying to kill us...

"No time," our mouth said, the voice strained. It was foreign, too high to be Gen's but too rough to be mine. We kept low, stopping to look around a crate.

In the dark, there was still nothing much on this side of the compound. Beyond, I could hear the faint sounds of the great river, the far end that split from the fork around the Del Tor compound, and our eyes scanned the dark woods ahead. There was no sign of movement. Yet.

We needed to create distance, and we needed to create distance *fast*. I didn't know where we could go, but at that moment all that mattered was getting the hell away from here.

A shout, and lanterns rounded the building, lighting up the piles of crates around us. We were out of time.

"Fuck!" I tried to say at the same time he tried to swear *"Enyk!"* and a strangled mangling of the two was shouted instead. *"Fyenuk!"* Then we were moving, running, racing with only wild air and darkness between us and the woods and the warriors behind us. *Move or die* our instincts screamed, and oh how we *moved*. I had never run so fast in my life, and I wasn't even aware someone *could* run like this. Our legs pulled us forward with long, powerful pushes away from our pursuers and away from danger.

Danger didn't have to run quite as fast, though, when they had bows and throwing spears.

Arrows wicked past us in the dark, embedding in the dirt in a series of hollow *wups*! A spear snapped past our leg,

close enough to burn our skin with the long pole. I wanted to scream in fear, or brace for impact, but we needed our muscles loose and our lungs pulling in oxygen to escape.

Suddenly we were at the tree line, crashing through the brush as the forest engulfed us.

The moon finally escaped the tower's shadow, but it wasn't enough to fully see our path ahead. Branches attacked our torso, legs, and arms relentlessly as deep shadows came to life. The ground suddenly climbed up in short shelves, causing us to grab and vault up every few feet like a kid hopping an auditorium stage. The light of swinging lanterns followed us, illuminating us one second and then leaving us the next as we raced ahead of them with a familiarity I suddenly recognized.

Where are we going? I asked the void that was our mind, and our mouth said "Trust me!"

Where are we going? I asked again, and our teeth gritted in pain as we took a particularly girthy branch to the stomach. It turned us around for a moment, dropped us to our knees, and then we were up again, turning, and racing towards the growing roar of the river.

Gen! I suddenly saw it, as clear as a memory in our mind. "Gen, Gen there's a cliff ahead!"

"I *know*," we shouted. We came out of the cover of trees to see a large, hauntingly bright sky and the clear outline of the wild, racing river falling away into nothing. The ground dropped away into open, deadly air, the roar of the falls deafening us.

There was nowhere else to go. Then Gen pushed through my panic and ran straight for the cliff's edge.

Chapter Eleven

Gen, Melded,
Western Falls

Gen! His voice screamed in our mind, but I didn't stop. We ran with the wind to our back, pushing us forward. A shout chased us but I ignored it, ignored everything but the rapidly approaching cliff.

I had never done this at night. But this was the only chance we had.

Our legs pushed us, our shoulders and back rippling with each step. All at once, the ground ran out into open air. The night sky greeted us. I leapt to greet it.

For an impossible moment we were aloft, the freedom and terror of the fall forgotten as our sight filled with a hundred stars scattered through the darkness above. We were hovering, weightless, free from gravity.

Then we were falling fast. Too fast to comprehend.

Something hot seared our right thigh. I didn't—*we* couldn't even see what it was. It was a struggle to get our arms to listen to me through Simon's panic, our mouth opened in a shrill, endless scream as black water raced below, but I threw our arms out like extending wings as fast as I could, keeping us upright, our feet out and ready for the impact—

It was like hitting solid stone. For a moment I was terrified we *had* hit ground and the next feeling we shared would be a ripple of shattering bones from our feet to our pelvis. Then the water's surface broke, and we plunged into the depths.

There wasn't time to register the impact before we were beneath the surface, choppy rapids slamming us from all sides. Our scream was ripped away in the water. All sense of direction was lost. *Are we upright? Sideways? Have we breathed in water? Will we—*

With effort I again shoved Simon's panic to the side. There were times to think, and times to do, and right now I just needed to *do this as I've always done!* I screamed in desperation inside our mind.

He was pushed down, away, but not gone. Unfamiliar with navigating a meld he was powerless to stop me.

I gave into my body. It had never done me wrong, even if it was now shared. I pulled away from conscious thought and let instincts take control. It was the one thing I was good at.

Bubbles danced on our skin. We shot downwards with speed until our feet hit riverbed. It was not a gentle touch. Pain slammed through us on the impact, one of our ankles buckling awkwardly. I didn't allow the pain to dissuade me from scrambling for purchase on the lakebed, forcing ourselves to kneel flat footed in the mud. I didn't have much time. I aimed our body diagonally in a direction that was—I hoped—further downstream from where we'd entered the water.

Gen, Simon's voice came again through his shrill babbling, *Gen we can't breathe!*

Our legs tensed in memory of the move I wanted to do. We kicked off from the bottom with all our might and shot upwards like a spear, up and over with our hands at our sides, faster than if we had just swam up to the surface. Please, I prayed quietly, *no rocks, no trees, no—* The river's surface broke around us in an explosion. Everything was a blur of shadowed trees, spraying water, and stars. We sucked in a breath, but before we could take a second the rapids plunged us back under.

There was nothing to grab onto but water. It was all I could do to push above the surface again. This time, we glimpsed the cliff we'd jumped from far to our right and high above us, disappearing in the distance. *We made it downstream,* I thought in relief, pulling in another choked gasp of air before we went under again.

Water pushed into our nose, our mouth. It choked our lungs with the acrid taste of fish and mud. Sheer primal panic screamed through our mind with the clang of bells and the roar of our pulse in our ears.

No, one of us thought, and the other fought to hack away the river threatening to drown us in its indifferent rapids. Every wet warbling cough only sufficed to pull in gargling mixtures of surf and air on the inhale, doing nothing but continue the torture.

We're going to die, we realized, arms uselessly slapping what we hoped was the surface, desperate for purchase on land. *We're going to drown.*

No, I pushed through, making one last desperate thrust towards something, anything. Air, a rock, a tree root, anything—

The boulder greeted our body full on. The shock ran up our back, forcing us to spit out our breath and the water we'd breathed in. The rapids pelted us mercilessly against it, the spray flying into our eyes. With effort we got turned around and pulled ourselves onto the boulder. The water didn't want to let us go, but I dug into any reserve of strength I could find and pushed. I could feel Simon doing the same, working with me to climb out of the waves.

Laying on our side, pulled fully out, we collapsed against the stone. We pulled in breath after breath of cool night air, chasing the water from our lungs with wracking, desperate coughs.

When they subsided we were alone in the dark. The moon shone silver on our soaked skin. Jorel's Kor hadn't killed us. The river hadn't drowned us.

We still stood a chance.

We turned back upriver, but no lights from lanterns greeted us. Only black moving water and an endless moonlit sky. The river had taken us far out of sight from the cliffs.

"We.... we need to get to the banks," I said through our lips at the same time Simon's voice howled in our head *you could have* killed *us, Gen! We nearly drowned!*

"We were about to be killed anyway!" I yelled back at ourselves. "It was all I could do! I have made that jump many times!"

In the dark? At night?

He already knew the answer. "We need to get to the banks." I said again, and before he could think to argue I took a breath and pushed us back into the river. Now oriented , the water couldn't fight us as mercilessly. I kept with the current to swim diagonally towards the eastern banks. Kicking, pulling, breathing.

Our arms propelled us forward in long, practiced strides. A weariness pushed around in our bones, but I didn't pay it any mind. No thoughts came to either of us. There was only the wicked, whining sense of loss, and numbness, and regrets and fear that lingered.

And then, there was land.

River gravel found our feet, then our knees, then our palms as we crawled out from the water on a well sheltered bank. We caught our breath kneeling on the shore, the water tracing over our soles and calves. Then, we stood, shakily, on our own two feet. I wasn't sure which one of us managed the feat. I didn't think it was me.

I'm going to be sick, Simon thought with absolute conviction, and the tensing of our stomach confirmed it. I pulled away from him, my mind and body stripping away from us like overstretched tar, pulling and pulling until we—

Chapter Twelve

Gen, Downriver

I spilled out from our body. I hadn't practiced unmelding in a long time, and it was less than a smooth transition. I stumbled gracelessly to the ground while Simon staggered and caught himself against a tree. His eyes closed shut and he moaned, doubling over to throw up bile. His wretches were awful, bodily things, but they were just background noise to me. The thoughts I had desperately tried to drown in the river found their way in, swarming my brain and pulling me down. I was helpless to stop them.

Mael is dead. It started, *Jorel killed her, and you did nothing. You could have stopped him, could have done* anything. *You let her down one last, final time...*

I laid on the stoney beach, lost, overwhelmed, and falling deeply, endlessly, into despair. Regrets rolled in my stomach and choked my throat with every thought. My body screamed to get up, to run right back into the water and let the river swallow me whole, and to not fight to come back up. I wanted to slip away from myself. From the horrors of that night.

I had never wanted to meld again. The fact that I had should have kept me throwing up right next to Simon. *Simon.* Oh, *Haliz,* I had brought Simon into a meld. What had I done? What had I subjected him to?

There was no going back from this. Not the meld, not Mael's murder, not the deep loathing and fear that now coursed through my bones.

My fist came up, slamming into the ground. River stones flew away on impact. I hit them once, then again, again.

"Enyk!" I swore, *"Enyk enyk* fucking *fuck!"* I grabbed a handful of stones and rolled, throwing them into the trees beyond. They crashed into the brush, shattered branches, disappeared into the shadows. My chest heaved in breaths as all my strength left me just as suddenly as the burst had come. "....Fuck." I breathed, rolling onto my stomach to put my face in my hands, elbows propped painfully on the stones.

*I'm sorry...*I wanted to tell her, but it was far too late. The night stretched out for what may have been minutes, but felt like one long, endless eternity. An eternity of a moment of hopeless failure.

"....he said," Simon had spoken, and somewhere in the midst of it all his voice reached me.

"...*what?*" I asked, turning my head to see him. Simon was standing still against the tree, his arm perpendicular to the trunk as he leaned his weight into it, his fist clenched.

Thinking.

He'd lost his glasses somewhere between here and the temple, and without the dark frames his face seemed foreign in the shadows. Open, unprotected.

"What was it he said?" He repeated, something hard and... and concerned in his voice.

"What who said?"

"*Jorel.* What was it that he said back there? About humans?"

Simon had something very serious in his eyes. He was lost in some thought he was clinging to. I was drowning in myself, but Simon hadn't forgotten where we were or why we'd ended up here.

He stared at me for an answer. I didn't understand why it mattered. Not yet. "I... he, he said—he said that Mael had let the humans crawl over the land... and... and I don't know the words in human.... taking from the land?" I swallowed the lump of emotions in my throat. I could barely speak around the choking swallows of tears I took every few words.

"Gen" He said, "You melded with me."

I didn't answer. It wasn't a question.

His eyes watched me. I was expecting him to demand answers, wanting to know how I had done it, who I really was, and what the meld was.

Instead, asked me something new. Something worse.

"Can you do it again?"

It was a hard question. It rolled right into me and knocked me down again.

My mouth opened. Stayed open. Stammered. No tangible words came out.

I couldn't think. I couldn't speak.

I was undone.

"Simon," I pleaded. "I cannot... I will not, Simon, please—"

He took a step towards me. "We need to, Gen—"

"You do not understand," I cried out, kneeling and digging my fingers in. They stung from the cold, gritty mud. "Please, please no... please do not ask this of me, you do... you do not know—"

His knees crunched in the stones before me. He walked on his legs to me, taking my face in both of his cold, wet hands. "I don't. I don't know anything about you. I don't know who you are or how you did that, or who Jorel is or why he did what he did. But I know that you are the fastest, strongest man I know and I have this...this gut feeling that something is wrong."

"They chased us over a waterfall," I said, "They killed Mael, they are trying to kill us *everything is wrong—*"

"Gen *listen to me*," He commanded, and I shut up. I don't think I had ever heard Simon speak like that. It came from some hidden strength deep within him, born from something I didn't understand and wasn't sure I possessed. "Jorel has killed the only kriest of power who favored the humans," he spelled out for me, "He's the commander of the Kor. The temple has fallen to him and he's made it clear Del Tor won't aid my kind anymore." He swallowed, connecting the dots even as he spoke. "If the Kor or Asterel led an attack on New Caramel there is no one in power who would care to hold them accountable, let alone stop it. We are the only ones that know what's going on, and we've gotten a head start on his men. We need to get to New Caramel and warn them..

"If anyone can get us there in time, it's you. And if anyone can say the right things to get them to believe us it's—" his eyes pulled away, but I saw something there. Something he didn't want to admit. "—It's me."

I had no strength left in me to run from this. But I could stay for him. He was only in this mess because I was too much of a shameful coward to stand with Mael and face the reidship head on.

I didn't want to see Simon's body next.

He was all I had left.

I closed my eyes. Opened them again. Then I took his face with my hands as well. "Alright," I conceded. He met my gaze with a mixture of emotions and resolution.

"Hold tight," I said softly. "This time...might not be as quick." Reaching down into myself, I began the meld.

Chapter Thirteen

Simon, Melded

The first few minutes of the meld were smothering. Unimaginable guilt and pain crushed down on our chest, Gen's misery folding into my barely stifled panic.

We had to get to Tess. She'd been right this whole time. I was a fool to doubt her.

Gen found our bearings from the stars and tree line alone. We ran at a far more paced speed than earlier, both to keep from hurting ourselves in the dark and to preserve our energy, but we made good time. I could have sworn an arrow had hit our leg when we'd jumped from the cliff, but no pain or blood came from the spot.

It was hard to not slip into the familiar motion of running in our body, and the almost therapeutic thrum it sent through us. Slowly, the overbearing depths of emotions I had slammed into when we melded waned away, and I was able to explain my concerns properly.

Gen had been right; there was something powerfully simple in exchanging information with another part of your own mind. Gen replayed the spectacle Jorel had started at my request, and there wasn't a need for translation. Gen understood the meaning and his words, and now I could, too.

I grasped the weight of his actions, that he was Mael's son, what kind of man he was. I gleaned all of this as we paced towards the city, and then some. I understood his speech, I felt Gen's unrelenting guilt for failing to protect Mael. I felt her as he felt her. A maternal figure, a mentor, a comfort. I felt Jorel as he did as well. I felt him as an unrelenting bully, an intelligent man, someone who made Gen's hair stand on end anymore. Someone he was endlessly cautious about, even if I couldn't see what events had made him such. The information Gen gave me was less images and memories so much as emotions and feelings, ones that I just...*understood.*

Sentiments that would otherwise have taken long, in depth conversations to convey passed between us in minutes. There was hardly room for misunderstandings when you shared a mind.

I learned that Gen's thoughts tended to get very crowded, at times, and that was when he would back off and revert to feelings. I would feel his ache, I would feel reverberations of memories. He never told me Mael was the closest to a mother he knew, but I felt what her image evoked within him in real time. It was very different from my own mind and thoughts. I had never truly thought about what reading someone else's mind would be like. Old books and movies had it like a phone system, where you could transmit or hear clear, concise words, but that wasn't really how minds operated. Emotions, sensations, memories in familiar but blurry colors, they all came in at once. It was less two voices in one head so much as two heads together.

Most anything I thought, he received. Most anything he thought, I received. What I sometimes lacked, though, was *context.*

As we ran through the woods our feet were sure with the familiarity of traveling in the dark, cautions of roots and low hanging branches were reacted to automatically through practice.

But not my practice. I'd never been in any forest after dark outside of a tent, and I certainly had not run through one. There was a level of comfort Gen exhibited that clearly showed he'd done something like this before. But when, and where, and how I couldn't say.

It was less like we were melded into one than stuck together with many strips of scotch tape.

Whatever we were, though, was good enough. Our body was piloted almost purely by Gen, each movement foreign and strange to me even as I felt it all. With the same absent process you use to breathe, he ran carefully through the dark forest.

He pushed me back again just enough I could get familiar with the odd co-pilot feeling and relegate most movement to him.

I pulled our hand away from a branch. He moved our legs and stepped around it with grace I could never have possessed in my own body.

What I mostly did in our meld was replay the night over and over and over again. I desperately needed to catalog it, understand it. I replayed the melding ceremony, and Jorel's murder of Mael. I thought of the melding I had witnessed, the fishmonger family, and how unsure their movements were at first, how guided they needed to be with every step.

I found myself comparing it to now, to how easily we had melded, moved, ran in our first moments as one.

"You've melded before," we said to ourselves, quiet and accusatory.

"Yes," we answered. Simple, precise, without context, memory, or further answer.

Frustration—my own for his lack of answer and his for my question—rose within us. Our feet sidestepped the root of a particularly ugly tree.

"When? With who?"

"Does it matter?

It very much did. Now that my life was no longer in immediate danger, the pieces of the puzzle that did not fit together mattered very, very much.

I didn't say that out loud, didn't really think it, but the part of us that was Gen could taste the edges of my emotions and figured it out. He still didn't offer up the information. Frustrated, I sort of— *pushed? Pulled?— concentrated*, in the same way one would when you were trying really, really hard to recall where you left your keys. It wasn't my own memory I tried to pull up, but Gen's. I could almost see it there, somewhere on the trace end of his non-answer. Something

familiar, and not so far back—

"Stop," we said. We stopped, physically, in our tracks. The night was cool on our drying skin, but a sweat had begun to build from our pace. The forest around us was just as dark, just as black and shadowed as it had been only a moment before, but something seemed sharper about our surroundings. More defined.

"Don't...please don't go there," we spoke, and our voice was barely audible. It was low, and quiet, and full of a pain I was horribly familiar with, but registered wasn't my own. "Not now, not tonight, not after everything I've been through."

I felt what it took out of us to have Gen ask that. I felt for one horrible moment how low he'd sunk the moment that elusive memory had begun to pull towards me. It felt heavy, boggcd down with threads closely tied to so many other painful, heavy memories. I didn't see whatever it was he was trying not to think about, or to have me not think about—God, what a strange thing to say—and I was suddenly aware of two dreadful things.

Whatever truth Gen had, whatever secrets lay just behind a veil of ends that didn't tie together and stories that didn't line up, it was larger than I could have ever imagined. It also carried tremendous, relentless agony.

The second thing I suddenly gleaned was that Gen carried it with him *always*.

I'd never felt so close to this man as I had in that moment. Understanding came in how I related to the terrible, sinking weight of my past. The one I was trying so hard to move on from.

In that moment, standing unnaturally still in the silence, we shared that moment. Then came the understanding that someone else had just walked into our minds and bodies and brought something deeply personal out of the darkness and into the light.

It was exposing. It was terrifying. It was done.

"Okay," we said, and I didn't know who spoke. Maybe both of us.

We moved suddenly, rolling down and to the right and solidly into a pile of brush that clawed at our skin and clothes. It was a blur, nothing I had done on purpose nor anything by Gen's design. I recognized that his instincts, far sharper than mine, had screamed at us like a firework in our veins. Perhaps it had been a sudden flash of light, or a change in the air that had notified him but I would never know. I don't honestly think he did, either.

We rolled to the right and inches from where we had been standing, away from a movement directly to our left. We tumbled on the forest floor, stopping gracelessly and forcefully upright against a tree. Our eyes fought to focus on the thing, searching the darkness for whatever had spooked us.

A bolt, black and wicked, had lodged itself into the ground where we had stood.

There was barely a second in time for us to register the thin shadow when another lodged itself aggressively into the tree above our head. Angled differently from the way we'd come, we heard footfall.

Heavy, multiple, purposed.

The search party had arrived, climbing through the blackened woods with speed and ease that betrayed familiarity with the path. *Practice.* It tasted of soldiers applying a drill they'd mastered a hundred times. It was coordinated. It was pointed. It was here.

A shout rang up, something in kriest I had yet to learn but something we understood all the same. *Found them.* We didn't wait for the words to finish before we were moving again, that impossibly keen instinct of Gen's rolling our body around the tree for cover and then sliding us down a short and nearly invisible embankment. Trees clawed at our face and brush scratched at our hands and feet. We felt it all. Sweat lined our brow until it was smacked away by a stray leaf. The devout came after us immediately, coming down the same slope at the moment our feet hit the solid ground below. Another bolt came past us, a sickening *snick* embedding it into something very close by.

Towards the city, I managed a thought, *we need to head to the city, lose them in the streets, find help—*

Our body turned sharply, and Gen drove us forward at a reckless run. We didn't try for silence, there was no point in it anyway. Not when they were this close. There had to be at least three pursuers, calling out in the dark. Taunting us. Hunting us. We were nearly blind in the forest, less prepared, without the thick soled boots to protect our feet or any weapon to fight back.

The only thing we had was Gen's speed and dexterity, and he gave us his all.

The woods were unforgiving. Unfamiliar. Branches caught us, roots tripped us up, but we ignored all of it. Kept going, kept running. Another bolt came to our left, another only a hair to our right. It had been so close we'd felt the change in air right against our thigh. Faster we ran, more reckless, desperate.

And then the ground opened up under us.

We fell without control down a sudden steep cliff face. It was hardly an embankment so much as a sheer drop, only the slightest angle keeping us from going fully airborne. It was from this brief, disorienting moment that we looked *up* for the first time, up into the sky through the trees that thinned this close to the city line. Into the open darkness above.

Into the worst thing we could see.

We hit the ground hard. We didn't roll so much as tumble at the end, and it was all Gen could do to keep us rolling over our shoulder instead of our head. Rocks dug into our flesh and roots pressed painfully into our sides and back. Panic overrode my mind at the horrors above.

The sky was filling with smoke, and a lot of it.

We came to a stop mostly upright between two trees. We'd missed them both by only a hair on either side. "No," our lips said— I said— my mind swimming. Dread soaked my bones, chilled me in the rolling smog. "No," we repeated, pushing ourselves up. "*No...*"

We crashed further through the brush, slid heavily down short ledges, slipped and fell and righted ourselves again and again and again. We followed the smoke, stumbling blind and reckless until the tree line opened up to us above a short ledge no taller than a man, one that led to more step-like embankments beyond the trees to the clear, unobstructed view of the destruction.

To New Caramel, ablaze.

The presence of fire came hot and fast through the air. Heat rose our skin to an uncomfortable low burn from even this distance. Smoke rolled into the forest and darkened the sky, obscuring the moon and stars.

We could taste the buildings it consumed. Wood and plant ash fell like snow from the new residential zones to the east, just beyond old main street. The stench thickly coated our throats and choked our lungs. The strange breeze tossed some our way, little petals of gray and black barely visible against the smothered sky. They smelled smokey, almost pleasant like a campfire, or a hearth in winter. Underneath it all was something darker, more metallic. Bitter and meaty. It smelled wrong. Its unbearableness crawled along our skin and shook our bones. Everything in us told us to run away, to turn back to the forest

The skyline glowed amber, but it was far too soon to be the sun. The attack on New Caramel heated our face and burned our fear.

We'd been so wrong to assume we'd had time. We were already far, far too late.

It was all we could do to stand there and face the work of a man who, in a single hour, had upturned the entire world.

This wasn't a war. This was a slaughter.

Chapter Fourteen

Jorel, Mael's Home

"Sanra, Reid Jorel," Vaga knelt before me, her face lowered to the floor. Her voice was far less calm than I had hoped it would be. I was standing in the very room I'd argued with my mother that evening, having repurposed the sitting room space into a base of operations. We were alone.

"Sanra, Captain Vaga. What do you have for me?"

"We have closed off the temple at your request. No one else in or out, save our own. The accolades are gathered in the food hall as we speak, under watch until you can speak to them as requested."

Just as planned. "There will be pushback, but do not punish them for it. Change is, at face value, fear inducing. We can hardly blame the temple for reacting to such a sudden upheaval of every truth they'd held.. I will speak to the congregate and ease their fears, but advise our own to handle them with care. No unnecessary force. Remember our true enemies."

"That is very considerate of you, Reid Jorel."

"I am a considerate man. I consider everyone, everywhere, all at once."

"That you are." There was a pause, and then she continued her briefing. "The southern skies are amber with fire, just as you instructed the twins. It seems their cleanup campaign is going just as intended."

I heard something bitter in her voice. A dark longing to be out there, in the squatters town they called a city, cleaning out the human lives she so despised. Doing the work she wanted most over the work I needed her to do most. But she did not voice it. So I asked.

"You would prefer to be there?"

"I would prefer," she said carefully, "The blood I am owed for the lands I have lost to the pests and for my son's life I will never recover."

"And you will get it all," I assured her, "in the days to come. The battle to reign in the humans and repurpose the lands will be an exhaustive one, and it will take time. Tonight, the hardest part is under the capable hands of the twins. It is messy, and brutal, and it may make you feel better now but it will only hinder our goals to have you waste this important evening culling pests." I knelt before her, touching her shoulder. "I need you here, doing what you do best. I can trust no one else with this delicate situation."

Her eyes flicked up to meet mine, light catching a hound's tooth necklace she normally kept tucked in her shirts. It was from the dog that took her young son's life four years ago. A dog that should have never graced our world, a wild menace plaguing our lands gifted by the humans themselves. I may not feel strongly one way or another towards the existence of the humans, but on the matter of the dogs I stood firmly against. It was why she'd even entertained the idea of the work I'd given Chelsea.

Vaga searched my eyes, and then nodded her assent.

"Of course, Reid Jorel."

I stood again, grabbing my boots and taking a seat in one of my mother's sitting room chairs to pull them on. Now for the unpleasant part.

My voice came out low, displeased. Venomous. "...and the melded?"

Vaga paused, a long, drawn out silence that ended just a hair before too long.

"...there has been no further sign of them, either in the river or along the banks. The search is still ongoing. They did go over a waterfall, Reid Jorel. There *is* a chance they have drowned and half washed out to sea by now."

I valued Vaga for her willingness to say to me the things others might be worried would upset me. Telling me that we may have lost such a vital asset to a simple drowning definitely fell under that header. A nice, final punch in the gut after an otherwise successful usurpation. One that was too easy. From anyone else, I might have responded with violence.

"I *know* Gen." I said, more to myself than her, wrapping the leather bindings around the boot and tying it off. "He's base jumped from there dozens of times. If anyone could survive that fall in the dark, it's him."

Vaga said nothing, waiting for me to continue. I chewed on it all as I put on my second boot, hoping she couldn't see the way my hands shook ever so slightly at the possibility I was wrong. What a joke this all was. All of my work—no, the very *future* of my people— now hinged on our ability to capture one single imbecile alive and bring him back to me. Without the knowledge of how to complete an unmelding, I and *Haliz Fundir* were both useless in the face of the north's existing might.

To unmeld improperly was to guarantee death. I'd known that to be true since I was a child.

"Send word to the twins," I ordered, standing at last. "Gen is to be found and returned at all costs. He is a threat to the security of our people should he flee back to the north and inform them. I do not care what condition he's in as long as he is returned alive. He will live to see punishment for his crimes against the temple, and the affront of Haliz Fundir he has done melding with a *human*."

"And what *of* the human?"

I'd thought of this.

"Keep him alive, for now. I think his death could be of great use to our cause if timed right."

I stepped over to the desk my mother kept and pulled out a mostly empty scroll, writing instructions hastily with a deep purple ink. It dried fast, and I was able to roll it up and tie it off, handing it to my captain.

"Ensure this is given to the twins with the following instructions: should they fail to locate and return the traitor and his human by sunrise, they are to read and follow this *exactly*. Do you understand my orders?"

She eyed the scroll warily. "....yes, Reid Jorel."

"Then see it done," I dismissed her, handing her the scroll. She stood, leaving without a second glance back into my mother's home.

Alone in the space, I felt Mael haunt me in every corner of the quiet room. I felt her eyes on me, and the weight of her death on my hands.

My hand collided with the inkwell before I could think, shattering the ceramic cup against the wall and spraying a deep indigo all over my mother's precious tapestries. It splashed my hand, the ink cool like old blood.

Mael's death was a necessity, I willed my thoughts to reach Gen across reality and time, *but if you continue to defy me— yours will be a joy.*

Yours and the human standing in my way.

Chapter Fifteen

Gen, Melded, New Caramel

We stumbled down the next embankment with jerky, uncoordinated steps. We'd found ourselves at the edge of the city, near a long-empty building and the fence that ran the length of the property. We'd lost the Kor pursuing us momentarily in the drop.

The horror of Jorel's larger plan began to unfold before our very eyes. If he'd wanted to flex his new strength, he'd succeeded.

God, Simon said quietly in our mind, our bare feet touching the first stretch of broken blacktop, *what has he done?*

The fires illuminated the town in harsh, flickering shadows. This close the smells and sounds were added to. Screams of pain, and fear, and shouted orders created a din of chaos. It was coming from the town center and the residential zones to the east.

Above all that, somewhere in the far off distance, a cacophony of wild, animalistic braying filled the night. It was haunting, and primal, and somewhat painful to listen to. It sent our teeth on edge and shook our bones, filling our gut with something deeply instinctual. Something we had never felt before, but recognized regardless.

The fear of being eaten, of monsters in the darkness. Of beasts with sharp teeth and dripping jaws.

I chastised myself for ever thinking we'd stood a chance of doing something right. Simon...Simon learned. He now understood what kind of man Jorel truly was, and what kind of man now hunted us across the island.

And it scared him.

It scared us both.

Our fear turned to copper on our tongue. And then we were moving, hand over hand along the fence, clinging to its links. Rust pinched our fingers and coated our palms. Our feet shuffled around each other, not quite a shimmy, not quite a jog. Just... moving. Moving to the left, to the open end of the fence a few sections down.

A memory flashed between us, something unbidden, of a day in elementary school climbing the playground fence for the first time. A memory of falling, of landing on my back and the wind getting knocked from me. It wasn't *my* memory, and it came to me more in feelings, a passing, intrusive thought. Something for our minds to cling to, desperately. Something that was safer, and simpler, and somewhere far, far away from here. From this world. From this reality.

His city burned and bled and all Simon could think about for a long moment was being back...somewhere else, climbing a fence at a school and falling back into the deep pea gravel and feeling the wind escape his lungs. Of the Florida sky, so wide and clear and blue, and being anywhere but here.

Our feet were not my own. They were driven by him, by something conscious and calm, a level of rational thought that flowed under the panic and grounded him—ground us both, really— despite everything else. Rationalization that came to him and pushed our feet forward.

"This was coordinated," he voiced through our lips, pulling together thoughts from the mess in our mind. "Planned.

The power is down, they probably blocked off the main roads..."

"Simon," I breathed, "What now?"

Neither of us answered at first. Simon's thoughts raced, turning over everything he could find, every aspect of our situation and any cards we may have left. My hand felt painfully empty.

I couldn't go home, to turn back towards Torrel was suicide, and to advance forward was surely meeting the same fate. The forest was nasty at night, full of plenty of its own dangers, from sudden cliff drops to the few major predatory animals. Wild dogs desperate for a meal or worse, if legends were true, of The Great Bear further east. Hunter snares or traps invisible to the eye. In the day I could have reasonably taken that gamble, but deep in the night...

I felt the exact moment he stopped shuffling his options. Hesitated. I felt him mull something over, something heavy and unpleasant, something he shielded from me by sheer will alone.

Our heart raced. He didn't move away from the thought. Settled into it. Found resolution.

"We need to get to my apartment."

"Why?"

"We need supplies," He said through our lips, "and we need to find Tess. She's our only option now. If I know her, she'll be in the thick of this mess. So is my place."

"Who's that?"

I felt something sour in the back of our mouth. Simon's feelings for her. All he said, though, was "...someone I hoped you'd never meet."

I didn't push, but he felt my unanswered questions nonetheless. I felt him recognize it and wall up, digging in his heels. Simon never withheld anything. It was a hard pressed challenge to get him to stop sharing his thoughts on a good day, and since occupying space in the same mind the constant barrage of line after line of information was staggering. Now, however, all I met was a wall.

There came more shouts behind us, and any further conversation quit. I didn't know if it was the right choice or not, but he seemed sure of his answer, of this Tess person. And I trusted him. More now than ever, feeling him live inside our head and body. I'd also asked for a lot of trust from him, jumping us both over a literal cliff. So despite all logic and instinct, I conceded.

We ran for the road. That was also the direction of the majority of the screaming, but it wasn't as if we had any better options. All that was left was forward to Simon's apartment. To the madness and unknown ahead.

With no idea what awaited us we ran into the shadows of the building's walls, towards the flames and screams, towards the darkened streets below.

Chapter Sixteen

Simon, Melded, New Caramel Streets

Darkness has a way of changing the familiar. Shadows shaped the world around me in harsh black swaths. The fires downtown created a red glow that licked the tops of buildings and sent the deep pitches of darkness to a dance. Familiar places now stood in obscurity, forbidding and foreign.

The night had become anything but silent. In the distance the howls and screams continued their keening, and the roar and snaps of bone and fire permeated the air with force. Then there was us, our breath, our pulse, our feet on the blackened ground. The fires seemed to deepen what darkness they could not illuminate. The blues of the night were gone, erased by the smoke climbing in the sky and the haunting orange glow.

Gen's voice wasn't speaking to me. He was too concentrated on moving, following my feel for the city layout. We stuck close to the buildings, our heart hammering in our chest. What would we find when we turned the next corner? The next street?

The Kor were hot in pursuit again, only a block or so behind. We weaved through alleys and under awnings. Every time we thought we may have lost them, or ducked fully out of sight, one of them would round the corner behind us or jump over a fence with ease and call to the others.

Please, Tess, I begged, *please be where I need you to be tonight.*

Fear and a drive for survival were all I knew. Our ears perked up and moved at each tiny sound. It was amazing, the directionality the Kriest ears had over our own. It was like being immersed in the most superior surround sound system in the world. If only the listening options were better.

Our leg muscles were tense. Our back was tense. Our arms were tense. Everything ached, begged us to slow. Gen didn't listen to it. Tuned it out. *Was this a runner's high?* I'd never felt the full effect of fight or flight taking over. Not like this. It all felt so familiar to Gen, though.

Like an old friend.

I didn't have time to think about it.

Nothing appeared before us for the first few blocks. No humans, nor kriest, nor whatever was making the horrible howls. Then time seemed to warp. All there was was the darkness, shortening with every step, every heartbeat.

Fear, cold and slow licked our bones. Something deep within us, something primal and old, warned us. Warned us to go back, that death was around the corner.

Death was also behind us. Their boots fell heavy, arrows flying past us wildly as they fought to aim in the dark. None of them were familiar with street warfare. Not that either of us were, either, but Gen knew how to run through a city. It was the only edge we had.

We barreled into a crossroad, skidding, sliding, so close to home I could taste it. The heat of flames licked our face. The golden light exploded upwards from a building down the way to expose how horribly wrong we'd been to think there was safety in the city.

Hell, truly unimaginable, lay before us.

They'd started in the row. It was once a collection of quaint outdoor shopping centers with matching New England brick facades and white capped molding, back in the old world.

Many of the buildings had been repurposed into apartments when the main business hub had moved further north to allow for easier trading with Torrel.

I had never seen a street run red with blood. Neither of us had. It pooled under the dead and splattered the brick facings, gathering in low points between the paved stones and gutters. Bodies of people— real, normal people, who only hours before had been asleep in their beds— littered the brick road. A lifetime of old world horror movies hadn't prepared me to see true bodily carnage. The movies had done it wrong, romanticized and played up this idea of gore for the audience. True death was unapologetic, almost unreal.

No one here had died an easy death. But everyone here was dead. There was not a single living soul on the block, no kriest or humans or obvious source of the howling. Through doorways left cracked and open we saw prone hands and feet being swallowed by flames or darkness. Those in the roads or propped unnaturally against walls were dressed for bed, barefoot and in comfortable clothing. Many had taken wounds from bladed instruments, their throats and chests opened up in clean, efficient sweeps of hatchets or spears. One man, old enough to be well into fatherhood, lay on his side with his head cut almost fully off, only a grisly bit of spine holding his body to his skull. The picture inside was surreal, a perfect vivisection of muscles and windpipe, drained of most blood. It was like a diagram in some far removed anatomy book. On closer inspection, a few of the dead had this wound, the decapitating calling card of someone with no mercy and a horribly heavy hand with their blade.

These were my neighbors. This could have been me. They'd died by knife or hatchet.

Many more had been ripped apart.

A woman with red hair and a sloppy black cavern where her throat had been lay on her back in an almost angelic pose, her hazel eyes open and trained on nothing. Her lips were parted and her jaw slack in death, almost as if in silent surprise. Jacqueline Clay. Our stomach rolled but only a low, horrible moan came out at the recognition. Her arms were torn up by claws in defense, but whatever had done this to her had managed to push her back on the ground and tear out her throat. The meat that had been there was unrecognizable, like a flesh colored sack filled with ground hamburger. Chunks of her were dropped like breadcrumbs in violent spatters across the street. They led our eyes to another body, and then another.

That morning I had seen her shaking blankets out of her windows, opening her home to the chilled early air. She'd hemmed my pants earlier this month. She'd had a daughter.

We stepped around her. The ground was wet, helplessly wet, and neither of us wanted to think about what we were stepping in. The air was thick with a throaty campfire smell, and the coppery musk of spilled blood. From the burning building across the way another smell came, one that rolled our stomach again and again. It smelled like cooked pork.

Behind us the boots stopped. We turned to the left, down the way we had come. One of the three, the leader, was saying something in panicked Kriest. *The line,* I heard, *the monsters.*

Something fell to the street with a clatter, a burning part of some building further down, and as if they'd seen a ghost, two of the devout turned and ran *back the way we'd come.* The third made a halfhearted jog back, raising his bolt, looking between us and the glowing red of the street beyond, and in quick succession dropped his weapon down to his side and ran after his comrades.

"*Why?*" I asked softly. There was no one to answer, only the crackling flames that danced in pools of my neighbors spilled lifeblood. "*Why?*"

From a dark and broken door across the street, an answer came. Two low, guttural growls rose from the shadows, horrifyingly close. A shape began to move away from the darkness, bulbous and misshapen, towards the street. Towards us.

Chapter Seventeen

Gen, Melded, New Caramel Streets

My father had taught me that running from a predator will only make it chase you. Stand your ground, arm yourself, and fight. It's your only chance of survival.

I'd never been much of a fighter, though. He'd also never been much of a father.

I didn't wait to see the monster in the shadows. We hadn't been very far from the opposite buildings and as soon as that form moved we did too. We turned with a lunge, racing with everything I had in us towards the broken brick buildings. The beast howled, two separate hollow sounds that sounded shrill and guttural at the same time. Claws scrambled against the wet ground as it came for us, chasing our exposed back.

Breathing when you ran this fast was almost painful. I threw everything we had left in that run, desperately fleeing the last ten steps to the wall. Our feet slapped hard on the ground but I hardly felt it. Our pulse screamed in our ears and chest as I begged every star in the sky and every leaf on *Haliz Fundir* that we could be just a little faster, just a little quicker. Simon screamed in our head *"Go go go!"* and I was fucking going. I had never run so fast or so hard in my life.

That thing was faster, though. In only eight quick steps it nearly caught up to us, its own taloned paws coming down in the same bloody puddles our feet had just left. Its shrieks were all we could hear, filling the space around us. Heat and snapping jaws chased our legs and raised our flesh.

The wall was so close, a somehow intact window just before us. The body of poor Jacqueline was closer. The thing at our heels was matching our step, no doubt watching and lunging for our exposed vitals as any hunter would do so close to their prey. I didn't think about it so much as I felt it. So much as I *knew*, it wasn't watching our legs.

I did not leap over her body. I stepped over it, just barely clearing her and landing on the ground opposite her with a single stride. A stride I turned into a desperate jump. A jump I aimed to grab the top ledge of that large picture window.

The unknown beast behind us ran head on into the mutilated corpse. Exposed and slippery innards tripped it up, slid it out from the dead run and momentum did the rest. My hands slammed home on the ledge and I threw our legs up with a desperate scream of our own. They didn't catch on the sill to the side, but it was enough to give the beast clearance under us. In a loud shattering of glass the howling beast crashed through, just barely swiping our left foot where I hadn't pulled it up quickly enough. Wet fur left a sick grime on our skin, and the large form pushed our leg painfully to the right. We cried out, in fear or disgust or pain I didn't know.

Crashing sounds of furniture and glass followed it out of sight into the room below. I didn't wait for it to reemerge. I scrambled desperately for handholds and footholds, digging the tips of our fingers and toes into the bricks and sills around us. Our feet slipped just as often as they found hold.

We couldn't breathe right. We were out of synch, every breath clawing and jerky, fast and unhinged. We could hear our voice in every inhale and exhale. Thoughts screamed in our mind, wild and stripped back to the barest of instincts. *Climb! Faster! Fasterfasterfasterfaster!*

There was an open window on the second floor. Simon nearly turned us into it at the same time I tried to jerk away from it. We ended up in a spasm,

What if it can jump?

It's inside *the building! What if it can climb stairs?!*

Snarling screams came to us through the inside rooms, bouncing around the halls and pushing up to the second floor to reach us. Howls of anger and pain chased us off the sill and back outside, jumping to the next window over and scaling the wall to the roof. It was an effort to pull ourselves up and over the concrete ledge. Our arms screamed. Our legs screamed. We could still barely pull in a breath.

We collapsed on the flat surface, our face to the skies. Who was screaming right now?

Was it him? Was it me? Who was breathing? I can't *breathe, I need to breathe, I need to—*

Chapter Eighteen

Gen, Partially Unmelded

—I began to pull away from him, our upper bodies forming into themselves again, arms pulling apart but not all the way. Desperation grabbed us and gave us both our lungs, separate. Apart. I gasped for breath like I was back in the river, pulling us up from the water for the hundredth time. Campfire-scented air filled my lungs, I took in one breath, two, and he did the same.

Great, panicked, gasping breaths and then it wasn't enough. I wasn't strong enough to fight the meld fully. I wasn't able to regain my own arms, my legs, my stomach my hips— I was a monstrosity, I was him, I was nothing, *I was—*

Chapter Nineteen

Gen, Melded, Row Rooftop

We screamed when we came back together. Horrible pain wracked our core. His arm came into mine again, our shoulder. His lungs and ribs scraped into mine, pulling over and under and then into itself until we were— Whole. Melded. Sobbing in unison.

Breathing again. In sync. As one.

We lay prone on the rooftop. Our ears rang. The sky hung heavy and choked with smoke above us. Everything shook. Or was it us who was shaking? Our hands trembled so badly it pulled away loose bits of gravel used to pave the surface. We were immobilized by the waning pain and the survivalist terror we had just ran through.

The air cooled the blood on our legs. Dried it. Clumps of flesh cemented themselves to our skin. Awareness of the touch grew within us, swelled and roiled into our stomach. I was the one to turn us on our side as we retched, but only bile came up. It looked black in the night.

We curled up painfully, shaking. Helpless. Unsure. And then a voice spoke within us.

Simon's voice. A voice of reason.

We need to get up, it said softly, barely a whisper in our mind. *We need to move away from here. Before that....thing comes back.*

I couldn't argue with that if I'd tried. No thoughts formed, and any that tried slid away from me into our mind. I was so tired. So afraid. So horrified at what we had seen, what we had escaped. At myself. At the growing recognition that I had tried to unmeld us...and *failed.*

The thought paralyzed me. The memory shook me. Simon's voice came again. *Gen. It is not safe here.*

It's not safe anywhere, I managed back.

I know where we need to go next.

A plan. A goal, a place to go. *Where?*

My apartment, he reminded me, the voice coming through a little louder. A little further out of the grips of fear. Back into logic. *To find Tess.*

I wanted to ask who. I wanted to ask why. I couldn't care to do either. Not at that moment. Instead, when our arms gently pulled us up onto our elbows, shaky and unsure, I helped him. I helped move us upright, sitting up slowly. Brushing away the small rocks—the *pea gravel,* the word came to me again—from our arms where they'd dug in. Pulling our feet under us.

Standing.

Cautiously we flexed our arms, rolled our shoulders, bent our knees and moved our hands. We were one again. Whole. Unbothered. Our right foot felt bruised, but nothing seemed broken. Honestly, most of our body felt bruised, but not broken. It was just the latest in the collection of abrasions tonight. It was good enough.

An ache of exhaustion flooded our muscles from the expelled adrenaline, but I ignored it.

It wasn't the time. Simon was right, we needed to move.

"Where to?"

A map came to mind, a feeling of direction and location much clearer than I had expected. An image of a building with metal doors and thick brick walls formed. It was only a few blocks from here. Closer to the fires, but simple enough to travel by rooftop if Simon's feel of the city was right.

Together, we took the first step. From the streets below a chorus of howls followed us, but stayed below. Neither of us dared look over the side to see what had chased us from the shadows. Simon figured it wouldn't be safe to give away our position. I didn't care to see it.

The flames called us east, to Simon's apartments and the directions of the screams and fighting. It seemed as safe as anywhere else.

My sense of self came back as we walked. The gaps between the buildings were negligible to nonexistent. Some areas were impossible to see in the dark and we moved by feel, others were cast in flaming golden brilliance, and we had to be careful to stay out of sight. People so rarely looked *up* that it was a safe bet no one would, but tonight we couldn't think of a reason to push our luck any further.

Heading closer to the center of it all seemed suicide. Simon reassured me deeper in was our only way out. There was something he wasn't telling me. Something he wouldn't let me see, no matter how much I wizened up to it and pried. He was impenetrable, and it was infuriating. I had the feeling he wasn't leading me into danger, though. Just something he did not want to tell me. Something I wouldn't like.

Thoughts of moving shadows and hatchets filled my mind, fear at what may be lurking in the building as we grew nearer. No sooner had I thought it did an image come to us. Metal doors, reinforced, to the apartment building he resided in. Security that was rare to find in New Caramel anymore, a luxury.

We stepped over the side of a flat roof to a seemingly slanted one. I leaned into the angle, pressing against the tiles. They gripped our hands strangely.

"Nothing would have gotten in," Simon said, sure. "If they did... the chances they made it to the apartment is nil at best.

"Why do you live somewhere so...."

"Secure?" he finished seamlessly for me. "....because I needed the protection when I moved here."

From what?

Our lips formed a thin, hard line. Something painful traced the back of our mind. A bitter memory I couldn't make out.

From whom.

A scream, horrible and in pain exploded through the night. It was close. Very, *very* close. We moved away from it instinctually, ducking low into the shadows of the rooftop. Our breath caught in our chest. We didn't move. The scream came again, full of words we couldn't make out, and then it stopped, clean and jarringly sudden.

No further sounds came. I held us still against the shingles for almost a minute before slowly moving forward, peeking up and around the angled rooftop to the streets below. The fire hadn't come this far down the lots yet, and there was little visibility. If there was someone down there, it wasn't anyone we could see. Cautiously, we stepped down from the top of the slope and turned back towards his apartment building.

There was no more talking as we moved on.

There was nothing special or different about the roof we stepped on at last, but Simon's voice said: *This is it.*

We dropped low on instinct, Simon had long given me reign of our movements, helping only to turn our ears to the sounds around us. The roof was flat and dark, but across the street a fire raged. It seemed most of the fighting was two blocks over, with plenty of buildings between us and it. It didn't stop the sounds from reaching us.

Screaming, bloodcurdling cries of anger, rage, laughter laced with bloodlust, they all rose over the city line. More of that damned animalistic howling came, and something between a bark and a shriek. Crying, begging, something Simon recognized in the cadence of *praying*.

The access door opened easily for us, it was never locked, Simon knew, and we slipped in. He liked to come read up here sometimes, and he'd never considered someone scaling the walls to break in through the roof. The heavy metal door closed behind us with a slam. The sounds of the massacre below stopped with it.

We breathed out in relief. Guilt came with it. We descended the—*concrete* stairs. I found if I concentrated hard enough on something new, a word would sometimes come to me. One that seemed right. This was new, but not worth dwelling on.

We went down one landing, keeping our footsteps as quiet as possible. Holding the cold metal railing in the dark. Chips of paint flaked and fell away. If anyone was in here with us, waiting in the flights below, they were just as lost and in the dark as we were. That fact wasn't enough of a comfort. We went down one flight, two, felt the landing with our messy feet and stopped. Simon reached us out, feeling along the wall for—

A doorknob pressed into our hands, and quietly, slowly, we turned it. It opened to an apartment hallway beyond, illuminated blissfully by a single window. I saw three doors in it, and relief washed over us. Recognition. It was untouched. Whatever had broken into the apartments on the row hadn't made it in here. Or at least, not to this floor.

Unmeld with me, Simon requested quietly. We slipped into the hall and closed the door quietly behind us, not letting it latch all the way in fear of the sound. *I—it will be better if we're separated for this part.*

I didn't move. *It's alright,* his voice came, *it will go better this time. I know it.*

What if it doesn't? I asked the space in our mind, but he didn't reply. Waited. Finally I took a breath in, feeling my panic rise and claw at my throat. At our throat. But it was only me. Simon remained calm, soothing, as his voice came again.

Unmeld us, Gen.

We swallowed painfully, and just as before, as I had been trained, I reached down into us, down into the tangled hold of the meld and soothed the binds that formed us, released them and began to pull away from him. From us. It came smoothly, and all at once. One moment we were one and then—

Chapter Twenty

Gen, Simon's Apartment

We stood in the hallway. Simon's first few steps were unsure. Then, as he got used to being in his singular form again he moved with more confidence, aided by routine. I watched quietly as he went back to the door and kneeled, pulling up a loose floorboard with practiced ease. His fingers shook as he pulled out a single silver key.

There was something so human and simple in his movements, a sense of normalcy that came from something he had done a hundred times before. But to me it was almost foreign. Seeing him here, in place against the unfamiliar backdrop of a human home, was far from anything I had ever gotten to witness him do. I began to wonder what his life was really like outside of our translating sessions. I wondered if I even had the right to ask.

He slid the bit of metal into a slit in the knob and unlocked the door.

"Stay low," I advised, unsure if motion in the windows would give our position away.

He nodded, clearly drawing the same conclusion.

We entered the dark apartment together, him venturing further while I closed the door as quietly as possible and stayed near the entrance, listening. I couldn't help but turn from my guard post for a few moments to look around, though.

The space was small, one large room sectioned off sparsely with furniture that didn't match. It lacked the warmth of decor that Mael's did, and was clearly built with efficiency instead of aesthetics in mind.

The walls were nearly barren, and what was hung appeared mostly functional or second hand. The windows had sheer blanket-like materials draped across them, and not all in the same color or form. An old clock hung by a small kitchen area, unmoving. The face was cracked along the bottom. The furniture had a similar quality as old world human furniture, dated and worn and repatched. A small wooden table sat in the corner, two mismatched chairs faced each other. Most of the soul of the space came in the form of wooden boxes stacked in the corner. Human printed books lined most of them, or binders with handwritten spines. A random assortment of items was next to them, including some human thing they called an umbrella, an old walking stick with carved designs by either an unskilled craftsman or a child, and a trash bin filled with crumpled papers.

There was a couch against the inside wall with a haphazard nest of blankets laid across its length. A low, long table was between the makeshift shelves and the worn couch, and strewn across its surface was many familiar notes, books and translation materials.

It seemed the heart of Simon's living space was that couch and table. However he stepped past all of it to a small door next to the couch and opened what appeared to be another bedroom.

"Wait here," he said. "Keep guard at the door. This won't take long."

"Sure," I gave him, watching his back as he left. It felt strange, like I was purposefully being kept from the room, but...but I was probably thinking too much. I could still barely think at all. I turned away, pressing the heels of my palms into my eyes. I'd always been so *bad* at thinking.

I desperately wanted to do anything besides think. Besides remembering. Besides being here, now, after everything we've gone through this evening. After Mael...

The room was silent. Painfully, dreadfully silent. The dull ringing in my ears seemed so loud. I'd never felt so helpless, so alone, as I did tonight. I desperately wished to go to Simon, to go to him and press against him and press *into* him until I stopped being me.

Even that thought sickened me. Melding. *Melding.* I'd sworn to myself so long ago that I would never become the reid. That I wouldn't ever use the power of melding, not on myself, not on anyone else. Especially not... not on someone I cared for so much.

Not after I'd learned the truth.

Simon...please, someday, forgive me.

Something soft thumped beyond the hall door. My body seized in place. A chill rose along my spine. There *had* been a sound, hadn't there?

I crossed the space in two long, painfully quiet steps. I leaned against the frame, holding my breath. Peered through the small crack in the door. It hadn't closed all the way behind us.

And through that sliver... I saw.

Heaving itself up the final step was the shadowy nightmare we'd faced at the row. There was nothing outright to tell me it was the same monster, but something deep in the base of my spine knew it was true. It was the same beast that had chased us up that building, the same one we'd sent hurtling through a glass window. Somehow it had found us, followed us from rooftop to rooftop from the darkened streets below, waiting.

Relentless.

And when it staggered into the light of the window, lifting its mangled unholy head, it was all I could do to not weep.

Death had come for us. Death had stalked us through the night and came into Simon's home. Death now raised itself up, staggering within its own trail of eviscerated gore, the same mess it had slid across in the row. In the firelight of the kitchen window, I saw its form at last. Death had two heads.

Chapter Twenty-One

Simon, Simon's apartment

I would have brought Gen in here with me if I could have stomached it. I would have stayed melded with him, perfectly in form in that strange place of existence. Unmelding was like taking away a sort of safety blanket I didn't know I needed.

The problem was that Gen could read English perfectly enough. And I had my true notes in here. My work for Tess.

Gen...please, someday, forgive me.

The attached bedroom was small, and I'd never decorated it. It was mostly filled with boards and hung notes, visible maps of Torrel del Tor from my memory overlaid next to existing archives. Names and descriptions and Tess' own meticulous notes. Not just mine and hers, either, but every informant under her employ. Information that needed to be compiled and organized, cross checked, confirmed.

Tess called it *insurance. Important work for the continued survival of us all.* Her *just in case* project. I knew it made me no less of a spy for a paranoid master. I knew she'd been no less than right. I knew now more than ever she needed everything we had, and that meant the work in this room I hadn't yet finished and passed along to her capable hands.

The flare was my first stop. Quickly, hoping the sound of it would be drowned out by the chaos outside, I pulled the strange orange gun from the case on the wall. *Please,* I silently begged to anything that would listen as I pulled open the window and pointed it out to the sky above.

Please see this and know it's me...

I'd never pulled a flare before, and I was shocked by the sound and the pushback. A large red ball shot upwards to the flaming skies, higher and higher above every building around. I dropped the launcher out of the window, pinching my fingers in the sill on my way back in.

I didn't wait for the flare to come back down. I was already moving, grabbing my existing survival bag—another idea of Tess's I was now thankful for—and began pulling down every hung note, map and text and shoving it inside. I didn't care if it wasn't all annotated. She'd need everything I could bring. She'd be pissed if I didn't. I had to remove a bottle of cologne from the pack to make room. It was an old gift from my family I had left back in the old world, and it was something I'd kept with me through every move. But it wasn't important anymore.

I stopped at the last photo on the wall. It was older, an instant polaroid from years ago. It was a photo of a younger me, a more vulnerable me, a me I hated to remember but needed to never forget. It was a photo of me taken at a high angle by the woman whose arm circled my throat, almost choking me but pretending to have a playful air. Her curly red hair was a wild mess, her lab coat stained with the same inks that coated my own hands and shirt. She was laughing in the photo. It didn't reach her eyes. It didn't reach mine, either.

I hesitated at that photo. At Chelsea's eyes boring into me from the paper. *It's probably the last polaroid on the island,* I could remember her saying, *and I want to remember this moment forever.*

The day of your biggest fuck up.

I tore it from the tack and shoved it without regard in a backpack pocket. I hated to remember, but I couldn't afford to forget what she was. What I'd been through. Why I'd sold myself to Tess.

I just hoped Gen would understand.

The front door to my apartment exploded in and sounds of chaos came to me all at once. The snapping of the wooden frame as the hinges gave way. The solid *thap* of the doorknob embedding itself in the drywall. Gen shouting my name, terror in his scream. I threw open the door in the same motion I grabbed up my bag, searching wildly for him. Praying it was Tess.

Knowing I was wrong.

Nothing could have prepared me for what greeted me on the other side. Gen was sprawled on his back, something long and dark—*my umbrella*—lodged lengthwise into the jaws of a massive and deformed monster on top of him. Blood was smeared along the floor, and I didn't know if it was Gen's, or the beasts, or someone else's entirely. Saliva and gore ran down yellowed fangs wrapped around the umbrella, only that bar of metal stopping it from coming down on Gen's arm and face.

I didn't know what I was looking at at first. It was a mass of legs and body and matted fur, and then all at once I knew what I was seeing. My stomach rolled.

It was a dog. Or more accurately...it had been.

Five years ago, most everyone who'd gone to sleep in their respective beds of Caramel, Vermont woke in the early morning to find we weren't there anymore. Chunks of our town had been picked up and slathered on the face of this foreign island. One with new stars, new people, and unfamiliar seas around us. It had been chaos. It had been disorienting and maddening and impossible. But everyone who had made it was whole and fine. Adaptable.

The dogs had not been so lucky.

Whatever power had brought us here and kept us whole hadn't been so thorough with the animals. Pets especially. When we awoke on our first day on the island there wasn't a single cat that had come across. Some birds that had been local came along, although their numbers were more sporadic and many of them did not survive the first few years with newer, larger predatory birds around. Rabbits went much the same way, although they've had more success in the lower lands near the bay. Fish tanks sat empty. Beloved pets were gone, left behind in the old world.

While a majority of dogs did make it through, the ones that did weren't quite right anymore.

It started small; disobedience in the face of commands, howling at all times of the day or night. And then the break-outs started. The dogs wouldn't stay still in their homes. They began to chew through their tethers, doors, and hell even dry-wall to get outside.

It wasn't all at once, but one by one and two by two the dogs tried in frenzied desperation to flee their masters. When they did, it wasn't a mystery where they went. There was a call, something on the island that no human nor kriest could feel or comprehend but the dogs all understood. The island called, and they answered. Then they ran for the woods.

The dogs became feral, living deep among the trees, refusing human companionship, and becoming an overall menace to the towns at times. They would hunt livestock or game, steal wins from hunters and break into more rural homes for food.

They became scavengers.

When we came here, we all came whole. But the dogs left something behind that we kept. They abandoned their humanity, for lack of a better word. They lost their domes-ticity and became scrambling, scavenging beasts. They were hardly recognizable as the beloved animal I had always known. Too often you'd see the new generations slinking about, every image a wild mutt breed. They were all thin in the way street dogs were back home, covered in battle scars and haunted by whatever had driven the first few away from civilization.

The thing before me was beyond imagination.

The lower body was simply a large dog somewhere around the form of a german shepherd. Patches of its fur had either been torn away or sloughed off. It was as if someone had taken another dog—something gray and unrecognizable anymore—flipped it upside down and melted it into the bottom dog. If it was a meld, it was incomplete and trapped that way. The two heads merged at the forehead at a strange angle. Two of the four ears combined into a mass of ear-like flesh with two distinct canals visible, and the other side of the head had two ears separately placed. The top dog was missing one eye, having had it completely submerged into the other's skull, and the other sat just above the bottom dog's left eye. It looked like the eye socket of the top one had crushed the eyeball, and it had oozed out and down the fur long ago, drying there. Its torso began to follow down the spine, then twisted a full one eighty and sank into the bottom dog. Paws had melded only partway down the bottom dog's legs and stuck out at awkward, painful angles. Shoulders and legs that looked more like a fur-covered sack of double the bones and tissues fought for space. Out of its back hips a fifth, useless leg protruded into the air, twisted at a horrific angle Two separate tails sprouted from its hind end.

It was physically twisted, like a child had taken two colors of playdough and spun them together. It almost fascinated me. It made me sick to my very core and afraid even beyond that.

There was horror in the sacrilege of its creation. There was horror in the inhumanity of its agony, in the constant, bone-sheering pain of its existence that drove it mad and drove it forward. No animal should ever be pushed into a life so feared and pained its instincts only drove it to fight. For all reason to leave its mind. I understood that, the fresh memory of Gen and I'd incomplete unmelding on the rooftop surging again.

There would be no reprieve for this monster. Only pain, and madness, and eventually death.

And the endless, frenzied drive to kill before that death came.

Its lower jaw snapped around the umbrella, tearing apart the metal and plastic frame. The upper jaw snapped uselessly in the air, emitting a high keening wail like a teakettle. Gen was screaming, from concentration or pain or fear I couldn't tell, and tears ran down his face. Behind them both the hall-way had begun to fill with thick smoke, the fires having finally reached us.

"Run!" He screamed in human, but I couldn't. I couldn't move. I knew, deep down, that it was useless to run. I couldn't outpace this thing. I wouldn't even make it to the door. It was blocking the way. Gen screamed again, the jaws reaching around the umbrella and nearly closing on his forearm. I saw blood begin to pour down his skin and onto his chest and the floor as the dog tried to bite him over, and over, and over again.

I couldn't fight. I couldn't run. So I did the only thing I could do.

I turned back to the bedroom.

Gen's struggle continued. The window was still open to my left, and if I tried I could maybe make it out and kick the fire escape into place... get as far away from here and the monster as I could.

I abandoned the idea. I lunged forward, my hands clos-ing on the only thing I could think to grab.

Gen screamed again, something in Kriest I didn't know. It barely sounded like words. I unscrewed the cap in the same motion I turned back to the living room.

"Hey!" I shouted, catching the monster's attention. *"Get off of him!"*

I reared back and threw the open cologne bottle as hard as I could. A spinning trail of old, pungent sandalwood slammed directly in its face, shattering on impact.

The beast howled, rearing up and away from Gen, clawing his arms in the process. Gen closed his eyes and swore, scrambling backwards and away from the dogs as fast as he could. Perfume had sprayed all over, aromating the room instantly. The dog howled, all of its senses overwhelmed and its vision obstructed by the stinging liquid in its eyes. Gen coughed violently, almost retching at the onslaught.

I ran to him, grabbing his arm and attempting to pull him up.

"The building's on fire," I said. "We need to get out of here!"

"What was that?!" He choked, wiping furiously at his eyes. Tears continued streaming down his face. For the first time I saw the puncture wounds in his arms, not life-threatening but not pleasant either.

"Desperation," I said back. The dogs howled and screamed together, backing away from their own faces and crashing into my coffee table, my shelves, my walls. All of my belongings began to fall around it and crash to the floor.

"We need to go, I'll get us to the door–"

"Wait!" Gen screamed, and I looked up to see what he saw. In the door stood a figure, tall and foreboding. At its side was a crossbow, haloed by the firelight behind.

The dog screamed and reared its dual heads towards us. Our backs pressed into a wall.

We were trapped.

Chapter Twenty-Two

Simon, Simon's apartment

Tess appeared through the smoke like a dark, bloody angel. Trails of smog parted for her, shrinking from her skin like the hands of an old lover. She looked like she'd been through hell twice and won both times. Her boyishly short and untamed curls were plastered to her skull from blood or dirt or both. Her green-hazel eyes were wide and sharp, taking in the room in seconds. Me, Gen, the upturned furniture and the hound howling in pain between us, kicking against the air and floor and wall all at once. Her muscles tensed under her skin, and she pulled up the old and familiar crossbow nearly half her size. Without mercy or prejudice she dispatched two bolts in quick order into the dog, once in each skull. *Snik, snik,* and the braying stopped.

Fire licked the hall behind her, haloed her form. Her shoulders were clawed, something having torn straight through the black mesh to the hard flesh beneath. Her boots were smeared with gore and viscera, her pants stained but otherwise in good condition. Once they may have been military fatigues, or some functional cargo style, but now they were black with dye and blood and darkness.

"Chief! Is he in there?" A voice shouted somewhere in the smoke behind her, deep and familiar. Stone.

"Affirmative," she said, "he's got the translator with him as well."

"Then let's get the *fuck* out of here!" Boomed the man, and in the same breath he appeared, a solid slab of muscle and shoulders that filled the doorway in shadows. His salt and pepper hair was plastered back with the same grime hers was, his eyes a steely blue.

"The building's burning around us."

"Heard, commander." She said, crossing the room to pull the bolts from the dogs with a sickening *squelch*. She had to press the heel of her boots against their skulls for leverage. It didn't appear to be the first time she'd done this tonight.

"Agent," she spoke over her shoulder, "do you have anything to report that could explain what the *fuck* is going on?"

A beat of silence followed. Gen was looking directly at me, confusion and a small iota of understanding on his face. Of who she was talking to. Or, perhaps, why she'd called me *agent.*

I closed my eyes. Tried to choke in a breath in the smoky air.

"Yes, Chief," I said. "You were right to be worried...there's been a usurpation of power at the temple. The same man who did it is behind this attack and, somehow, the dogs."

"And him?" She motioned to Gen.

"Chief!" Stone bellowed from the hallway.

"The only person who can help." It dawned on me when I spoke how right that was. "He comes with."

Tess eyed him. Eyed me. "Prove it." She crossed her arms, a stubbornness about her.

"We don't have time—"

"If you've been outside at all you'll fucking forgive me for being a little skeptical of a kriest," she snapped. "Especially one from the fucking temple."

I glared at her. Helpless. She stared back. Unmoving. Gen eyed us both, bleeding and on edge.

We didn't have much time. I swallowed hard and turned to him.

"Gen," I asked, and he cut me off.

"No."

"Gen, it's—"

"Why did she call you agent?" He asked, and I saw by the set of his beautiful, stubborn jaw all of his barriers were up. That I was so close to losing him. That the truth was written on my face.

"Desi," I said, and I had never known how a single word could be such a plea. It came out raw, desperate. Begging. *Please.*

He hesitated. Like he wasn't sure to trust me.

"You've been spying on the temple," He concluded, "On me."

Tears stung my eyes. "It's complicated."

"We've got to *go*," Stone snarled again. Gen took me in, stared at my outstretched arm, and made his decision. His hand came out, clasped mine solidly, and squeezed. He didn't initiate the meld right away. There was a second of silent intense understanding between us.

"I'll explain everything," I said quietly. "As soon as we're safe. I promise. You can find it yourself, I'll open my mind willingly to you. Please, Gen—she can help. She's the only chance we've got."

Tess watched our exchange with her arms crossed. Stone called out again and she ignored him completely. I saw her finger tense on the trigger.

Gen watched my face. Searched it. Squeezed his eyes tightly closed. Fought something within himself and settled on what to do.

Without another word, he reached into me. He took my hand first, then silently slipped his own hand forward, up my arm, into my arm, and we—

Chapter Twenty-Three

Gen, Melded, Simon's blood-stained living room

"I'll explain everything," He'd said. *"I promise."*

He was a traitor to me. A spy.

Yet still there was relief when the meld slipped into place.

Why am I incapable of leaving him behind?

"You've got a lot to answer for, Holiday," she snarled. The meld had spooked her, but proven whatever point Simon had been trying to make. There must have been other dogs like the one dead on the floor, because she swallowed the reality of the meld in seconds and was all business again.

Tess hauled us up by the arm, dragging us upright and out into the hall. Her strength surprised me, and the ease at which she pushed us around. She was pure muscle. She picked up the bag Simon had dropped and all but shoved it against us.

"Move," she barked, propelling us in front of her.

The hulk of an older man, *Stone,* Simon confirmed, caught our fall. In the thickening smoke it was impossible to make out his features, but I knew what to expect all the same. Broad, silvering temples and hair he kept pinned atop his head. Hair that was raven black where it wasn't aging. He was, as always, clean shaven. From memory we could recall a few round scars in his right shoulder and ear, which was missing a considerable amount of flesh. He was wearing something dark and tightly woven, or maybe a kind of textured leather. He had long twin blades, both sheathed at his hips. One was longer and far more curved than the other. *His sons*, he called them.

Stone caught us and looked us over once, something close to bewilderment filling his expression. "What the hell is this," he asked Tess.

"*Answers*," she pushed at us from behind, and we staggered back into the older man. "But not here. Keep him alive, that's an order."

"Them," Simon corrected, "Gen and I are both in here."

Tess snarled again, baring her teeth like an animal.

"*For now.*"

I glared at the wall. Simon understood that the look was meant for him. Our hands clenched and unclenched in rapid fire. That was all his nerves.

Please trust me, they'll make sure we're unharmed... At least until they get whatever they need from us.

It's no less than what anyone else is offering, and at least they aren't trying to eat *us.*

I couldn't argue with that. I *had* said I would trust him on this...although that was proving harder to do than I'd originally thought. I wanted to lay down and give up. I wanted to scream. I wanted to weep. I wanted to wake up and find out this entire day, or even my entire life, had just been one long, bad dream. Through our meld I could tell that Simon felt the same.

He longed for Florida.

I longed for a warm wrapping of blankets in the corner of Mael's home.

We got neither.

Stone shoved up the window next to us in the hall and the heat of reality blasted our faces. The fires were close, if not upon us. He stepped out quickly, and began to descend down a ladder we'd previously missed. Either that or Tess had stashed it away for just such an event and came in clutch. That felt more like her.

"Faster, Holiday," Tess ordered behind us, but it wasn't Simon that moved.

It was easier for us both if I did the heavy work.

I slung the pack over our back, our ruined forearms tugging at the motion. We stepped out sideways onto the ladder, ducking through the window. I grabbed the sides and slid down with ease, forcing Stone to move out of the way. It was satisfying. It was petty. It impressed Tess, who came down the same way.

I hated the way I saw her through our eyes. With familiarity. Every tensing of her shoulder, every tilt of her head, it was all familiar and as easy to read as a picture book. Simon knew this woman and knew her well. Knew her in ways I now did. *Chief Tess, head of the underground police. Ex-military, in the old world. Spy master, now.*

She called you agent.

I'm sorry, Simon's voice came back. *It's not what you think.*

That you have been working as a spy against the temple the entire time I've known you?

"*For* the temple," he begged for me to understand, the force of it forcing it out of our lips. Tess' head snapped up from her new position at the building's corner, looking around into the street beyond.

"What?"

"We are not talking to you," I said flatly, then moved against the wall.

"It's not the time to explain," Simon said plainly to her, lowering our voice. "We need to get out of this mess. I trust you can manage that?"

Stone stared at us openly. Tess ignored us again, turning to the street. "Don't get cheeky with me, Holiday."

"It's been a long goddamned night, Tess."

"For all of us," Stone finally said, warningly. Stone always thought of us——of *Simon*— — as a kind of younger brother. One that needed guidance, and sometimes to be knocked around.

"It's clear," Tess cut in.

"Now what?" We asked.

"Now we *run!*" Tess said, shoving our shoulders again. *"I trust you can manage that?"*

"Can *you?*" I snapped back, not bothering to hide my distrust and annoyance at her. That gave her a second of pause. I knew how jarring it could be to watch someone meld, to see two people in one body. She'd been expecting Simon. She wouldn't find him in our face right now.

I didn't wait for her to finish her searching glance to turn away. To turn east, just as Stone was. East, towards the deeper woods. East, towards the old ruins. *East*, I suddenly understood, towards the old school. *The fortress.*

Simon knew we didn't have time to sit and debate things. But we *did* have time to *know* things. So he began to make good on his promise. *I'll explain everything.*

I could see it in our mind, flashes of the farthest eastern outskirts of New Caramel, the parts of the city that hadn't fully come through. The buildings were spread thin, disappearing into the tree line and beyond. Roads had come in partway with long sections fully missing or buckled over stumps and falling down embankments and hills. Some buildings that should have been there were absent entirely, while others were there in the roof, cellar, or walls only. Many of the buildings had become claimed by the woods, and others stripped for their resources to repair other more commonly used places deeper in town. Mostly they'd been left to sit alone to rot, many dangerously unstable or overrun with wildlife.

It was an area of New Caramel presumed abandoned. Even by other humans. I knew now that was far from true. Jorel had come to slaughter an unsuspecting people. Tess, against all logic, had suspected this was coming for a long time. She had spent years building and preparing various bases of resistance against such an attack. One sat out in the woods, in a building Simon said was once called *a school.*

Simon showed me——no, not *showed*, let me *experience*——the truths of it.

When we all rounded the corner, we witnessed the fruition of her planning.

Where the Row had been a slaughter, the main roads were an all out war. Absent the upper hand surprise had given them the kriest were no longer taking on unarmed people in their beds. Humans in varying states of dress, some in pajamas and others in what practically amounted to full leather armor gear, had taken up arms and were now fighting back. Some of the Kor had come into town on deer, but only a few of them remained. The slaughtered bodies of the others lay strewn in the streets where they had fallen, their throats slit or legs disassembled. The humans had not taken up arms randomly, instead they were provided with a large assembly of swords, or hatchets, or both. It was clear Tess had been building up arms in secret over the many years, and this was the time for their use.

The main fighting took place in the streets, walls of people refusing to allow the kor into the remaining buildings, or evacuating all at once. Fires tore through the surrounding buildings, but the Kor hadn't seemed to turn it on the humans as a weapon yet. Burning rubble fell heavily from the upper stories, adding to the chaotic terrain of brick and bodies and blood.

The humans may not be fighting unprepared, but it was clear the Kor had been given far more time to ready themselves.

They fought with practice, taking on the newly armed militia of the human resistance with the skills of those who have seen battle before. All their skirmishes with the north played into their hands, and for every fallen kor we saw we witnessed three or more human corpses littering the ground. It was still chaos, and it was impossible to tell which side truly had the upper hand.

There was no winning. Not tonight.

Dog melds appeared from the side streets, grabbing people alive and dragging them into the darkness to tear them apart. Their screams were the worst.

A Kor soldier broke away from the crowd, racing towards us with purpose. We knew this one. We'd come face to face with him and his brother only hours before.

Dimi wore the black and purple military wear of the Kor, smeared with blood. His hatchets were fisted, raised and swinging down on anyone that got in his way. He barreled through the carnage, directly for us.

Stone stepped in the way, deflecting the blow with an effortless swipe of his own sword.

The metal hit with a sharp *clang* against the Kor's weapon, and anger flashed deep in his eyes. Stone squared up, moving into a practiced slicing motion upwards. Tess saw the motion of the second kriest before we could, shoving us into a small alley between two buildings.

"Go!" she shouted, dodging the blow Herris pushed towards her and turning to hit the man with her own unsheathed blade. His eyes were wild with hate and excitement, his spear stained red halfway down the hilt. "I'm right behind you!"

No other choice ahead of us, we slipped into the pathway.

No sooner were we two steps in did the first dog emerge. Its dual sets of reflecting eyes found us in the shadows, stepping forward with two low, reverberating growls to greet us. We came to a stop, never taking our eyes off of it, but still slowly reaching to the side for something Simon had noticed on a crate.

The pole fit firmly in our hands. We tightened our grip. Flexed it. *It isn't right,* we thought in tandem, even if the flavor of the word tasted different to us both. The thought of violence sickened him. The immobility of having my hands tied up paralyzed me. Against all logic we abandoned the pipe, throwing it away with a reverberating *clang!*

The noise distracted the dog just enough. In three long strides we were at the opposite wall, then lunging for it, catching it at about waist height in an arching wall run that landed us just beyond the beast. Our feet hit the pavement hard just as it noticed our trick, turning to us with a dense bark of rage. In the same second we heard the familiar *thwap* of a bolt entering meat and the beast made an entirely different sound, one of pain and collapsing lungs. *Thwap, thwap!* It came again, and we turned only long enough to see Tess fully caught up, disposing of the melded dog in three hits.

"Simon!" She shouted, *"Get to the science wing! Protect that pack! I'll come for you in the morning!"*

Her image was obscured as more of those dogs closed around her, chasing her down the alley. We didn't look back again, climbing the chain link fence with torn fingers and soles and making a break for the forest line.

Our breathing was ragged. Our fear had become palpable, and exhausting. We were nothing like the men we'd been when we'd entered the city behind us only an hour before.

The blackness of the woods enveloped us once again, closing its shadowed fingers around our back. We turned towards the east, and solitude greeted us with hollow reprieve.

Day Two

Chapter Twenty-Four

Jorel, Mael's Den

The night had not gone as planned. Rarely one to drink I nonetheless found solace in a fur berry wine, the bitter taste pinching my nerves all the way down. It was potent. It wasn't enough. Between the briefings, the meetings, the grandstanding that was necessary to gain full control over Del Tor, I was exhausted. The work was never ending, but it was my burden to bear. And it was far from over

I had found myself in a hollow pocket of solitude sometime in the desperately late hours of the night. Or was it the desperately early hours of the morning? The night tasted different at this hour. Quieter. Lonelier. Most of the island was fast asleep, from the deer in the woods to the children in their beds. Tomorrow would bring a new dawn over Torrel, one where my people would awake to a new Reid and a new promise of the future. A future where Asterel would no longer be a threat over our heads. A future, for better or worse, with the subservience of humans and far more resources to go around.

My hand clenched the cup. New Caramel had not gone wholly as planned, but it was nothing outside the margin of error I had expected. If my loyalists had thought they could go in and cull an entire people in their sleep with no resistance they were fools, not that I had done anything to dispel that delusion. Further resistance was to be expected, and was already planned for.

There was still so much work to be done. Work that could not wait until the morning.

Work that gnawed at my insides far more than the wine ever could.

Gen.

The awaited knock came at my door. I did not need to ask who it was.

"Enter," I spoke, using my native tongue. The good doctor could speak at least that much.

Chelsea, if she'd ever been to begin with, was even less of a welcome sight at this hour, in my own home. In the home that had once belonged to my mother. To my father. And now, rightfully, to me. I had glimpsed my own reflection not so long ago. I was tired, but not quite haggard. I desperately wanted and needed to crawl into a bed and sleep until dawn, and it showed.

Dr. Ashley Chelsea looked as if she had rolled straight from a full night's rest, bright eyed and unaware of the time. Her hair was pulled back as it always was, but in place of her usual lab coat she wore a long dark cloak over similarly deep toned clothes. She'd worn the same boots as always. She looked put together, functioning, relatively undisturbed.

Considering that until only an hour ago she had been sleeping blocks from a massacre of her own crafting, I'd bet she'd slept just as fine as any other night.

"Sit," I spoke in human, motioning for the chair beside me. She chose instead to wander about the small den space, feeling my mother's collected tapestries with her delicate hands. "Bold of you to call me here, considering the circumstances." She started. "Me, being a human and all, in the heart of your domain...and especially tonight of all nights. How dangerous. I'm quite the small, pitiful target outside of my labs. A perfect toothpick of a woman."

I had no desire to entertain her whimsy that night.

"I sent a competent guard to fetch you, and you're here in one piece. You wouldn't have come if you didn't know you'd be fine. You are quite the capable woman. Even without a guard you'd have been just fine."

She showed her teeth in something resembling a smile.

"*Why* am I here, then?" Her boots clicked on the ground as she circled around me, ever the predator. It would normally set me on edge, but now it was why I'd needed her. It was the same reason as all of our meetings before.

"I missed your company," I said dryly. It felt petty. I hardly cared. She didn't appreciate the joke. At her disapproving glance, I met her eyes and held them. "I have need of your work."

"You're already *using* my work. They're out roaming the streets, hunting down all the little insects you need to squash to keep your forces happy. And they're working splendidly, I might add." A proud smile found her lips. "Did you know the row is actually running red with blood? I'd never imagined how beautiful such a thing could be."

"You delivered everything you promised." It wasn't a compliment. It sickened me, what she'd created. What they were doing. But I could at least admit it was effective. And I was the one who'd ordered it done. So what was one more?

I wonder what she's done with Jask.

I tossed back more of my drink. "I need something new. Something specific. I already gave you the materials, assuming one of them is still alive"

At this, Chelsea paused. I watched her watch me, her standing height barely above mine sitting down, the fireplace's glow haloing her hair's flyaways. Her eyes were dark, unyielding. In perfect juxtaposition to her ominous stance, her voice was casual—no, it was downright glib when she asked "Oh, did something not fall into plan?"

I hated to hand her the satisfaction, but that was the truth.

"My key wasn't where he needed to be."

"Oh *dear*!" she exclaimed, drawing it out in a long, mocking tone. It sounded so false, the care and concern she put into it. Satisfied. "The perfect, cunning, infallible man before me made a mistake. Oh, how awful that must be!"

She flopped back suddenly, landing in the large cushioned chair across from me.

"How *human*."

I said nothing. Betrayed nothing. Entertained the idea of enclosing her perfect, tiny neck between my hands and squeezing them tight. Even more than I hated her, though, I had a greater goal to achieve.

"Are you finished?" I asked flatly.

"I had my fun. Consider it my price for dragging me out tonight," she said, settling back in her chair. "So what, you lost your key? I fail to see how that's my issue. If I remember correctly, that was part of the *temple* plan, not New Caramel. And I covered my bases there, I've done my part. I have delivered exactly what you've paid for, nothing more, nothing less." Her voice dropped in tone, her patience waning. "Our contract is through, *Reid*."

"I am willing to pay more."

She let out another bark of a laugh.

"You have nothing that I want! Nothing in the world. I already *have* everything I could ask for. I have your branch, I have my research, and I have an army of dogs I could turn around on you at any time if you keep wasting mine. What more could you *possibly*—"

"Do you know a man, a human, named Simon Holiday?"

Her body froze. Her mouth was halfway around the next word in her sentence, rounding over the next condescension. Dr. Ashley Chelsea's entire body seemed to still; no breath pulled her chest, no muscle moved a twitch. It took me a moment to realize that I had succeeded in what I had hoped to do—catch her off guard.

Then something shifted. Changed. I felt the ghost of a blade against my throat, but nothing was there. It was just something behind those dark eyes of hers. Something very, very dangerous. I wasn't sure it was even truly directed at me.

"...why do you ask?" She hedged.

Watching me.

"You said there was nothing I had that you wanted as payment. I'm asking if Simon Holliday is the exception to that." It was a gamble, a desperate one with the very last chip I had, and I prayed I was right to play it. I had no guarantee my intel was good, or that the name would mean anything to her anymore.

Her hand opened, pushed up her glasses. Obscured her gaze for just a single moment.

"Explain."

I leaned forward. Steepled my fingers. Watched that hand hiding her eyes. "Gen has all the last knowledge I need, and he wasn't where he was meant to be tonight. Instead, he was stowing away with that blonde human of yours. Do you know where he is now?"

"You don't?"

"I don't," I said, levying all the intel I'd gathered on Gen's pitiful human in the last few hours on this one sentence, "since he's run off in his newly melded form with Simon Holiday."

The hand didn't move. Then, it shook. So did her shoulders. Quiet, nearly inaudible laughter rose through her, growing until it became something louder, unhinged. Haunting.

I felt fear, true, primal fear seep into my bones. I had only witnessed one monster in my life as dangerous as the woman before me, and that monster had eaten my father many, many years ago.

I had let her into my house.

"He's a *meld* now?" She exclaimed, her hand moving away from her face to grasp something invisible before her. Her eyes were unfocused, distant, somewhere else. Then, something in her stiffened with.... anger? *No*, it was something darker than that, deeper.

Personal. *Territorial.*

"Your key melded with Simon Holiday." A statement, not a question.

"I need him, Chelsea." I pushed. "I need Gen back at all costs. At any cost." I set the wine down, leaned forward into her space, and steepled my fingers. Being so close to her right then was the second most terrifying thing I had done in my life. "For your assistance, I'll give you Simon Holiday, no questions, no complaints. We get Gen back, and he's yours to do with as you please, and I promise you no one will ever interfere with that work, so long as I am alive. Do this for me, and he is yours."

Chelsea moved suddenly, barely waiting for the offer to sink in. She tossed my notes, cup and pitcher of wine from the table in one single sweep, climbing across it on her knees. Her hands grabbed for my shirt, her eyes wide and menacing, full of a hunger I had never seen on a human's face.

"If you get me Simon Holiday, I will give you anything you need, anything you ask for, my lab, my soul, my body, my mind is at your disposal!" She took my chin, dug her fingernails in. Her voice was unhinged, something between desperation and lust. "I will do anything. Anything at all. Anything to get my Simon back."

It was all I could do to not recoil. Blood pooled at her fingernails where she dug into my jaw. Quietly, with little motion, I handed her the design, my next unforgivable sin. The back pocket contingency meld we had discussed last season. The one I had hoped to never see come to life.

"Let's start," I said, "With this."

Chapter Twenty-Five

Simon, The Science Building's Rooftop

The early hours before dawn brought a stillness. The air turned cooler, and far off in the town a silence settled like a low fog. It rolled emptily through the streets, tracing over the unmoved dead and filling the gaps where crickets and early birds normally resided. Even murderers had to sleep sometime, and after the high of felling Del Tor and the first successful ambush of new Caramel, Jorel's units fell back into the darkness and left a still, deathly haunt in their wake.

We sat on the roof of the old school, desperate and frozen. Desperate to sleep, but every time our eyes closed the previous hours would replay behind them like a broken projector. Desperate to leave but not sure where to go. Desperate to wake up from this nightmare. Desperate for tears that would no longer come.

The building was once an outlier of a college campus from the old world. It was three stories tall and gutted nearly empty over the years since our arrival here. Many walls were stripped down to the frame, and most of the floorings and all of the furniture had been scavenged and repurposed elsewhere in the early years. Marble had become a special kind of luxury, and the old building had been rife with it.

Most of the lab equipment had been moved to the industrial plant to the west when the medicine project had been erected. It had been a successful attempt to find alternatives to needed medicines and other chemicals lost to the old world. I'd helped move and set up part of the project myself. It wasn't anything I wished to dwell on anymore.

I was glad to have my mind to myself again, even for a minute. There was a lot to think about, and none of it was anything I wished to share with Gen. About my old job in the labs, about my current work for Tess... about Chelsea.

He hadn't asked me for anything more since we'd left the town. His silence was worse than his demands for the truth.

Maybe he'd already found them inside of us.

I leaned against the rooftop's fence, shivering in my makeshift cloak of an old blanket I'd found in a corner somewhere. It smelled like dust, but it was better than nothing.

Out in the distance I watched the black void that should have been New Caramel. The sky was a deep indigo, and through a faint contrast I could barely make out the shapeless horizon of my town. The fires and smoke had all dwindled into nothing. It was all so silent.

Gen sat next to me on the blanket pile. He had one knee pulled up, his arm resting against it and his head cradled against his bicep. His other leg sat straight out, both half covered by a small plaid sheet. I couldn't see the tear streaks tracing his cheeks in the low light, but I'd felt him shake with silent sobs from the moment we'd pulled apart.

We'd found our way here in silence, terrified at any moment another dog or Kor would find their way after us, chasing our hasty run through the brush. None had come, but every sound, every movement of the dark trees became something in our mind. Fear haunted us, clawing at our chest and legs like the very branches we pushed through.

We'd run along the city's upper tree line, out of sight of the streets beyond. We'd run for somewhere between a few minutes and a few lifetimes until we'd stumbled upon the paths of the ruins. Darkness had threatened to twist the places around us into the unfamiliar, but I had been out here many, many times in the dark. Broken roads cracked upwards, and vines had long overtook the shells of buildings remaining.

Gen did not question it, just picked up on my memorized path and got us where we needed to go. To the old science building, square and dark and as hollow as our own chest.

The shadows that terrified us obscured our ascent through the old stairs in a deep silence. Only our footfalls, uneven and exhausted, echoed in the space around us. No Kor, no dogs, no life.

The roof was flat, populated with an old storage shed Tess used for her own needs, and ringed by a fence that had fallen in disrepair. It was my usual relay point. It was open to the sky, but unassuming in its dilapidation. It wasn't true safety, but for the night it would do.

We'd come apart, unmelding into two separate, equally gasping piles. My lungs and legs screamed. My arms *hurt*. With shaking hands I held them up, witnessing them in the faint light from the fire-touched sky.

Scars, deep and old, in the wicked shapes of a dog's teeth pocketed their length. The skin was shiny and closed. It could have been from wounds received years before that had never quite healed right. Beside me I saw Gen, doubled over, sobbing, barely holding himself up with his arms.

Arms that bore identical scars.

I'd tried to reach out, to touch him. He'd shrugged me away, retreating without words to a spot along the fence that had somehow withstood the trials of time. My hand hung empty and cold in the space he'd been.

I understood.

Tess had left the same blankets and survival kit in the shed I'd seen last time we'd been here. *Always prepared.* Opening the lock in the dark and rooting around for the supplies gave me an excuse to give Gen time alone. Somehow, despite being unmelded I had a fairly good idea what he was thinking about.

When I offered him a blanket and the water she'd stored, he didn't push me away. I sat next to him in my own blanket, silent. Giving him time.

An hour passed. More. The city's fires began to dwindle, the distant shouting growing faint. Gen sat beside me, just as he had in the temple's alcove a lifetime ago. I let him. I wasn't sure what to say, anyway. How to process any of this. Something had become numb inside of me, dampening the pain I should have felt. It was probably just sheer exhaustion, everything from the night finally catching up to us. The melds, the base diving, drowning and running for our lives again and again.

The night grew still. The sound of insects faintly returned around us. The air began to taste different. Sleep did not come to either of us.

When Gen finally spoke, it wasn't what I had been expecting.

"How could Jorel do this?" He asked finally, his voice barely a whisper. It carried to me all the same.

"You know him." I said it as a statement, not a question.

His silence seemed to stand on the edge of something, as if he was chewing over how much of the story to tell me. I was too tired to care. Finally, he said "Reid Mael was his mother.

We studied together at the temple growing up."

"You studied together?" I asked, "As accolades?"

He hesitated again. Flexed his fingers. Looked away. "As apprentices."

I heard his voice choke. That admission took something out of him, opened something irreparably deep and painful.

I reached out in the dark, missed, then met his arm. "It's okay, Gen."

"Apprentices for Mael's position," he carried on, "to lead Del Tor. To be in charge of *Haliz Fundir*. To learn to meld."

A shiver passed over my skin, goosebumps erupting down my arms. "Wait. I knew you were a member of the temple, but you're telling me you were in training to, what, take over the whole thing someday?"

He nodded.

"What were you doing translating old books with me then? That seems.... A bit beneath someone training to run the whole thing?" Against my better judgement, I asked "Did Mael suspect me?"

Gen was quiet at this. It was a silence akin to the city beyond. It was too quiet, too unnatural. Heavy.

"She believed in you with everything she had," he breathed. "She did the same for me. It never mattered, though. I was always running away." Something shook from him—a sob, but deeper, more hollow. "I couldn't take the responsibility, so I ran from it. Like I always do. And now Mael is dead."

"Gen..."

"She was the only mother I've ever known."

I didn't know what to say to that, or to the way his voice finally cracked. Should I even say anything at all? *I'm sorry* didn't seem adequate.

My eyes tried to focus on the dark sky beyond him, but there was nothing to find. "I never asked for her, for *this*. For *any* of this."

"Gen—"

"She trusted you!" He said suddenly in anger, pain emanating in his voice. "*I* trusted you, and you have been...you've been spying on us, on me, for Tess this entire time! I took you to the ceremony. I brought you to Mael's *home!*"

There it was. I knew it would come, but it didn't hurt any less. "I swear to you it was never to hurt you...I never would have told her about tonight. Not Mael's home, not about the ceremony, or melding. Tess just wanted eyes in close to make sure Mael truly had humanity's best interests at heart...everything I have given her has confirmed that."

"You gave her maps," he said, "and names, and faces. Details from within the temple, in case she ever needed to attack us first! All under the guise of helping bridge our cultures together."

I flinched away from that truth. "I know, and I'm sorry. It was part of the agreement..."

"You think I don't know that?" He said angrily, "I've been in your mind! I know... I know and I understand so much..." his voice broke, a choking sob escaping his chest. "I understand you never gave her anything that could hurt us...that no matter why she sent you there, you couldn't do something that would hurt me. That you believe your cover story and hoped...and hoped to make a difference."

I didn't have anything to say to that. He was right, and he was right because he had pulled the thoughts directly from my mind. Just as I had begged him to do.

"You came to me as a spy," he said achingly, holding himself. "You lied to me...but you're all I have left."

I moved closer to him. Touched his arm gently. This time he didn't pull away.

"You feel so lost..." he whispered. "So displaced..."

I'd never felt so raw, so open without cover, as that moment on the roof together. As the moment he told me the deepest truth I knew about myself. I had willingly given him a place in my mind, opened myself up to the meld for him to understand what I had been doing working for Tess. I hadn't known it would open up more than that, let him in deeper than I'd ever meant anyone to go.

His dark eyes found mine in the low light. "Simon," he asked, "Who's Chelsea?"

Ice ran down my spine. "...I don't like talking about her."

"I need you to." he said. *If I'm ever going to trust you again*, he hadn't said. I weighed the pains of my past against the pains of my present, against losing Gen and everything we'd had. Weighed Chelsea's cruelty against giving up the only good thing I had found in so, so long.

The first good thing I'd allowed myself to fall into.

"...It's a long story."

"Then give me the short version," he said. "Give me the truth."

I took a deep breath. "She's a scientist, one who specializes in microbiology. Sorry if you don't know that word it's...uh, an old world term. One I'm too tired to explain."

"Who is she to you?"

I hesitated at this one. "...once, she was my girlfriend."

He didn't say anything for a long second. I hated to admit it. "Why isn't she your girlfriend anymore?"

I didn't know how to explain that long, painful story. Nor did I want to. But I needed to give him at least something. "Because she... because she was cruel. Because she never killed me but she definitely tried. Because she was more interested in owning me and the power that gave her than caring for me. By the end of it I was so desperate to get away from her I was willing to do anything...even give myself over to Tess."

He thought about that for a second. "She sounds a lot like Jorel."

"In a weird way," I said, "I think they'd be friends."

He snorted. Then, finally, he leaned into me, resting his head on my chest. Satisfied by some answer I'd said. Too tired to dig any further. I wrapped my blanket around us both, comforted by the touch. "You found desperation at the face of a monster. That's why you agreed to spy for Tess."

"You could say that."

"I understand that," he added, "more than you'll ever know."

"I won't ask for your forgiveness."

He leaned closer. "You saved my life tonight. I think you'll have it, in time."

"Gen..."

"I still have so many questions."

"I do, too."

"I'm afraid to ask them."

"So am I."

"Tomorrow?" He asked, and it was all I could do to agree.

"If we live that long."

Chapter Twenty-Six

Gen, The Storage Shed

We slept fitfully for a few short hours until dawn inside the storage shed, crammed together as single beings. The sleeping bag we had found prevented us from having to lay on the bare floor, but we were still forced to lay pressed together for warmth.

Simon was restless from what I could only assume were the same nightmares that kept me from staying asleep. Midway through the night I woke up again from the images that had followed me into my dreams only to see his shoulders move. He began to shake in muffled, helpless sobs. Without thinking, I placed my arm around him and held him from behind. Neither of us acknowledged the touch. To my surprise, he didn't move away. My heart thudded in my ears until I finally fell back asleep holding the man I had only that day before barely touched at all.

The nightmares didn't stay away, but I was allowed to sleep through them until dawn knowing at least I was far from alone.

Even apart, his pulse matched mine as we made it through that first night in hell.

Chapter Twenty-Seven

Jorel, Torrel Del Tor

The kriest who looked back at me in the mirror looked every bit the part of who I wanted to be. His new uniform was flawless; the top kept the layered, tunic design of a warrior, one asymmetrical starched collar casting a dark shadow across his neck, but the bottom length was gathered at one hip and left to hang on the other side like the skirts of the previous Ried. The artists had made quick work of the embroidery, and rare red and yellow threads lined the fires of last night as well as an imposing sunrise scene. A new beginning, born from fire and might. He wore his warrior leggings beneath, the deep purple fabric tight and fit for quick movements. He looked every bit the leader he was.

Every bit the leader he should be.

But I am not that person yet, am I? My overtaking of the human settlement was, as expected, only in its beginning phases. You can never rid pests with a single burning. They find cracks to hide in, they avoid the smoke. Now it was a matter of flushing them out, and even if a few refused to accept their fate laying down, it was only a matter of time.

New Caramel was exactly where I needed it to be right now. Still on schedule for desolation.

The temple had bowed after Mael's death to me. How could they not? I was a born leader, the rightful heir to the reid status and in the end, I had left them no choice. I was right that there would be outliers, but my followers had wasted no time isolating any bits of dissent.

Just as planned.

In time, even they would fold. The logic of the path we all must now take will sink in, eventually.

I should be celebrating. With this, the true path to our strongest era in Torrel had begun. We had an overwhelming majority of everything go exactly according to plan. As the third phase began, there was nowhere to go but up.

But an overwhelming majority of a win was not a win. I needed this to be absolute.

I needed *Gen*.

I stared at my reflection. His fists tightened at his sides. His jaw tensed. He looked like nothing more than a dressed up *failure*.

My hands were, at the moment, tied. I forced my fists to unclench, my jaw to relax. The temple need not see me in this state. I needed to project the very image of a successful leader on my first day. I needed to trust that my plays to get my one errant player back would resolve. I needed to trust in the monster I had asked Chelsea to release, and that her fixation on Simon would be enough to keep her in line.

Of course, I couldn't trust her fully, which is why I'd had a backup plan at the ready. One that was already laid in place.

A knock came to my door.

"Sanra, Reid Jorel," they said, "We are ready for you."

I pushed all doubts away from my reflection's face and turned to the door. Gen could only run so far, and so fast. But there was nowhere to run to on an island with no friends.

As my father had shown me, when all else was taken from you, the only place left to turn was the eager, waiting jaws of an old, familiar predator.

Chapter Twenty-Eight

Gen, Rooftop

The tail end of a dream chased me awake. A memory, more like it. Mael's arms had held me tight to her chest as I sobbed uncontrollably, the last time I had cried before to-night. It had been pitiful, clinging to the woman I considered a mother as a grown man, wailing as if from a nightmare. But it hadn't been a nightmare. It had been the truth. It had been the final, awful truth of it all. About *Haliz Fundir*, about the island and the reidship.

Now you know, she'd whispered, petting my hair. *Oh, Gen... I'm so sorry. I'm sorry it's too late to turn back...*

It's too late to turn back...

My eyes were open. The dawn was calm, swaths of pink and red chasing the sky I could see through the open shed door. Right outside of it I saw the shadow of Simon, awake before me and hunched over. His back was to me, and I could see him working with something on the ground before him.

He must have felt I was awake, because he offered "Tess is almost here" over his shoulder in explanation.

It didn't really explain anything, though. He was hur-riedly pulling items from the storage shed and into his bag. Maps, notebooks and other things from his apartment littered the ground beside him, as well as a rolled blanket and other odd supplies I'd seen in the shed the night before.

"What are you doing?" I asked, sitting up stiffly. The ground had not been kind to my aching body. I moved forward, joining him. The sight of my new, tattered forearm scars greeted me in the light. They ached like an old bruise. The older, ringed ones above them ached like an old friend.

"Overthinking, probably." He muttered, shoveling the last of the maps into a new cloth bag he must have found in the shed. As he had with the other backpack he cinched it tightly, then held it in his free hand.

"About what?"

"About how you're the last person on the island who knows how a meld works. I mean, really works. That's power, and that power is what Jorel is after. Power he'd do *anything* to get back." He paused at that, looking somewhere in the distance and getting lost in his own thoughts. "...maybe it's a power we can use in our favor."

"I don't understand." I said, "What do you mean?"

"I'm not sure yet," he answered, dropping the bag over the side of the building to the ground below. His eyes turned to meet mine. "You said the meld was used to transfer knowledge, right? Like how you learned about my work for Tess, or knew the way to my apartment."

"Yes," I hedged, not sure where this was going.

"But it isn't just a transfer of knowledge, is it?" He came up to me, took my arm. Held it up to his. Our scars sat there, perfectly copied between us. "There's something physical that's exchanged. The bite marks on your arms healed over through the meld, and now I have them, too. I lost my glasses back in the river but I've had no problem seeing at all. There's a bruise we've both got on our shoulders now from the fall in the woods."

"How did—"

"I checked, and it's not the only one." he said, and I felt my face heating up at the image of him examining me closely when I was asleep. "When we unmeld, we take something from each other, just like how we bring things together into it. Your Human has gotten noticeably better...you've finally started using contractions, when I know you've had a lot of trouble with those."

"I haven't been—" I paused, hearing it when I said it. *Haven't.*

"There's abilities within *Haliz Fundir*'s influence that you haven't told me about. Abilities I think you know. Things that probably get stronger the longer we're melded, right?"

I didn't answer. Couldn't. But he was right. He's always been so damned smart. He dropped his voice down, quiet. Low.

"I don't blame you for not saying them...I think you have your reasons for abandoning your training, but that never turned you into a traitor. You loved Mael, and the temple, and you've always kept this revered respect for her work and position. I don't know what happened, or why you left that path, but I couldn't be upset at you for holding your values close. For protecting a craft that's far older and far bigger than yourself."

He looked me dead in the eyes, the gray of his own turning a strange indigo in the morning sun.

"It's honorable."

I swallowed around something hard.

"Simon..."

"What happens if we stay melded together too long?" He asked. A wall began to come up in my mind.

"I've never seen it."

"But you know."

I bit my lip. Looked away.

"Yes."

"Then answer this..." he pushed his hair away from his face, thinking. "Between the risks of a long term meld and the risks of Jorel catching you....which would you rather face?"

"Whichever one keeps you safe." I spoke before I could think, and felt my whole face light up in embarrassment. Simon didn't react.

"Then when the time comes today," he said, "know I choose the same."

The hatch to the stairwell opened, slowly at first, and then faster as Tess emerged. She was in the same dark clothes of the night before, but they were significantly more haggard. Her left pant leg had been cut to her upper thigh, and her knee and part of her calf were wrapped in stained bandages. She had a long dark cloak wrapped around her, trailing on the floor and obscuring most of her form in shadow until she pulled down the hood.

Simon and I stood, letting her come to us. She stopped a few paces away, leaving our backs to the edge of the rooftop.

"Morning boys," she started, putting a hand on her hip. "Sleep well?"

"Awful." Simon said. "You?"

"About the same." She looked exhausted, and her voice was lower and more weary than it had been the night before. "It was all we could do to hold the line last night, and we barely did that. Dozens of those damned mutts are dead and littering the street, but so are plenty of kriest who invaded."

"And the people?" He asked.

Something dark filled her features. She ran a hand through her hair, a very similar motion to what Simon had done earlier.

"...we haven't had the access to sweep the streets and collect the dead," she said, "but our estimates are in the hundreds. More. There were only around four thousand of us at the yearly census, and I can't tell you how many unaccounted for are dead, or hunkered down somewhere, or unaware any-thing even happened if they're in the farming towns to the south. We don't know if the attack included them or not."

"How many survivors do you have?"

"Less than eight hundred spread between the ware-house, the front lines, and the old bank." She answered honestly.

Simon closed his eyes, tilted his head upwards.

"God..." he said, and it was the closest I'd ever seen him get to human religion. The numbers felt like a punch to the gut for myself. Less than a quarter of the human population alive and accounted for...and what about those who lived in Torrel? What other work had Jorel sent his men to do last night?

"Tell me some of the documents survived," Tess im-plored. Simon opened his eyes, remembered himself and threw the bag to her.

She caught it one-handed.

"Take it," he said. "That's all I had left in the apartment."

She felt the weight of the sack.

"This isn't a lot."

"What *else* would I have?"

"*Answers!*" She growled, taking a step forward. "More than half the city is probably dead, Simon, and we don't have a single god-damned clue *why*!"

"Your lives were sold," I said, speaking up for the first time since her arrival. Both their heads turned to me. "A man named Jorel allied with the anti-human extremists in the Kor to overthrow Mael. He killed her and now has control of Del Tor. He's using this attack against you to both fulfill his fol-lower's wishes and send a show of strength to Sol."

Simon had puzzled most of this together when we'd been melded, but speaking it out loud solidified the truth in it.

"Why take over?" she asked.

"To use Del Tor in a war against Asterel," I answered honestly.

Tess watched me. "He sold our lives for control of Del Tor?"

"Yes."

"So it's true," she said, more to herself than me, "about *Haliz Fundir*. He wants to use melding against the north.

I opened my mouth but Simon held up his hand to stop me. He was tilting his head, giving her an odd look. I picked up on it a second after he did, what she'd said.

"How do you know about that?" When Tess said nothing, he added "I was the first human to learn about melding, Tess, and I never told you about it." He took a cautious step towards her. "I was the only spy you had with access to Del Tor. It's a bit of a jump to just figure that out on your own, and you know it."

There was a long, tense moment between them. Tess looked at him, made a strange motion with her jaw, then looked to the side with a small exhale of disbelief. Something fell away from her then, a mask she'd been wearing.

A lie.

We don't have a single god-damned clue why.

"You can't blame me for being conservative with my knowledge, Simon." She said, shrugging her shoulders. "I wanted confirmation that my intel was good. You know who I am."

"*Tess*," he said, something very tense in his tone. "What aren't you telling us?"

I looked between them, warily. Tess took a cautious sidestep, almost a nervous shuffle.

Almost.

"Last night, one of my eyes came down from Torrel just before the attack. The merchant's guild was overthrown by a majority of its members, all now hailing under the new rule of *Reid Jorel.*" S

he took another step, moving her eyes between us.

"The Kor have become more than just the warriors— the name has become a sect of extremists all following the same ideals: to take the fight to Sol in the north, and to remove us humans off the island." She looked at Simon, an old point clearly resurfacing between them. "Something I feared would happen from the moment we got here."

"What happened to the merchants?" Simon asked, turning ever so slightly towards her as she circled us.

"Five of them, led by Merchant Zorren, locked the other four in cells below the merchant's hall. Their businesses have been overtaken if they did not cooperate. The Kor insignia is now raised above the guild."

"Jorel is trying to cut off any chance of trade or assistance to us," Simon realized. "If the wealthiest merchants have pooled their support behind him, others would have to risk their lives or livelihoods to bring supplies into the city."

"There is now a barricade along the main routes," she confirmed. "We've been told no one goes in or out without the Kor's consent."

Simon looked troubled.

"...you said you heard this from your eyes," he said, "what eyes? I didn't know you had anyone working the merchant's guild. They don't allow humans into their folds."

"I never said I only employed humans, Simon."

Another shadow rose from the hatch and stepped onto the roof. She was dressed in a similar cloak, her square glasses cracked down one frame. She was in the same clothes she'd been in the night before, if not now crusted in dark brown blood.

Something crossed Simon's face, something between betrayal, pain, and a soft, accepting sadness.

"...Dora."

"Simon," She said, "I'm so, so sorry.... I wanted to tell you for months now—"

"Dora." Tess snapped, and the girl went silent. Anger rose in me from the pain Simon was showing.

"Why?" Simon asked.

"She's been working for me for years, keeping an ear to the movements of the northern merchants." She said, "Her father attempted to indoctrinate her last night. She managed to escape him and made it back down to the city. Told me all about the attack, and about the things you've kept from me."

Her eyes found me, angry. Accusatory.

Simon looked as if he'd been slapped.

"You told her about Gen," he spoke. "You knew who he was on the cart. You came straight here and told her who he was and his position at Del Tor—it's why she wasn't surprised by the melding—*Christ*, Dora! You decided you were going to tell her even before the attack happened! Do you have any idea what you were going to give away?"

"He's the reid in training, Simon!" Dora shouted, the very force of her words driving her body forward. "If Mael had sent him to watch you, if she'd known our plans then he could have been feeding you false information this whole time! I didn't know how he could have been involved in all this, it put everything we've worked for at risk—"

"We?" He asked, anger hot in his voice. "*We?* I've had this position for less than a year.

"How long have you been working for Tess?"

Dora hesitated. Simon didn't back down.

"You were worried that, what, Gen could have been spying on me, *too*? Just like you were?"

She didn't answer, barely able to meet his eyes. His next sentence almost broke me, it was so painful and raw.

"How long have you been pretending to be my friend?"

"As long as I needed her to." Tess answered for her.

Am I the only one here who isn't *a spy?*

"How did you get back through the blockade?" Simon demanded. "The last cart in?"

"Y-yes," she replied now, unsure. Her eyes flicked to Tess.

For a spy, she isn't a very good liar. Even if I didn't know what she was lying about.

"Tess," he said now, and his voice was hard. "*There was no last cart in.* When I rode into Torrel last night, it was the last one traveling the main roads."

Tess shot Dora a look, and her ears went down. I was having a hard time keeping up, but I could see Simon pulling bits of information together. It set me on edge. He pressed on.

"If Dora didn't come by the main road, and no one else has been allowed in, how the fuck did you know about the blockade?" He stepped closer. "*Who else have you been speaking to?*"

"For someone so smart," Tess said, "you sure have a way of being so, *so* fucking stupid."

Simon had picked up on what I should have been wary of the whole time two seconds before Tess pulled her crossbow from its harness and pointed it directly at my chest. It was loaded.

Everyone tensed.

"Don't," Dora said, "you said we'd find another way—"

but Tess ignored her.

"Jorel sent an ambassador," she said calmly. "A messenger, more like. A ceasefire until tonight at midnight. We bring Gen to them and they end the attacks, call back the dogs. This is our only chance for mercy."

I froze in place, taking this all in. Simon's eyes widened in fear.

"You *know* that's bullshit," he said quickly, "killing Gen won't—"

"They want him alive," she said, aiming lower to my stomach. "This won't kill him."

"Selling him back to Jorel is only going to hurt us in the long run! It's exactly what he wants!" he shouted, "He's only called back the dogs so they don't accidentally maul him. Once he has what he wants, he'll only start the attacks again!"

"You think I don't know that?" Tess asked, in the same tone someone might say *do you think I'm stupid?* "This is our chance to get close, to distract his forces during the handoff so we can advance forward again. It's all we got."

"You'll be walking him to his death, to all our deaths!"

"*Our deaths are already promised!*" She shouted, and it was hot and angry. Desperate, but wholly in control. "Jorel and his Kor aim to kill us all, with or without Gen. At least by giving him over we stand to change the situation. We can only hole up in the ruins for so long, Simon. We don't have enough supplies to last more than a week sheltering the remaining townsfolk, we have no avenues for trade to get more, and they've got god-damned monster dogs hunting us down and eating us alive! There is no survival in sheltering him, and with Mael dead all hopes of diplomacy are dead with her. He's going to kill us all, Simon. And I'm going to do *everything* I can to stop it."

"It's murder."

"It's not personal."

Dora looked between the two, horribly unsure. Simon clenched his fists.

"I won't allow this."

Tess stood up straighter.

"You don't get a say. It's my call to make, and if it's not me someone else will do it." She looked me dead in the eyes. "Word is out. The whole town wants your head. There's too many desperate people willing to do desperate things after last night."

"Are you one of them?" I asked.

"I always have been."

"He's the last one on the island who can harness *Haliz Fundir*," Simon tried to reason, but she let out a barking laugh.

"Damnit Simon, if *Chelsea* somehow figured it out all on her own, we can too. Knowledge is never unreachable."

Simon looked sick at the mention of Chelsea's name.

"You don't know that she—"

"Who else?" Tess hissed, "Who else would be so cruel, so twisted as to create those *mutts?*"

I could see in Simon's eyes he knew she was right.

"I don't know how she did it, but she got her hands on that power and used it against us. If we can get to her, we can figure it out ourselves."

"*Those dogs are an affront to creation,*" I barely managed to whisper. Rage made my hands shake, an indignation at the thought of creating more of those things. "Their existence is agony. They can never be unmelded without dying. All you'd be doing is more torture—"

"Torture that may prove fruitful to our survival," She countered, "that's all that matters anymore."

She took another step towards me. Simon took another step towards her. Dora shook in place. Tess stilled.

"Don't you dare," he snarled, and it really was just that. A *snarl*. I'd never heard his voice do that before.

"This is bigger than you."

"I'll fight you," he said, "I will fight you and drag you down until the bitter end. Every step of the way if you so much as hurt one hair on his head."

"You couldn't fight back against the woman who actively beat you for years on end," she said coldly, with an impatience one usually reserves for an unruly teenager. "Do you think you could manage it against me here and now, when you know I'm right? When you know this is the only way?"

"Tess—" Dora breathed, finally taking a step towards her back, hand extended.

"*Tess,*" Simon said simultaneously. Her name was a threat.

"If we survive this I will *personally* find you a new boyfriend, Simon!" she snapped, lining the bolt back up with my stomach. I didn't think I could move quickly enough out of the way having seen how dead of a shot she was last night. "One with *much* better hair."

"*He's got great god-damned hair!*"

Something flew from his hand, a small rock he'd picked up off the roof earlier. It hit her hip and bounced harmlessly away. A snarl of frustration overcame her at last, and she forgot herself, turning away to face him. It was the first moment her eyes had left me since this began.

"Stop throwing a damned tantrum and think *rationally,* Simon!"

Simon didn't waver. The morning breeze pushed his hair from his face, the golden light of dawn rimming him in an ethereal halo. I realized that he had, in the moment of distraction the argument over my hair afforded, moved much closer to me.

"I am."

"Simon, don't!" Dora screamed, but it was too late.

He dove right at me. His body blocked Tess's chance at a clear shot, tackling me, wrapping his arms around my chest as we fell back, back, back into the open air beyond the rooftop. Tess swore, the sound being ripped away from us by the wind. The ground was coming up impossibly fast, and it was all I could do to—

Chapter Twenty-Nine

Gen, Melded, Freefalling

—We righted ourselves in the fall, our feet launching out to greet the ground beneath us. The grass came up quickly, and we hit it with loose muscles and bent legs. The shock of the impact ran right up our core, and before it was lost we were rolling to the side, over our shoulder into a somersault through the rough dirt and overgrown weeds.

If it hurt we hadn't felt it yet, only the pressure of our bones pressing into one another on impact. It jammed our joints and felt more like a sledgehammer to our heels than anything else. Rocks and dirt clods had jutted into our skin from the roll, and old bruises from the night before acted up on impact. We didn't wait to see if the fall had broken anything, or if Tess had men on the ground waiting for us. In a movement that impressed Simon, I had us upright and running for the woods, swinging our arm down to pick up the bag Simon had tossed down earlier.

Tess wasn't the only one who'd kept her cards close for that meeting.

Her voice came after us.

"You're out of options, Simon!" She shouted, "There's nowhere to run where they won't find you next! You're selling us all to delay something you can't stop!"

Dora said nothing. We weren't sure there was anything she could ever say to repair the trust she'd broken. Or to change our minds. Tess was right about one thing, though; we really had no one else to run to or rely on.

Just ourselves.

If Simon had time to think about that, I didn't. So I pushed him into the depths of our mind and ran fast, and far, and deep into the woods.

Again.

Chapter Thirty

Simon, Melded, The Eastern Woods

One of our ankles finally slowed us down. We began to stumble, pain needling its way through the urge to survive until we couldn't ignore it.

We slowed, then collapsed onto a fallen log. A tangle of blood flowers curled near its shape. They'd covered a fallen bird's nest, telling a sad story of life cut off at the onset. There was so much death on the island today.

We found our breath first, and our survival bag second. It was my hands that shakily undid the zipper, digging for the first aid supplies within.

"We need something to eat," Gen spoke, and our hands pulled out a wrapped bag of jerky and fruit leather.

"...and drink," he added, reaching himself for the canteen strapped to the side.

We ate in silence, alternating between wrapping our lame ankle and grabbing another jerky stick. It didn't seem broken, just sprained, and walking on it felt wobbly at best. It wasn't until we'd searched for, and found, a decent walking stick that we ran out of things to occupy ourselves with and had to face the question neither of us wanted to.

"Where do we go now?" I asked bleakly. I'd grown comfortable in the meld, and on feeling out Gen's thoughts.

I could tell he was rolling through options, images of people, faces I didn't know, places I couldn't begin to recognize. They came in flashes of sensory feedback; the warmth of the sun on his face, the scent of spiced goods, the feeling of cool coastal stone under his bare toes.

"The only place left," he said finally. We looked away from the direction we'd come, deeper into the forest. "We head east until we reach *Eten Barra*...what you call the eastern road. Then south to the fishing towns, and pray Jorel has overlooked their existence for now."

"How far?"

"Under a day's walk. We should reach the path before sundown."

I realized that I really had no sense of scope for the size of the island. It wasn't as if our merge with the world had come with a map and mile conversion, and in honesty I'd not really traveled much past New Caramel and the lower parts of Torrel. I tried to conjure an image of the full island shape from above, and it was Gen that filled in the gaps.

The high peaks at the top of the island came to mind, with bluffs that ended in nearly 100 foot drops straight to a rocky sea below. That was the location of Asterel, Sol's city built into the bluffs. Then the forest that encased most of the central and eastern isle, desolate of civilization and considered mostly wild, and the river to the west that ran through Asterel and Torrel until emptying in the southern crescent bay. Along the east, just inside the coastline, was a long, winding path that ran from northeastern Asterel all the way down to the bay and the main fishing towns therein. It was forbidden to the humans, controlled by the north, and this time of year was rarely traversed.

If we walked to the path, we could follow it all the way to the allied fishing settlements that had long pledged their allegiance to Mael and *Haliz Fundir*. To *Et Sporrel*.

To maybe our last chance at sanctuary.

"Let's go," we said, but there was no excitement in the action. Only the long walk from my betrayal of Tess's trust, of Gen's death sentence, and towards a fraction of a hope neither of us truly held anymore for safety.

For a reprieve from this nightmare.

Together, we leaned on our stick, and took the first steps forward.

It was a long day. Longer than it had any right to be. The shadows shrank and stretched again with the sun's progression until we were only an hour out from sunset proper. The forest's trees grew darker, the sky a deep orange. It reminded us of fire. Even when we closed our eyes the light came through, tinting our lids red.

We had a lot of time to think, between rests and long walks. Our ankle throbbed, but Gen paid it little mind. It wasn't as if we had another option. I let him control our pace, admiring the ease at which he moved through everything. He was a perfect runner, an excellent climber, and even the night before he'd found such sure footing running through the woods in the dark. I only missed getting to watch his movements, no matter how much I enjoyed experiencing them together.

You aren't so terrible to look at yourself, Gen thought in the shared space we had allowed ourselves. It was easier to communicate thoughts and feelings when we lessened the walls between us. This pocket between let us both feel the start at a moving shadow and resolve it as a grounded songbird in the same space of thought. It hadn't taken us long to give up on speaking words out loud to maintain a safe silence and find a way to talk. His thoughts were always in a kind of duality; he had them in Kriest, but at the same time could rethink it in Human and push them forward to me. I still heard the whispers of his original language, and rather than hearing his words like a sound, I understood them as he did. As I understood my own thoughts. As he'd just understood mine.

Our face heated up. *You've been spying on me too, huh?*

Dora's betrayal still stung. But humor helped ease the blow.

You make it hard not to.

I'm far too awkward.

It's endearing.

Above us was a spray of branches with needle-like leaves that reached out far from the main trunk. Nestled under each section of needles were clusters of blueberry-sized fruit, each a peachy tone with dark purple speckles. They looked enticing. I loved berries, but I wasn't sure about them. I'd never seen them before and had enough bad memories about ingesting unfamiliar wild berries to try them.

But this body was not just my own.

Despite my hesitation our hand reached up, plucked one, and popped it in our mouth. The berry burst between our teeth, and a taste somewhat tart and yet powerfully sweet crossed our tongue. Gen didn't like it much, but a wave of something almost nostalgic crossed our mind.

Something from his childhood. We chewed, swallowed, and a lingering sweetness stayed behind. I gained the understanding that he'd felt my hesitation on its edibility and showed me rather than told me, despite not liking the flavor much. Our chest felt warm, and a sweetness that had nothing to do with the berry settled in.

We kept walking.

It's going to be dark soon, he observed, *we shouldn't be on the ground once the sun sets.*

What's on the ground?

Plenty of things we don't want to face alone in the dark, he answered. *Jorel is not the only predator native to the island, wild stags or dogs live this way. Not just that— I haven't known the north to set snares this far from the capital, but I do not want to risk stepping in one if I'm wrong. Harder to see anything following us either, and the Asterelian warriors are trained for stealth in the woods.*

You know an awful lot about the north, I ventured cautiously, *more than I would have expected you to.*

Gen didn't answer. Not at first, anyway. Then, quietly, he said through our teeth "It is just another thing I've run away from."

Anger and grief hot and fresh from Mael's death filled us, stomping out the sweetness of the berry and clouding my ability to read into his emotions or thoughts. It chased down our arms and clenched our fists. I didn't push the question further, only moving to stop our forward advancement and hug our arms to ourself. The pain and resentment had been rolling through Gen all day, and it was all I could do to try and ease them back when they arrived.

"That's not your fault, Gen," I said, holding our body there. "There wasn't anything you could have done even if you'd tried. You know that, I know that. I know you're feeling helpless but you did what you could....you saved me."

I swallowed something hard in my throat.

"Thank you, for that."

I hadn't said that yet. Thanked him. For saving me. For *anything*, really.

No, he said into our shared space. *Riel veit desin.*

I should thank you, he'd thought in Kriest, and I'd understood.

Gen...

Gen brought us to a standstill. We held our breath. The forest was deathly quiet. The normal songs of birds and insects and rustling leaves had gone, leaving us utterly, eerily, in silence.

The skin on the back of our neck raised. A chill slipped into our bones. Something was wrong. We were no longer alone.

Our eyes scanned the woods, never moving our neck. Instinct clawed at our sides and stomach and this time, we both listened. The desire to tense and run flooded our lungs and threatened to choke us, but something stronger, more practiced held us in place. We weren't just alone, we were being hunted. Whatever was out there was close, and out of sight.

Time stretched. The silence grew louder. I had never felt so exposed. The woods seemed to close in, and I had the sense of being surrounded by an unknown enemy somewhere in the trees around us. Nothing moved. Not even the wind.

It waited for the moment we blinked to lunge.

The brush exploded outwards in a spray of broken twigs and leaf fall. It was all we could do to abandon our stick and lunge forward for the ground, but it wasn't enough. Something with the heft of a boulder and the sharpness of steel caught our shoulder blade, sending us spiraling into the air. We rotated in a helpless spin right into a tree, the trunk knocking all breath from our lungs.

We could barely think, or register what was before us, but the part of us that was Gen's impeccable survival instinct kicked in again, throwing us bodily to the right just as a thick, meaty paw raked the tree we'd met not even a second before. Claws as long as daggers shredded the trunk, splintering it.

Our hands landed painfully in the dirt and Gen pushed us up, again all in the same motion. Blood, our own, splashed our hand from the fresh wound on our shoulder. It burned, and our skin screamed at the raw air scraping the wound.

Finally we turned, looking at the beast that had found us now.

It was no dog that stared us down, nor a Kor soldier. The looming mass of muscle twisted over bones was beyond imagination, but there was also no mistaking the snout that turned to us, or the clawed hand that shone with our own blood.

Chelsea had found a *god damned bear*. And she'd worked her magic.

Chapter Thirty-One

Jorel, The Best Cells
Money Can Buy

The cart that took me to the merchant's hall was gilded with mainland silver. The only way to obtain it anymore was through the scavenged shipwreck leavings that would crash below the bluffs of Asterel, or by smelting the heirlooms our ancestors brought to the island a hundred years before. Silver was a rare commodity, second only to true gold, and one that the general public did not come to lightly. Del Tor rarely utilized it as the north would refuse to trade with us, and the rest lay securely in the hands of the highest merchants of Torrel.

That they'd deemed it fitting to escort me to their hall in such splendor was nothing too unpleasant.

The holding cells beneath the grand hall, however, were far from splendid.

The dark walls were damp with earth long rotted and stagnating beneath the stone walls. It had a deep, earthen smell that clung to the back of your throat, right next to the sticky odor of unwashed bodies and excrement. Where the hall above was a gleaming testament to the beauty architecture could reach, the cells I found myself in front of only served to show the cruelties money could buy.

Metal bars, forged from smelted ship ribbing from the mainland stronger than any stone a hundredfold, stood steady and thick. The room I stood in was a round cavern lined with these formidable cages, large enough for a man to stand comfortably but never lay down fully. The ceilings and floors were carved of deep volcanic stone. The cages were fully round and visible from all sides, allowing no privacy.

Inside three of them leaned the familiar, if tattered, forms of once powerful merchants.

When Zorren and the others had taken control of the hall and the city's economy, these men had stood against me together, and they had fallen together.

Three stood nervously, unsure. The fourth, a man by the name of Hen, sat in his cell, relaxed. His back was pressed to the bars, his arms at his side. He watched me just the same, but something in his gaze was different from the others. I didn't realize it yet.

"Zorren has called me here to answer a question you have all posed," I began, walking between the cells. Their eyes were on me, watching, studying. Uncertain of my position or power. I meant to clarify that to them tonight. "Regarding my mother's treachery to our people that I have so claimed."

"She served this city well." One man—Twell, a middle aged stick of a man with premature graying hair and a patchy tail he normally hid with ribbons—spoke up. Such luxury of ribbons and adornments had been stripped of him when he was captured and led here. "She followed her duties as Reid and took care of the people. She was an honest woman."

"No one is ever truly honest," another voice arose. Even I was surprised to hear it, and turned to face the man who had decided to sit. Hen. "You of all people should know that, Twell."

His eyes moved slowly to his fellow merchant, unwavering, until Twell could no longer hold his stare and turned, squirming away.

"No," I agreed, leery as to why Hen was speaking in my favor, but trying not to show it. Hen was the youngest on the merchant counsel, having spent his working life keeping trade open with Asterel despite their feelings against *Haliz Fundir*. He was middle aged, a thin, tall man with dark circles beneath his honey eyes and long thick hair he braided back. His features were sharp, and he had grown into himself in his years.

Truth be told I was not sure what Hen dealt in, *truly* dealt in, or what his nature was with the north. Only that his relationship with my mother was familiar, but not close.

"My mother never spoke in full honesty. She never behaved in honesty, either."

"So you claim," Twell spoke up again.

"So I have come *here* to claim." I turned, walking slowly around the four cages, well out of arm's reach on the middle path. "I have left my duties at the temple unattended to answer your request. I have done so because I understand your trepidation—no, because I *respect* it. I had hoped for nothing less from four of the most successful men this city has to offer."

I knew a little flattery could convince anyone my words were their own thoughts, if played right. I'd learned it from the best.

"Success does not come by blindly following new ways. It comes from tenacity, it comes from cunning ability and caution."

All eyes were on me, listening. Unsure. None had seemed to expect the compliment I threw in. None, it seemed, save for Hen.

"It is hard to feel respect from behind metal bars." He said simply. I got the feeling he was not addressing me, but the others. Reminding them of their position. Undermining me. None of them spoke.

"It is easy to believe in freedom without them," I countered. "An illusion my mother was always very good at instilling in us all."

No one said anything to that, either. They waited, watching and listening for the answer they had requested of me. So I gave it to them. My mother dealt in secrets. Today, I dealt in truth.

"My father was a quiet man," I said into the silence, pacing evenly between them all. "A devout man. He came from a family of hunters, and he was one of the best. His lineage had worked with Del Tor ever since we had settled on the island, and his quiet complacency and reverie for the ways did not go unnoticed. He had been trained since childhood to follow the reid— to follow my grandmother, then my mother—without question. To revere her for it, cling to her every word, follow her every request."

"I often think about how convenient that was for her— ideal, even, to find my father. A man who was beloved and well known within the community, who was successful and attractive in all the right ways, and also clung to every word she spoke without question."

I allowed the slightest hint of a bitter tone to enter my words. It wasn't as if I could tell this story without it.

Even I had my limits.

"My father was the happiest man alive. All who followed her ways are. He was married to a reid, and his first and only child was a son, myself. My mother allowed him his hunting trips, his sense of honor and freedom. She had a way of handing those out on silver platters while keeping you under her foot. She even allowed me to go with him.

"My father taught me the ways of the forest, the honor and care in taking the life of an animal, and all the ways it could be useful. A deer's bones were for marrow, their hide for boots and clothes. There was no limit to the ways a skilled artisan could use each piece. Clothing, stews, decorations, tools, page folders, toys, there is no end of ways to use one in death. This sentiment was one he failed to see my mother use against the living."

Jask's prone body, laying under Chelsea's hungry claws.

Their eyes followed me. Heard my points. I continued.

"Their marriage was blessed under *Haliz Fundir* itself, by the hand of my grandmother before her passing and my mother's ascension. It was all my father wanted. It was all my mother *needed*."

I found a spot to watch on the floor, a single crack in an otherwise perfect stone block. It was thin, barely noticeable, but others had begun to spread from its center.

"My mother had first met Sol as a young woman. Far younger than she had met my father. He had long since placed himself in her favor."

Unease settled in at that accusation. But I knew it to be the truth. Soon, they would as well.

"You've heard of the powers *Haliz Fundir* affords." I'd made sure Zorren and the others educated them. "You know Sol's death toll from this last year alone. It has only gone on unchecked by my mother's hand."

"When Sol first rose to power thirty years ago, my grandmother saw him for the threat he was. My mother, newly wed, rose to power herself that same year. With her mother dead, it was easy enough for her."

My mother had never outright claimed love for Sol, nor confessed to the murder of her mother. She would have been stupid to do so, and my mother was no fool. Many things, but not a fool. Still, I let the implication lie at their feet.

"After her rise to reid," I continued, "All texts and ideas of using *Haliz's* power in any manner that may actually threaten Sol were swiftly locked away, and she began to convince us all it was for the best that Sol was left alone. He tested our borders, killed our warriors without mercy, disrupted trade and economy and all that time we believed under my mother's word that it was the best we could do against him."

"Under her lies, we believed we lived in peace. We believed we were free, and safe. My father, more than anyone else, believed this with his whole soul."

"Until."

I took a breath. A moment's pause for my words to sink in for my, quite literally, captive audience. But I also needed a moment to prepare. To ready for the half truths they needed to hear. To sell what needed sold if I was to hope for a single gained follower from these four. I had no intention of spending the time nor energy to replace the merchants if I could afford not to.

This show was also to reaffirm the loyalty of Zorren and the other four upstairs, who had followed behind me only in their hatred for humans. Once the humans were removed from the island, they would need another reason to rally behind me. Shadows of doubt over my mother's allegiance were just the way to get there.

"He discovered the truth."

I saw their thoughts racing on the *how*. They were all reasonably intelligent men, if not crafty nor creative. Their own minds could fill in the details far better than I could.

"He realized what he was to her. What he had *always* been to her: second best to a man who hated us all, to the brutal, violent king in the north. A fool kept blinded by peace and pleasantness to Mael's negligent inaction and the reasons behind it. As we all were." My voice raised, genuine anger rising. "I was only seven years old when he confronted her in our own home. He begged her to let it be wrong, to turn around and do what needed to be done. Do you know what her last words were to him?"

All eyes were still on me. Another merchant, Dern, actually shook his head, morbidly enraptured in my tale.

"*You are only in my way.*"

I turned away from them. Closed my eyes. Most of that had been lies, obscured details to lead them where they needed to go.

This, though, was the truth. That line, that damned line, haunted me to this very day. But now was not the time to relive this pain. I needed to gather it.

To harness it.

I clasped my hands behind me. Swung my tail low and purposefully.

"My father, at the behest of my mother, went hunting the next day. It was a trip he would never return from. It was the trip that gave my mother her greatest public sorrow, it was a trip that shaped her reid crest, the very crest I still carry."

I turned, holding up the metal symbol of the great bear, the one my mother had adorned Del Tor with. The very great bear that had vexed all hunters the island over.

"You know that my father died by the great bear. What you did not know, what no one is *willing* to accept, is that my mother sent him out knowing this was the exact outcome he would befall. You ask me here to speak of my mother's treachery. She has robbed us countless times again and again of our safety by convincing us it is there. She has weakened our resistance, dulled our fighting spirit, and all the while encouraged Sol to grow ever stronger, just out of sight and just out of mind. She has given up rations to the humans who steal from our markets and offer no value in return. She has given up the lives of her mother, my fellow soldiers, and even my own father in favor of a man who would kill us a hundred times over and burn down Haliz at the wave of a hand!"

"You ask me of her treachery. I ask you how much time do you have? How many times will I need to return, how much proof will I be asked to bring? I could come back every day for weeks, seasons, years, and every day tell you a new story, no less true than the last. I can bring you texts, journals, testimonies. My mother sold her life to Sol, at the price of us all."

"If this does not answer your question," I said, tossing the worn journal I had found years before on the floor before Twill's dirt stained feet. "Then ask for me again. I understand your trepidation. I respect it. If my words are not enough to convince you of the truth, then let the voices of the past speak for themselves."

Twill kneeled slowly, picking up the small, leather bound journal. He flipped a few pages. Sucked in a breath.

"This is a log book," he whispered, his hand shaking ever so slightly at the knowledge, "meldings, recorded for—for years, decades, who and why and by whom."

I had gifted them forbidden knowledge. Any true merchant knew information was worth its weight in gold.

"You'll see first hand what a meld can be used for, what it *has* been used for. What my mother refused to do now. Take your time," I added, "think carefully. Zorren has assured me you will all remain unharmed down here, as long as you need. I would think you will all do with it as you please. I hope you will use it wisely. As I must do with mine."

Zorren nodded at the cue, knocking on the door to the cellar. It opened with a heavy clang to reveal the same stairs I had entered from.

"Take care they are fed soon," I said to Zorren on the way out, not sparing them another glance. It was up to them now to follow the path I had laid before them. I could not guide them there any further. "Twill looks as if he hasn't eaten in years."

"Sanra, Reid Jorel," Zorren said in salute, and I began to make my way up the stairs to the hall above.

"Your mother dealt in lies," Hen called after my departure, the first words he had spoken in a long while. "a trait I see her son follows in, as well."

I paused. My hand gripped the railing, but I did not turn.

"We both know that isn't true," I lied, "don't we?"

I left Hen the only dissenter in the room, knowing by morning the other three would fall in their place behind me, granting me all the funding I would need to move forward. I would lead them into the great era, all while Hen, the proudest of them all, rotted away in his cage, too corrupted by Mael to be of any use to me.

For now, at least. In the end, even Jask had served his purpose. Once I had Gen's final knowledge, I'm sure I could figure something out.

If Chelsea could find use for the bear cubs I had gifted her, surely she could find use for Hen, as well. I hated to admit how many of my problems could be resolved simply by throwing them at that woman.

Perhaps I was too much like my mother, throwing bears at anyone who stood against me.

Although I doubt my mother could have ever been as creative as Chelsea had been.

Chapter Thirty-Two

Gen, Melded, The Eastern Forest

The bear stood on its hind haunches, growing to nearly another head over our height. It wasn't fully grown, barely into its adolescent stage. Its fur was a light black tinted a strange shade of olive in its darkest parts. The skin at its snout and paws turned into a pale flesh color spotted with dark freckles. Its face was long and generic, two rounded ears turned downwards on either side. It was lengthy and thin, each leg ending in a flat paw with four knife-like claws extending far from the center. At the sight of those talons an image came to mind of a creature I had never seen before.

Sloth toes.

We would have been properly screwed if that was all to the animal before us. Of course, the craftsman had really only used the bear as a base. Rising out of its back like a shrug was the splayed body of another dog, barely recognizable. The fur and skin of the bear had slunk around it, as if the dog had wriggled its way under its pelt. Its lower jaw was completely absorbed by the bear, hinging below the bear's own like a high necklace. What did appear atop the bear's head between the ears was once a face, now stretched and held in place by the butchered meld. Its eyes were shut, seeming to sink in on themselves. Around its nose was a strange muzzle made from familiar white sticks that warped into their skin. It held something made of fabric tight to the dog snout with no worries of coming dislodged.

Simon recognized it with horror. *That's one of my shirts!*

The blinded dog head made strange snorting sounds into the cloth, and the bear threw its head violently to and fro. It stomped its front feet like it was trying to shake itself into control. We took that second to get our feet under us, slipping in the leaves that had fallen from our abrupt stop.

The moment we moved the bear's eyes shot up, locking us into a terrifying stare. Under its regular set of eyes were a second set, smaller but unbelievably vibrant. Those brown eyes looked at us less like prey and more like a destination. The bear's, by contrast, were dull, nearly vacant. Responding only to our movement out of habit.

The dog's brain was in control of its actions. This didn't seem like a better deal for us.

It moved without warning, Running on all fours with unimaginable speed. We had barely turned to our left and tried lunging away when it was upon us. We dove arms-first into the air, but we hadn't been fast enough. We'd never had a chance.

A jaw full of large yellowed teeth closed around our right calf, snatching us out of the air. Our vision became unintelligible blurs of ground, trees, sky, and the ground again as we tumbled about, anchored at the leg.

We screamed. It was impossibly loud in our ears, coming from the very depths of our chest. The meld did not bite down fully, our one saving grace, but its teeth still punctured our flesh and held us firm. Our face and shoulder slammed into the unforgiving ground, cutting our first scream short and blinding us with the white hot pain of a concussion. There was no adrenaline to cushion the brunt of our new wounds.

The bear adjusted its hold, digging its teeth in deeper and refused to let us go. Another scream replaced the first as new waves of stabbing pain rocked our body. We could hear its teeth against our bones, a horrid wet scraping that grated our ears from the inside of our body. Blood ran down its jowls, dripping onto our face and trailing from our leg to our hip. Our pants, a cargo short monstrosity Simon had rescued from the science building's stash, stained red with alarming speed.

We threw our hands out uselessly. They grasped at the beast, pulling at fistfuls of impossibly thick fur. It ignored our awkward flailing; we had neither the angle nor the strength to land any consequential blows

Having us secured it turned towards the way it had come. It was all we could do to pull ourselves up away from the ground, but when our grip failed we fell back to earth face first. With every movement the bear's teeth seemed to chew down on our leg, giving us all new horrific experiences of pain and sounds. Wet squelching of our flesh. The movement of our bone, being pushed away from teeth embedded against it. The horrid endless ringing in our ears. Our screams, uncontrolled and unrelenting.

The bear began to pull us along, walking briskly back towards the west. We hit, pulled, and screamed against our hold. It didn't matter. Single-mindedly the creature drug us on, refusing to stop or let us go.

We're going to die, I couldn't keep the thought from my head, *we're going to die, we're going to die we're going to die—*

Worse, Simon's awful, logical thoughts came. *It's dragging us back home.*

To Chelsea.

To Jorel.

We didn't know what was worse. Panic took hold, and our thoughts short circuited out into a cacophony of overlaid doomsday noise. We wailed, we begged, we fought and went limp, and nothing deterred the creature.

It seemed like an eternity. It seemed like a minute. The clearing ended and we began to descend into the tree line, further and further away from the eastern path. Fat drops of our own blood followed us, our head and ear scraping painfully on the ground when we couldn't pull it up.

"Please," we said finally, half choking on dirt and our own spit. "Please, not this..."

With an impossibly loud crash of a tree being *shattered in half*, our prayers were answered. The bear that held us had no time to react as a deep shadow separated from the woods around us, exploding into the clearing and tossing the meld onto its side with a perfectly aimed body slam.

The meld took us along for the beginning of the tumble, ragdolling us into the air in a hellish arc.

Our leg felt as if it was going to rip down the center from the

Our leg felt as if it was going to rip down the center from the pull of its teeth. At the topmost part of the ark it let go, and we were flying unguided into the branches above. They gave easily under us, and it felt like we had been thrown into a bed of needles that clawed at our back mercilessly. In less than a second we were falling again, spinning towards the ground.

The floor greeted us again on our back, the slam we received knocking the air from our lungs. Stars filled our vision again. Our lungs seemed to cave in on themselves, and for a long, horrible minute, we were sure we had broken something. Our spine, our neck, our ribs. The air came back to us, but it was like sucking in through a straw. Every breath was a wheezing labor, each one barely better than the last.

We had almost forgotten about the bear until our senses came back to us and the stars seemed to subside.

With no small amount of effort or pain I pushed us somewhat upright, looking down our dirt and blood covered body to the meld that had hunted us and the large mass of fur and muscle that had released us from its grasp.

In awe and reverie, in terror and respect, I recognized the animal before us for who she was.

The Great Bear.

Her fur was no longer dark, having bleached an impractical gray with her old age. It was not that the legends had exaggerated her size; it was more accurate to say they hadn't done her mass *justice*.

She was as wide as three of the young bears that had captured us only minutes before. Her height was on full display now as she rose to her hind haunches, her head pressing the branches of trees back effortlessly. The trunk of one tree groaned with the effort, bending away from her might. Her talons were chipped and stained, each as long as one of our legs. Her body was covered in scars, old and well earned, from deer and bears and the many hunters who had faced her before and died at her might. She seemed eternal before us, something that had been here long before me and would be here long after I had gone. She was a legend. She was a force of nature.

She was ten feet away from us, her teeth bared, her silvery eyes locked on the meld that wasn't nearly far enough away from where we lay.

From her mighty lungs came a sound I had never heard a bear make, but could translate regardless. *Anguish.* Deep, emotional pain from a depth far into her very soul. She looked upon the bear at her feet and wailed, crying out at the sight.

A mother's anguish, Simon thought, almost absently, *at what her child has become.*

That may not be a sound I had ever heard, but somewhere deep within us, Simon understood.

Once, a lifetime ago, in another world, he had had that very look turned upon him. It was something I now understood through the meld. It was something we had no time to dwell on.

The younger bear almost seemed to ignore her as it returned to its feet, jaws open to scent the air around it desperately. In a single moment it caught our scent, turning away from its once mother to find us barely sitting up on the ground, prone and helpless.

Before it could so much as step towards us the great bear had swiped it back down with one of her paws, pushing it with force. The meld only turned to get up again, eyes locking in on us. Once more the great bear turned it over, and once more it turned from her to find us, now desperately backing into a tree and hoping to get distance from it.

At this third rebuttal, the great bear seemed to become desperate. It unleashed an agonized cry once more, using both of its paws to push the meld aside. Finally it acknowledged the larger animal, releasing a warning, annoyed hollow howl from its lungs. It was more dog than bear, and a pain I had only seen in someone's eyes once overcame the great bear's. The reflection of Mael's last gaze echoed there, witnessing what her son had become.

That look was soon overtaken by determination and a horrible, horrible anger I did not know an animal could wear.

This time, the great bear did not push the creature made of her child to the side, instead baring her full set of teeth in a deep roar that shook the very ground beneath us and hefted her full weight downwards, encompassing the entirety of the dog's partially melded body in her mouth and biting her jaws.

Blood sprayed from her closed teeth, soaking her own fur and the surrounding trees. The body of the bear under her began to jerk uncoordinated, the power of Haliz only capable of withstanding so much damage within a meld to hold its own. The great bear did not swallow, instead throwing her head to the side and expelling the mass of flesh and blood in a long arc into the clearing. It landed with a *whump* and an equally messy *squelch*, spraying half of its contents into the nearby trees.

Not waiting for the younger bear to attack yet or to even realize it was dying she swiped at its extra jaw with one of her impossibly long claws. The younger bear roared in pain, but it came out strangled and jittery. Whatever autonomy Chelsea had left in this monster had apparently resided in the dog's head, now splattered halfway across the forest floor. With fangs and claws the great bear tore at the mangled remains, ripping away any section that had come under the meld with violent precision. In the attack, we were all but forgotten.

Not one to look a gift bear in the mouth we clung to the tree, pulling ourselves into a standing position hand over hand. Blood gushed out of our leg, our shoulder, and a hundred cuts along our back, but it didn't matter just then. All that mattered was getting distance between us and the great bear, currently locked into the emotional disassembly of her own child and the superimposed invader on his back. It was a surgery where there would be no survivors.

Walking was an effort, more of a stumble. Together we worked to pull ourselves away with the trees for support and dragged our useless leg behind us. Her screams filled our ears like a hammer. We didn't care what direction we were going, just so long as it was away from the clearing.

The sounds of the bear faded behind us the further out we got. Breathing was difficult, each pull of air into our lungs a shaking, near sobbing event. Each step sent jolting pain up our body with the impact. With foggy realization, I knew that we were not going to make it far. We were too slow, and too low on blood. The world was pulsing and growing fuzzy on the edges.

Gen, Simon said inside of us, *we're going to die.*

We stopped walking. We leaned into a tree, stumbling against it. Our hands smeared our own blood on the bark, a deep red darkened in the setting sunlight. Leaves had begun to stick to our leg where the blood acted like a glue. We could barely make out the definitions of puncture wounds anymore with the mess our flesh had become. We had no idea how bad our shoulder and back were.

I swallowed. Closed our eyes.

"No," I tried to say, but our voice barely came out past a low crackle. I tried again. "No, we aren't dying."

I found us a thick, sturdy looking stick. It had to be decently sized to make sure we didn't bite through it. This was our last option. A desperate, painful attempt to stop the bleeding, one that came dangerously close to admitting the truth of the meld, and everything I had learned on the final day of my training. Some part of me still clung to that loyalty, to the vow of silence I had sworn so long ago. Another was beholden to the fear that refused to let me go. I fought against them now, knowing that surely even Mael couldn't fault me for revealing this to Simon now, under these circumstances.

A rise of panic flooded through us as I thought the process through, biting down on the stick and clinging to the tree to hold us up. Simon, through my thoughts, understood what was about to happen. We bit the stick harder.

Sticking out our injured leg to the side and fighting off the haze of our consciousness trying to fade away, I isolated the meld that held us together, grabbed hold of Haliz's will binding our leg together, and *pulled*.

Another scream came forth, unbidden, louder than any before around the log we gagged ourselves with. The branch's girth took the force of our teeth well, but still threatened to break. The meld pried apart, our legs pulling away into two messy, goopy visages of legs attempting to separate through the blood. Our bones reformed, our muscles tearing away from the other only to reach for their new ligament holds, pulling tightly. Our skin doubled and rolled away, leaving our muscles open to the elements for a blinding second of pain. We could see the teeth marks on our bones, like a knife had been taken to a tree. Pulling at the meld this slowly, we could watch the way the flesh fought to reassemble until two sloppy, blood soaked legs sat below our knee, our kneecap fighting to remain whole and migrating along the path.

It was only about five seconds, eight at most. It was the worst pain I had ever experienced in my life. In either of our lives. And once they were whole and alone I let go of the reins, letting the meld take back over, greedily forming us back to-gether. It was barely a second, and in that second the pain eased, soothed by the invisible will of *Haliz*.

It was all we could do to not collapse into a heap on the ground. Where raw agony had laid only moments before a chilled numbness entered. Our breathing steadied, our heart rate slowed.

Simon moved our hand, reaching down to wipe the blood and dirt and leaves from our calf. Where there had been opened wounds only horrid scars remained. The wounds had closed hastily, the flow of blood stopping. I focused on our breathing while he gently set the foot down, wincing.

Why...? He asked, then out loud, "How?"

Haliz Fundir keeps its victims alive, and the meld will do anything to mend you together to keep its meal full.

Concern rose from him.

"What...what do you mean?"

"You don't want to know," I said softly.

"Now you know," Mael's voice echoed to me. *"Oh, Gen...I'm so sorry. I'm sorry it's too late to turn back."*

Simon, for all he was worth, understood my fear. Still he said

"No, but I need to."

We stood in silence for a long moment, collectively thinking. Debating. Weighing options and understanding them all in the same instance. Suddenly, from afar, another mournful cry of the great bear shook the woods.

"Later," I finally agreed, shoving the stick back in between our teeth and repeating the process for our shoulder, focusing more on the area with the claw marks than the smaller scratches that were already closing on their own. This time we doubled over, clawing at the ground and desperately trying to muffle a scream as fire consumed our back and arm. I didn't need to fight the meld as long this time, and within seconds we were together again, whole and riding the pleasing aid of the meld washing away our pain.

As soon as our breathing returned we were up, shaking but standing mostly on our own. Our stomach rolled, then heaved and we doubled over, vomiting up what was left of our last meal. The forest shook, and the sound of breaking trees echoed across the island.

We were up again, moving, following the pointed direction of the long shadows now to race for the east. To race for the path, and hopefully to gain enough distance between us and the great bear that she would forget all about us in her grief.

Running in a straight line was nearly impossible. We stumbled, tripped, and landed against the trees over and over. The spots at the edge of our vision returned, reminding us that no matter the influence of the meld, not all of our blood had returned, and it wasn't so easy to shake off the trauma of our attack. The scars on our leg began to burn, the new flesh not used to being stretched and released over and over again. Our back burned just the same. We weren't achieving nearly the speed we'd had before, but we were moving. Noisily, in distress, we were moving.

The forest opened up to us all at once. One moment we were in the thick of it, roughing over what we now recognized were many trees long felled by The Great Bear, and the next we were tripping over nothing, falling on a wide flat path. The ground was paved with bricks of a petrified wood made from the jask trees. A northern staple of ingenuity. Hitting them with our knees somehow hurt worse than the forest floor ever had, but we hardly cared. We had made it. We had left the woods and finally hit the eastern path, and if we could just get up and keep moving, we would be on our way to salvation.

Assuming the creatures of the woods didn't eat us, first.

There really isn't much left to eat, Simon thought for us. *Can't be a juicy bite if most of our juice got left a mile back.*

It was the worst joke I had ever heard. It was the best thing I could hope to hear then. Simon, us, thinking. Alive. Albeit less juicy than we had been. Together, we burbled into a bewildered, unhinged laugh. It sounded nothing like either of our normal laughter. It was unhinged, far too loud, and somehow brought up tears that dripped a watery pink on the ground below. Our face streaked clean with them, and our hands came up to wash them away, only to smear more dirt and drying blood on our cheeks. This sent us into another fit of laughter, giggling helplessly through our teeth as we crouched on the road, flaking bits of forest muck and gore off of us with each shake.

"You're right," a voice spoke behind us, decidedly deep and in an inflection of Kriest I had not heard in many, many years. Before we could move two impossibly large forms came to either side of us, gripping our biceps in vice grips and pulling us upwards until our feet could no longer touch the ground. We were already struggling, wild, frenzied motions that did little good against the two far stronger men. The voice moved around us, standing before us both with a terrible, familiar smile.

"This is *funny."*

Chapter Thirty-Three

Simon, Melded, The Forbidden Eastern Path

We strained against the two kriest holding us, but the hands around our arms might as well have been welded steel. We were fast, but speed couldn't help us now. I felt our legs flail

uselessly in empty air, our shoulders and core pinned bodily in place.

"What a spectacle," said the larger kriest standing before us. He was a man of early middle age with graying whiskers hiding in his angular black beard. His eyes betrayed no emotion past his bored expression, but his taught mouth and disapproving tone said it all.

What a spectacle, he'd said, in the same disgusted tone one would use to say *what a joke*.

He was large, but not imposing. He was broad chested, with an overall square shape made more prominent by the taxidermied dog heads that rode on his stiffly-postured shoulders. His outfit was far removed from any kriest attire I had ever seen before. His chest was half covered in plated armor, his abs wrapped in a dark cloth. The many belts at his waist were made of colored leather that wrapped around his waist and then thighs. Colored cloth squares were tied along the belts, in a noticeable pattern I figured denoted some kind of rank. His boots were surprisingly thin, favoring flexibility and stealth over wear and strength. All of their boots were. His knees had a kind of leather pad on them, and his leggings were a thickly woven cloth interlaced with straight embroidered lines in the same color pattern as his scarves.

His eyes were a strikingly familiar dark tone, his skin tanned from time outdoors and his hair as dark as ink. His ears and tail matched the deep black tones, and I noted the way his tail flicked steadily behind him. Aggravated.

We recognized him immediately, even though it had been many years since Gen had seen him last.

"*Corten*," he said, our voice low and on edge. At his name, Corten's tail stilled and at this he took a step closer to us. To scrutinize us.

His face came in close, but outside of striking distance. His eyes roamed our face, taking in every angle, every crease. Recognition flashed in his own eyes.

"*Well*," Corten said, slowly pulling back from us. "*If it isn't the prodigal traitor, returned back to us. And as a* meld, *no less*"

The way he'd said *meld* was a slur. It dripped venom, invoking an image of the lowliest, most vile maggot one would find crawling around in the muck. I'd never heard anyone say anything with so much vitriol in my life.

"*With a human.*" Gen added, our voice filled with barely contained anger. Our tail twitched behind us. "*One who is ten times the honorable man you'll ever be.*"

"*Don't you speak to me about honor,*" Corten growled, "*I will not be preached to by the child who ran away with that witch and disgraced our father's blood.*"

"If you'll recall," Gen spoke slowly, *"Our father lost me to Mael because he owed her and she came to collect. He could only ever hope to be half the warrior she has ever been."*

"Your head will make a welcome gift at his feet," Corten sneered, rearing back just as the soldier on our left spoke.

"Your highness," he said, *"They smell like smoke. They must have come from the human town."*

"So?"

"They might have valuable intel on the rumors we've been getting from our scouts," the left warrior said. *"Intel that your father, Our Lord and King—"*

"Our Lord and King," both Corten and the soldier on our right recited at the same time.

"— would probably prefer to weed out of them himself."

Corten chewed this over, and the prospect gave us a renewed sense of panic, Gen's unwillingness to stick around for *whatever that meant* causing us to violently throw our weight about. It was no use, the two on either side of us only held tighter, keeping us elevated above the ground. Anywhere our feet landed on their legs and sides were completely ignored.

At this, Corten smiled. He was a handsome man, but there was something unattractive behind this smile. Smug. Dangerous. It pulled the corners of his mouth wrong.

"Welcome home, little brother," Corten said, rearing back with his staff and slamming it home in our temple. A blinding burst of pain flooded our head and scrambled our mind, and in the same instant everything went dark.

Day Three

Chapter Thirty-Four

Gen, Melded Internal

Together, we dreamt of the past.

It was late spring. Outside of the temple the island sang with the cries of freshly hatched songbirds. The first round of seasonal flowers had already died out only to be replaced with later blooms. Where the southern fields leading downhill from the city had lay a darkened green for the previous months, they now exploded in vibrancy as the spring grasses came and the fresh flowers painted the hills in reds and pinks and blues.

Spring always came on the tail end of winter storms. The seas around the island would swell into a deep blue and crash against the bluffs alongside sideways sheets of rain. Winter storms were cold, but never frozen enough to fully erase the hearty plants around us. The thick woods protected the city proper from the brunt of the winds, but offered little protection from the sweeping rainwater rushing down the mountainside. By the time early spring came the river was already fat with water and the flood season would begin. Ponds would fill and the river would overflow at the slightest provocation, turning the rapids by Torrel deadly. The island's mountainside had a natural slope that would help keep water from gathering in the cities as it would all run southeast to the bay by any path it could find. No one wanted to stand in a foot of rainwater for a whole season.

No one except for *Haliz Fundir*. The central room surrounding the great tree was enclosed in a large circular courtyard, the bottom level made with solid black stone to keep a permanent water level around the tree. In the spring, the rains would pour down through the open roof or the various rain tunnels higher up to gather at its base. For most of the year the water sat at ankle depth, barely enough to cover the winding coils of stone-like roots, but by the end of spring it would amass a pond as deep as I was tall. The midpoint of spring was when it was its highest, heralding the offerings. Gifts of hunted deer carcasses, the rare funerary services and unused butchery leavings were brought and gifted to the tree. It was a near nightly occurrence to see candles lit inside every wall crevice and along every walkway while the offerings were brought in a procession. I used to sit in an alcove on the third floor and watch down at the processions below, out of the way enough no one ever bothered to comment on my presence there. Baskets and platters of the offerings were brought in covered in lines of spices, herbs, and freshly sprung flowers attached with scented wax drips, each a decorative touch to the otherwise wasted meat.

The garnishing helped to cover up the scents of flesh and give a touch of elegance and ritual. Of course, this fact wasn't something advertised to everyone. Mael had always called the sacred and symbolic garnishings *decorative at best,* if only behind closed doors. She had earned my trust secret by tiny secret since bringing me here from Asterel. Now, I see her actions for what they were—a simple ploy to get the lost child she had gathered on her side, to give me a feeling of belonging to this secret little club of which we were the only two. *Aromatic herbs help with the smell,* she'd said while we worked, showing me how to tie the weighted stones to the offerings with sinew ropes and place them in the basket, *And the wax adds a task to do. People like to be busy, Gen, to feel they have a place and a purpose. Someday, I hope you find that solace.*

Did you? I'd wanted to ask, but Mael's eyes gave me the answer without ever speaking.

The waters that covered the roots of *Haliz Fundir* had receded greatly that week alone, and it wouldn't be much longer until they reached their lowest summer point. The light of the setting sun turned the water red and indigo from the leaves above. Water dripped on the walkways and the shrinking pool from the rain the night before in rhythm. The thunderstorm had been one last hurrah of the season. I could still taste the electricity in the air.

Or maybe it was my own nerves.

This late in the evening, there was no gifting procession for *Haliz*. Where my past few weeks had been spent watching over the embroidered hoods of the monastery's devout, today I had only dancing twilight spots to watch on the water.

"What do y'all do with the butchery offerings?" a voice asked, familiar yet unknown in my dream.

A memory came of the devout walking along the paths just above the water, their voices singing and humming songs of praise and our history.

"Glory to life, at the binding of our blood, Haliz Fundir, gifter to us all..." Some would kneel on the wood, unafraid to get the leaves and dirt on their perfectly embroidered robes and lower the gifted meats down to the waters below. Others would belt their song lines and throw the offerings far into the pool, trails of petals and herbs flying behind the rock-tied meats. Down, down to the roots below the meat would sink, and where the garnishing may rise back to the surface, the stones would not. In the summer we would all pitch in to clean up the stones from the roots, the only things left behind.

"What happens to the meat?" The voice came again, barely brushing my ear and sounding as if a great distance away. I didn't think to answer, but the answer came to me all the same.

It never comes back up.

The voice had nothing to say.

My solitude broke with the sound of patient, even footsteps on the path below. I didn't need to look down to know who it was. Not only because I had been expecting her, but because no one else moved with such a practiced step. It was rhythmic and familiar. Comforting, even.

Mael walked to the main platform before the tree, the one I had seen her perform on dozens of times over. It was the very same platform where Jorel and I had kneeled before her for most of our late childhoods, witnessing her meld two of the temple's accolades to get a feel for it. We had stood before it for ceremonies, in song. We had decorated it ourselves in abundances of flowers and offerings and spices. It now stood empty, the spring ceremonies over. She stood at its base and looked beyond it to *Haliz Fundir*, a solemn expression on her face that I couldn't read.

After a long minute she turned her head to find me, knowing exactly where to look in my favorite alcove.

"The sun is about to set," she said, her voice echoing in the room, "are you ready?"

My heart threatened to outpace me, and I took a deep breath to quell it. Regardless of how unprepared I was for that night, I descended the wall and made my way to her side.

She was dressed in uncharacteristically dark clothing. It was a plain wrap dress of deep indigo, and I noted the lack of embroidery on it. It was the most simple dress I had ever seen her wear, and I couldn't even begin to guess why she'd chosen it. Normally she was swimming in an ocean of cloth, her skirts pooling around her like blankets on a bed when she kneeled on the floor. I could remember napping in those skirts some late nights when I was a child, drifting off to the soothing sounds of her readings. Some of those memories had Jorel in the background, sitting just a distance away but never leaving the room entirely. You could feel his eyes on his mother as she read to us stories from the mainland, intense and watching.

He was decidedly absent tonight. As he had been from all of our training sessions since his outburst a few short years before. It was just Mael and I now, alone at the final lesson of my reid training.

She had held this night in secrecy, and I was unsure what to expect when she produced a long serrated blade from her skirt.

Her eyes held mine, more solemn than I had ever seen.

"Gen. Tonight is a night I have spent half of a lifetime preparing you for. It is also a night that nothing could prepare you for. I have taught you the history of the reids, of our devotion to use the power *Haliz* has for the betterment of our community. You have learned the ceremonies, the pictures we paint for the people around us, and why we do both. I have taught you all I can about being a reid...all of the lies, how to say them, why we tell them."

Her voice was flat and serious, almost as if she wanted to be anywhere else. It gave me a sense of unease.

"Tonight," she whispered, so softly I could barely hear her, "You learn the secret we protect."

"Mael..." I said, suddenly very unsure about this whole thing. Before I could say more, her free hand reached out and took my face in a gentle, almost motherly caress.

"Follow me."

It was a command and a condemnation in one. I heard it in her voice, but I did not understand yet why it was there. It was a lesson I would learn the hard way.

She led me down the stairs to the base of Haliz, and its roots. I had been down here once or twice before, but I quickly realized she was leaving the small area at the end of the stairs and venturing further, stepping over wet roots to reach the trunk itself.

I had never been so close to its base. Haliz Fundir's core was considered very sacred space, and keeping a far distance from it was one thing Mael had been very strict on without any further explanation beyond its sanctimony. Knowing what I knew about the religion built around this, it was easy to see there was some other reason for it. One Mael had never explained to us. Jorel, for the duration of his training, and I both had just received the same lie.

It is sacrilegious to venture that close to the sanctity of Haliz.

Still, like all rules put in place by Mael, I had followed it. Until tonight.

We came to its massive base, and Mael began to walk around it. The roots were large, thicker than my leg at the thinnest, and walking around them was a challenge. Still, she moved with a familiar ease that led me to believe she had been down here many times before. I followed her footfalls to the best of my ability, rounding the large trunk's circumference to the area just out of sight of the stage we'd left behind.

The light was fading away, the red glow filtering through the leaves turning a deeper indigo, just like her dress. I noticed she had not brought a lantern of any sort, and I idly wondered how long this would take.

She stopped us in front of a surprisingly gnarled section of the base where two burls twisted against each other. There was a divot in the center of both, shaped like a sideways eye. It was a shocking mark on what had always appeared to me, from the front at least, a nearly flawless plant. Many cuts long healed over scarred Haliz, including a few I knew had to have been for spigots to gather the sap we used in ceremonies. I had never thought about how it was collected.

Mael reached out to the tree with her hand, caressing its surface with a flat palm. She looked deeply lost in thought, her face turned up to the leaves far above.

"Gen," she spoke again, not looking at me yet, "do you know why the north favors obsidian for their blades, despite how brittle it can be?"

That was easy enough.

"It's abundant and extremely sharp. Even the smallest shards can be sharper than any blade made in Torrel."

I found myself parroting the words of my father and brothers, who'd taught me all I knew about the material. Obsidiancraft was an Asterelian specialty. I still had scars on my legs from the *demonstrations* they gave with their lessons.

"Both are correct," she said, slowly pulling her hand back. "But not the first reason. Those in the north chose obsidian because it is the only thing sharp enough to cut the flesh of *Haliz*."

Her blade glinted red in the low sun, and for the first time, I saw it as the obsidian craft it was. It shone like smooth black glass, the jagged edges wicked against her small, smooth hands.

I didn't know what to say.

She turned the blade over, not admiring it so much as studying it. Avoiding my eyes.

"Tonight's lesson will be one from *Haliz Fundir* itself. I cannot go in with you, but I will be there to bring you back. You will give yourself to it, and in return, it will take something from you." She opened her lips again, as if to say more, then closed them. Finally, her eyes found mine. I saw resolve in them.

"This is the last truth I have to tell. After this...after this I won't be alone as the only reid anymore. There will be two of us."

I saw something that wasn't said. That she wished there had been a third. I had never truly understood why she had cut Jorel out of the training, not that I hadn't been relieved by it, but something told me that after this I would understand. Tonight, I would find out what it was she was truly keeping from him.

"I only hope you're strong enough," she whispered. I didn't think I was meant to hear it.

She turned to the tree, and with surprising brutality she plunged the dagger hilt-deep into the right burl. Sap began to bleed in a slow, dark red line. Just as quickly, she pulled back the blade and drove it home in the other burl.

When she stepped back two bleeding wounds greeted me at waist height. She lowered the blade to her side, not bothering to wipe the sap away.

"Kneel," she instructed, "and reach as far within as you can."

I hesitated, curling and uncurling my fists nervously. She did not move. I eyed the openings. Nothing sprang forth from them. No sounds emerged. Obediently, I kneeled between the protruding roots and raised my hands to either entrance. The air was still as I pressed my fingers in, then my hands and forearms, coming to rest with my elbows jutting out in the stagnant air.

It was cold, unbelievably cold. Like sticking my arms into the river in the last weeks of winter. From the depths of that coldness something came forth, more a will of mind than a physical movement, that sought out the heat of my body and began to bond with me. My heartbeat quickened when I realized the easy give of the tree's flesh when I had pressed in was gone, my arms now locked in place. I could not move in deeper. I could not pull them out.

The tree began to heat around me. It had been feeling me out, deciding what I was, and now that it had gotten a feel for me there was no chance of escape.

It is going to take something from you.

Understanding crawled into my mind from somewhere deep in my core. It was a primal knowledge, something left in my blood from a time where civilization was a far away concept.

I was being eaten.

I thrashed against the wood, but it held on tighter than stone. My heart had never beat so fast in my life, it began to knock around in my ribs like a bird against a cage. Desperate. Panicked. It was far too late.

There are no words to describe the agony that began. I could feel myself being *unwound* within that mass of flesh. My skin was dissolved away, my nerves flayed open and connected into something else, something outside of me. To *Haliz* itself. My finger muscles moved in ways I had never imagined they could go, prying away from my bones in delicate filets. In their place the suckling meat of the tree came, wood wrapping where the flesh had once been and rising through my veins like vines. It entered me. It soothed me. The beating in my chest began to slow, and then steady. It matched the rhythm of life deep within the trunk.

The pain eased and then tempered away entirely. I was held somewhere between feeling odd, invasive pressure and feeling nothing at all.

The vine-like trunk began to slither around me, a movement nearly imperceptible except I could *feel* it through me just as sure as I could feel the twitch of my own tail. It was becoming a part of me. I was becoming a part of it.

It pulsed and squeezed gently, like the reassuring touch of a lover's hand in yours. It settled into a feeling of comfort, and I, too, began to settle. My body relaxed just as it wanted me to do, falling out of my kneeling position onto the side of my thighs. I leaned into it, allowing it to work its way ever so slowly into my arms. I could feel my hands, or what had once been my hands, were long gone. Sap and blood both ran from the gashed bark. What I felt instead...

What I felt instead...

I could feel the mass of my form, the sturdy weight of all of my cabled vines coalescing with each other. I could feel my trunk formed firm in their tight wrappings. I could feel my blood rush with anticipation. It had been a long time since something so filling had attached itself so close to my core. It took no energy at all to open the flesh and set the connections we needed to feed.

I could feel our vines reaching outwards, further and further from our core like roots, spreading long and far along the island. I could taste the copper in the soil, miles and miles away where a doe had fallen dead. I could feel the give of the earth as we had moved up towards it, pushing myself to the delicious blood above. Our vine pressed up gently, tendrils of our flesh pulling away and up to slowly snake into the deer's body.

Our flowers bloomed, dyed with the sap that ran through us and the blood we consumed. Beautiful flowers that took in the sun for energy to fuel the feast, large, temporary blooms that would grow in number with the bodies we ate.

My arms were gone to my elbow now. My face rested gently against our trunk, pressed to the cold surface. I would continue to push into this meal, taking my time and using care to keep it alive as long as possible. I would regulate its blood, coax the body to produce more to feed myself. A body like this could feed me for days, weeks, even longer if I took good care of it. If it didn't fight.

I no longer knew where I ended and where Haliz began. I was Gen. I was being consumed. I was a part of it. I *was* it.

Pleasure rolled through me. Through us.

"Gen," someone said, softly.

Gen! That alien voice screamed fearfully.

"*Gen,*" came the first voice again. Familiar. Motherly. *Mael.*

I thought to turn the face of this body up to see her, but the will wasn't there. Her warm hands found my chin, turned it to her. Her eyes were even. There was pain there, but also something harder. Resolution. Grief. Remorse.

"I am going to end the meld," she said evenly, the way you would announce entry to a room. It was a warning. It was a statement.

Mael reached *into* me. No, reached *past* me. It wasn't me that was the link, it was *Haliz.* And *Haliz,* greedily, accepted her addition. She reached into the feeding tree and I felt her through both my body, and *Haliz's* flesh. Our bodies began to meld, but it was not the smooth transition I had expected. She held our meld at bay, refusing to enter us fully. Pain from before began to burn inside of us like fire.

I couldn't breathe to scream. Mael had felt it before, and she gritted her teeth against it, continuing to work. Haliz felt no pain, only the pulling loss of its food leaving.

It was new.

It was all the same.

It was regret, remorse, hunger, fear.

I no longer knew where I began or ended, who I was, who we were.

At long last Mael pulled us back. She severed the connection to Haliz with a surgical precision passed down by so many reids before her. It was the memory of her mother, who had pulled her own arms from the tree. Of her great aunt, and her father, his mentor, further and further back it went, a deeply shared memory passed down through this very ritual a dozen and more times over. It seared into my mind, coiled in my muscles and raced into my veins. Our hearts beat together, and through us all I imprinted the steps as if I had done them a hundred times before.

My mangled arms came back, the thick mixture of my own soupy flesh and sap and boiling blood spilling across my lap and the ground around us. Haliz's roots sucked it up greedily, leaving nothing in the thin layer of water we knelt in. Long, sinuous lines of pulp fell from what was left.

It had stripped me of my meat, and in the moonlight my own slick, exposed bones greeted me, pockmarked where it had begun to eat into them, too.

There exists a place beyond fear. Beyond all responses, rational or otherwise. At that sight, I found that space. My breath felt hollow. My eyes could produce no tears. The world fell away and for a long, terrifying moment that felt like eternity, everything I was and everything around me was only the bones gleaming in the moonlight.

Mael, fully herself again, moved in quick fashion.

She used the blade to chip two long splinters from the trunk, putting each in her hands.

"It's almost over," she'd said, pressing my back to her chest and reaching around to take what remained of my arms. In a single, practiced motion she pushed the small slivers into the stumps of my flesh, between the bones of my arms.

I felt the now hauntingly familiar pull of *Haliz Fundir. Haliz's* chips felt my muscles and explored in, beginning to connect to my tissue and memories. The part of me that had been connected to its main host remembered the meld, how to pull another into itself and keep the body in good standing. It remembered me entering its folds, it remembered the layers of muscle and tendon and tissue it had pulled away, and it recognized that without them my body, its meal, would die.

It became a part of me. Something I could feel, connect to, but was not fully absorbed by. Together we pulled the resources from other parts of my body. We followed the blueprint in its being until my arms began to reform.

The bleeding quickened as it forced me to dump my energy into replicating my blood, and then stopped when it thought to close up my wounds. Muscles and nerves, raw to the air, pulled along my bones. Skin expanded from the existing strips, and soon the resemblance of hands was uncanny. Not complete, not perfect, but there.

In my body, *Haliz* still pulsed. Its sap ran through my veins, my blood feeding the small implants forevermore. They would never gain the strength to grow, They would never be given the chance to die. But in me, just as they were in Mael, they would always, always hunger. They would always cling to their carnivorous nature to feed, and to keep their victims alive and together as they did it.

Just as their host did to me.

Just as I would allow it to do in the future any time I initiated a meld.

I understood now. I understood what a meld was. I understood what Haliz was, and why we needed the Reid.

The tree was not blessed. It was no gift. It was a monster. A monster that fed on blood and flesh just as surely as a normal tree fed on water. Its roots spread out over the whole island, not just the enclosure around us. If it found something dead it would scavenge its flesh, pulling its nutrients back to the core to help feed the massive system. And if it found something alive...

...if it found something alive, it kept it that way. Welcomed it into its own core, keeping the body in good standing and letting its victim's own body keep it alive longer. Taking its time.

Taking all you had to offer for as long as it could let you.

It does not want. It only feeds.

I, now a reid, was all that held our people back from its endless consumption with the thin veneer of tradition and lies we had built around it for generations.

At that revelation, at the final truth, I began to weep. I understood the horror I now sat upon, the reasons why my father and his father and all the kings of Asterel back to our settling here had forsaken its ways. I understood the weight Mael carried, and the burden she had been preparing me for in half of a lifetime.

"Deida," I called to her, weeping openly for the only person I could think to ask for.

Mama...

Mael's body pulled mine close, holding me in her lap and pressing my face to her shoulder like a child. I clung to her desperately with my still shifting hands. My muscles rolled, figuring how to fit against my bones again. It scared me.

At that moment I was not a grown man, nor anyone with pride. I was a scared, helpless child, broken in the awe of the first true monster I had ever seen.

The walls closed in on us, darkening the roots in the shade of night. The sun had long since set. I had no reference for how long I had been in the mcld. That very wall I had spent my life climbing around suddenly looked very foreign. Haunting. It was not meant to keep this space sacred. It was meant to keep people away from the trunk. From the heart. It was meant to protect us.

"Now you know," she'd whispered, petting my hair. *"Oh, Gen... I'm so sorry. I'm sorry it's too late to turn back. It is a part of you now, and you it. You understand what it is and what it is we do."*

"No," I'd said, my voice raspy, unfamiliar. *"No, I don't understand why we do this, why...why we...why you...why we live so close to this...this thing. Why we–"*

Words failed me. She softened her look, understanding.

"Even poisonous berries have their place as medicines when condensed properly," she explained, as if to a child. *"That doesn't mean someone ignorant of the danger will not stumble upon the brush and eat freely if left outside. If someone responsible took all the bushes and locked them away, the ignorant would only covet it more, believing it is kept from them because it is valuable. We as the reids walk a fine line between the two. We hold this monster safely behind enclosed walls, but we put on the show of sanctimony and religion to let people think they know the truth. People enjoy the lie, Gen. They enjoy keeping busy, feeling like they are a part of something. We keep their hands and their minds idle with tradition and tasks so they will not want for more. It keeps them all safe."*

Why meld at all, then? That disembodied voice asked, and as if I had said it Mael responded.

"If we parade the berries around for their rare medicinal properties, no one will look beyond it to learn of the poison. If no one knows of the poison, no one will use it."

Jorel wants to use it. The voice said again, and this time Mael looked up and over my shoulder to someone standing just beyond. Someone that wasn't here the first time this happened. Someone beyond my memories.

"I pray he never does," she said, *"or he will learn when you unleash a poison in the river, it is not only your enemies who will drink from it. He is a fool who sees a poison for a cure. And for that, Simon, Gen, I am sorry. Where I have failed I must ask you to try."*

Aware that something in the dream had changed I pulled back from her chest, only to feel something hot and wet follow me. The deep cavern of her wound stared at me, just as it had been on the night of her murder. Blood dripped from her lips, turned down in a solemn grimace.

"Stop him," she pleaded, *"or* Haliz *will consume us all."*

The ground that greeted us when we awoke was cold. The black stone of our cell was laid in uneven slabs, and the edge of one cut up to dig into our hip. Our hands were still bound, but that wasn't an immediate concern of ours.

Sitting up was a fight through stiff muscles and a lack of two usable hands. The fog of sleep faded slowly into something akin to a headache. How long had it been since we'd slept fully through the night? Had we truly slept at all since this all began?

Behind us a heavy door sat imposing and solid. The room was small, taller than it was wide, and composed on three walls of the stone cliffside the north carved most of their dwellings into. The fourth wall, though, was a short half wall of stone that came to about hip height, and the rest was metal bars open to the sheer drop to the sea below. The room was damp with rain and sea spray, and the back of our throat tasted like salt. The sun had not come up yet, but we had no real gauge of what time it was. Either very late or very early, that was for certain.

The only light came from a slim sliver of moonlight coming through clouds rolling in from the sea. It cast something of a silvery glow over the damp stone.

Upright we could feel all of our pains return. Our head didn't feel as woozy, but we were struggling with thirst. Our ankle had become stiff and a bit swollen, but the pains of it had ebbed against the cold stone. The feeling in our leg and shoulder was indescribable, not pain exactly so much as an unwelcome tugging under our new scars. There was an unpleasant throbbing behind our temple, and we could feel a deep bruise forming from where we had been knocked unconscious. Our arms, somehow, were the only things mildly okay, although the scars from the first dog's teeth shone differently in the moonlight.

"Where are we?"

Simon's question came in Human. Our voice was parched and unfamiliar. In search of that answer we moved to our feet, our cut-up bare soles stung on the cold stone. Clinging to the wall we made our way over to the bars, looking first up to the moon, and then down into the darkness below. We must have only been a few stories up for the spray to still reach us, peppering our face and wearing the metal bars with time.

"*Entrell Jor.* The Eastern Hold." I translated for him, but got the feeling it was unnecessary now. We'd been melded long enough the barriers of our languages were paper thin.

"Where is that?" He asked warily.

"It's an old stone fortress along the eastern bluffs. It's a ways north from where we were, a waypoint between Asterel and Eten Barra."

With a sinking feeling, we both realized we would never reach the southern fishing towns. Maybe we'd never even had a chance.

I continued.

"It was built long ago during the wars as a fortress and lookout for ships rounding the isle to make for calmer southern waters. The holding cells are built directly into the cliffs. Even if someone made it out of the bars, the fall would kill them. Sol always preferred to gift its control to his favored son each year, letting his warriors venture further and further south to patrol against smugglers from Torrel."

"What would they smuggle?"

"Anything relating to *Del Tor,*" I said.

"Gen?"

I'm not ready to talk about the dream, I said silently. Understanding came, although I knew in time there was a lot to answer for. The thought of that discussion exhausted us both.

"Then, Gen?" he asked again.

"Yes?"

"You know so much about the north because you're from there."

I didn't have the constitution to fight against his perceptiveness any longer.

"Yes."

"It's more than that, isn't it?"

"Yes." I knew he'd pieced it out hours ago. I could only keep the mental wall between us so strong.

"Sol is your father, isn't he?" I nodded, words failing me. "You didn' leave on good terms, did you?"

I shook our head.

"Mael took you?"

Sol ended up in her debt, I answered internally in Kriest. *Mael never said how. When she marched herself directly into the middle of the northern castle, declared that she had decided on her payment, and demanded he line up all of his sons, he ordered the guards to stand down.*

"What did she do?" our lips asked softly.

She went down the line of us, one by one. I don't know why she settled on me, the youngest. She announced to the whole court and Sol himself that she was taking me on as her apprentice, and that would be his penance. That if he let us go without a struggle she would call both sides even, and nothing further would occur.

"You watched your father weigh your own life," he said in understanding, reliving the same memory I was.

Yes, and I watched me die to him the instant Mael touched my arm.

I swallowed. Simon gave me a moment to collect myself, feeling our throat choke up. *He let us go, but promised that if he were to ever see me again, I would die the traitor I was.*

Why did he let her do something so bold?

Because my father feared Mael.

I knew it to be true. As did Mael, and not many others. It was something Jorel had never believed in, preferring to think of her as weak. It was something deeper than even the threat of *Haliz* hanging over their heads. Something well before my time.

"And now your brother is taking us to him to be tortured for information regarding Mael's death."

The only true thing holding him back from his bloodline mission to destroy Haliz Fundir *and all who live by it.*

So we're fucked, Simon concluded, leaning us bodily against the bars in defeat. I said nothing. It didn't matter, we still shared a mind. He heard the outlines of my thoughts as I pulled them together.

...Gen?

"...There *is* a way out," I spoke carefully, pulling us back from the bars. Our hands had been working at the ties while I spoke, and within a few seconds more I had slipped us from our bonds. *Corten always sucked at restraining anyone.* "There are plenty of paths out of the hold, ones I am familiar with. I spent plenty of time here when I was a child, avoiding the abuse of my brothers."

"Then it's moot. There's no way out of the door." I rubbed life into our sore wrists. "I'll open the door."

How?

"From the outside," I said.

"How do you—" He asked, and our eyes focused on one of the bars. One of the *weather worn* bars closest to the wall where years of sea and salt and winds had worn it truly thin.

Thin enough to have a wider gap between it and the wall. Wide enough to possibly fit a person through.

"We can't fit through there," Simon observed.

I can. I thought in response and sat back mentally to let Simon's thoughts run. He was a thinker; I was a doer. I had already gone through the motions and was ready for action. Now, It was up to him.

I could hear it come to him, could feel the growing unease and fear as he put the pieces together.

"Gen—" He said, to start to dissuade me, but—

Chapter Thirty-Five

Gen, Cells of Entrell Jor

We unmelded, pulling apart into our single selves again with a little more ease this time. The off-balance staggered us both, and immediately I felt very, very alone.

Simon looked at me, his blue human eyes reflected dark in the moonlight. My hand was still on the bar, ready to go. Both of our legs mirrored our new scars. Apart, I would be able to slip through the gap with a little difficulty, but not impossibly. Pressing my side to the space, I was now sure of it.

Simon opened his mouth. Closed it. Swallowed. Opened it again. It felt hollow not to hear his thoughts in my head, but I could see them running in his eyes.

"That drop will kill you," he whispered.

"If we stay here, we will both die," I answered, pulling myself up and on to the half wall sideways. "It's not a matter of if we die anymore, Simon, it's just a matter of when and how. Too many people want us dead, or mauled, or worse. I will be damned if Sol gets that honor. If I stay, we die. If I fail, we die. If not..."

"Gen," he started again, and floundered. I was already squeezing my body through the gap, feeling my ears tug back against the metal.

"Gen," He said again, but I was through, grabbing another bar from the other side and holding tight to find a hold for my feet. Outside the winds were worse, and everything was so cold it burned to the touch, but I was already in so much pain from everything I just added it to the count.

"Gen!" He said again, covering my hands over the bars with his own.

I looked back at him, at his bruised, scared, perfect face in the moonlight, half blocked by the shadow of my own body. His blonde hair was a hopeless mess from another night sleeping on the ground, and I could only imagine what mine looked like.

He stared up at me, helpless, trying to find the words and then failing again. Finally, he took one of his hands and placed it on the side of my face, his rough skin a welcome warmth.

"Come back to me, damnit," he said. "Don't run from me. Don't run from this...from us."

A deep ache wracked my chest. I knew what he meant when he said *us*. He meant the truth we now both carried on our shoulders, and the burden of dream-Mael's request. He meant the insufferable loss that weighed me down to be away from him. He meant the parts of me that I had allowed to be digested into him with every long minute of our meld, and the parts of him I had absorbed into myself.

I also just wanted it to mean *us*, the way it could have meant if Jorel had never attacked the ceremony. If we had gone on to Mael's chambers and sat up into the late hours discussing the melding and the larger changes we could all usher into our world. If I had never learned that he had been sent as a spy for the human militia. If he had never learned of the burden of truth placed on my shoulders I had been too much of a coward to bear.

If I had, instead of letting him walk to one of the guest houses, invited him to my room like I had wanted to do for many, many late nights translating together in the libraries.

I couldn't run anymore from what we were now, couldn't live with the *what ifs* that I would never wake up to. Tomorrow, if we lived that long, would only bring more torture, more pain, and a road neither of us were ready for but needed to go down. No...I wouldn't run from us. Not in any capacity. Not anymore.

I leaned forward, kissing him deeply. Our skin was chapped and my forehead hit the metal bar with a soft *clang*, but I couldn't have cared less. As if it was scripted his mouth moved with mine. I could feel his pulse racing through his palm, and I felt mine speed up in perfect sync. We both drew it out, fumbling for the first second then finding our rhythm. It hurt. It was

bliss.

Slowly we pulled apart, studying each other's eyes with matching intensity. The kiss had tasted like a promise.

"I'm done running," I said simply, fighting the urge to slip back into the cell with him and kiss him again, and again, and again.

"I love you," he said quickly, seeming to speak without any form of careful thinking for the first time in his life.

"I know," I answered. "I've always known."

Before I could second guess myself I reached up to the wet stone above, beginning my impossible ascent along the prison walls, determined to make it back to him so I could reply properly in kind.

I love you, too, echoed in motivation in my mind, back and forth over and over with each treacherous hand and foothold, my legs and arms shaking from the strain. Hand over hand, I climbed.

I love you.
I love you.
I love you.

Chapter Thirty-Six

Simon, Cells of Entrell Jor

I didn't move from my spot at the bars for minutes long after he had gone from sight and sound. The ocean spray covered all noises he might have made, and from my angle inside I never would have hoped to locate him above me.

His lips had left a warm impression on mine. It felt like finally grasping something you had needed your whole life. It also dredged up old, painful memories of my last lover that I would rather not dwell on. Instead, I retreated to a sitting position against the far wall and thought back to more recent events.

Days ago, or maybe it had really been a lifetime ago, I had stood precariously on a roof with Gen I'd been made to climb myself.

"Someday," I'd said, *"I'd like to know more about you. About all of you, and all your mysteries. To get inside your head a bit."*

"Someday," He'd answered, *"I might let you."*

Now, alone in the darkness of the cell, I freely explored the memories Gen had given me.

Even apart, it all came back to me as easily as my own. He had opened himself up to me fully, and the parts he had shown me he'd left behind. I could recall the meld with *Haliz,* or the warmth of Mael's skirts on a chilled winter's day as a child.

Some memories were fainter, but still there. A childhood spent on the beautiful stone floors of the palace, playing quietly by himself. The pain of an older brother stepping on his hands, breaking his toys in the process. The metal rings that he had decorated his tail with and the hard shoes on his feet. I found if I dug more I could recall other things. I could reference texts I had never read, remember foods I had never eaten.

There was a comfort there I hadn't known I needed, living someone else's life. Feeling experiences so vastly different from my own. There was also a dissonance, and a frame of reference I had never experienced.

Along the eastern path, the son of Sol's latest guard kneeled beside a far younger Gen, teaching him about the berries safe to eat. *There is a freedom in the knowledge,* he'd said, a young face smiling at him. *Just knowing you'll never go hungry or mistake a* karif *plant for a* denwar.

In the labs I so rarely left for my work, Chelsea sat on her chair patiently, staring with fascination at the dark blood I had vomited in the sink basin. *We might want to work faster, my love,* she said, her voice painted in concern I still believed she had. *There's got to be a way to extract an antidote from those berries you ate.*

The boy had been Gen's first kiss, a season before he was taken to the west. It tasted like tart berries, a flavor Gen still held on to in his mind every time he saw one.

When Chelsea had kissed me awake the next morning, flakes of my own dried blood had come away with her like old lipstick.

You did it, she'd smiled, *you pulled through. I knew you could, my sweet, smart boy.*

I hadn't known she'd had the stem extract the entire time, and the tea she had given me had been the true neutralizer. I had been sick for days after, weak and barely able to move. She had brought me more of that tea every time I ate, knowing it was never meant to be taken in excess. She had learned to read Kriest far before me, and with the resourcefulness she'd always had she'd been reading on the poisons of the island for weeks.

Gen had reached up, plucked the familiar *karif* berry from its branch, and popped it in our mouth. The berry burst between our teeth, and a taste somewhat tart and yet powerfully sweet crossed our tongue. Gen didn't like it much, but the memory of his first kiss played behind the wall of our thoughts. He wondered what it would taste like to kiss me, instead.

The smells of Mael's kitchen had wafted up to him in her home's rafters, the promise of warm food finally enough to coax him down for the first time since his arrival. He hadn't eaten in two days. Mael had looked up from the bowl she filled to meet his eyes, and against all expectations she smiled warmly.

"Come sit with us," she'd asked, her son looking up from his own food with a tired detachment. *"You should never have to eat alone."*

"I'm sorry," my father said, sitting a now long cold plate of dinner before me. The portions were miniscule, clearly only a small part of what had been offered when he and my mother and sister had eaten without me. The smells of homemade roast had flooded the whole house for two hours, but I'd been made to sit alone in my room and go without that night.

"You know she means well by you. If you'd just stop fussin' and behave in church, she wouldn't need to do this. Yer just too much sometimes."

"I only asked why—"

"That's yer issue, ain't it?" he asked tiredly, *"All you ever do is ask questions. Stop tryin' to be some brilliant something and just be the son we and God need of you."*

"You're brilliant!" Chelsea had exclaimed, pressing her body against mine in the bed we now shared. Working with the scientist many years my superior was no new thing since coming to this world, but sleeping with her sure was. As was the constant compliments she'd bombarded me with since our very first meeting.

"Yeah?" I'd asked carefully, not sure yet if I believed her, but warming up to the idea.

"Truly," she breathed, running her hand down my bare chest. *"It's just a shame no one can see it but me. Stay with me, kid, and I promise everyone will know soon enough, though."*

"How?"

"I have my ways," she'd smiled disarmingly, and for the first time, I bought into her isolating lies.

"May I please have two deer rolls?" Gen had asked in carefully practiced Human. Jorel had stared at him, his latest growth spurt finally putting him taller than Gen since they'd met only a few years before. They were in the market, running an errand for Mael and had stopped to eat on their way back.

The human teller, a newer hire at the stall, gave him an equally surprised look followed by a quick smile.

"Sure thing, cutie," she said, turning to make the food.

"When have you been studying Human?" Jorel asked.

"Study?" he answered, then shook his head. *"I hear them speak every day we run out for Mael. I just pay attention. It's not too hard, really."*

Jorel squidged up his nose. *"I don't like how their language sounds,"* he said, and Gen shrugged.

"Sometimes it's not about what you like, right?" Gen answered, taking the food from the teller with a polite nod. *"If*

you don't want to do something anyway, might as well be better at it than everyone else so you can enjoy some *part of it."*

"Says who?"

"Says you, all the time." Gen handed him his food. It was more of a shove towards his chest. *"So next time you want to shove your ideologies down my throat, I'm going to just repeat them to you in Human. Because I'm better at it than you, and I'm tired of listening to your grandstanding."*

Jorel looked at him with great annoyance and...something else. It was almost admiration.

Respect for the gall he'd needed to stand up to him. Then it turned into something new. Fixation. He looked at Gen for the first time, really, truly looked at him, and did not dismiss him as he'd spent years doing.

Chelsea looked down at me in the dark with a look I had then learned all too well. She fixated on me with empty eyes and a scowl that told me she was far from pleased with me. It meant pain was going to come. Those days, there were less and less of the times she *wasn't* hurting me. She had broken me of the thought of leaving years before, convinced me I had nothing in this world outside of her labs waiting for me, and no one to stop her from bringing me back if I tried.The worst part was that it was true.

"You're thinking about screwing her, aren't you?" She asked, her voice even and dangerous. She had me pinned to the bed, digging her knees into my wrists.

"Screwing who?" I asked, and figured out it wasn't the right answer pretty quick.

"Tess," she hissed, pressing her weight down even further. *"She's putting dirty thoughts in your head, I know she is."*

The glint of a small blade caught the moonlight. The same reflection was in her eyes, sharp and threatening.

"If she's going to put bad thoughts in your head, love," she said now, her voice changing to something soft, almost

soothing. Concerned. *"Then I'll just have to cut them out, won't I?"*

The blade traced my temple, and it was all I could do not to move.

"Don't make me do that. You know I hate hurting you." She lied.

"She's a monster!" Tess argued with me. We were on the second floor of the labs on her biweekly pickup. Chelsea had been out for another job, leaving the passover of the medicines to me. The chief of our town's little militia was pacing angrily in the space, her eyes never fully leaving me.

"The city counsel won't recognize it because she's the only one who can run this damn lab and we need the medicines she produces. You and I both know the lives she saves by proxy are not worth the lives she ruins on purpose. We can find someone else to run the lab, dammit! We need her gone. You're the only one close enough to her, there's got to be a way—"

"I won't kill her!" I said back for the third time. My heart was racing. *"I want out, I need your help but I won't pay that price."*

"She enjoys hurting people!"

"I don't!"

"Even if others will die if you won't?" She snapped back.

"I need to save my own life, Tess," I said, desperately exhausted. *"Please...isn't one enough?"*

Mael's eyes had connected with mine. The intensity she pushed into that look felt almost separate from the dreamlike memory around us. It felt real. It felt grounded. Blood dripped from her lips, turned down in a solemn grimace.

"Stop him," she'd pleaded, *"or Haliz will consume us all."*

I stopped there, opening my eyes to look at the space Gen had slipped through, now empty of all but shadows. I could still feel his lips on mine. *Isn't one enough?*

No, I thought. Not anymore.

Something scraped the outside of the door. Quickly, unaware who would greet me from the other side I launched myself up to my feet, regretting the spots that danced over my vision. The heavy wooden lever on the outside was lifted, and with an effort the door opened inwards to me.

Standing silhouetted by a single low torch was Gen, shaking from exhaustion and wet from the sea spray, but alive. He was alive, and here, just as he'd promised me.

He took two quick steps to me, and I did the same. We met together just inside the room as I enveloped him in my arms, kissing him just as deeply as the first. He melted into the embrace, his cold skin like ice to my fire.

We pulled away finally, his hands gripping the back of my shirt.

"I love you, too," He breathed. "Lets get the fuck out of here."

"Really? I was just beginning to like the ambiance." He snorted, gently pushing against my chest.

"Come on," he said, "while it's still dark."

Together, but unmelded, we slipped out of our own cell, replacing the bar and entering the dark maze-like expanse of *Entrell Jor.*

Chapter
Thirty-Seven

Simon, Entrell Jor

The fortress was a testament to the resilience of Asterelian architecture. It was carved into, around, or inside of the tall black cliffs that made the eastern shelf of the island, but the vast building was no listless cave. Any of the black stone that had been carved out from the cliffs below had been used to build up the great domed levels above and all of its vast storerooms, bed chambers and halls. It was both built atop of and built as a part of the steep bluffs overlooking the sea.

As Gen pulled me through the dark hallways an odd sense of familiarity came over me. Gen had spent a lot of his childhood seasons here. Sol valued a warrior's hand, and he had worked relentlessly to push such sentiments into his many sons. This hold had been a well kept resource in his family for trade, training, and quiet parliament meetings away from prying ears. Each season he had personally sent his hoard of sons out here in turn to learn the land and how to hunt. Away from the constant eyes of the court, they had found ample time and places to let their competitive and cruel natures try and one up each other.

Gen, ever the helpless pacifist and the youngest of the clutch, had used the vast woods and halls as a sanctuary, allowing himself to get lost and hide from his older brothers and their torment. It is where he'd found his love of climbing and hiding away in small, safe spaces. More and more I began to understand that the speed and athleticism I admired in him came less from his time in Del Tor and more from his bullying family in the north.

With each new hallway tiny flashes of memory would come to me, alcoves I had never seen making themselves known in the dark, good handholds to get in and out of windows quickly, loose stones to avoid. Now he had returned, and once again was desperately trying to avoid detection by those same brothers. Corten, being one of the oldest, had been the most cruel to keep his favor from his father. But he'd never been the smartest.

Before I could finish that line of thought, and discover more about who that person was, Gen grabbed me. He swung us around in a full circle to press tightly against a nearby pillar. I folded against him, trying to take up as little space as possible. His hands held me firmly in place. In the hall we had just about turned down voices came, talking in unhurried Kriest. With his ears he had heard it a second before I ever could.

I was fully aware of Gen's body against me. His own heartbeat in his chest, his pulse elevated and yet calmer than mine, steadier. I could feel it everywhere we touched, and I found my own calm to match. We may not be melded, but we were still together. As long as I had him there, it was going to be alright. I needed it to be alright.

The alcove enveloped us in darkness as Corten and a new voice entered the hall. It was one I did not recognize. They spoke in Kriest, not bothering to pitch their voices low. They had no need to; it was extremely late at night and this was their own playground. To them the thought of prying ears was absurd.

"...intel has sent word," Corten was saying, *"that the temple is still in transition. Scouts from the human settlement say there is a strong resistance to the new reid, and the conflict is dragging out longer than they had expected."*

"Our Lord and King—"

"Our Lord and King," Corten spoke with him.

"— was not wrong," the second voice added, *"when he advised us all to hold and observe."*

"How do you figure?" Corten snapped in frustration, *"We could be entering right now and taking over the temple, burning that damned tree to the ground as we should have done a hundred times over!"*

"Yes," the second voice said, clearly used to deploying patience against the older prince, *"or we could wait out their fighting until there is only one tired, depleted group remaining. Either the humans win and the temple is left defenseless, and we finish the new reid's job of wiping them out, or...?"*

He trailed off, clearly trying to get Corten's gears going. After a painfully long second, Corten spoke with a dawning clarity. *"...or the humans are gone, and most of the reid's forces will be taken out with them."*

As their voices disappeared down another corner and out of hearing range, I could just barely make out the soldier's voice saying

"Yes sir, I believe that's an invaluable insight..." as if it had truly been Corten's idea all along.

We waited for three breaths after silence fell to slip back into the hall. Gen lingered against me before stepping back, a stray patch of moonlight catching him from a high up window.

"It shouldn't be too far now," he advised, turning his head towards the direction Corten and his companion had originated from. "If we just..."

Again, Gen seemed to hear something only a second before me, but it was a second too late. From the darkness behind us something fast and nearly silent ran at him with pointed speed.

It was all Gen could do to turn, let alone put his arms up defensively, before it was upon him.

Something long and thin jabbed forward, hitting Gen in the chest before swinging in a perfect arc to sweep at his feet. One moment Gen was standing, barely thinking to react, and the next he had fallen bodily onto the ground, someone standing over him with the business end of a spear turned to his throat. In the window's glow I saw a kriest about Gen's age with deep eyes and a ferocious scowl. He had been so silent, so fast we hadn't even known he was there until he was upon us. Despite the low light, Gen seemed to recognize him

"Lias." Gen said flatly.

"*Gen.*"

Lias spoke Gen's name like a curse. It was low and deep in the back of his throat, as if to keep the foul taste of it out of his mouth. His teeth showed a little too much.

Neither said anything else, almost as if they were waiting for the other to make their move. Gen's body was coiled like a snake, his muscles wound tightly as if to lunge him away at a moment's notice. I'd seen him like that too many times since this all began. Lias's stance was, by contrast, perfectly still. Where Gen was a cornered animal, Lias was a practiced hunter.

Gen was no threat to him. Something they both seemed very, very aware of.

"And Simon," I interjected, my hands still up in defense. When no one got stabbed, I took one slow, careful sidestep to be more in the new kriest's field of vision. Worse yet, closer to stabbing range. "At least, for now. *Nice to meet you?*"

They both stared at me. They didn't know what to say. I didn't know what I was saying. I just knew there was something between them that was thick with the promise of violence, and I'd had half the thought that maybe, just maybe, if I put myself between them I could stave off whatever deep seeded fight was threatened. Against my very instinct to run, I'd done just that.

Without Gen's quick wit and reaction times, there really was nothing to act on but my own, poorly guided thoughts. I saw Gen flash me a look of condemnation. I could practically hear him shouting *what are you thinking?!!*

That's just the issue; I wasn't thinking. I was just.... acting.

Lias looked at me in shock, like he hadn't even noticed my presence. Like he didn't care to notice. Then he shifted, just barely, out of the murderous stance he'd held above my beloved. Right out of that stance and into a new one; one pointed more towards *me.*

Lias looked me over once more.

"He speaks our language." A statement, not a question.

"Poorly." Gen offered.

"I'm improving." I sniffed.

"Poorly," Lias confirmed, *"but still Kriest."*

Lias. I could feel memories of him, hazy with age but crisp with warning. Gen had been the youngest by only three days. Lias, born to a different mother, was the next oldest. Each brother in the long line of Sol's children had found their hierarchy through age, as it was far easier to punch down than it was to fight someone far older and stronger than you. Gen had survived his place in the food chain by learning to run and hide. Lias, on the other hand, had found his by keeping a sharper wit and a quicker blade. The wit kept the older brothers passive, mistaking him as less than a threat. The blade taught them how wrong they were.

More than Corten, we had just ran into the most dangerous brother we possibly could have. It was a situation we had no hope of fighting out of, and even less arguing through. So instead, I tried something different.

"You don't sound very upset by that," I noted, taking another careful shuffle closer to him. The tip of his spear followed me.

"....no." he said. Thinking. Weighing something. Gen still hadn't moved, but his eyes were screaming at me. I stepped again to get between them, my hands still up. He followed me, but made no move closer.

"I thought the kriest of the north killed humans on sight?"

"The thoughtless ones."

"You were following us," I observed, seeing the direction he had been coming from.

"You were looking for us in the cell?"

"Perceptive," he mocked, *"Aren't you?"*

"Simon..." Gen warned, but I did not take my eyes off of Lias.

"Getting mauled by a bear tends to bring out hidden talents." I shrugged. Lias made a face, and I thought at first my translation had been off. Instead, I realized I had caught him slightly off guard. *"Gen and I would be dead if you wanted it."*

"Yes."

"Why isn't he?"

"Simon!" Gen breathed, aghast.

"I need something from you." He said to me, pushing the tip of his spear forward more. At my chest. It was a gesture, but no less a threat than it had been a moment before. I tried not to look terrified.

"Yes?"

"And you need your life."

"More or less," I concurred. "What's left of—*sorry, what's left of it, anyway."*

Lias held the spear steady, not speaking for a long, weighted moment. I all but held my breath. Gen had gone impossibly still on the floor, not daring to move a muscle.

"Then I'll offer you a deal, human." He kept his weapon trained on us, but his eyes were only looking at me. *"I need knowledge only you humans keep. If you have what I need, I will spare your life and let the woods be your executioner."*

Gen narrowed his eyes at him in suspicion. *"And face Sol's wrath for letting us go?"*

"Corten is the head of Entrell Jor," he said with a sneer, *"A lost prisoner is his responsibility, not mine. My tracks will be covered."*

Something bitter and long formed was there. I was beginning to grasp the competitive, cut-throat dynamic of Sol's many sons. I had also grasped something else, something he'd said.

Or, more accurately, *not* said.

"Let us *go,"* I countered. He tightened his grip on the spear. I stood firm. "Us. *If you want my help to earn my freedom, Gen comes with me."*

"The prince goes nowhere."

"I don't see any princes here but you." I stepped towards him. He didn't move. His eyes were stuck on mine. "Our *lives,* our *freedom. Not mine. If you can't agree to that, then kill us both and be done with it. I won't go on living without him."*

Gen took in a sharp breath. Lias said nothing at first. His fingers flexed over the staff, once and then again and then settled still. He was weighing whatever it is he needed from me, a human, against his desire and duty to kill Gen and myself. I knew when I said it I'd had nothing to wager—hell, I didn't even know what it was he needed from me or if I could do it, but it was all I could do to try. I'd meant it.

I couldn't live on without Gen.

More than the melding, or the kiss, something had changed between us, and there had been this horrible, black ache in my chest when he'd left me in the cell. It was a feeling I would rather die than repeat. My life meant nothing without him beside it.

"Besides," I said evenly. *"It's Corten who would take the fall for Gen's escape, isn't it? If your father wanted you to care more about keeping the prisoners in, maybe he should have bequeathed the hold to you, instead."*

Lias looked as if he had just tasted something sour, but his lip quirked up in a slight resemblance of a smile. That long black tail of his flicked in amusement. He looked up through his eyelashes at us, studying us one at a time in a different light. His long fingers flexed with familiarity against his staff, and up close I could see the blades he wore on his arm cuffs in black, glinting detail. They shone like glass around the leather bands strapping them down. I was no weapons expert, but I could imagine the simple practiced flick of his wrist he would need to dislodge those blades and put them into someone. Call it imagination, or intuition, or both. We were lucky he'd only used the staff. And the blunt end at that.

"Your kriest isn't half bad," he gave, stepping back at last. *"Tell me what I need to know and I'll walk you both to the forest myself."*

Something relaxed between all three of us. Gen looked as if he could hardly believe I had pulled that off. I sure felt the same way.

"Thank you," I said, then caught myself when he gave me a quizzical and slightly more hostile look at my language. Right. Northerners. I switched to Kriest, finding it a little easier than I would have expected.

"Thank you," I tried again, *"For not killing us."*

He snorted out a single huff of a laugh. There was no humor in it.

"*Yet.*"

"*For not killing us...yet.*" That earned me another partial smile. It was gone just as quickly as it had arrived. Those fingers flexed on the staff again.

"*Don't push it,* human." he said, glancing through the crack in the door.

"*What do you need to know?*" I asked, offering Gen my hand to help him off the floor. He took it, pulling himself up with ease.

"*Not here,*" Lias said, pushing the door open quietly. He turned, motioning for silence and then for us to follow.

Gen and I shared a look. Gen was far from thrilled by this plan. I knew we had nothing better to choose. Silently we followed, praying this would work out alright.

Not that anything else had for days.

Lias's path took us further away from any exits, back towards the seaside. It also led us up many access stairways half hidden in the walls. At one point we all had to turn sideways to ascend, fumbling in the dark. Not even Gen had known these corridors, but from our general direction he seemed to guess where we were heading.

"*What's waiting for us in the south tower?*" he hissed to his brother, still not trusting him in the least.

"*A place where no sound travels back to the main keep,*" he answered. It was both a serious answer, and a thinly veiled threat.

"*Boys,*" I chastised, "*Behave.*"

Neither seemed to appreciate my wit. The silence remained tense.

Eventually a spiral staircase led to a single heavy door. Light spilled through the bottom cracks. Lias easily found the latch in the dark and pulled it open, stepping to the side. His spear was still visible in his off hand.

"In." he commanded. Unaware there was any other option, we obeyed.

The tower was wider than I had expected. The stone was dark, like everything else built on the bluffs, but it was about eight to ten running paces long. The room was open with no windows and no other ways in or out. Once, it could have been a storage room, or a meeting area.

Now it was clearly an undisturbed retreat for the man beside us.

Lanterns cast a golden glow around the room, illuminating repurposed weapons racks, a large pile of beddings that had turned into an extravagant sleeping nook, far more scrolls and collected tombs than I would have expected him to care for, and a basin for water or washing. The floor had a mix of old and faded rugs covering the stone, and there had been attempts to create sitting spaces, a few tables for different purposes, and some mismatched storage chests were aligned in an almost wall separating the bed area from the weapon area. A few large and wicked looking blades lay out on a table next to a bowl of cleaning solvent and many arrows in various stages of being made.

More than just the space, I took the opportunity to study Gen's older brother. In the light, it was impossible to ignore the family resemblances between them. Lias and Gen shared the same squared jaw, the frustrated downwards turn at the corner of their mouths, the impossibly messy mop of dark brown curls. Lias's eyes were lighter, more of a honey brown to Gen's dark ones, and it was hard to tell if the narrower appearance was the shape or a distrusting squint. Lias's nose was also a tad thinner and had clearly been broken and reformed at least once. A feature Gen was lacking. They were about the same height, it was hard to tell with Gen's lack of shoes if there even was a true difference, but where Gen was lean like a runner Lias was lean like a fighter. His muscles were not overly promised, but they were thicker, more coiled, and gathered in his arms and shoulders more. There was a mutual tension of distrust between them, and they both wore it in their tensed shoulders and the sets of their jaws.

The large pile of beddings and furs moved suddenly, a bulge of something hidden shifting its weight. Gen and I both froze at the same time, equally on edge.

"*Who is that?*" Gen asked, judging the distance between us and the door, and us and the spear.

"*The reason I brought him here,*" Lias motioned to me with the blunt end of his spear, poking my side. I took an awkward step forward, and then another, before finally walking half of the room to the bed. The closer I got the more the pile seemed to move, now less like a person and more like many small things. Hesitantly, I reached forward and pulled the topmost blanket back.

At first, I thought I had only uncovered another fur. But then the fur lifted a pair of large, sorrowful eyes at me, and I understood.

"Oh," I breathed, *"She's beautiful."*

I meant it. The dog before me was a mixture of a golden retriever and something larger that I couldn't quite identify. A mutt, but I'd recognize a goldie anywhere. She had short burnt yellow fur and large, trusting brown eyes. They looked back and forth between me and Lias, unsure but not afraid. I kneeled down slowly, extending my hand for her to sniff. She truly was gorgeous, but she'd seen better days. Her back right leg was extended out at a slightly awkward angle, the bone having been broken and reset from what looked like a trap. A homemade splint held it in place, and healing scabs and scratches could be seen around the bindings. She was thin, not quite emaciated but far thinner than a healthy dog should be, and it was only when I realized that the blanket was still moving that I discovered she wasn't alone.

Carefully, as to not startle her, I lifted the blanket back further. Three little squeaking balls of puppy squirmed against her stomach, too small to open their eyes but still on the larger side of puppy. Whomever the father was must have been a large breed himself.

Lias, it seemed, had been keeping a pet. One whose birth had clearly been tough on her.

She was exhausted, but her tail still thumped happily after she was done sniffing me.

"Oh hello," I said in my own language, talking to the dog. Her tail thumped more, and I reached out to scratch her ears with both hands. "Hello there mama....hello...did you make all of these? You did, didn't you? All these sweet babies.... You did a good job....Oh what a good goldie...."

"*What is he saying?*" I heard Lias ask Gen with an accusatory air in Kriest. I could practically hear Gen roll his eyes.

"*He's cooing to the thing, all nonsense. Asking if it made all those puppies itself.*"

Lias scoffed.

"*Of course she did. Is your human defective?*"

"*The human is not defective and can understand you,*" I said back to them, pausing to look over my shoulder. "*How did you acquire her?*"

At this Lias breathed out, a familiar look of frustration on his face. I'd seen it on Gen's a few times before.

"*Some Torrel idiot had been setting traps closer and closer to the border,*" he explained, "*A useless, lanky stick of a man. He honestly got himself trapped up in his own snares more than he caught anything, but I was still keeping an eye on him, deciding if he was going to be an issue. One night, his trap caught her, but he crossed the path to get to her. I scared him off—I really couldn't stand to kill him. He was just so pathetic— but then I was left with the dog.*"

"*What made you save her?*"

At this he looked more frustrated, but it was almost flustered. Like this was his first time admitting something insanely silly out loud.

"*I almost didn't. I went to put it out of its misery— those things are menaces—but instead of being its usual manic self when I went over to it the dog...well, it did* that.*"

That was, in fact, what she was doing right now, giving me large, sorrowful puppy eyes and raising one eyebrow, and then the next, looking unsure but very harmless and very, very adorable.

Lias seemed to melt just a bit at that look, but Gen wasn't moved. He crossed his arms, addressing me in Human.

"I always knew he was knocked around too much as a kid."

"There is *nothing* wrong with liking dogs!" I said exasperatedly.

Gen clapped his hands together.

"They have been trying to *eat us* for days! Or have you forgotten?"

"Look her in the eyes and tell me she could ever hurt a fly."

Gen crossed his arms, looking at the dog. It didn't move him.

"*Useless things,*" he muttered, and in a single instant Lias had turned his spear in his hand, pointing it back at Gen's throat.

"*Speak another word against it,*" he threatened, his voice lower and filled with more anger than I had yet heard, "*And you will never speak again.*"

Gen sniffed indignantly, giving his brother a death glare.

"*Lias,*" I said carefully, still petting the dog with my off hand, "*I'm here. What is it you needed from me?*"

Lias nor Gen moved for a long minute, seeming to dare the other to move first. Finally, he lowered his weapon.

"*I don't have access to human texts,*" he said, "*Nor has anything else I've found helped. It's getting weaker, and I don't want it to die.*"

Ah.

"*So you need someone who knows about dogs to teach you how to take care of one?*"

There was another pause.

"*...yes.*"

I breathed out, not believing the luck we had fallen into. "*So if I help you with her, we can go?*"

"*Yes,*" he said, not happy about the prospect. "*I stand by my word.*"

"*Then let's start with the basics. What's her name?*"

"*Name?*"

Now it was my turn to get frustrated. *"You haven't even named her?"*

"Why would I name it?"

I see the stubbornness of Gen is a family trait.

"Dogs are not objects, they're animals, and fairly intelligent ones. You wanted to learn how to take care of a dog. Well, how you talk to her—and she is a HER, not an it—is part of it. Dogs pay attention to your tone of voice. She may or may not understand your words but she'll hear how you say things and watch your body language. See how happy she is?"

The dog's tail was still thumping on the blankets, and she was making half an attempt to wiggle closer to me and rest her head on my palm. I let her. Lias looked warily between us both, caught between hating the prospect of me being right and what I gathered was a desire for me to actually be right. To give him answers he needed. I pushed forward.

"She's underweight, scared, and nursing. Besides telling you what dogs eat and how to help her and her pups you need to learn how to handle a dog, how to get her to trust you. She clearly wants to. Naming her is a good place to start. How much do you want to keep her healthy and safe?"

Gen, already exhausted, sat on the floor. Lias chewed my words over, then decided on something.

"Essel."

Snare.

Well, I thought, there have been worse dog names.

"Come here," I said, motioning for him to kneel next to us. *"We can start with how to touch her and go from there."*

Lias cautiously lowered himself to sit next to me, setting the spear to his other side but no less armed. I had no delusions that he couldn't pick it back up and be done with me quicker than I could think to grab it myself. There was no other way out of this than through.

"Hold your hand out," I said, *"palm up. Let her sniff you. Dogs have very strong noses, and smelling you is a great way to gain trust."*

After showing him myself, he gently reached forward, palm up, with a look of intense concentration on his face. Essel looked up at him, then began to press her nose into his hand, scenting him deeply. After a few seconds she did the same as she'd done to me, pressing her snout into his hand and thumping her tail.

"What is she doing?"

"The tail means she's happy," I said, realizing this was going to be a long night. *"Dogs like being praised. Tell her good girl, Essel."*

"...good girl, Essel," he said, his voice softer than I expected. Essel, in kind, began to wag her tail with more ferocity.

Gen watched on as I bought our lives from one of the most dangerously cunning Asterel kriest one dog fact at a time. The night stretched on, the lanterns dimmed, and through careful negotiations we stayed alive one more night.

Chapter
Thirty-Eight

Gen, Entrell Jor
Northern Tower

Lias had us sleep on the floor. I was too exhausted to complain. I drifted off to the even cadence of Simon's voice explaining the stages of puppy life in my own tongue, chasing vague dreams of falling away from cliffs and shattering at the bottom.

I had nearly died a dozen times climbing up the side of the bluffs. My fingers had frozen completely numb by the time I reached a higher access door, nearly sobbing from relief. It had cost me every last amount of reserve energy to pull that off. I barely kept myself from passing out in exhaustion as soon as I hit solid ground. It was only my drive to make it back to Simon that kept me awake and upright.

A few short hours after I had finally drifted off I was awoken again by a nudge to my side. The first thing I made out was warm, familiar arms laying across my chest, and the blanket someone had put over me. Simon's head rested against my shoulder, his eyes closed and his breathing even. The next thing I saw was my brother standing over us, studying us both with an even, unreadable expression.

I searched him for weaponry, but at some point he had set aside the blades and spear.

Now he only carried a few spare rags and a cloth sack.

"Get up," he ordered. "There's food in the bag and water in the barrels. Use one of them to wash yourselves down. You both stink of blood."

"Good morning to you too, asshole." I managed. His lip curled up in a slight sneer, but there was no real bite to it. He may not like me, but whatever information he had gotten from Simon seemed to ebb his desire to stab me. I reminded myself to properly thank Simon for that later.

"Quickly," he said. "It's almost dawn. We need the last covers of darkness to get you both out."

"And after that?"

"Not my problem."

"You haven't changed at all." I said wryly, gently pulling Simon awake. He grumbled, fighting to bury his face into my chest again.

"You've done nothing but change." was his reply. Something in his voice was on edge again, but more uncomfortable than violent.

"I don't know what that meld has done to you...to both of you...but it terrifies me. I want that stain out of my home."

With that he turned away, heading back to his comfortable pile of bedding, furs, and dogs. I didn't quite understand what he meant, or what he had seen with the both of us to make him say it, but I couldn't argue the sentiment.

In only two days, Simon had become nearly fluent in a language he had struggled to learn for years. And that was only the beginning.

A meld was never meant to be held this long. We were in uncharted territory.

Simon was a nightmare to wake up, but the promise of food and water and a bare basics bath roused him. The water in the basin was blissfully cool on the back of my throat, and I drank more than my fill. Simon did the same.

Lias laid with his back to us— no doubt still within reach of any number of hidden weapons— when we scrubbed ourselves down. I heard him mumble softly to the dogs under his care. Essel and her brood. After the horrors of the row I never wanted to be this close to any dog ever again, meld or not.

Any excitement of seeing Simon undress was dampened by our circumstances, but it was a great way to catalog my new scars in his mirrored flesh. I helped him clean off his back, tracing a finger absently down the large, ugly mar that came from the bear meld's claws. Smaller more frequent lines laced the rest of his back from the tree limbs and falls. I knew the same marks would be on my own, which he helped clean.

We found the bag Lias had given us contained not just food, but extra clothing around our size.

"Come on," Lias pushed us once we were dressed, "Eat while you walk. We need to be out before first light to avoid the patrol."

"Who patrols the morning?" I asked.

"Me," he replied. "I'm not being late for this."

The walk through the keep was silent. Lias kept us to strange pathways to avoid running into any other patrolling soldiers. He had their movements memorized, just as we had done since we were kids. I wondered absently how many of my brothers might be roaming the halls. Then I reminded myself they had stopped being my family long ago.

We left through a door half hidden behind an overgrowth of bush.

"Keep your heads down," he instructed.

We listened, walking through a natural tunnel of trees and shrubbery until we entered the woods. Lias guided us easily, his spear at the ready in his hands. I never once heard his footsteps, even on the forest floor.

In no time at all we reached the area just before the path. "This is as far as I go." he stated. "I've kept my word."

"Thank you," Simon said. This seemed to almost catch Lias off guard.

"...As far as I am concerned," he said to him, "We are even. A trade of services. May we never see each other again."

I expected this to be the last word, but he hesitated, flexing his fingers around the spear handle.

"...that being said, human, I won't forget what you've done for me."

"Nor I you," he replied, "And my name. It's Simon."

"Simon," he said in farewell, then looked at me. "Gen."

"This better not be poison," I motioned to the bag.

"Worse," he said, "Deer stuffed rolls with karif berry paste. Your favorite."

At my disgusted scowl he laughed, a bark of a sound that was not entirely pleasant. Stepping back, he let the shadows take him, leaving us alone in the dark woods. Again.

The atmosphere was beginning to lighten, the trees turning from a deep black to a hazy blue. I looked to Simon only to find his eyes already on me.

"Where to?" I asked.

"Nowhere good."

I reached out, touching his face.

"Together?"

He leaned into the touch, then moved forward to press a single slow, tired kiss on my lips. I matched his movement, feeling his hand cover my own.

His eyes were worn and weary when he pulled away.

"I wouldn't have it any other way."

Through our touch, I pushed together with him, melding once more.

Chapter Thirty-Nine:

Gen, Melded, The Eastern Forest

We felt our feet move in rhythm and silence. The towering spires of stone disappeared past the trees just as true dawn broke behind our back. It was only minus before we found the eastern road, and for a single, fleeting moment we both stared down it to the south.

We stepped onto the path, leaning on our new walking staff to cross it, heading west for New Caramel once more.

Alone and one step at a time, the woods swallowed us whole.

Day Four

Chapter Forty

Jorel, Mael's Home

Morning came with the news that Chelsea had failed.

It arrived on a single sheet of yellow paper, folded twice. She hadn't chosen to encrypt anything. Two bold, clear sentences in Human stared directly at me:

Our monster did not return home.

They did get the message, though.

Staring at this note in the early dawn, my dress robes only half pulled up, something new began to creep into the pit of my stomach. A feeling so foreign to me I almost didn't have the words for it.

The fear of failure.

I closed my eyes against the note in my hand. Counted the mounting problems. The humans had been proving themselves a far more worthy opponent than I had originally anticipated.

They had failed to betray Gen to me, and had managed to hold the line against Dimi and Herris.

We hadn't gained any new ground since the first night. The Kor were getting restless to quash them, more demanding to change their posted positions from here at Del Tor to the front lines in New Caramel. Vaga had been tasked with keeping the temple, the execution of the Humans, and our line in the north adequately staffed. Frustrations were rising that we would not allow too many to leave their spots and go south.

The temple, while slowly returning to the routine of days past, had entered a silent battle of wills against me. Large numbers of congregants actively kept to the opposite side of Del Tor as me, approaching me only when needed. There were still murmurs of uncertainty in the face of my mother's execution, and small shrines in her honor were beginning to erect themselves around the temple. I had ordered my Kor to leave them be, no matter how much it sickened me to see my people still clinging to the past, their blind trust in my mother not so easily dispelled.

As many as I had swayed there were still just as many who turned away.

Asterel had seemed to pull back from the forest over-night. The line they'd worked to hold was vacant, their posts drawn back.

None of my scouts could offer me any concrete an-swers, and those we sent further in did not return. Sol was still up there in the bluffs, watching.

Waiting.

Seeing what force I would offer against him.

The answer was none until Gen was found and returned. *Or,* a small intuitive voice said, *none that you can unmeld. Yet.*

That thought stirred about as I set the paper down next to the other correspondence I had received that morning. It was a report from the city guards of a disturbance in Torrel the night before. The southern markets had raised blue banners in solidarity with my mother and with Gen, recognizing him as the true reid. They had asked how they should handle the organizers.

Tests of my will came from all sides. My enemies, my allies, and even my own people.

That letter from the guard had already been responded to. It was one I did not need to think long on, and could answer in three simple words.

Make an example.

It felt right.

But it didn't feel good.

So rarely what needs to be done does, though. Chores do not feel good, but they are necessary. The acts and tasks of the world that keep society going for the betterment of all. Right, but not Good.

I wonder, often, which my father felt when he walked forward, unarmed, to his death all those years ago.

I wonder if it felt right. I wonder if it tasted as sour as this did.

I wasn't ready to venture there just yet. So, instead, I tucked the thought away and finished dressing, thinking back to a question Chelsea of all people had asked of me.

Do you ever feel remorse? Does it bother you, keep you awake at night, to do what needs to be done?

I no longer had the luxury of losing sleep. A leader needed his rest, after all, to keep up his wit and charge his body and mind for the trials he faced.

To that end, I slept fine.

If only Gen's face didn't chase my dreams as the visage of my failures.

I began my morning with the final words of my mother playing over and over in my mind, wrapping again and again around my throat as I began yet another day as reid, incomplete.

You are a disgrace.

It only doubled my will to find him. By tomorrow night, I knew I would have him in my grasp. I had no other option.

Chapter Forty-One

Simon, Melded, The Eastern Woods

The eastern ruins of New Caramel greeted us by dusk. The shadows had once again grown long, the trees black against a deep amber sky. Dark clouds had begun to roll in from the sea. By the time we reached the old science building the pain in our hastily healed leg had worsened, but it wasn't anything we had the luxury of handling.

The prospect of sneaking into a city under siege and searching the streets for Tess was daunting at best, impossible at worst. Luckily for us, Tess was smarter than anyone had given her credit for, and she was always prepared.

A single shadow pulled away from the rest as we approached. The silhouette was decidedly human, and unmistakable.

His sword was drawn in one smooth, silent motion. It was not until we stepped into a stray beam of light and he saw our face, or more specifically our light hair, that he paused.

"We need to speak to Tess." We said, our eyes not leaving Stone's.

"She knew you'd be back." he said, his voice even and empty.

"She was right."

"It's too late to do us any good. They've already resumed their attacks. You've robbed us of our only chance at gaining any leverage against the Kor."

"You've never had any," we said slowly, "and from what we've learned, it's only going to get worse."

"Then why come back at all?" He snapped, stepping forward. His sword was still at the ready, but now we could see the mess that had been made of his face. Something had caught him from temple to chin, cleaving his cheek in a mess of torn tissue and skin. His eye was, barely, saved, but the swelling was keeping it closed. He'd received one hell of a stitching job, and from the discarded and bloody scraps of fabric at his feet we'd caught him changing them out.

"That's for Tess to know."

"Hundreds more have suffered for your selfishness," he spoke directly to me, ignoring the part of us that Gen occupied, "*again*. As if letting Ashley Chelsea live wasn't enough, you left us all to die so you could get your dick wet with the one chance we had to spare countless lives!"

We shrugged. It was me that replied.

"What can I say, I've got a weak spot for romance that leads to the inevitable deaths of hundreds."

His hands tightened on the hilt of his sword. His voice shook with anger.

"This isn't funny, Simon," he said, "how can you sleep at night with what you've done to us, to your own kind?"

"Who said I've been sleeping?" Heedless of his sword or the anger in his voice we walked to stand beside him, facing the town. We spoke once more with finality, our voice tired and unwilling to fight his fury any further. "Take us to Tess."

The look in his eyes burned.

"I should kill you where you stand and save us all the trouble."

"You won't, though," we replied, "because Tess sent you here to wait for us. She knows what we are and what we offer, and she knew we'd be back. All of our deaths are coming, captain. Do you want to face it with or without the knowledge we offer? Tess never took me off the payroll. I've done my job as eyes. We need to speak to her."

Stone was never a dumb man. He was loyal to his people, he cared so damn much, and to that end he was never against getting his hands dirty to keep innocents safe. It was an honorable trait from a man who had lost everything when we first arrived here. He had regained his purpose working for Tess, I knew, and in keeping people safe from all the dark things they didn't need to know happened in new caramel.

To that end, I didn't blame him for hating me now. He had never voiced his true thoughts on my mistake to not poison Chelsea last year, but I knew it had kept him at arm's length from me. He was the hand that held back the tides. Tess was the all seeing eye that directed him.

Her intuition made her an infallible general. He knew this. I knew this. She had asked him to be here and to bring us to her when we arrived, and for that I knew he wouldn't go against her. Because no matter what he thought of her direction, he trusted it.

"If ending your life will stop this," he promised, his voice low and threatening. "I will not hesitate to take it."

"If you think our death will stop this," we replied, "it's no wonder you're only captain."

Something changed in his eyes, but he said not another word. We turned towards the south, following his lead back to the graveyard my city had become.

The humans had gained far more ground than either of us were expecting.

We walked well into the city, passing a few blocks away from the first battle and north to a long abandoned daycare.

The absence of fighting sounds was chilling, and now sadly foreign in this town. Stone kept us in silence.

It wasn't long before I recognized the building we were heading for. The old daycare had been a mid nineteenth century installment with few updates through the decades after. It was solid, boxy, and made of classic red brick, chain link fences and asbestos. It had been in dire need of a tear down and rebuild long before we came to this world, but from what the native Caramel citizens had told me the city had to fight historical societies at every turn to repurpose it. So instead it had been left to sit, its outdated metal playground rusting slowly behind a waist high metal fence that ran the perimeter. By the time we had arrived in this world, we ran out of uses for it.

It had sat in dilapidation for a long time, many of the windows boarded up or bricked over. Stone took us through the gate, two guards waving him in. They looked young, maybe no more than their teen years, and very tired. One wore a cooking pot on his head like a helmet. Through this observation I accidentally taught Gen the other meaning of *pothead*. We stifled a chuckle. The guards glared at us, but we were too far gone to pretend we were beyond humor.

The doors opened for us and he led us past many rooms and offices to an old classroom. Along the way we passed the cafeteria, easily the largest room in the building, and through the door we glimpsed rows of people huddled together. They huddled about, attempting to sleep on any surface they could find. Cots and blankets and makeshift tents lined the space, a final refuge from the onslaught of attacks they had faced. Grimly we turned away and followed Stone to our final destination.

In the center of the room, gathered around a makeshift table of many small desks pushed together, was a group of survivors all worse for wear. Their clothes were stained with dried or drying blood and torn from battle. Many had suffered injuries ranging from deep bruising to bites or slashes, but none looked lethal. Someone had outfitted most of them in the dark outfits of Tess's inner circle, benefitting from the tougher materials or leather armor sets. Others sat around the walls of the room on chairs or makeshift stools.

Standing by the center of the table, a lantern suspended above her head and pouring over maps of the city both professional and hastily scrawled, was Tess. She had dark circles beneath her eyes, but the fire in them was far from dim. She was nodding to something someone was saying, and while we couldn't hear her words we could recognize the cadence. Whatever was being said, it wasn't good. But it wasn't anything she hadn't been expecting, either.

At our entrance, flanked by Stone, the room went silent one by one. Stone pushed us forward, causing us to stumble for a step. In that step we had closed the distance to the lantern's glow, and it illuminated us for all to see like a spotlight.

"The traitor has arrived," he said flatly for the entire room to hear, "wrapped in one nice, travel sized package with the translator."

Murmurs went up, but no one moved. They all seemed to be waiting for Tess to react, to decide how they should move in the face of our return. I began to recognize some of the faces around us. Tanya Herring, a woman who had worked for Tess for years as a peace officer. Her son, who had just hit high school age, stood beside her with a spear tightly clenched in his fist. One of his eyes was bandaged over. Sully, the local garden expert. Maya, a well known petty criminal with a history of pickpocketing. Torris, who had once been an engineer and now worked in sanitation for the city.

I didn't see many of the hardened fighters Tess had reared over the years. Almost everyone that stood in this makeshift war room were everyday citizens, ones who had somehow survived the days before and wore a deep, haunted look about them. I wish I could say I didn't know what they had gone through to change them so much in such a short time.

Sadly, I think I did.

Tess's eyes searched us. They saw our scars, noted the stick we still leaned on for support. Finally she locked our gazes together. If I had returned to Tess expecting admonition, or rage, or sorrow, I was horribly let down.

In the same even tone she had asked me dozens of times before on my return trips from Del Tor, Tess simply asked

"Report?"

We couldn't help but swallow. "You'll want to hear this alone, Tess."

Before we could even finish our sentence her hand came up, cutting off our words.

"No," she said. "Too much has happened. You're lucky I'm entertaining you at all. Convince me what you have to say is worth my time, Simon. Everyone here has earned the right to listen and judge for themselves."

"Tess—"

"And they deserve the respect of hearing it from you *directly*, Simon." her hand motioned to our melded form. "Not from whatever this is."

We stared at her. She stared back. We knew that she was the only chance we had. She did not yet know we were the only chance *she* had. More than anything, we needed to tell her this.

To convince her. If she wanted to hear that horrible truth from Simon as a singular, then so be it. It was easy this time, pulling away from each other to—

Chapter Forty-Two

Simon, The Daycare

—Stumble carelessly apart. I fell away from him, nearly slamming into the table beside me. I braced for the impact, but none came. Instead, warm and familiar arms caught me across my chest and I was held back. Gen released me slowly, letting me catch my balance.

"*Thank you,*" I mumbled quietly in Kriest.

"I hope you know what you're doing," he said back in my own tongue, offering a flash of a smile. There was a joke there, because he already knew the answer. We'd had all day to think about it together.

I did not, in fact, know what I was doing.

When he handed me the walking stick, he let his hand linger over mine a moment more. I needed this. I needed him. It was disorienting, being separate again. I was lost in the feeling of being a singularity for the first time in over a day. Getting to feel his touch was a trade that almost made it worth it.

The moment passed, I righted myself on the stick, and Gen stepped away carefully.

"I don't have good news."

"No one does anymore."

"Asterel has taken notice of the situation," I began, never looking away from her. "Sol plans to let the conflict drag out long and then eliminate whichever side remains."

"The north has never had any reason to attack us." Stone rebuffed.

"Neither, seemingly, did Del Tor." Tess reminded him.

"It was *not* Del Tor that attacked us." I snapped. "It was *Jorel* and his psychotic cult followers. Del Tor does not stand with him. The temple has not fallen gracefully into his lap. The sentiment of most of the temple favored humans, or at least they weren't hostile, more neutral. Mael was a respected Reid and no matter his birthright he is still the man who killed her."

"What do you expect me to derive from this information, Holiday?" Tess asked, again without breaking that flat, even cadence. Her tone gave nothing away.

I took a steadying breath. Here came the hard part.

"The only way out is through."

"Meaning?"

This was the hard sell.

"*Meaning* that our only chance of survival is to break the line and take the fight to Del Tor. If this drags out any longer we face eradication, either from Jorel who had months to plan this and gather resources, or Sol who has prepared longer. You're the one who told me you barely had enough rations to last a week. We don't stand a chance against a second army. Our one and only shot is to take all the resources we have left and put it into a single forward offensive maneuver to enter the temple and overthrow him."

"That's suicide," Stone argued, but Gen was quick to turn to him in my place.

"Staying here is as well," he said, "but attacking the temple directly gives us a chance."

"You don't speak for us, kriest."

"No," he said, straightening up despite his injuries. "I don't speak for you, I speak for Del Tor. I speak for *Haliz*, and for Mael's wishes to unite our peoples and recognize you all for the steady, unrelenting force you all are. This is your home, this is my home, and right now my home and name have been taken and destroyed by a man who will kill us all, including me, or leave us for dead against Sol himself."

"Who do you think you are?" Stone hissed.

"I am Reid Gen," He spoke clearly in strong, perfect Human. "I am the true and only heir to the truths of the melding power that is being used against you. I am the last and lost son of Sol, his name a besmirchment on my own and the last and lost son of Mael, the Reid none of us deserved and whose name and kindness will die with us all if we don't act now."

"And what does that mean for us?" Tess asked.

"It means I know all of the secrets of the temple, every hidden passage and safe entry. The one thing Simon never gave you was knowledge of the temple's inner workings. I can give that to you, every last bit. Maps, names, Jorel's sanctuary exposed. I can give you the fighting chance you need."

"Tess," I said directly to her. "This is our only shot. You know the line cannot hold here for long."

Tess's jaw tightened, relaxed, then tightened again. Almost as if she was physically chewing on that information, rolling it around on her tongue, seeing how it tasted. Thoughts solidified behind her stormy eyes as if on a typewriter; every letter perfectly done, no mistakes, the hammer pressing in a permanent impression on her mind with every stroke. She took my words in, made them something permanent. Irrevocable. There was something almost methodical about it, another perfectly recorded page for the vast filing cabinet of information within her mind. Tess was dangerous for more than her muscles or weapons. She was smart, a survivor, and damned cunning too. I had never quite seen her in action before though. I whispered a silent prayer that I never had to be on her truly bad side, assuming I lived long enough to meet it.

I could almost hear the moment she closed the drawer, settling on something. She turned her focus back on me.

"We're all up shit creek, huh boys?" She put one hand on her hip, the other relaxed at her side. Despite addressing both of us verbally I could tell all of her attention was on me personally. "And not a single damned paddle in sight."

"You forgot to mention the canoe is on fire," I managed, "but not hopeless, seeing as how you've got a few hundred men and women at your disposal to help with the endeavor."

"That's just the problem though, isn't it?" she came around the table to stand before us directly. "Look around you, Holiday. I don't have hundreds of able men and women, I have a few dozen unprepared and aged out soldiers and a few hundred displaced refugees at *most*. Among both we have casualties, not enough medical care for everyone and no clue what we're up against. I need all the damned hands I can manage just to keep the wolves at bay. And that's not a metaphor, those fucking dog nightmares outside keep sniffing us out."

"So you'd stand here and die?"

"I don't intend to die. We can take them here, just as we have been. We've been gaining ground every hour."

"Your pride will lead these people to a slow, terrible loss!" I boomed, catching her by surprise. "If we stay here, we will die slowly, one by one until Jorel can overwhelm us all. If we hold our ground and take him over time Sol will be waiting with a fresh army from the north, fully supplied and trained in the art battle their whole lives. They will come in and take everyone out, and I can promise you their methods will not be as kind as Jorel's."

"Jorel has sent hellhounds to tear our children limb from screaming limb, what worse can the north do?"

"Jorel wants you dead," Gen said, "Sol wants you to suffer. Do you think this is hell, Captain? You know nothing of the north. You are a waypoint towards Jorel's goal; killing you is only a means to an end. If Sol gets here and takes you, there will be *no* end. He does not need to get through you to find what he wants. You *are* what he wants. He will take you, your women, your children, he will order his men to rally up the strongest of you, the ones who still hold a fighting spirit, a defiance in their eyes, and you will be marched up to the bluffs. The lucky others will be killed for sport and glory by his warriors and sons, but those of you taken up there will pray for death."

Something dark flavored his voice.

"It will be a death he will not grant. He likes to break the strong ones. Take his time. Make them listen to the others. None of you have seen his ways because no human has come back from him alive. Do you think they were all killed swiftly? Have you ever seen any bodies?"

"Liars!" Stone growled from the side. He stepped forward, looking at Tess but addressing the room at large. "I'm more ready to believe that you have sided with your father to lead us to our death when you ran away and realized you had no other allies on this hell of an island."

"We are not lying," Gen said through gritted teeth.

"You want me to believe the word of two cowards over the expertise of our leader?"

The few humans around us shifted their weight, looking at each other and speaking in hushed tones. Tess, not ready to step in, stood firm with her arms crossed over her chest, as impassive as ever. But I could see her eyes watching this all unfold, waiting for something.

"I will speak for them" a familiar voice called out from the crowd. Her voice wasn't the steady boom of confidence that could have benefitted us most, but Dora stepped forward from the throng of people around us and it was like an angel coming down from above. Even if the angel was shaking like a leaf. Even if her clothes were torn down the arm and brown with her own dried blood. Even if her wide, curious eyes were haunted by the same terrors we had all seen that night.

Something had changed inside Dora. These last few days had broken something not so insignificant inside of her. Still, she stepped forward for us.

"I will speak for them both."

"Dora," I breathed, a lot of emotions swirling around in me. Relief she was alive. Pain that she had lied to me for so long about who she was. Understanding that I had done the same.

"They are not cowards, nor are they liars," she pleaded, coming to stand across the table from Stone. She put her ink stained hands on the table, stamping a paper there. "I over-heard Merchant Hen speak with Mael when she took Gen from the north. His mother was one of the victims of his father's torture, was she not?"

Gen looked painfully caught off guard at this. There was no way to fake the look of deep seeded hurt that came over him.

"...yes," he said after a moment.

"Mael rescued him, and raised him as her own. The same Mael who spoke for all of you when the arrival happened, who has spent five long years bridging the gaps between us and finding places for you in our community, offering aid in food and supplies year after year. She never spoke lowly of him, and he is known around our city for being her spitting image. He volunteered time for over a year to translate knowledge for you, knowledge you all took greedily with your own spy. He is not the kind of man who would *ever* run back to his father, nor subject any of us to his hand."

"He ran away when we needed him," Stone countered to the much smaller woman. This did not intimidate her.

"You asked for his sacrifice! A sacrifice of which you did not fully understand the weight, and one we all knew wouldn't even do us any good in the long run! Would you have given yourself up for the same?"

"Yes," Stone said, "I would do anything for my people."

"Oh stop it, Stone," Tess said, tiredly. "Not everyone is as self sacrificing as you."

It was the first sign that the tides might be turning in our favor. At her interruption, Dora whirled on her next.

"I am absolutely appalled that you would stand here after everything I did for you and after all you know about Simon and dare dismiss him so easily."

"He's failed me before."

"You asked him to commit a murder," she countered, fire in her normally docile and sweet eyes. "You've asked him *twice* to commit a murder. Both times of his own lover! You lauded him for his intelligence and bemoaned him for his humanity. And yet it was his humanity that brought him back with a chance to save even some of our lives."

"He chose to leave in the first place—"

"And look where that got him!"

Tess didn't need to look again, but she still glanced at me. I didn't know the full extent of the sight I was, but I knew it wasn't pretty. Scarred, exhausted, wounded and changed in ways I couldn't even quantify. The rest of the room also turned to take a longer look.

"Whatever he went through, whatever he's ever been through, he has prevailed. Simon is a survivor, through and through, and one who has proven to care for other's lives. Gen is the rightful Reid of Del Tor and a resource not even I could get close to in my time working for you. If they are both here before us in our final hour saying what they're saying, I know it to be true and I want to hear them out, damn it all!"

Her last words echoed through the room. I didn't think I had ever heard her cuss. Gen was staring at her in open awe. So were a lot of people. Tess included.

"Please," Dora added, softer, begging. "Hear them out."

Tess wiped her face with her hand, smearing a bit of ink on her cheek. She looked over at Stone, who was emphatically shaking his head no. She looked back to Dora, who had her fists clenched on the table and her eyes strong and sure staring back.

I saw her jaw move slightly, really taking in her two trusted advisors on this matter. Then her eyes turned back to us, settling on Gen. Studying him. He stared back at her openly, not trying to hide anything, even if he was uncomfortable under her gaze.

"I will hear you both out." She said at last.

"Everyone clear the room, you know where your orders lie. Maya, bring me back some of the larger papers, and the half maps we've had Dora on. Torren, before you go bring some more chairs before they both fall over on the floor. I expect maps from you, I expect you to explain everything you know and how you know it. And," she added, "I expect you to tell me what the hell happened to you since yesterday morning."

Gen and I looked at each other. Relief flooded us both, but even without the meld I could feel the tension there. The resolution to what was to come.

"This doesn't mean I am agreeing to storm Del Tor," Tess added, her voice low and serious. "I will take what you know, I will hear you out, and I will think on it. I will guarantee both of your safety at least through the night while we deliberate."

"That's all I ask," we both said in unison. Tess blinked, frowning at us.

"And that creepy shit has *got* to stop. If you pull it again I'm kicking you both out in the streets."

"Yes Ma'am," we said together.

We spoke to her for hours. Gen worked with Dora, who had the steadiest hand by far, to draw detailed maps of Del Tor. I could see he was keeping a few secrets from them, but he was giving her more than enough to gain her trust and use, just as we'd agreed on our way here. I gave her a detailed recount of our time in the east, even admitting Lias's dogs to her. I doubted they would ever meet to reveal I had given his secret away. Not without trying to kill each other, at least. She was horrified to learn about the bear encounters, and not even her leadership facade held the sheer concern for me she showed when I recounted that bit.

Tess may be a hardass, and a certified badass on the level of a Valkyrie warrior, but she's also been a kind of protective older sister to me since we'd met. I had looked up to her, respected her, but we'd butted heads constantly. My leaving with Gen had hurt her deeper than on the level of a simple commander desperate to help her people; it had been a betrayal by her own family. I had recognized what it would mean that morning on the roof, packing before Gen awoke. I did it anyway. She knew that I'd understood what I was doing. She hadn't forgiven me for it, yet, but if we lived through the next few days perhaps we might.

We ate premade food they brought us, dried fruits and stale bread slices and questionable rain water. At least there was enough for us to get our fill. Gen gave her information on Jorel, and what he knew of the Kor. I spoke to our knowledge of Asterel and what they knew and how they planned to act. She wanted to know our proposed part in this, and the answer was simple. We would be there with her, executing what needs done. We spoke, in a restrained sense, to some of the things

Haliz was capable of. How it had been used in the past for war, and how important it was to take that power back from him.

"Then who does it go to?" she asked, "You?"

"No one," he said, "Just as it was for Mael."

"She held that power."

"She never used it," he said, "as it should be. As is right."

"And if I were to take control?"

"A human outside of the reidship with no experience taking over a temple?" I asked, bemused. "Might as well hop into a helicopter and try to fly it with no training while the owner's family is outside, pissed as hell."

"What's a *helicopter*?" Gen asked.

"I *did* have helicopter training," Tess said, a slight look matching bemusement on her face. "You're so quick to forget that."

"And I used to know the names of every bird native to Florida," I said flatly, "and look how much use that is to me here."

"What's a *Florida*?" Dora asked.

Finally, after going over everything again and again and again, she decided we had earned the right to sleep while she deliberated all we had given her. She promised us a private office to sleep in for the night, and some soap and water to wash off. Beyond exhausted and immensely turned on by the words "soap" and "water," we both stood to follow Dora out.

I was halfway to the door when Tess's voice called out my name. It was sudden, and as sharp as a dagger. I turned to face her, and there was something in her eyes. Something that I knew all too well.

"A word?"

I caught Gen's gaze. He nodded, even if he looked less than thrilled by it. *Go,* he seemed to say, and I nodded back. I took a seat on an old car bench by the wall and waited. The room emptied and all that was left was Tess, with her hard, weary eyes, and me with my aching body and full yawn.

Tess waited for the door to close, then crossed the room to sit beside me. She pulled one leg up to rest her foot on the edge of the seat and her arm on the protruding knee. Casual. Comfortable. Confident. I didn't know anymore if it was posturing or if she just felt at home in times of war. Or if she was thinking of something far more familiar but equally horrendous.

"There's one loose end you haven't brought up tonight, one you've been avoiding."

"Yes ma'am," I said, knowing there was no point in lying now.

She seemed surprised by that, and it took her a second to respond.

"...you're going to go after Chelsea, aren't you?" She asked finally.

I said nothing. Just leaned forward, resting my forearms on my knees and steepling my fingers. There was an answer enough in that silence.

"...what do you plan to do with her?"

I stared at my hands.

"Stop her."

"How?"

I didn't answer at first. I knew what she wanted me to say. I didn't know that I could.

"Going alone is suicide," she said, "and I need to know its done this time. Once and for all. She cannot keep living, not in this world or any other. If you can't do it, then I'll send one of my—"

"*No.* No one else goes but me and Gen. I need you and yours to be ready for the temple. You have your place, we have ours."

"You aren't abandoning us."

"We'll be right behind you."

"I'm not going to let you walk into her den of spiders naked, Simon!"

"You *are*, because it's the only option I'm giving you."

"Why?" She growled. "Why are you putting your life in the hands of this kriest boy over me—"

"Because I need her focused on me, Tess." There was no bite in my tone, just a deep frustration. "You know how she is, *what* she is. We both do. And you know what I am to her. Anyone else will only serve to infuriate her, push her to violence and put more lives on the line that we both know she'd take. Or worse. It needs to be me, and I trust no one else in the world more than I trust Gen to walk in there with me."

I felt my shoulders sag.

"...we've both got some unfinished business in her labs."

I could feel Tess's eyes on me. Feel her back down. I seemed to pass some sort of test, but not fully.

"Damnit Simon," she shook her head, "don't let me regret listening to you."

I wanted to feel success in those words, at the admittance that she was truly listening to what I had said all night and falling in line. But something about the way she said it was off. I couldn't shake it.

"What does that mean?"

"...you've changed, Simon."

"We all have."

"I see him in you now," she continued. "I see his restlessness in you. You never used to bounce your leg like that. Sometimes you used to get so damned still I would check if you were breathing. You were statuesque."

I stopped bouncing my leg.

"You speak their language now, and it's only been three days. But you don't just speak the language, it's almost as if he's the one talking when you open your mouth. Same pitch, same tone, same mannerisms. It's more than just a few things, Simon. It's *everything*. The way you stand, the way you breathe... I barely recognize you anymore."

"You're not alone there." I closed my eyes, rested my face in my hands. She didn't let the silence settle long.

"If you can't do what needs done, Simon....could he?"

I stared at the floor. She continued.

"Could he kill Chelsea? You aren't... *you*, anymore, Simon. You're not him, either, but parts of him exist in you even when you two aren't melded. Can the you I'm talking to right now do what needs done?"

I felt her weight shift, as if to touch my shoulder. I stood up, out of her grasp. It was a wobbly motion, my leg still not liking the abuse. I couldn't tell if her question truly upset me or not, but I moved on instinct to avoid the moment all the same. To avoid that touch, that human connection, to feel the weight of her hand on my shoulder and the weight of what she needed me to do. Needed me to say.

To say I could and would kill someone with my own hands. To kill someone who was truly evil, for the lives of hundreds. Or at the very least....if *we* could.

I thought of the blood of my ex lover on Gen's hands. I thought of Mael's blood on the roots of *Haliz Fundir*. I thought of the look in Gen's eyes when he stared down Lias and Corten and the deep, boiling rage I saw in his entire body. I thought of his sadness, his depth, of the edges of him and me both that have worn painfully down over these last few days. I thought of his strength and resolution now. I thought of taking a life.

"I don't know," I told her honestly. "But I know what he'd say to your question."

"What's that?"

"*Simon always finds a way*," I spoke, turning back to look at her over my shoulder. "That's always been enough for him."

She studied me. Her eyes wavered over my face, her jaw setting and shifting, rolling the words on her tongue. Tasting an idea in that way she does. Her eyes never left mine when she asked.

"Who are you, anymore?"

"I'm still me," I answered softly. "And yet...so much more than myself."

I watched her chew that over. Slowly. Carefully. Unsure. She finally nodded, then stood beside me, resolute.

"Then let's hope it's enough."

Chapter Forty-Three

Gen, The Daycare

After hours of hard travel and days of hell, soap had never felt so much like a luxury. It didn't even bother me that the water was cold. As I had the night before I stripped down and used towels and water to rinse off, but unlike last time Simon was not present, and instead Dora stood in the small shower room with me, she turned her back to offer me privacy while her presence offered me security.

"Thank you," I said to her in Kriest.

"It was the least I could do," she replied, "for my best friend."

"He's hurt, you know, that you spied on him."

She was quiet for a second. I rinsed out my hair.

"I know," she finally replied. "It is something I'll need to make up to him for the rest of my life."

"However long that is."

"Unlike you," she said back, "who keeps trying to die at every possible convenience, I intend to live until I'm 83 years old and retire in a northern Torrel estate."

"Yeah?" I couldn't help but smile.

"Yeah! So, what will you be doing with the rest of *your* life?"

"You mean tomorrow?"

"Humor me."

Now it was my turn to be silent.

"I don't know," I answered honestly. "I guess I'll become Reid. Rebuild and repair the temple and New Caramel."

"Well you'll have to share custody of Simon with me."

"Oh?"

"Yes," she said, "I want him every other week to ensure I make my appointments and get my readings done."

The image made me smile.

"Thank you, Dora."

"Sanra, Reid Gen," she said in response. I was glad our backs were to each other. I didn't want her to see the fat tears that spilled over at those words. I wonder if Mael had ever cried over the nuance of the greeting before.

All is well due to you, and all you do.

Dora let me finish in silence, giving me the time I needed to allow myself to break apart and scoop the pieces back together. In the absence of Simon's calm voice in my head, my own thoughts flooded back in, uncertain and chaotic.

Could I really do this? Could I really become Reid?

In the emptiness of my own mind, no one was there to reassure me.

Simon joined me in our makeshift bedroom later in the night. They'd pushed together two old cots in the corner of an office for our use. A pile of mismatched blankets sat on the floor for us. I had the sense that Tess had kept many supplies such as this around the city in various holes for any emergency. It was a far cry from my own bed at the temple, or even the soft lounges I'd used around Mael's home growing up, but it was the most forgiving surface I'd laid on in days. Combined with the soap from earlier, I was in the lap of luxury. I nearly felt like a person again.

At the same time, I'd never felt so far removed from myself. I'd lost something since

Mael's death, and whatever it was had never returned. Being alone in my mind, the void I had been feeling felt endlessly vast and incomplete.

Simon slipped in quietly, probably worried about waking me. He was wearing new clothes, and his hair was damp and smelled like soap. Our eyes met when he sat down, and he softened considerably. He took my hand and entwined our fingers with a soft squeeze.

We laid facing each other, wrapped in borrowed blankets and the illusion of safety. It was damn near domestic. The fate of our plan now lay in Tess's capable, calculating hands. One of her advisors argued against us. The other for. We had no way of knowing which she'd listen to. Regardless of her decision to join us in Del Tor, though, we both knew the weight of responsibility lay on both our shoulders.

He for Chelsea. I for Jorel.

I didn't have the strength left in me to wonder if moments like this were what we had missed with every unanswered flirt or glance over the last year and a half. How many nights we could have spent laying next to each other, studying each other's faces in the darkness, holding each other close.

I couldn't even bring myself to pretend things were alright. I'd long been stripped of any sense of security, or hope for life after the night was over. It was a horrible place to be. It was better, somehow, knowing I wasn't alone through this.

"I live for you." I said quietly, the weight of tomorrow heavy on my mind. I felt him squeeze my hand tighter. I needed to get the words out now, or I may never say them again. "I have been for a long time. Now, though, I don't think I could go on without you. Being apart is agony."

He nodded, knowing I meant in more ways than one.

"I don't know who I am anymore without you." His eyes were wet and red-rimmed, and he swallowed hard. "I don't know that I'm really Simon anymore. I feel so vacant, and all

I can think of is melding together again. Even knowing all I know, what the meld is... I crave it."

I felt myself swallowing too, a painful sense of understanding filling even my bones. He didn't need to elaborate. Pulled apart, it felt like we had not come apart wholly ourselves anymore. I felt my thoughts coming in steadier than they ever had before. I felt words come to my lips quicker than they ever had, and I knew that was only the beginning of what we had shared. I wasn't sure anymore if the decision to stop running had really been my own, or if I ever could have gotten there without his mind inside me.

"The emptiness is worse than the price." I agreed, and my own voice sounded choked and unfamiliar to my ears. Was I crying, as well?

He swallowed hard again, making a low and involuntary *"mm"* noise. Another tear slipped out and ran down his nose.

"Do you want to know the darndest thing?" He asked in a hoarse whisper. I didn't say anything. I had a feeling I didn't need to.

"As much as I can't stand being separate," he continued, "I can't stand the thought of melding back together and losing you again." More tears spilled freely, and his shoulder jerked in an inaudible sob. "I've missed looking at you, talking to you, t-touching you... it's not the same when we're in the same body."

"I know," I didn't need to elaborate. He'd said it all for me. "Simon.... I know."

His laugh was hollow, somewhere between sobs and silence.

"What have we become?"

"Friends," I said, cupping his face in my palm. "Partners. Lovers. *One*."

"*Gen*," He breathed. No more words were needed, no more words were wanted. I pulled him closer, and we kissed for the first time since the woods outside Entrell Jor.

I turned my head so he didn't have to lift his off the pillow, supporting my weight on one arm while I pulled his face closer with the other. I felt his sigh against my cheek, felt his lips part so I could deepen the kiss. I moved my mouth against his hungrily, desperate for his touch.

"I love you," I said in my language. "*I love you*," I said again, in his.

"You're perfect," He'd breathed, and I pulled him into another long kiss to hide the emotions on my face.

So are you.

We had little use for words after that.

I knew there would never be anyone else I could love in the immeasurable ways that I loved him. Whether that time came tomorrow, or the next day, or a lifetime from now, I would spend every moment of it devoting everything I had and everything I was to him.

He was all I'd ever needed.

Chapter Forty-Four

Simon, Melded, The Daycare

When we melded back together, it was only after too much time had passed wrapped in each other's arms. Exhaustion had finally overtaken us, and the illusion of safety could no longer stave off the grim reality of our plight.

We'd held each other's hands. I'd kissed him one last time, and we'd slipped back together with practiced ease. I felt no resistance of flesh, nothing but the fusion of our bodies and minds.

The separate memories of the event we had just shared rolled into each other, and we experienced it from both sides. Emotions, touch, words and feelings. We sat on the makeshift bed, alone in this experience with no one to see us through it but the tangled blankets. I felt our hands twine together in our lap, a shallow attempt to hold the other's again. But there was no warmth of his skin with the touch. There was only a feeling of holding my own hand.

When we cried, tears of relief mixed with deep, wracking sobs for what we had lost. I didn't know if it was me, or him, or both of us who wept. All I knew was this moment, this existence of us together, and not even our precious memories were spared the melding. What and who we were as individuals was gone, for better or for worse, and all that waited for us outside the door was death and pain chasing at our heels.

"I love you," we breathed through our lips in perfect, aching unison. "I will always love you."

When sleep came, it came without dreams. All that there was was us, together, opening the meld into a depth neither of us had yet ventured. When we awoke the next morning, I didn't know who I would be, or who he would become. But together, we would be something new.

Something perfect.

We were one.

Chapter Forty-Five

Jorel, Torrel Del Tor

The night was too quiet. From over the sea deep clouds rolled in, electrifying the air and dropping the pressure. A storm was coming to the island, a late rain for the season. Through the branches of *Haliz* I could see heat lightning far off in the sky, highlighting the branches and leaves in sharp bursts of white. Thunder reached us like a low echo. To-morrow would be a mess. People would hole in their homes, trying to stave off what was sure to be a long, drawn out downpour. Further to the coast, my scouts had reported, the sea had turned wild, crashing near to the top of the cliffs at points and entering the woods at others.

More than the storm had me on edge, though. The merchants held below the hall had not yet folded, no doubt due to Hen. I was sure my words would have been enough to break even his influence. I had been overconfident.

It was another over confidence I now found myself correcting.

Sol's patrols had ceased in their entirety. Like a tide pulling dangerously back to the sea, I knew it could only mean something big was heading our way. He was keeping his men close. Watching.

Waiting for something.

Ready.

Without Gen, I had no answer.

Standing under Haliz Fundir in its might, feeling the tightening lines of threat around me, it was not the wisdom of my traitor mother that graced me, nor my own doctrine that eased my nerves and offered guidance. It was the final words of my father that teased my mind, caressing my ear like an old, tired ghost.

"You'll understand someday," he'd said to me, ruffling my hair as he always had. A small but empty smile played on his lips. *"You'll understand, as I do now, that I am only in the way."*

"Jorel," had been the last thing he ever said to me. It was not my name. It was an order, the only one I'd ever received from him.

Hold.

Leaving me obediently in place, unsure and afraid, he'd stood in the brush, rising to his full height. There was honor there, honor I wish he could have seen. Honor in doing what he felt must be done. Even if it was gruesome. Even if he was only following the orders of another.

I am only in the way.

My father left me there, kneeling in the wet mud beside the boulder, as he walked away. The image of his back, holding his bow he would never draw, and the dagger he would never reach for, is one that haunts me to this day. It was swallowed by the blackness of the cave, the darkness welcoming him in like an old friend holding open the door.

My father walked into the den of the great bear, alone and unwilling to arm himself. He did not die a quiet death. He did not die a quick one. He did not seem to regret it.

There is honor, he'd taught me, *in facing a monster greater than yourself, and there is just as much honor in dying as there is surviving.*

I was no longer the child who had listened to his father's death throes. I had not been that child since I had returned home, his final words in my mind.

I am only in the way

He had believed them. Believed them so, so deeply that he had chosen death rather than face continuing as a burden.

That truth, that manipulation of my mother that had broken him so deeply as to take his own life, was the catalyst for all of this. For seeing her as she truly was, I gained the ability to question all around me, to seek the reasons of the world and to bend them myself. If it took a monster to hunt a monster, so be it. I would never be like her, to overlook the life of her people for her own gain. I would be stronger than my father had ever been, and better than my mother ever could be.

I had replayed this memory hundreds of times. My father's last command is what reached me now.

Jorel.

Hold.

I was the strength this world needed. I was the one who could make the hard decisions for the betterment of others. So I would, no matter the cost. No matter what I had to do to get there.

I was now as old as my father had been, all those years ago. Standing before a monster larger than myself. It was the same monster my mother had sold my people for. It was the same monster that had spoken through her, pushing my father into ending his own life in its stead. *Sol.*

Dimi and Herris kneeled behind me. The platform was illuminated in the late night with sparse candles. There was little ceremony in this event. It was private, only the twins and my closest hands stood around. At their side lay their favored hatchets and spear, the weapons by which they had fought so hard for me.

The humans were only prolonging the inevitable. I had begun to realize that their coordination and actions were no accident. They were calculated, and must be acting on knowledge they should not have. There was not a single human smart enough to rally the people and hold such a coordinated counterattack. Someone must have been there feeding them information.

Where I'd initially had every intention of playing the long game and simply starving them out, things had changed. The north was now anticipating something, and I no longer had the luxury of playing a lengthy game with the humans. Abandoning the front was a simple enough idea, but the kor would waver in their devotion to my cause if I did not fulfill the promises I had offered them. They wanted the humans removed, killed and subjugated. The threat of the north, as it did for too many of my people, was of second concern.

Walking away wasn't an option. Prolonging the effort was unwise with Sol plotting in the reserves. I had balked for the full day on what to do regarding the situation. I could not afford to send more of my kor there and leave the temple unguarded, but without the capability to unmeld I was incapable of creating the true soldiers I needed, the ones that could turn the tides of the war against the humans *and* serve as a message to Sol of our power without ever exchanging direct blows.

Someone had been giving the humans information. It was someone who would have no qualms selling the sanctity of his people for his own security. A coward with nothing to lose and a mentor who had taught him all of her ways of selling others for gain.

The humans had Gen. They were housing him, giving him sanctuary in exchange for information against me and my men. Of this I was sure.

Hold, my father's voice whispered in my ear once more.

I turned to the twins, facing them at last. Before them two empty bowls of sap mixed wine sat empty. They kneeled patiently, their heads bowed, their tails extended long behind them, their hands shaking with anticipation.

"Tonight," I said to them, "history will be made."

The human problem needed to be erased. Gen needed to be found. Chelsea had failed me, and I had no one to turn to but myself.

In the face of such impossible requirements, it was I who would hold strong against the weight of the world. I did not need the power to unmeld my soldiers now. When they succeeded in finding me Gen and bringing him kicking and screaming into my hands, I would have all I needed to undo what was done then.

For now, I needed strength. I needed to end this.

Those around me hummed a deep, old song in honor of this momentous moment. Sleep may at last evade me for this decision, but I would make it regardless.

My hands on their shoulders, I began the first meld under my rule as Reid.

Day Five

Chapter Forty-Six

Simon, Melded, The Daycare

Dora's soft hand knocked on the door sometime just before dawn.

"Tess has decided," she said through the wood, hearing us sit up. "They move on Torrel Del Tor at dusk."

We closed our eyes.

"Did she say why the wait?" we asked.

"She said you'd know," she replied, and we heard her slip from the door and leave us there.

Morning had come. It was time to face the dawn. Tess knew our part was not beside her, not yet, anyway. She trusted us.

She trusts you, Gen corrected as we hurriedly dressed. We both thought back to my conversation with her the night before.

Let's hope her trust is in the right place.

Sneaking out past the others holed in the daycare was surprisingly easy, considering we should have been under watch. It was also simpler to leave a place in the same body than in separate. Tess had no doubt called her people away from the path she figured we would use. It was clear to me that she was giving us every opportunity to leave, and it was an opportunity we were quick to take advantage of.

We'd just left through a side door into the back play area when a voice called out.

"Simon! Gen!"

We turned fast enough to have a small bag thrown into our chest. We caught it on reflex, looking around to find Tess herself leaning out of an upstairs window, a solemn look on her face.

"You'll need that," she said, keeping her voice low enough to only carry to our ears. "It's the good stuff, don't waste it by dying on me before the final show."

We pulled the canvas bag open, finding more stale bread, fruits and plenty of jerky there for us. It was more rations than she could afford to lose. Beside them was also a carefully scrawled map in Dora's penmanship and less carefully marked notes by Tess detailing the safest route to the labs.

We swallowed around a lump that formed in our throat.

"Thank you," we said.

"Thank me by being at the temple when we need you," she said, and then, after a brief consideration, "and by kicking in that bitch's perfect fucking teeth for me."

We managed a smile.

"Yes ma'am."

"Go," she ordered, "before I change my mind."

We hopped the short chain link fence with ease. When we looked back just before turning the corner, she was long gone from the window. No raised alarm went out, and no one followed us as we followed the path outlined for us into the depths of New Caramel, eating what we could.

We were right to eat quickly, before our nerves failed us. We were only a few short blocks in before the sweetly acrid stench of rot burned our throat. Our body pushed out a breath halfway pulled to our lungs in a desperate attempt to save us from pulling in more, but it was no use. The next shallow breath was just as bad as the first, and then the next.

We pulled our shirt collar over our mouth and settled for shallow, disgusting pulls of air while death and decomposition wafted from the streets around us.

I was used to the smell of decay, or at least not unfamiliar. For me, it was a hot trashcan in July, ripe and ready to be taken to the curb. It was a dead animal on the side of the road. It was the unfortunate outcome of a sink full of dishes left unwashed for too long. This was something different— an entirely new beast all together.

Insects swam through the sky, ravenous. Excited. The streets of New Caramel had become a haven for scavengers and decomposers alike. With the threat of Jorel's forces still roaming the town no one had risked venturing out to clean the roads of corpses or gore. Much of the street debris had gone into the gutters, and animals had done their part to pull some of the corpses out of sight for a more private meal, but these were not enough to wash away the carnage.

Mingled in with it all was the sickly sweet smell of the blood flowers that now choked the city in their numbers. White vines from *Haliz* had sprouted up, pushing through dirt or stone or concrete anywhere it could find. Thick leaf-like petals of the flowers turned the city indigo and wound along streets, in and through gutters, up the sides of buildings and into windows high above, and everywhere else we looked. The offshoots of *Haliz* drank the city's spilled blood with no remorse or distinction for where it came from.

Haliz hasn't eaten this well in almost two hundred years, Gen thought absently.

I'm sure that's nothing to be concerned about. I added.

Passing the local bakery, I couldn't even remember the glowing aroma of freshly baked bread. I wondered if I had ever smelled them at all. The memory was shoved violently away by the acrid decay around us. Somewhere underneath was a darker, heavier scent. It was defecation, the aftermath of corpses both human and kriest vacating themselves during death. All of it had cooked in the sun, rotted for days and spawned thousands upon thousands of flies, gnats and more.

The stench burned in our minds. It was a memory worse than the horror of the slaughter itself.

We stuck to the shadows of side streets and empty houses. The quiet sank into the rooms of abandoned homes and businesses like a plague. If we'd thought the streets were bad, the homes were worse. Many were only in disarray; furniture overturned, boot and scuff marks on the carpet or floors, even a smear or two of blackened blood in places. In one home further past the center of town we found an arm, green and bloated, with no body attached to its end. Something black and slimy had seeped out of it, destroying the floor and welcoming a hoard of maggots into its sludge. It was too small to be an adult's. Our stomach rolled at the sight, and it was all we could do to keep our breakfast down.

Clues that the dog melds—hellhounds, the humans had taken to calling them—had been by were all over. Claw marks marred doors or corpses when we found them. Piles of shit were all around, a testament to Chelsea's meld of the beast's digestive systems. Bones picked of flesh wore their teeth marks for all to see.

Not wanting to be spotted, we stuck to slipping in and out of windows and using back yards to navigate the suburban section before the edge. We both pushed on in abject silence, taking in the remains of the first night but unwilling to speak on it. To solidify its reality. Most of it did not bear remembering.

Chelsea did this, I thought at last, *she did all of this.*

This isn't your fault, Gen thought back, *you were trying to save your own life when you left her. There was no way you ever could have foreseen what she would do. This is beyond imagination.*

Her cruelty has always been beyond imagination, I answered. *I of all people know that very well.*

And your compassion never wavered.

I knew what he meant. But as the streets gave way to silent dirt walking paths and a familiar shell of a building arose beside the western woods, I couldn't accept his words for the compassionate complement they were.

It's wavering, now.

The labs, as they'd always been, were unassuming. The building itself was about three stories tall, tan brick instead of the traditional town red, with the upper levels housing mostly renovated living quarters. Single pane windows ran the length of each floor, many of them covered up with wood or curtains as the years had gone on. The first floor was the main lab and working space, and the basement had always been storage, officially. I knew it to be her true labs.

At the beginning of the project, a few people with backgrounds in medicine or biology had gathered to live here, to help establish it. Over time, though, the residents dwindled as the projects took off or ran into dead ends. It had been started with the best of intentions; the absence of modernized medicines had left many of us to die in those first crucial years of arrival. Things like insulin, antibiotics, and pain relievers were in short supply and running out fast. Illness or a lack of medication did plenty of us in during the beginning. Attempting to understand the local flora and create substitutions was the task the labs were repurposed for.

Chelsea had been an obvious choice to head the project, with her known accolades in the field, and I had been hand selected by her to be one of her workers. The rest, sadly, was history.

Chelsea's collection of windmills and dwindling solar cells kept the lab in power at all times, separate from the rest of the town.

Every single light in the building was alight. The golden glow against the cloud-darkened morning was like a beacon, and it all seemed to beckon us in.

A chill ran down our spine. Everything was far too quiet. The glow from the window turned sinister in the silence, far from the inviting images of home we both held.

Remember our goals.

Right.

Gen replied.

We get in.

We unmeld.

I distract Chelsea.

I find the source of Haliz she'd been using.

We shut down the labs.

We take care of the good doctor.

"No," I said out loud, turning our chin up to stare the building down. "*I'll* take care of her."

You won't be alone.

I know, I replied, brushing some stray hairs behind our ear. We'd seen ourselves in a mirror for the first time that morning. Long, shaggy blonde curls. Dark gray eyes with honey flecks.

His cheekbones, my delicate jawline. Tawny ears and a tall athletic form. We looked ethereal.

Even apart, we're still together.

I'd like to explore that even further, when this is all over.

I felt our face heat up. *We could have last night.*

When I have sex with you, he practically purred in our mind, *it's not gonna be in some cot in a warzone. It will be in our own bed, with no interruptions. I want to take my time.*

Our face was unbearably warm. "You'll be the death of me, Gen."

"Everyone wants to kill you," He reminded me, "*I* also want to sleep with you."

"What a refreshing change of pace."

"I try."

We're stalling, I thought finally.

Yeah, he thought back, as we set our bag down and began climbing the chain link fence along the perimeter. *But I could spend all day stalling if* that's *what you wanted to talk about.*

You are despicable.

You love me for it.

Our feet dropped on the other side, the boots we'd been given holding our ankle in place well enough to only send a mild amount of pain up our leg.

I love you for a lot of things. I know, he responded, *and helping you murder your ex lover better be one of them.*

It's pretty endearing, I thought absently, trying to keep up the positive internal banter.

With every step towards the side basement doors we took, that got harder and harder to achieve.

The sounds of dogs braying became less muffled as we approached the door, telling us we'd come to the right building.

Simon? He asked.

Yeah?

Be careful.

Our hand hovered over the handle to the top of the stairs, the metal door's lock a numerical keypad Chelsea had kept working by sheer spite alone. My fingers danced over the familiar code, knowing she would never change it. With a magnetic click the door unlocked, and we pulled the handle.

We never got a chance to be careful. The instant the lock came open the door was pushed outwards from the inside, and something long and chittering shot out from the shadows. The stick slammed into our side, and every single nerve in our body lit up in a blinding, incohesive scramble. It was like getting punched in the gut, only ten times worse.

Unwarranted, the meld recoiled from us in force, expelling us from one another with prejudice. We lost control of our muscles, I falling to my knees as Gen stumbled dangerously forward. Unable to do anything, I watched him disappear into the space of the door, the loud bangs of his body rolling down the cement steps registering as the weapon was pulled away.

"Gen!" I tried to scream, but it was barely a breath that escaped me. The door swung in and Chelsea stood to her full height above me, the taser stick she'd modified still threateningly alive in her hand.

"So this is who the dogs heard." she smiled, stepping over my prone form. Ashley Chelsea tilted her head at me, excitement filling her eyes.

"Oh, *Simon*," she said, a look of admonishing reproach on her face, "Did you really think it would be that easy?"

Chapter Forty-Seven

Gen, Chelsea's labs

Everything hurt again

The room was groaning around me. My eyes tried to open, and against a harsh white light they closed again. The groaning, it turned out, was me.

Light filtered through my lids and gave my vision a soft red tint. I tried to turn away from it, a mistake. My whole mind swam like it was going down a drain, and I had to turn on my side to dry heave against the pain. Luckily for me, Simon must have kept the food when we separated, because nothing but bile came up.

Simon.

I could feel his absence. I was fully, utterly myself again. Or at least, whatever constituted as myself these days. My only solace in that fact was that he wasn't here to feel the deep ache rolling through my entire body. Whatever had hit us when we opened the door had left my muscles numb and barely responsive, and I felt like I had fallen down a flight of stairs. Maybe I had.

Simon.

Where was he?

Against the pain in my head I opened my eyes. The light burned, but I was able to squint and adjust slowly. The first thing I learned was that I was on a hard yellowed tile floor. The grout was dirty and stained to the color of rust. I flattened my hand against one, slowly willing my arms to hold my weight and push me up. After a few long seconds of struggling, I managed.

Upright I could see I was in some sort of room lined with cabinets. There was a countertop island between me and the rest of the room, and from my half-prone position on the floor I couldn't see around it. The cabinets were a sage green, and many locks kept them all tightly shut. Around the corner of the island, on the floor, I could see a long chain coiled in a perfect loop. It was pristine, clearly recently washed off, but the puddle of water under it ran russet from whatever had been cleaned away. Each chain was the size of my palm.

I did not like the sight of that.

Trying to move into a sitting position, I heard the groaning again. This time, it wasn't me. My ears shot up at the noise, my entire body freezing in place. It came again, louder. It was a pathetic sound, as far as pained noises went. It was deep, and yet still managed a nasally tone.

Whatever it was, it wasn't a hellhound, at least.

I turned my head, looking for the source. Cautiously, with the slowest movements I could manage, I pulled my knees under me and pulled myself up to lean against the counter, peeking over the top.

The rest of the room also housed the countertop islands. A part of me I had taken from Simon registered that I was in one of the working lab rooms they'd set up in the basement. The lights buzzed overhead, and I could see the space had not been kept in the same careful order Chelsea had once demanded of her labs. Items were strewn about, carelessly left on the floor or other surfaces. Piles of tools, some I recognized, some I did not, were scattered on the island tops on stained towels.

I saw new additions on the walls; hooks had been added to hold up more varying sizes of chains, ropes, and electrical wiring that had been cut and spliced into long loops. One table had a long string of bleached vertebrae arranged in a perfect line. Others had small dishes filled with things I couldn't begin to identify from this distance.

They looked organic.

Chelsea clearly hadn't been using this lab for its intended use in a long time.

The source of the groaning was laid on the far left island, nearly unidentifiable in the state he was in. My heart sank to the bottom of my stomach at the thought that the mess of dried blood could be Simon, but then I saw the ears. A kriest was laid on the table like a bed, curling up on himself like a small child would. His entire body shook, his bloodied hands opening and closing in a nervous and uncoordinated way.

It was hard to see through the bruises, but I would know that long, beakish face anywhere. He had been turned to our temple years ago by his own mother in a last-ditch attempt to find any use for him. After managing to set fire to the kitchens not once but *twice*, and even failing to not drop baskets of bread every single time he was handed one, Mael had told him that perhaps the best way to support the temple was by *not* helping the temple.

It seems Chelsea had found a use for him at last.

"...Jask?" I asked, finding my feet under me to stand against the counter.

His stormy eyes flashed over to me, and I knew I was right.

The groaning turned to mumbling, and I took a careful step around the counter. My legs were starting to feel less watery, but I was concerned with how numb my body still felt. Jask's eyes followed me, and by the time I took my second step he spoke.

"What?" I asked, unable to hear him.

"I can still hear the wind," he chattered, "I can still hear it rolling through the forest. I can still hear the howls, the damned howls..."

It didn't make any sense, but then again Jask had never made sense. Whatever little bit of coherence this man had clung to for his adult life was long gone by now. Chelsea had seen to that.

Unsure what to do with him, I took another step into the room. I had a feeling that getting any closer to him would be a bad idea. The pitiful husk of a man wrapped in what amounted to a tied off sheet set my teeth on edge. He looked every bit a cornered animal.

"Stay here," I said, "I'm going to find a way out."

No sooner had I said that did he sit suddenly upright, scrambling to get his feet under him and moving with alarming speed. My muscles were still working against me, the bear-bitten leg especially so, and I couldn't move out in time. His gangly, sharp form came barreling into me at top speed, throwing us both to the tiles below. I cracked my head against a counter, sharp pain behind my ear making me cry out.

With the speed of a man possessed he grabbed my left, gripping me tightly around the knee and using his other hand to plunge a long wooden stake of some kind deep into my thigh.

"What the fuck?!" I shrieked at him, shoving him away. He pulled the stick out with him, tearing my flesh and letting blood flow freely. I found the counter, pulling myself up. "What the hell is wrong with you?!"

"I am the keeper," he replied nonsensically, and I realized I had to get the *fuck* away from him.

I kicked at his legs with my stabbed one, trying to keep my good one under me. He went crumpling down like a doll and it was all the advantage I needed. Pain spotted my vision.

Willing any part of myself to work I dashed towards the door, trailing fat drops of blood in my wake.

My hand lunged for the handle and found it, pulling down on it desperately.

By the grace of *Haliz*, it was unlocked. I flung it in and staggered into the hallway, looking left and right for somewhere, anywhere to go, but all four doors were closed. I ran to them one by one and grabbed for the handles, only to discover they were all locked. One end of the hall was closed with an imposing metal door, a small light glowing red above it. Locked as well.

The other end turned to the right, leading somewhere else.

Jasks's incoherent shrieking still came from the room, but it didn't leave the room. I wasn't sure he was capable, physically or mentally, of following. I had just begun to turn when I saw the shadow.

From the open end of the hall a light shone, pushing the silhouette of something large and animalistic against the back wall. It came into the turn, stalking towards me.

I was trapped.

Facing the shadow I took a single step back, then another, finding myself instinctively moving away. It wasn't as large as the bear had been, but it was far from small. I could hear its taloned feet click on the hard floor with each step. Breathing, even and heavy echoed in the space.

It turned towards me the same instant my hand grabbed the doorframe to Jasks's room. I realized our mistake in assuming we had seen all Chelsea had to throw at us.

She'd kept the worst creations for herself.

The hellhounds we had seen in New Caramel, and even the bear in the woods, they were all just mockups. Rough drafts. *Practice.* I had come to the labs with one single job; to find the source of Chelsea's *Haliz Fundir* access and ensure it could no longer stay in her, or anyone's hands.

Anticipating this, and in a cruel twist of irony, she'd sent it directly for me.

A singular animal meld—a perfect blend of the very deer I had grown up with and another wild dog— fit into the hallway. It had the height and length of the deer, a young doe by the looks of it, but the thick fur of a canine. Its nose was wide and black, its design somewhere between the two, and when it opened its mouth a deadly row of salivating fangs and black gums greeted me. What had once been cloven hooves split into four sections, each ending in a wicked claw that looked almost welded to its toe. Its legs and thighs were bulked with muscles, and the way it moved was an unimaginable stride somewhere between the grace of a doe and power of the hellhounds outside. The tail was long and held low. The only imperfection in the meld was the ears. One side was canine, the other doe. Both were twitching and turning, gathering sounds together. Listening to me.

I wished I could speak for its eyes. As awful as that blend would have been, there was no way it could have been any worse than what protruded instead.

Somehow, Chelsea had discovered Haliz's penchant for slowly growing into a source of fresh blood, and she'd used this poor creature as a farm. Flourishing in its new host the vines of *Haliz* had grown exponentially. They coiled under its skin, breaking out only to turn back in on itself and slither back underneath its pelt. The back had become a fleshy copy of the main tree's trunk, thick white branches tightening together to give it a kind of organic armor. The vines had grown up the neck and into the head, exploding out of the eyes and turning back and into itself once more.

Dried blood flaked in the fur around where its eyes had been.

I could see chips taken out of the vines from its back, spilling a red mix of sap and blood down its pelt when she'd extracted her amount for the day.

I'd come here for the branch of Haliz she had been given. It had found me.

I took another step into the room. Jask had gone suddenly silent, but I didn't dare turn my head to find out why. At the movement the ears of the deer twitched, turning to hone in on me. I froze. So did it. Then, slowly, it lowered its blind head to the ground and opened its lips, scenting the floor. Scenting the blood I had left behind.

Blind or not, it was not deaf or without a sense of smell. I'd left a dripping trail right back to myself, and from the way its ears went down, it had locked in. Abandoning stealth I lunged into the room, slamming the door behind me and trying to throw the lock in place. Always one step ahead of everyone, Chelsea'd had it removed, and recently.

"It's coming," Jask moaned, pressing himself back into a nearby countertop island. The spear of wood he held had clattered to the floor, abandoned. "*It's coming....*"

No, I thought, pressing myself to the door and holding the handle. *It's already here.*

Chapter Forty-Eight

Simon, Chelsea's Labs

I woke up suffocating. My eyes shot open at once, the feeling of hands holding a rag to my face enough to make me fight back. Chelsea was on top of me, her knees digging into my arms just as she'd done two years before. The hard ground of the lab did my back no favors as I struggled to lift her off. I was far taller than she was, and had nearly fifty pounds on her, but Chelsea had never played fair.

Whatever she had on the rag was pungent. It choked my lungs and coated the back of my throat with what little air I could pull through it. More of her homemade smelling salts. I had suffered this before.

Her hands held firmly down for ten long, agonizing seconds after I woke up. Her face was impassive, as blank as ever. I kicked my legs, I tried to buck my hips to throw her off my arms, but nothing seemed to move her. All the time she stared down at me with dark, empty eyes. I was fighting to keep my food down against the smell, terrified if I threw up while laying on my back I'd aspirate my own vomit. I wasn't sure it would have been any worse than what I already choked on.

Finally, ten horrible, long seconds later, she pulled the rag away and I sucked in gulp after gulp of clear air. Her eyes watched me, setting the rag aside. She did not move off of me.

"Oh, *Simon*," she began, casually pushing a stray lock of sunset red hair behind her ear, "I'm very cross with you."

I choked in another breath, coughing for a second before I could look back up, not understanding her words.

"W-what?"

"You've been nothing but trouble for me, do you know that?" her voice was softly admonishing, but there was no hint of anger there. It was the same tone you'd scold a child with. *You can't help it,* her voice seemed to say, *you don't know any better.* "You've also been running all over the island causing trouble for my friend."

"You don't have any friends." I managed, and at that she shrugged.

"I'd like to think I could," she said, "If I could stand the man."

"Jorel?" I guessed, but it wasn't much of a question.

A small smile came over her face. She looked downright angelic when she did that. It set my whole body on edge. Carefully, she reached down to boop my nose.

"So you do still keep a brain in that pretty little skull of yours," she teased, petting my hair back from my forehead. Her hand was unbearably warm. "For now, at least."

"I'd like to keep it that way."

"We'll see how things go," she allowed, reaching over my head to grab something off of a nearby table.

Up close, I could now see the details of the taser she had hit us with. It was home brewed, a single cabled battery pack stuck on the far end, with two long wire prongs on the other. Wires ran from the battery to the black casing, and she'd created a switch from an old bicycle brake handle. All together it was around two feet long. It was archaic, but functional. She grabbed it now, holding the business end lazily near my face.

"For you and your *pet.*"

Something cold wrapped around my stomach.

"Where is he?"

"Exactly where you wanted him to be," she whispered, something twisting in that impassive smile. "Right where you brought him. *To me.*"

"You can't hurt him," I tried to reason, but it came out as more of a plea. "Jorel needs him back alive, he'll kill you if you hurt him."

She leaned forward, her hand squeezing the trigger of her taser. The end arced in bright blue light, an impossibly loud crackling filling the space between us. Her smile never wavered, but something darkened her eyes.

"There are many definitions to *alive,* Simon. No one knows that better than I."

Chapter Forty-Nine

Gen, Chelsea's Labs

"The wind was whispering, *whispering* down the cliffs," Jask bemoaned, tugging at his patchy ear hair even more. "It was like a warning, I should have listened! I liked the whispers, though, it was so much better than the fucking *dogs!*"

"*Is now the best time?!*"

I snarled at him through teeth gritted in pain. I could barely hear him over the sounds of splintering wood. I also couldn't be bothered to care thanks to the deep wound in my leg. The blood pouring out made the floor slick. My bare feet could barely get a grip on the tiles. My ankle screamed. I wanted to scream.

Jask *would not shut up.*

The door to my back meant nothing to the beast on the other side. Relentlessly, it bodied itself against the wood. Once, twice, and then again. With each barrage the frame and door bent inwards, threatening to give at any second.

"Jask!" I screamed, as if I actually expected him to help, to do anything but stand there uselessly and monologue.

Or stab me again.

"The dogs were always the worst!" He shouted back. "The bloody fucking mutts, always screaming, always braying, like they knew, like they were telling me off, like they could climb into my ears and stab into my—to my fucking brain *we knoooowwwww, we knooooww and you're nexxtttt!"*

Jask had lost his fucking mind. Whether it was at the sight of the monster trying to eat us or the untold tortures he had been through, it didn't matter. I couldn't even bother to care.

He'd stabbed me.

In that mess of a moment, all I could think was how much I resented him. How much I resented his sickly, sallow skin and deepening bruises and pathetic inability to ever see past the end of his thin, lengthy nose. The beast must have backed further from the door this time, because the next barrage sent splinters into my back. I barely registered them, just slid uselessly out from the door in my own blood before pressing my body back in the way again.

"Jask!" I shouted, but when his eyes met mine they were swollen and wild and vacant.

The fur on his ears was matted and patchy, like a deer who'd suffered too many ticks. His fingers reached up to tug on them, to pinch and pull out even more dark fur in his mania.

"Weeks," he moaned, "for weeks I had baited them in the woods, the traps, and set them and captured every single one of the mutts the humans left in our woods, I really..."

He began counting on his fingers, flicking dried blood from where his fingernails had once been with each unhinged motion.

"One by one... by two by two and I muzzled them and dragged them, screaming, *braying*, unrelenting down the woods to the lab, one by one by damned doomed one until the night I was told to come with the whispering wiiiinnndddd..."

He moaned the last word as if in agony, his knees buckling inwards and his eyes rolling back into his skull. With every word he spoke, a bloodied pink spit flew from his lips and ran down his chin. His overgrown, greasy black hair caught in that mix and tugged when his jaw moved.

Another hit came. The door wouldn't hold much longer.

"Jask," I wheezed, pleading, begging. I didn't even know what I was asking for anymore. I was eyeing the sparse lab room for anything that could help. Coming up empty. The chains wouldn't do me any good, the spear of *Haliz's* wood on the floor was *far* too close to Jask for me to try for it without possibly getting stabbed again, and every other cabinet had been meticulously locked or cleaned out and left open to mock us.

Jask suddenly snapped to attention, his dark eyes rolling to focus on me for the first time.

"I've always felt humans were wrong. That they didn't belong. They're a... a scourge on the island, Gen, don't you see?" he didn't wait for my response. "I didn't know what she was doing to the dogs, Gen. I never asked, I didn't need to. It wasn't about me, it was never about me, Gen. It was about doing what's right—"

"Does this feel right to you?!" I motioned to the room wildly, to the lab beyond and the whole damned week I'd had. To my body, damaged and bleeding, to his own mangled form, to the monster behind the door. In response I got a low, pitifully pitched moan of a wail that ended in a choked, useless sob.

"I just wanted my home back, Gen," he wailed, "I just wanted... I just wanted to make them go away. The dogs. The humans. I'm so scared, Gen."

There came a long, gurgling howl from behind the door. My guts lurched at the sound, a deep, primal response. I was so sick of being afraid, of being helpless. It's all we had been for days right up until coming here. We'd run out of the *luxury* of fear.

Now it was anger I found myself holding on to, barricaded in a basement that would soon turn into my grave.

"Shut *up!*" I shouted, louder than I had meant to. Jask cowered back, whimpering and staring at me, finally, in fear.

Silence filled the air. The hall to my back was suddenly still, and it was more terrifying than anything else that night. There were no scrambling claws, no motion, no howling, no snarling, no growling. All I could hear was my own pulse in my ears, the labored breaths that shook my chest, and Jask's broken teeth clacking together in his jaw.

"I saw them, the humans, when they first came." he started again, breaking the silence. "When their *town* appeared, like a smear on the island, like a scourge on the land. They were never meant to be here."

"Something's wrong," I tried to cut in, clenching and unclenching my fists. "Something's wrong, I can't hear it anymore."

"There was a kid," Jask carried on, rocking back and forth on his heels as if I had never spoken. Gone somewhere in his head I had no desire to visit and had seemingly no choice in hearing about.

"He was hiding in the folds of his mother's skirts. I wish I could have gone back and clung to mine. Buildings crawled with the infestation, words I couldn't understand, poles with blue and red and white stripes that turned on their own..." he gasped, shaking his head. "It's all wrong, It's always been wrong, humans are wrong, if they'd just never come..."

All those years ago, he'd been facing the unknown. We all had been. Like too many of us, it had frightened him deeply, facing these strange people and the sudden change to our lives. Jask was still scared, years later. Fear had settled in him that day, and fear had never left. Fear of the unknown, fear for an uncertain future, fear now of the actions he took and the man he had become. Fear of the beast behind the door, one he had helped to create, even if he refused to lay blame on himself.

Had we not been inches from death, I would have made him learn to fear me, as well.

Jask may have been a worthless pawn in the grand scheme of things, just another bit following orders, but his small contribution to this whole endeavor had turned the tides and left hundreds dead. The *dogs*, the stupid wild dogs that had dwindled in numbers for weeks— the mangy beasts the humans had brought who had gone feral in our woods and that no one had seemed to care for or about— he had been ordered to take them and bring them here slowly over time, as to not capture attention to their disappearance. The kriest had never cared for them, anyway. We certainly weren't paying attention to the woods and the dogs who ran amok in them. It was brilliant. It was horrifying. And it was due to Jask's constant follower nature that it had succeeded flawlessly.

And to keep him from his other inevitable nature, the one of never shutting up, he'd been ordered to come here to die. And yet, he couldn't even do that correctly. Because he was still here, and he was still talking.

"I did everything for him. Everything. I followed his orders, I felt his words. It was the first lick of sense I had heard since those humans arrived. He is absolute, he sees things, things I can't even imagine, and I wanted to be a part of it. I wanted to be a part of the change, I wanted to see his words come to life."

"Jask, please stop talking," I tried, straining to hear through the door.

"Things are so beautiful, when he gets what he wants," he said, his voice choking. "I gave him everything..."

Then I heard it. A single, terrifying click against the door. A gentle scrape running down the wood, a hollow, haunting sound.

The meld was still there, just outside, sitting, thinking, doing.... something. Then another, diagonally down. Almost as if— as if it was marking the door with an X.

My body screamed at me, told me to move, to run, to get away from the door, and over the sound of roaring adrenaline in my ears I heard Jask again, screaming through his shattered teeth.

"He *sold* me, Gen! He sold me to her, he sold my body and my soul piece by piece for these *monsters!*"

My instincts screamed at me on my other side now as Jask snatched the stake off the floor, almost falling over in the process.

His eyes shone crazily in the fluorescent light, rimmed with bruises and tears and something completely unhinged.

"She is God!"

He lunged for me at the exact moment the monster hit the door, sending my body flying into the room along with it. We crashed into the island Jask had been leaning against, and all three of us crumpled into the shattered cabinets, splinters of wood and stone flying out in every direction.

The eyeless face of the creature turned to me, its fanged jaw opening to scream a long, braying howl. My death, come at last over the sound of Jask's unhinged screams.

So much for eighty years, I thought, as its mouth came to close around my neck.

Chapter Fifty

Simon, Chelsea's Labs

Chelsea was used to knowing the people around her inside and out. She had a keen way of reading you, trailing those misleading eyes of hers over you like the pages of a book and notating anything she could use against you. She'd had *years* to analyze me, pull me apart, memorize the cogs of my mind and poke the springs of each just to see what it did. She knew what I would say, what I would do, what I *wouldn't* do.

But she'd never learned the extent of what I would do for this man I loved.

No sooner had she finished her thinly veiled threat had I reared back my head and smashed it into her face. Violence, I'd learned, could be instantaneous. I seized that instant to attack, shocking her more than I hurt her. Blood exploded from her previously pristine nose, splattering on my chest. She came off balance, and I used that opportunity to roll to the side, throwing her away from me. Her hand came off the trigger of her taser and it had landed squarely between us.

Chelsea's eyes found mine again. She was *pissed*.

Murder danced behind that glare, or at least a thousand stages before death she would inflict on me. Her nose was freely gushing, and she wiped at it with the back of her hand.

"No," she snarled. I didn't know what she was saying no to, exactly. But the intent was clear.

I was not getting out of this basement alive.

We both saw the taser between us at the same time. She reached for it first. I used the longer reach of my leg to swipe an uncoordinated kick at it, sending it scrabbling along the tile floor. We were in her office, I recognized now, a room most of the way into the large basement where she kept all of her records under lock and key.

Snarling she turned to lunge the way I had kicked it, no doubt aware that without the extra protection of her taser she was physically outmatched. She hated being anything less than the largest threat in a room. Also aware of my disadvantage should she grab that again, and knowing there was no earthly way I would make it out of the room before she could get it, I also lunged for it.

Once again, my longer reach won out. My fingers closed around the makeshift handle while hers reached air, and I threw myself in a messy spin to face her, moving to press the nodes into her side just below her ribs.

I compressed the trigger, heard the taser scream to life, and all in the same second I heard it die.

It was out of juice.

Chelsea's laugh mocked me.

"Oopsie," she sneered, "I must have forgotten to charge it last night!"

Her laugh turned darker, more sinister. She wasn't bothering to mask her true self anymore.

"Good thing there's two more."

I didn't stick around to give her the chance to grab one out of whatever hidey hole she had them in. I was up in less than a second, moving with the speed I'd stolen from Gen for the door. She lunged to her desk, grabbing for something, but I was already out of the room, slamming the door behind me.

The hallway stretched in either direction. One would take me back to the stairs and the outside world, assuming the main door was unlocked. I severely doubted it was. She rarely overlooked things like that.

The other issue with leaving was that I didn't know where Gen was, and I wasn't leaving without him.

I turned to the right, racing down the long hall into the maze-like depths of the lower labs. The lights dimmed the further in I went, conserving energy and giving the space a low blue tone. I didn't know how many of her abominations still suffered in the depths of her labs, or what they might be. Danger closed in around me with each step. If not from her, then from the claws and fangs I knew I would find further in.

I was counting on that.

I'd carried the scars of her abuse inside of me for so long, and now they were carved into my flesh in the shape of teeth and fangs. I would carry those wounds for the rest of my life like a beacon for all to see. Worse than that, they were now on Gen's body as well.

For that, I could never forgive her.

For that, I would not let her survive.

I was barely a hallway down when the main lights shut off, red emergency lights coming on all along each hall. I heard the metallic clicks of door locks tripping all ahead of me. She was cutting off my outlets to hide, keeping me in the main pathway. She was herding me towards something. I had no illusions what would greet me at the end of the wing.

She'd been sending them to kill me for days now.

I tried all the doors I encountered regardless. Locked, locked, locked. I turned to the final hallway, a short stretch with a fire door separating this end and the final few rooms. It was open, the door slightly ajar.

I slowed when I reached it, stepping quietly to the opening and peering in. The space beyond was dark, only illuminated by a single red bulb in the back. It was a small hall with a few empty utility rooms in it, or at least it had been when I'd worked here. Nothing appeared in the emptiness of the hall, but under the doors I could see large shadows move, blocking the red lights coming from within.

Cautiously I slipped through the crack, tightening my grip on the dead taser.

Five doors greeted me. One at the end, and two on either side. Each had a small glass window, and aware I didn't have much time until she arrived I peered in. The first two had metal cages lining the room three high, all empty. The smell that came from them told me they were only recently vacant. The third also held cages, but in them I saw movement, and the low mutterings of many dogs reached my ears. I stepped away, checking the last two.

The one at the end of the hall was also empty, but had clearly housed something large and formidable. From the marks on the wall, I figured it was the bear we'd faced in the eastern woods. Deep gouges were taken from the concrete blocks. Why the door was untouched remained a mystery.

The fifth and last door yielded me the worst find possible. A large, intimidating black shape moved within, nearly blocking the window. All of my senses lit up in fight or flight mode as two large, adjacent eyes peered back at me. This was another meld of Chelsea's, and I recognized it for what it was immediately.

I dropped in a squat, out of sight of those eyes. I could see dark, course fur pressing under the door, and a single, dagger long talon scraped the floor. In a flash of inspiration and out of time, I wiped my hand along that fur, pulling back just as quickly as I had touched it to move far, far away from the door. The unfortunate beast within shifted its weight, pulling its paw back into the darkness.

Please, I thought, *let that be enough.*

Trapped between two monsters, I gripped the dead taser like a bat and turned to face the door.

No sooner had I turned away did the fire door push open, a small, beautifully porcelain hand closing its fingers on the side. It pushed in to reveal Ashley Chelsea, disheveled, coming undone, a sight I had never before seen.

Her hair was a mess. Fraying tufts stuck out at odd angles. Red emergency lights haloed her from behind. Her usually pristine clothes were stained with blood and dirt from the floor.

She paused when she saw me, swaying with what I hoped was a concussion.

A slow, pleased grin spread over her lips, and she straightened up into a poor imitation of her usually cocky demeanor. She didn't know who she was if she wasn't the largest person in the room. Likewise, I didn't know who I was if I wasn't the smallest.

But the blood splattering her blouse and the taser in my hands made it abundantly clear we were both in uncharted waters.

Her lips parted in a wide, cracked grin, her split lip and broken nose both dripping blood down her perfectly sculpted chin. It looked black in the light, like tar.

"Oh *please*, Simon. Is that your plan now?" she motioned weakly to my improvised weapon, clutched in my battered hands like a desperate lifeline. "To bludgeon me like some neanderthal?"

She managed something of a laugh. It was wild and unhinged, dripping with pain and a lack of self-control I had never experienced in her steady cadence. When she spoke again, her eyes lit like wildfires, and her throat let out a nasty, snarling growl.

"You don't have the fucking constitution to get your hands that dirty."

"You're right," I panted, and I hated how much my voice shook. "I don't. But I'm not really myself anymore, am I?"

Her teeth flashed in what I was sure would be another putdown in a long life of condescension, but I never heard it. I was a weak man with a weak stomach. They said you got used to violence, grew conditioned to blood and death if you spend too long wading through it. But I never had, not even through all the horrors of the last few days. Not even facing the woman who'd abused me—who'd taken advantage of me and stepped all over me like a fucking welcome mat, who'd torn my confidence and intelligence to shreds unless she could find a way they benefitted her—could change that.

No matter her crimes, no matter her sins and atrocities, no matter the pain and agony she'd caused, or the hundreds who had died at the teeth and claws of her work, I couldn't stand the thought of hurting her myself.

I was incapable of murder.

No matter how much I needed to, I couldn't kill her with my own hands.

So instead I turned, letting loose a scream of effort, and brought the taser's long shaft above my head down in an arc, putting all of my strength, my rage, my pain and fear and any reserve energy I had left behind into the blow.

It struck home on the door handle next to me, shattering the regular lock and mechanism with a loud metallic *crack*.

Fear was what kept these animals behind these doors. Fear was what had kept me locked away here for so long myself. Chelsea had never needed fancy locks or steel doors to hold anything in. It was her own flawless, horrible existence that kept you in place.

Complacent.

Trapped.

She was more than a person. She was a god, untouchable, infallible, unstoppable.

The scent of her blood, smeared along the door of its cage, was all the bear needed to see her for the mortal she was.

It slammed its shoulder into the door to break the handle the rest of the way and crash into the hall in a skittering, slobbering, agonized mess. She'd clearly kept two of the bears back and put them together.

Two heads on a conjoined neck, six legs and countless teeth turned to her now, goaded by the smell of her blood fresh on its noses.

There would be no mercy for her. Raw, animalistic vengeance stared down the first woman I had ever loved, a monster made from a monster she'd been all along. Because when the door had slammed open it rammed right into me, cracking my body back like a doll into the wall. Stars shot in front of my vision and bright circles of black and red pain blossomed across my skull, whiting out my vision for a moment. With my body hidden behind the door the bear had seen only one target. Razor sharp claws skittered and sliced along the concrete floor as it bodily pushed itself away from the wall and ran for her, clearing the space in a mere second.

I never saw her face, in the end. Never heard her final words. But I did hear her screams. I heard the deep, guttural shrieks torn from her just as surely as her flesh when the melded monster attacked. I heard sounds no human should ever make, and the agonizing crunching of bones and wet tearing of muscle as the monster pulled her apart with the very tenacity she had instilled into it.

I scrambled up weakly, abandoning the bent taser that had fallen from my hand where I landed. It was of no use to me now. The bear pulled her into the hall, then into one of the empty cage rooms I had left open during my search. Her hands, clawing desperately on the ground was the last I saw of Ashley Chelsea. I didn't stick around to see the rest.

Praying for a stroke of luck I bolted for the fire door, launching myself through and pulling it closed in a desperate attempt to stave the monster from doubling back for me next. In the darkness of the hallway, I heard a wet, terrible noise caught somewhere between a shriek and a caterwaul, and then, nothing. Just the muffled sounds of a great beast feeding, of jaws snapping meat in lieu of chewing and of claws ticking the floor as it moved for a better angle into its victim.

My breathing was labored. My whole body shook, and if I'd had time to throw up, I would have. I didn't mean to let a sob escape me but one came, nearly doubling me back over as I tried to right myself. I covered my mouth with one hand as I staggered for the door on the opposite end of the room. Hot tears streamed through my fingers and down my cheeks, trailing dirt and grime with them.

I walked back through the dimly illuminated hallway as my ex-lover's corpse was eaten by a monster she had created, and I couldn't even take in the irony through the sickening horror I now held for myself.

Still, I pushed on, back towards the rooms I hoped Gen may have been left. Time was of the essence, and whatever she had done with him I hoped I wasn't too late to stop it. Quickly I moved away from my past, and my sin, and my newest nightmare.

After today, I wasn't sure I would ever sleep again.

Chapter Fifty-One

Simon, Chelsea's labs

The halls were deathly still. Silence hung through every room I tried, all of it cast in that haunting red light. Nothing moved. No hellhounds, or bears, or people. I was running out of hallways to go down in my desperate search. Talons of fear sunk deeper and deeper into my stomach.

I wanted to call for him, but the thought that there might still be other *things* around kept me mute. I checked the labs, the offices, the storage rooms and the old break room we'd turned into a reading room. Neat stacks of books and cozy chairs mocked me, empty of all signs of disturbance. No Gen. Nothing at all.

I came to the last stretch of halls before the outside stairs. A fire door stood at the far end, ominous and locked. I knew all that lay behind that was a smaller lab and the exit.

I turned into the hall and stepped right into splatters of blood. My heart dropped.

My breath froze in my chest as I traced the blood along the floor from closed door to closed door to, finally, a shattered doorframe and a pile of long wooden splinters. Something had disturbed the blood there, smearing it with large, strange footprints I couldn't even begin to identify.

"Gen?" I wheezed, terrified of what I would find. Silence answered me. I took a step towards the door, then another. *Please let him be okay,* I prayed, *oh please oh please...*

Fingers appeared from the darkness of the room, curling around the broken door frame. They were bloody and indistinguishable. I slowed my steps, pausing in the hall. Something raised the hair on the back of my neck again. I didn't know what I was walking into, and I was unarmed and out of resources. There was a shuffling of weight, and a dark, blood-soaked head appeared.

"Simon?" it asked weakly, and it was all I could do not to cry.

He turned into the hall, bloody and disheveled, but alive. His dark eyes met mine, and tears streamed down his cheeks. For a moment I thought I would fall to my knees in relief, go completely slack and lay down under the weight of murder and relief and days of constant agony.

I live for you, I repeated in my head, racing to him. *Please, keep living for me.*

Chapter Fifty-Two

Gen, Chelsea's Labs

We met just outside the door, exhausted, more collapsing against each other than embracing. When I leaned my cheek against his chest his heart beat loud and fast like a drum, and that was all that mattered. Him, with me again, alive.

I shifted my weight on my good foot and pulled his mouth down to mine, caring less about how it stung my bruising and bloodied lip, or about the pain that shot up my damaged leg.

He kissed back in a similar fashion, desperate for the connection. I didn't care about anything else, only that he was with me again.

We pulled back, each assessing the other. His arms steadied me instinctively when I wobbled, and his eyes widened in panic at my appearance.

"It's not all my blood," I hedged off his question, pushing back my soaked hair from my face.

"What is, then?"

I hop-stepped back just a bit to show him the torn cloth I had used to staunch the bleeding in my leg. He hissed at the sight, seeing how more blood was already soaking through.

"How bad is it?"

I shook my head, swallowing.

"I don't know. Bad. But not enough to kill me."

"I'm starting to get used to that answer," he mused, attempting a smile. It didn't come.

"Can you... can we run on it?"

"I don't know," I answered honestly. "I can barely stand on it. We'll have to see how it closes when we meld. It's... it's deep. Where's Chelsea?"

"Taken care of," he said, and something soft and painful entered his voice. "Back the way I came...there's a few doors between us."

He didn't offer to elaborate. He didn't need to; I would live the memory on my own soon enough. Something in his voice told me it hadn't been a simple task.

"What happened?" He asked me. "Whose blood is this?"

"Come see for yourself," I said, turning back to the room.

Simon looked in cautiously, then supporting my weight we went back into Jask's tomb.

To the mess Jask had become.

Simon stiffened when we turned in the room, those beautiful blue eyes widening in the same bewilderment and awe I had experienced when I had seen. Together we made our way around the door remnants and smashed countertops to the winding white branches that pulsed across the walls, floor and ceiling. They turned a strange pink in the light with dark shadows cast behind them on the wall. In the center of it all was the origin of the mess: Jask and the deer.

The body of the deer and dog meld lay limp on the ground, roots spreading through the flesh and curling in and out of bleeding holes along its tortured form. What had broken through the door and lunged for my throat half an hour before was now reduced to a pile of flesh for the tree's new body to grow. Up from the mess a single trunk the thickness of my arm sprouted diagonally into Jask's shoulder, piercing his torso completely before branching behind him into snaking white vines that had already crept ten feet out along the walls and ceiling.

His left arm was gone from where the beast had taken it in its maw, the unfortunate victim to its first bite instead of my throat. Where a raw, bleeding stump should have been the branch had taken over, screwing itself into the flesh in a similar manner as it had my own arm during my own training. The vines ran from his stump down into the severed, half swallowed arm hanging in disassembled sections, as if the tree was attempting to become a new bone structure and slip the arm chunks up like a sleeve to the remaining limb.

It was trying to heal him, despite piercing him straight through the eye directly to the wall.

Jask had been dead a while now, but his body was too dumb to accept death properly. He hung limply from the branch, but his chest still moved in laborious, pained breaths. Simon's jaw dropped open in abject horror and awe, taking in the scene with fresh eyes. I could only stare on in weariness, tired of the constant barrage of nightmares we had faced, and of my own inability to prevent this from happening.

"...Jask was one of Jorel's followers," I said finally, leaning into Simon's chest. "I guess Jorel gave him to Chelsea to pay for the work he was doing. She'd been torturing him for... I don't know how long. Somehow he got a sliver of Haliz and he stabbed me in the leg when I woke up."

"And the...meld?" he asked, unsure from the body what it had even once been. The vines had overtaken it fully, obscuring most of its mass.

"It was how she grew more of Haliz to work with. Gave it a host to feed from and grow into. She left us in here and sent it to take care of us both."

"Looks like she failed twice today," he mumbled to himself.

"Barely. The meld lunged at us and almost took out my throat, but Jask fell into its teeth instead. It took his arm, drug him over to this side of the room. He finally did something right and stabbed it with the stake, but... well, it rammed forward, impaling him too."

Simon took in a sympathetic hiss of breath.

I'd only lived by sheer dumb luck. Or, perhaps it was better to say I lived by Jasks's terrible luck. Either way he had managed to both kill the meld and himself in a single stroke, leaving me bleeding out on the floor from my leg, but otherwise alive.

"God," he swore softly, and I looked up at him in amusement.

"Funny," I said, "That was his last word, too."

He studied the bodies in the dim light.

".... it's pulling his arm back together," he observed, stepping closer and taking me with him. "It's healing him...or, at least, keeping his body functioning."

"I think it's doing what it's always done," I said, hopping awkwardly to change the weight he had put on my leg. . "...it's melding. Haliz wants a host with a functioning circulatory system to feed on and grow. It looks like there was enough of the tree's will in the shard and vines to create whatever this is."

Simon opened his mouth, then closed it. He looked at me for a long moment, then back to Jask. I watched him reach over to the wall and, with no small amount of effort, snap off a piece of the growing vines.

He stared at the cold wood in his hands, thinking. Finally, he looked back up to me.

"This needs to end."

"Yeah," I said, "it does."

Chapter Fifty-Three

Simon, Leaving Chelsea's Labs

We didn't burn the labs when we left. I knew of a hundred ways to do it, but something held me back. A whisper of intuition that now was not the time. That we would need this place again, assuming we were in any place to return.

Gen hated the idea of leaving the evidence of her melds alive, but I argued with him.

"If there's any way that we can save those animals, we need to find it. There's a chance we can make something good from this."

"If we die, no one will be able to do anything good with anything down here."

"If we die," I reminded him, "It won't be our responsibility anymore."

Gen laughed at that, a bewildered, aching sound. "When did you get so cynical, Simon Holiday?"

"Probably about the time I learned what teeth sound like against my bones," I shrugged.

"Fair enough." He leaned his head on my shoulder. "Sorry I'm getting blood on your clothes."

"I'm used to it."

"I'm not."

"One of us has to stay sane," I reminded him, squeezing his shoulder. "And I don't think it's me anymore."

"You've always been too logical to be sane, love."

I smiled at the pet name.

"Then I guess I'll have to be the one to remind you we need to leave. The day isn't over yet."

"Right." He said. I heard determination in his voice, but also a dark, bitter bite. "Jorel."

"Jorel."

We make it past the fire door easily enough. The very room she'd put Gen and Jask in had another door to the first lab that would lead to the exit. She'd cleverly hidden it behind a shelf to give the illusion the fire door was the only way in or out. An illusion of entrapment.

"I don't know that I have the constitution to meld us together," Gen said wearily as we faced the steps back outside. I gently kissed his temple and took his hand.

"Then allow me," I whispered to him, reaching down into ourselves just as he had done all the times before to pull the meld together. Just another thing I had learned, another part of himself he had given me.

We became one again.

Chapter Fifty-Four

Simon, Melded,
Riverside

Rain greeted us outside, the first dregs of the late-season storm upon us. It less cleaned us off so much as it muddied the mess on our skin and clothes. The trails slowly dampened to mud, but did not become untraversable. It was as if the storm was holding itself at bay just long enough for us to arrive where we were needed the most. Where we didn't want to be.

The walk through the woods was hollow and silent. I lived his experience with Jask. He lived the end of Chelsea's life. The pleasant banter we'd tried to share throughout the morning was gone, and only a deep, pained silence remained. The relief of being whole again waned, and a sharp pain settled into our minds at last.

The sun was lowering further and further to the east, and so was the ability to keep ourselves together after everything we'd been through. Silently we climbed on, pushing through the pain of our scars and the odd way our newest leg injury made us move. It slowed our progress, but it did not stop us. No matter how silently we wished it would.

We found ourselves at the eastern banks of the river once more. It was the same place we had crawled ashore only four days ago, on the rocky beach. The dimming light of dusk cast everything in deep blue hues, and the river reflected the faint tangerine glow of a horizon far away.

With effort we kneeled in the shoreline's pebbles, the stones digging gently into our skin. They crunched almost inaudibly under our weight. The water accepted our hands readily. It was too dark to clearly see the blood washing away from our skin, but we imagined it. Long red ribbons floating endlessly downstream, pulling away the nightmares of that night with each cool lapping swell.

But the nightmare stayed. Silent by the river the screams played in our ears, and in the darkness we saw the flames and blood.

Closing them did nothing. Opening them did nothing. So instead we dug our knees and palms into the water and shook endlessly, feeling our stomach tighten and roll over and over and over again.

We couldn't stay there forever.

I knew. We both knew. But neither of us made to move. Drying blood flaked on our skin, causing tiny itches on our neck and face. We slapped at them wetly, swiping splashes of river water into our already ruined shirt. He whimpered. I sobbed. They both came out together in a choked noise I had never heard. We closed our eyes against the memories it evoked.

The sound of intestines squashed into the ground by the meaty paws of shrieking beasts. A true, low wail of agony, like a siren. The unhinged shrieks of the dying. The sounds of teeth shattering bone, like a cracking tree branch. The final gurgling screams of a woman I once loved.

The roar at the bottom of a river, the wet sound of a spear through flesh, the cheering howls of men lost to blood lust. The braying of dogs, sentenced to a painful, relentless death. The silence of the moments in between.

We opened our mouth. No further sound came out. Just a cracking squeak, like static on a radio. We couldn't breathe, in our out. Our chest grew hot with our sobs that cramped our lungs in place. Finally air came in, in and out and in and out until we were breathing again.

The river lapped our knees until we stood, leaning heavily on our walking stick. The cooing babble of water rolling between rocks found our ears, the sounds of insects in the night. It was so peaceful. So calm. We wanted to lay back down in the waves, stay here forever.

But we didn't stop. We didn't allow ourselves the luxury. Instead we turned our face to the north and began the long ascent back to Del Tor.

Towards our last chance to end a war and return some semblance of safety to the people around *Haliz*. Even if it meant giving up that safety ourselves. Even if it meant countless more would die in that pursuit. Even if we were two of them.

By now, Tess would have launched the smaller distraction team against the Kor in New Caramel, and worked the mass of her actual force along this very river to the tunnelways Gen had provided them. They would come out just below the great bridge, and surprise and lingering sunlight would aid them in gaining access. Take the bridge, take the power. No one in or out without going through Tess. She would take care of the majority of the Kor, crippling his forces to get us a path through or die trying.

The rest was up to us. All we needed to do was get to Jorel. And we knew exactly where he would be.

Chapter Fifty-Five

Jorel, Del Tor

The acolytes had gathered in the halls leading to the central temple in prayer. As Reid, I tried to brush off their unwillingness to conform to my leadership by beginning without me.

These things, I knew, would take time. It was just the one asset I was so short on these days.

They gathered in the halls, kneeling or standing, all holding candles before their chest. Many had brushed their hands with the same spices we used during the summer offerings, a symbolic gesture of them devoting themselves to *Haliz*. I was in my own ceremonial robes, the new ones made for me upon my ascension. None of them had moved to enter the main temple surrounding *Haliz*, and for the life of me I could not figure out why. Perhaps they were waiting for me to arrive at this event they did not tell me about?

I walked between them, heading to the doors. I opened them in, the night and light rain greeted us with the sight of the open walls surrounding *Haliz*.

"Please," I offered, "There is no need to wait out here. I promised the ceremonial times would remain the same under my rule."

Something seemed to shift in the crowd, something unsaid. Finally, a younger girl spoke up.

"We cannot enter," she looked away from me. "Not to-night, nor ever again."

I fought the urge to frown.

"And why is that?"

Marus, the very woman who had spoken in favor of my mother the night I killed her, stepped forward to speak for them all. She was wrapped in the same light ceremonial shawl as many of those who prayed to Haliz tonight, but I also saw she bore a sash of deep red I had never seen before. It had careful writing embroidered in it, and I knew I was staring at the leader of the inner temple resistance against my rule.

Sanra, Reid Mael.

"There is no reid to guide us," Marus said.

Before I could even formulate an answer a different voice rang out from the back of the hall.

"*Reid Jorel!*" It shouted, and the congregation parted to reveal one of my own kor standing there, his chest heaving from running a long distance to find me.

"The humans, they've arrived at the temple, they're attacking our own!"

White noise rang in the back of my head.

"What?" I said, wondering if I didn't hear him right.

"They've reached the main path," he said, "come quickly! They are attacking the grounds!"

How? I thought, incredulously. *How can they do this to me tonight?*

"Go ahead," I ordered, "find Vaga. Tell her to proceed with countermeasures."

I moved to follow just as he ran back the way he came, but someone grabbed my arm. I turned to find Marus gripping me with her aged hands. Her amber eyes looked at me with wild, unchecked emotion.

"You would spill blood on sacred ground?" she de-manded of me, not loosening her grip in the slightest. "Again?"

"*I* would?" I asked, incredulous. "Did you not hear of humans who've raised arms against our home? I am defending it!"

"As they no doubt are defending theirs," she countered. "Word has reached us of what you've done to them. How many have died for your inflated sense of self worth? How many more will die while you call it *protection*?"

"They have brought this conflict to our door!"

"Your mother never would have let this happen."

"My mother would have tucked her tail and hid away like the coward she has always been," I snapped, hardly having the time to humor this. "She would have balked at doing what needed to be done."

"Done for whom?"

"For all of you!" I motioned with my arm to the temple at large. Eyes were upon us, many of the same dressed devotees gathered in the halls and looked through the upper balconies, that same purple sash draped across their chest.

"*Regardless* of your loyalty to my mother, I have done this, all of this, *for you*. For everyone!"

"You claim this is all for our safety, but you have invited war to our doors!"

"Take up your arms," I said patiently, "Or it will be inside our halls, next."

"We will not fight a war for your pride," she hissed, "We will not raise our hands to the helpless humans you have ravaged to save your own face."

"Helpless?" I almost laughed. "They are here with swords, and knives for us all!"

"No," she said, "They are here for *you*."

Vaga's voice shouted my name, and I no longer had time to entertain the whims of an old woman.

"Draw your arms or die, the choice is yours. I choose to fight, as I always have, for us all."

"Only a coward chooses the easiest way," she shouted after me, "Only a coward chooses war!"

Eyes in the dozens watched me head towards the main entrance, and from their collective a single chant arose, mocking me as I left.\

"Sanra, Reid Mael!"

Over and over and over they chanted, their voices raising into a chorus at my back. I felt my blood boil, and my temper begin to overflow, and at that moment I wondered if perhaps opening the main doors and letting the humans *show* them how little they cared for which kriest they killed tonight crossed my mind. It would be a lesson hard learned for those who went against me.

Instead, I reigned myself in and ran for the window where Vaga stood, murder in her eyes.

"They've taken the bridge," she reported. "They're gaining ground across the campus."

"How could they have gotten past the western defenses?" I all but snarled. "Did no one see them?"

"The front liners haven't reported any more dogs loosed from their storage building since yesterday," she answered, "and with the increased patrols in the north we haven't had our forces focusing on that side of the city."

Damn it all, that's what I got for relying on Chelsea in any capacity. Either she had finally double crossed me, or she was dead. For her sake, she better hope it was the latter. I made a mental note to personally burn her building down with her inside of it when this was over. That was not a fight I wanted to take on willingly, at least not yet.

A sense of panic began to creep into the back of my mind. This was all too much, too soon, and too orchestrated. My thoughts raced with all of the strings that were unraveling, and all I would have to do to pull them back after this battle. My melded, stuck together. The temple acolytes, in silent support of those against me. Sol in the north looking for any sign of weakness from me, sure to pounce on this mess of a night. The merchants I had foolishly left alive, hoping to pull their support the diplomatic way.

There was a fundamental lack of understanding from everyone involved. No one *could* understand the threat above us, not like I could. And in their ignorance and fear they had turned against me, dividing us all.

Fine, I thought, *If this is the kind of ruler I needed to be to protect their sorry lives, then so be it.*

"Vaga!" I ordered, turning to my second in command. "Make sure everyone hears these words: those who stand against us stand against the life and safety of this very city. They are all branded traitors and followers of Sol. I want their heads on spikes outside the temple grounds by first light as an example to all who follow his ways. This ends tonight, this ends here!"

"*Sanra, Reid Jorel!*" she cried in unison with the Kor beside her. They both turned to run out, following my orders.

If the kor want blood, I thought, *so be it. I will honor it tomorrow as a tithe to the might of Haliz Fundir.*

Still, something felt off. The humans should have never been able to navigate their way inside like this. Not unless someone had spelled it out to them. Guided their hand.

Gen.

Frustration begets anger, and my own began to rise into the tips of my fingers and boil up my arms. He was so *simple,* so *useless,* how has he been such a consistent and evasive thorn in my side? He was always just one step out of my reach, when he should have been the easiest part of this all. Now it all pivoted on him, and he had sent a damned wild pack of humans here on our sacred homestead to ruin all I worked for.

I was not without one last trick up my sleeve. It was one I only needed to grab.

From the store room we'd set up beside the grand entrance I grabbed a simple spear. It was standard issue for the Kor and nothing like my favored one I had so foolishly left at my home. This would do until I could retrieve it. Boldly and with murder on my mind I strode to the front entrance, pushing open the great doors with both hands, heedless of the battle I was walking into.

If Gen thinks he can survive this night, I thought, setting out for my family estate, *he is wrong.*

This close to the main temple it was my own followers who ran about, darting this way and that for information, weapons, orders. Many of them saluted me or recognized my existence, but I was on a mission. No sooner had I traveled down the main path did I begin to see the human resistance in full.

They had brought spears with the head of Chelsea's dog creations on them and staked them into the ground like a macabre decoration. It seemed to be to make a point more than anything else. To show their strength? To leave a message? All I could do was speculate.

I doubted the humans were capable of the higher capacity thinking needed to engage in mental warfare. Maybe they were just as barbaric as the Kor wanted to believe. After all, it *was* a human who made those monsters to begin with.

They fought with swords, knives, and farming equipment. They wore strange leather armors, if at all, and nothing seemed to match. Their numbers were minimal, maybe less than two hundred if that, and although the response was delayed my own followers were now coming out to cut them down. If this was a game of numbers, it was only a matter of time before every last human was eliminated. I had followers to spare.

What I was surprised to see was the ferocity that the humans fought with.

Their weapons were improvised, but they still got under the reach of my men and around their guards. For every one human that was cut down they were taking two, or three, or sometimes four Kor down with them. The rain was coming down harder now, limiting visibility and turning the grounds into a mixture of blood and rain and silt. The kor fought with experience and valor, but the humans fought for desperate survival.

I saw Vaga engage with a tall man wielding a far longer sword than anyone else there. She used her trusted ax to batter the blade away, but where she overtook him with strength he overtook her with speed, moving too quick for her to get back on the offensive after each deflection and keeping her reactionary. Likewise, he couldn't seem to get an in, always going for a blow only to have it be knocked away.

Seeing my newest soldier enter the fray, I called to them. *"Dimi! Herris!"* I shouted to the towering meld, *"To Vaga!"*

The twins turned their head to me, and then looked over the slain body of the humans at their feet to see where I was directing them. In two long, easy strides they reached Vaga's side, pushing the sword away first with their own hatchet, then the spear they dual wielded. The shift was flawless and left the human ducking away, only to nearly roll into Vaga's next attack.

Masters of two weapons, I marveled, *in only a few hours.*

Secure in the knowledge this would be handled I turned again, slipping past the crowds to the short road to reach my mother's home.

A human, small and male, attempted to reach me, a long knife held like a short sword in his hand. I easily turned on him, thrusting my spear into his stomach and flinging him over me with no effort at all, tossing him back toward the battle. There was no personal vendetta against the boy, or really any original reason why the humans had to die, but now my stomach was filled with a sort of sick satisfaction to see another one ended.

Fucking pests, every last one of them.

The house came up quickly, and I bolted inside. I was foolish to leave my weapons here, so far from the temple, but the thought of an attack on my own turf— by humans, no less— seemed a far off joke until tonight. I found them just where I had left them: my ornate spear stood delicately against the wall of my mother's favorite office, the one I had taken over since her death. Beside it I saw the true reason for this journey, sitting black and ominous beside it.

My last gambit.

No sooner had I tucked it into my sash did a form break from the shadows, lunging for me with the glint of something long and metallic in her hand. I turned on instinct, using the hardened pole of my spear to block the blade, the metal surfaces coming together with a terrible clash of sparks.

A woman with short hair and dangerous eyes faced me down, blood from a fresh cut on her cheek rolling down her face.

"You must be Jorel," she said in clear enough human, flexing her off shoulder.

"To whom do I owe the pleasure?" I asked with no small amount of annoyance.

"Your death, come at last," she sneered. "But my friends call me Tess."

"Presumptuous," I noted, rearing back my head to slam it forward into her nose. It broke with a surprising gush of blood, knocking her back for just a second that I needed. "To assume you'd be either to me."

Tess didn't stay immobile for long. She yelled out a warrior's cry and came lunging for me, knocking me back into the hall. I punched her side, and she raised her blade to bring it down with deadly speed towards my head. Whomever this was, she was no normal human. She was trained, and she knew how to fight. From my reconnaissance, it seemed I had no one less than the leader of the resistance in my house.

How fitting. I needed to blow off some steam, and her death could bring me plenty of renewed clout with the Kor.

We grappled on the floor. She stabbed at my shoulder, and I knocked her off balance with a left hook to her face. Her fingers came down, clawing my jaw and ear in a painful mark.

Furious she had drawn blood on me, I used my full strength to throw her bodily away, standing and moving to hit her with a sideways cut from my spear. She dodged under it, not the least bit slowed down having been thrown, then came up to try and get within my range of attack. I stepped back, narrowly avoiding her blade and pulling the fight into the main living room. She lunged for me again, and it was all I could do to turn away from her speed and let her throw herself into the room behind me. She may be skilled, but I had far more build and muscle on her, and a longer reaching weapon.

No sooner did she turn to face me than I stabbed at her, forcing her to move to the side. A table she hadn't seen in the dark tripped her, and she fell backwards to the floor. I was on top of her in an instant, wrestling for that short blade she clung to so desperately. She struggled. I finally grabbed her hand. She bit my arm, and I pulled back two of her fingers, breaking them instantly. She cried out in rage and pain but loosed her grip on the sword, and I wrestled it away from her.

I kneeled over her, her own blade to her throat, savoring the moment we both knew she was beat.

"No wonder the humans fell," I mused, pressing the blade down, "when their own leader is this *weak*."

"Jorel!"

I looked up to see a silhouette of a kriest standing in the door. His hair was far lighter than any kriest I had ever seen, his clothing stained dark with blood. His pale eyes met mine, and his fingers gripped the door frame.

"Looking for us?"

I may not have recognized the voice, but I would know that cadence anywhere. Sliding the human away from me I threw her sword away and ran for them, knowing if I didn't grab them now they would be too fast for me to keep up. Gen and his human darted from the door, only to lunge for the wall of the adjacent building, scrambling up it with ease. They turned to look down at me, lightning from the storm illuminating them in a wicked white outline.

"This is between you and me, Jorel!" the meld shouted, "You want us? Come and get us!"

Just like that they darted away, faster than they had any right to be. I couldn't help the frustrated shout I let out, abandoning the human leader in my home and racing them on the ground.

There was no purpose in following them on the roof. I knew where they would go.

Back to where this all began.

Chapter Fifty-Six

Gen, Melded, Del Tor

It felt like if we had a plan, it was only half of one. Running at any speed was agony and an uphill battle to keep our ankle and thigh moving properly. We'd abandoned the boots for this final stretch of the run, knowing we wouldn't have time to remove them when we entered the temple.

Is Tess okay? Simon asked, the memory of her pinned beneath Jorel's massive form fresh in our mind.

I think her ego isn't, I answered. *But she'll live to fight another day.*

Do you think she'll try to follow us and kill him?

I think we got too much of a head start.

Down below, the battle raged on. The humans, at least those that were left, were clearly being overwhelmed. More and more kor appeared from between the buildings like insects, swarming the last stand of Simon's kind. Stone was taking on two fighters at once, and we caught sight of him just as his sword sliced through the chest of the female kor—Vaga, we recognized. He kicked her body into the massive Kor wielding a hatchet and spear.

My god, Simon thought, *the twins... he really did it...he really made a meld with no way to undo them.*

What has he done?

Resolve flooded our chest. Even if the humans couldn't win tonight... even if we had asked them to their deaths, we would not let Jorel live past the dawn for his crimes.

Then, with the temple in sight, everything changed.

Far in the distance, from the direction of the bridge, a long cry of a horn came. The battle seemed to pause, turning to the unknown source of the noise. For a long, terrifying second we imagined Sol and his troops come to overtake us all in this, our most chaotic hour. But the horn came again, and again, and we recognized the three note signal.

Dora survived the advance journey, Simon thought in relief, *she made it to the merchant's hall. She reached the people of Torrel.*

The reserves arrived in full, some of them regular city guards and many of them ordinary people. They came with torches that did not go out in the rain, and long spears and blades to assist in the attack. They ran forward from the bridge in droves, swarming any kor they could find and taking them down three to one. With renewed morale a cry ran up from the humans, taking the kor from the other side.

We didn't know what Dora had used to persuade them, or what allies she had found, but over our long talks the night before she had volunteered to go alone and do what she could.

Those in the temple might not raise a hand against the humans, she reasoned, but they wouldn't raise a hand to help them, either. Not on sacred lands.

But the townsfolk had long revered and adored Mael, and they'd long hated the bullying tactics of the Kor. It also wasn't far-fetched to assume that Jorel had made plenty of enemies these last few days with the townsfolk all on his own.

The humans now stood a chance. A kind of relief overtook us both, but it did not slow us down. Aware of Jorel hot on our trail we pushed through the worsening rain to the main temple doors.

Listening to Mael's words from before this all began, we took the main stairs. There was no point in hiding our entrance. We wanted to be seen. We needed the acolytes to view us and know that I was back, and that I may have left them but I wasn't running anymore. Simon was banking on their continued love of Mael and their recognition of me as her true heir to gain us immediate support and spur them to denounce Jorel in full.

More than that, the main stairs were just the fastest way to *Haliz*.

We could hear Jorel enter the building behind us, hear his shouts as he turned and followed our wet trail into the halls.

Many acolytes filled the halls, all in motion, all shocked to see us.

"It's Gen!" a younger boy called out, the very one I had seen trying to light the lanterns the morning of the melding ceremony. "Gen has returned!"

Cries of my name rang through the halls, and everyone parted to let us pass. I heard Mael's name mixed in there, shouts of warning and encouragement, or cheer.

"Sanra, Reid Gen!" another voice called out, someone older and female and unseen in the halls. The cry was taken up, and soon it filled every space we turned.

"Make way!" we cried, "We need to get to *Haliz*!"

Everyone parted, and we dashed forward the last few steps and through the open doors of the temple, back into the rain.

"Close the doors once he's through!" we cried back, "Don't let him out!"

We raced forward, nearly slipping on the slicked wood before reaching the stairs. We didn't descend them so much as slide down the railing, stumbling at the end. The roots of

Haliz Fundir greeted us, slick with nearly an inch of gathered rain water from the downpour.

From this point, we knew, we were truly winging it. We had no weapon, no fighting might or army behind us. It was just us, and him, and *Haliz*.

Our knowledge of the truth was all we had over him. If we stood any chance at all of overtaking him, it was here and now.

Behind us, we heard the great door close. We turned to face the stairs, but there was no need. Jorel leapt the barrier, coming down the full story to the roots beside us. His landing shot water up to our chest, and all too soon he was within arm's length.

"No more running," he said, pulling something long and black and horribly familiar from under his sash.

Our eyes widened, and it was Simon who cried "Jorel don't—!" through our lips, but it was too late.

With impressive might he slammed Chelsea's third taser into our chest and pulled the trigger true.

Chapter Fifty-Seven

Jorel, Del Tor

The weapon kicked back to me. Pain unlike anything I had ever felt spurred my chest like a deer's kick for the split second it took the weapon to die. Electricity, it would seem, did not play kindly with water.

Nor, as I had learned from Chelsea's research, did it with melds.

Gen and Simon the human pulled apart with a wail unlike anything I had ever heard. It was all I could do to remain standing from the weapon's kickback, and for them it was far too much. They both landed away from each other, kneeling over the ground. At last, I could see Gen as he was, and the mess he had become. His arms were full of scars, his hair a muddy, bloodied mop. Whatever he had done to evade me all these days, it had cost him. And now, it meant *nothing*.

"This is how it should have been," I told him, rearing back to kick him with all my might.

"You've wasted countless lives and time running from the inevitable. You. Are. A. Coward!"

He took each kick with a cry of pain. I heard something *crack* beneath my feet. A rib or two must have broken. He rolled away from me at that, from the force of my blow or his own will I wasn't sure.

"You've already failed, Jorel!" the human shouted, and I whipped my head to see him. He was standing now, taking careful steps back, closer to *Haliz's* trunk. "Can't you see that? You never stood a chance from the beginning! Chelsea is dead, your army decimated, and all of the temple and the town are after you. If they don't get to you first, Sol will in time. It's over, Jorel!"

I couldn't help but laugh. Gen got up, scrambling away from me and by attrition, his human. Pain wracked his face, and I could tell every breath was a struggle. Still, the human did not look away from me.

"What do you know?" I asked him, shocked I was even entertaining this.

"More than you," He said sharply. "I know what a scared bully you are, what a bully you've been your entire life. I know you failed your training because you could never see past yourself. I know the truth of Haliz, and the melding, and all you covet and I didn't have to destroy everything around me to get it."

He sneered at me, taunting me, taking another step back toward the tree.

"I've succeeded where you've failed a hundred times, and I wasn't even trying."

I saw this human now, *really* saw him. I saw his sharp wit, the calculating look in his eyes. The way he was clearly trying to distract me, get under my skin. I turned to Gen now, rage overflowing for the first time in a long few years of my life.

"So this is your plan, huh?" I asked him, "Hide behind your pathetic human and refuse to face up to your duty. Has your life truly been so privileged you think a few harsh words will be enough to keep me at bay?!"

I looked at Gen and saw years of wasted breaths. I saw the weakest mind in a room, constantly vying for my mother's attention and turning himself into her to get it. I saw the leech and parasite of the north bleeding my mother's goodwill dry to learn our ways. I saw the face of the very failures the human now threw in my face.

"Maybe you just need a reminder," I thought out loud, my voice turning to a scream without my consent, "of what it's like to *lose everything*!"

I reared back my spear, aimed right dead center for that *fucking human* he coveted so *damn* much, and threw it home with all the strength I had.

Right for his useless heart.

Chapter Fifty-Eight

Gen, Torrel Del Tor

I saw Jorel rear back his arm, illuminated by a flash of lightning from above. The spear glinted deadly and true in his hand.

I saw hatred carved into his face. I knew what he was going to do.

I knew what I had to do.

I'd never run so hard in my entire life. I turned for Simon, desperate to prevent the inevitable. I dug deep into myself, past all the pain and the weariness, the trauma and exhaustion and physical limitations I had. I ran just as Jorel brought his arm forward and loosed the spear.

I saw it all so clearly. The black obsidian blade hurtling for Simon. The look of panic on his face, knowing there was no way he could make it away in time. My own limitations, bound by the distance between us and the speed I could never hope to achieve.

I wouldn't reach him in time. I *couldn't* reach him in time. No matter how fast I was, there was no chance of getting to him to push him out of the way. With each useless, painfully slow step, I was only trying to fight off something inevitable. The spear drew ever closer, aimed right for his chest.

So I didn't run for him.

I lunged between them, throwing my arms out and turning my body to face Jorel. In that single, horrible instant the spear plunged into my chest. I didn't even feel the pain at first, only the choking sensation of the wind being knocked from me. It was like I had been kicked.

Jorel's eyes widened, and for the barest of moments, I saw fear and regret flash there.

Then the ground came rushing up to greet me, and I met it with uncoordinated force.

Chapter Fifty-Nine

Simon, Alone

Gen's body rammed to the ground, his blood spilling from him in messy, gushing pumps from the remainder of his heart. The rest pooled up and spilled around the spearhead, entirely too much too fast. I ran for him, eyes wide, a scream on my lips.

"Gen, no!"

His hand came to his chest, pulling back with all that deep scarlet red. His mouth moved as if to say *ah,* but no sound came out. Instead, more blood began spilling from his lips, just as

Mael's had.

"You useless fool!" Jorel shouted at him, as if it was Gen's fault he was dying. "You *fucking idiot!"*

I never reached him. Jorel got to him first, pulling the spear from his chest. Gen cried out, gurgling from the blood in his lungs. The same spear came sweeping out in anger, the wooden staff taking my feet out from under me. I fell hard into the roots, scraping my chin and hands as I went.

Water splashed into my eyes, and by the time I could blink it away it was too late.

Gen's chest spilled his blood out like a geyser, and he never sat up again. I watched the fight leave him, his muscles going weak, then slack, and finally empty of tension. His face lost all form of expression. His lips, stained with his own blood, parted involuntarily. His eyes, his deep, loving brown eyes that could pull you in from across a room suddenly faded. I watched as they dimmed and emptied into shadows. His pupils dilated, and while they were turned to me I knew they no longer saw. There was no soul behind those eyes, only the glassy haze of death.

My lover, my *love*, the man I had become one with in every way imaginable, was dead.

Gen was gone. He had died.

And with him, so did my heart.

And with him, so did my soul.

Gen...

My world shattered.

I shattered.

A moan escaped me, low and horrible. It was a sound that encompassed all my grief— my deep, endless well of pain and loss, my refusal to believe my eyes and the acceptance of the truth. From that sound, no sound a human should ever make, I learned the true meaning of pain.

A part of me was torn away and hollowed out by the deep gouge of a careless hand.

I couldn't have outran him if I'd tried. Without even giving me time to process, to mourn, Jorel was yanking me upright into the air. It was all I could do to find a grip with my feet on the flooded ground. His fists held me tight, digging into my flesh so hard I could feel my bones strain. Something mad danced behind his eyes, and I recognized it for what it was.

A man pushed over the edge.

"If I can't overtake Gen at the source," he reasoned, squeezing me tighter, his lip snarling with menace, "then I will pull his memories from you, strip by useless bloody fucking strip until there is nothing left of either of you.

"It's not ideal, but it will have to do."

Chapter Sixty

Simon, Melded, Del Tor

Jorel entered the meld like a bull through a gate. His body and mind tried to overtake mine, to overwhelm and crush my will until it bent to his. No protective barrier stood between us, and even if I had been given the chance to pull one up I doubt it would have yielded me any good.

His arm entered at my bicep, the will of Haliz greedily welding our bodies into one. The meld was slower than any of Gen's had been, and the now familiar agony of my flesh rearranging around another's came with it. My bones slid against his and then fused, my tendons snapped and my muscles warped to accommodate his.

The process came in long, excruciating seconds instead of the flash of time Gen had conjured. Our minds linked and blurred, and through it I felt the same pain echoing through him and his sheer determination stomping it down. His thoughts enclosed mine with a calculated precision that overwhelmed my own. I barely held back a scream at the onslaught.

He was going to learn the truth of *Haliz*. There was nothing I could do to stop him from entering that shadow of Gen still within me and pulling that knowledge into himself. The mental might of a man who could justify any action, any means, was never swayed. When the meld would finish I would be a mouse trapped in a snake pit. He would wrap and coil around me from all sides, squeezing my very life from me until he could swallow everything I was and the sum of all my and Gen's shared knowledge.

To that end, I did have one thing over him. And I had no intention of letting him fully meld with me.

In a split second decision I reached around his back with my unmelded arm, hanging on to my last gambit with a death grip.

You want to learn how the meld works? I screamed into our shared mind, our one melded lung pushing the words out of both our mouths.

Let me show you.

The branch of *Haliz* I had retrieved from Chelsea's labs plunged deep into his shoulder, his blood slicking my hand immediately. He howled in fury, attempting to pull the meld closed, but just as Gen had done after the bear attack I held the meld at bay, fighting the will of *Haliz* flowing through my very blood.

I was the one thing that he had overlooked to the bitter, bitter end. To Jorel I had never been anything but an obstacle, an annoying fly keeping Gen away from him. He'd never seen me as a threat. I don't think he'd ever even learned my name. Maybe in the beginning of this all, he would have been right. I would have never been any true threat to him or his goals. I was just a dumb human who knew nothing of the world I had resided in for years. Easily killed, overcome.

But I wasn't just Simon anymore. I would never be *just* Simon again. Gen was dead but he wasn't gone. Not truly. Not fully. Not as long as I survived as the person we had been to-gether. Not as long as I carried a part of him inside of me. It wasn't just a sentiment.

The shard that lived in my arm, passed into my body by I and Gen's many melds, howled at the resistance. The stake in his back pulsed with the beats of our hearts, adding its own nature into the fold. Where the shard in my arm had never been enough to truly consume anything, the collective will of both pushed that desire into a new intensity. Jorel struggled against it, screaming for me to let go, to complete the meld, but I would never meld fully with a man like him. Instead, I let the will of *Haliz* loose and aimed it for his mind.

A ried's training was to navigate a meld and direct Haliz Fundir's desire to combine and consume into a stable energy. This was Jorel's first true meld. He may have had the will-power, the drive, the endless walls of justifications to back himself up to and hold himself firm. He had the blood of hundreds on his hands, he had killed his own mother and sold his followers a genocide to gain a pardon. He had conscripted the help of a monster to create abominations in his name, smeared the very sanctity of existence with their agony and given them a passing grade.

He was ruthless, relentless, and seemingly unstoppable.

But I had practice.

And I no longer had anything left to lose.

Our minds crashed together, and in less than a second I had closed the venn diagram of our thoughts into one large, messy pool. Emotions flooded through the pain. Rage, betrayal, murder and bloodlust. Loneliness, fear, unwanted things he saw as weakness. Remorse for the death of his mother. Regret, not for what he'd done but for what he'd felt he needed to do.

Then I kept going. Each and every bit of him I found I pushed to the side, digging deeper and deeper into his mind. It was like what Gen and I had done through our dreams, but there was no willing participation in this. With a vengeance I did not know myself capable of, I violated the deepest parts of his mind, scraping them into the hungry maw of *Haliz*.

Jorel began to fracture, the shrill screaming from both of our throats becoming higher, and more keening. Pain mixed with a deep rooted fear I had learned so well since the melding ceremony. *The fear of being eaten alive.*

Through our melds I had Gen's memories. I had his experiences. I had years of the training he'd undergone as a Reid and the knowledge enough to understand what Jorel meant to do: to take me in, to overcome me and pull out the last true secrets of the meld from my mind and leave me shattered, broken, and somewhere between dead and worse than dead.

Jorel had undergone such training alongside Gen for a lifetime, but there was one thing he'd never learned. The truth of what it was. Mael had never taught him how to separate the melding safely. It was why he'd needed Gen, why he hadn't tried this on his mother. He knew melding with Mael would only turn the tides against him. She was strong, and practiced, an immovable object to his unstoppable force.

He'd only ever seen Gen as weak. As worthless. As someone he could easily overcome and devour using the very knowledge he needed from his mind. So he'd killed Mael and sought

to overtake Gen to gain his final training.

Gen was not weak. The last four days of his life proved that. He'd evaded capture, kept me alive through our time with monsters and Asterel and my own people alike, he'd run on injuries and grief and desperation all to survive and keep me safe. He'd given up his life for me. Gen was no coward. He was the strongest man I knew.

If he could stop running for me, I could get my hands dirty for him. I could do what needed to be done, no matter the cost.

I guess in that way, Jorel and I were not so different.

I began to not just touch his memories, but experience them. I was not a stranger inside his head, I was a part of it. I felt the warmth of his mother's cooking in his throat. I felt the kind, thoughtful hand of his father ruffling his hair. I remembered the day Gen first arrived in his home, scrambling to safety in the rafters of the very room he had just tried to kill Tess in.

Jorel screamed. He fought. I isolated the part of him that controlled his body and ate that, siphoning it away through the will of *Haliz.* I could feel *Haliz's* shards quivering with excitement to take in such aspects of a prey. I let it push itself on. My hand melded with the stake. My leg pushed further into him. It was a struggle to keep myself from being devoured as well, and if I had tried this a few days before I would have surely lost.

I had Jorel's repeated attempts on our life to thank for all the practice I'd gotten in the meld.

Jorel's thoughts cursed me, they screamed incoherent words, at first in my language and then his own when I took mine away from him.

Damn you, he shouted into the void, *I'll kill you,*
I'll kill you, I'll-

I took away even that part of him, and was left in blissful silence, only the last swirls of his emotions remaining. Chunk by chunk I explored his mind, and I pulled it all away and threw it into the open, happy maw of the meld. Soon the screaming subsided, the pain lessened in his body, and both his mental fortitude and physical capabilities folded under my cruel, careless hands.

*Mom...*the last dregs of Jorel's mind whimpered softly, then there was nothing left as I consumed even that.

Jorel was gone. I peeled the meld back from our bodies, and the hollow husk of his shell fell away from me into a crumpled heap on the ground. His face fell into the few inches of water that pooled around the roots. I watched his auto piloted body suck water in with each breath, jerking and choking slowly. With no dignity or honor the man who had killed two reids and countless numbers of my people drowned in a dirty puddle before the very tree he had coveted.

Rain pelted his stilled corpse and I was left standing, alive and alone.

Hollow.

The bodies of Gen and Jorel lay at my feet.

It was over.

We'd won.

All it had cost me was everything.

Chapter Sixty-One

Simon, Torrel Del Tor

Nothing moved.

Rain fell on his eyelids and lips and trailed into his mouth. There was no reaction, no movement from any of it. His ears lay limp, his head a heavy weight on my legs. *A dead weight.* I kept pushing his hair back, trailing blood along his forehead only for the rain to wash it away. I wanted to be able to see his eyes when they would open and focus on me, the same Gen I'd laid with that morning a lifetime ago, deep and dark and full of life. I wanted to see him blearily awaken, a soft smile on his face.

Are you alright? He'd ask me, completely ignoring everything he'd just gone through. I already knew what I would say to him, staring into those deep, loving eyes.

I am now.

Those eyes would never open again.

I didn't know how long I'd been kneeling in the water, cradling Gen in my lap. Time meant nothing to me anymore. My hands were bleeding from a dozen fresh cuts inside my palm and fingers. The very obsidian tip that had taken his life cut into my flesh, our blood mingling together. I sliced another part of root with it, not caring how much I bled. The cavity of his wound now held countless slivers of the tree, each pushed in one by one by my own hand. My fingers played restlessly with the thick wood chips I held.

The image of Jask's corpse was replaying in my mind again and again. I sliced another part of the tree away.

I pushed the pieces in one after another, slipping them through his cavernous wound and the spaces of his ribs. I poured my blood in as well, hoping that maybe the will of *Haliz* in my own body would carry through to him and do something, anything, to change this.

The water around us ran red.

Two shadows fell over us. Dora's soft voice parted the air.

"No," she breathed, "no, no Gen, oh *Simon...*"

I turned my head to face her. It was the first time I'd looked away from Gen since falling from Jorel's husk and reaching his side.

I live for you.

Dora's hair and clothes were plastered to her skin by the rain. She was finally wearing a new outfit, a dark wrapping that hid her shoulder wound. Tears welled in her eyes, and she covered her mouth with her hand. Beside her, where I expected to see Tess, was an older kriest with solemn eyes. I recognized him from the many memories I now held, Gen and Jorel's and my own.

Hen stood beside me, released from his prison and very well dressed. His bare feet were almost encompassed by the water pooling around the roots. If he minded the blood soaking into his pants, he made no indication of it. He wore an older style of white wrapping with gold sashes, and on the sash I saw an intricate embroidery of the night sky, very similar to the rug Mael had in her home. He looked impossibly put together for someone who had just walked through a battlefield, although there were dark, tired shadows under his eyes. He held his hands together respectfully when he spoke.

"Simon Holiday?"

I didn't know whether the answer to that question was *yes* anymore. So instead, I replied in Kriest with a flat note of recognition.

"Merchant Hen."

He nodded, seeming to read everything in those two words.

"What happened here?"

"What needed to be done." I choked.

Hen didn't have anything to say at that. Something akin to understanding washed over his face. Dora, however, looked stricken, like she might be ill. She followed my eyes to where Jorel lay, crumpled in a heap like laundry. I hadn't bothered to move him from where he'd fallen. I couldn't stand the thought of ever touching him again.

Looking at him brought fresh waves of pain, and anger, and sickness for what he did to Gen. Worse than even that, it brought sympathy and understanding for a man who'd only wanted better than the empty, fatherless world his mother had left him in.

I wanted to claw his memories out through my eyes.

"I'm sorry I couldn't bring them sooner," Dora said, guilt wracking her voice. She was openly crying now, stepping forward to reach out for me. "I'm sorry we couldn't—that we didn't get here in time."

"He chose this," I whispered, looking back at Gen's fallen form. I'd been playing with another sliver of root in my fingers, and in the absence of any reaction from the other shards I pushed this one into his chest cavity as well, slipping it between his ribs. Dora sucked in a breath, her grief turning to horror. Hen didn't react.

"Simon, don't." she stepped forward again, reaching to take my hand. "Simon—"

I wasn't looking up, but I heard her stop in her tracks. Hen must have put his arm out.

"Let him." he said.

She didn't move again.

"Simon," he addressed me, "there are quite a few things we need to discuss."

I watched the chip I had just added. It did nothing. I turned to face him again.

"No, there's not." I couldn't draw up any ill will to poison my words. They all came out flat, clipped, to the point. "I have no business with you, merchant."

"No," he said sadly, looking past me to Gen for just a moment. "But I do with you."

"Do what you want." I said, "Cut me to pieces and sell the parts. I don't care anymore. I don't have anything else to offer."

I have nothing to live for.

"This is only the beginning," said the merchant, ignoring my words. "*Haliz* has consumed too much too quickly. Jorel has upset the balance too far. The temple *needs* a Reid, now more than ever."

"Gen is dead."

My words hung in silence between us. It was the truth, but it hit home with the finesse of a hammer. Gen was gone. There was no one left to honor *Haliz*, or the traditions of the temple, or protect the people with small but necessary lies and a heart of gold. There was no one to scale the walls or sneak bread from the baskets, no one to read texts in the library or light up a room with a smile.

Heedless of the blood pooling around us, Hen knelt at our sides. His eyes met mine. That gaze was soft, but very deep. Just as Gen had seen in Mael's so many times before, I now saw the truth in his face. I knew he would not lie to me. Evenly, he spoke.

"*You* aren't."

I wished I was.

Gen's blood rose along Hen's outfit like ink blossoming over a paper, pulled up by the rain that already drenched him. He paid it no mind. His hand came over to touch my shoulder. It was a solid touch, rooted in reality and coming from a patient sort of kindness I had never experienced before. Dora stood behind him, trying desperately to hold it together.

"Simon," he said, "there is only one person left who knows the ways of Haliz, the will of Mael's work and the truth of this island. One person who understands what is at stake, and who has the memories and knowledge of a lifetime training for the role."

"It sounds like you know plenty."

"I know enough to know I know nothing," he answered, "and enough to see you're already thinking it through."

I was. The part of me that never stopped analyzing anything had already begun to move. I thought of Mael's legacy, and the chances to ensure New Caramel got the support they needed to rebuild and move forward. I knew no one else would care for the humans and the temple at the same time. I also understood that while no one would want me there, there was no denying that I was the only person for the job.

The threat of Sol had not disappeared just because Jorel had fallen. He would still be lurking in the shadows, watching, waiting for a sign of weakness to start this madness all over again. There was nothing to hold him back anymore, and no one to stop *Haliz* from growing too large to control.

"*Stop him,*" Mael had pleaded to us in a dream, "*or* Haliz *will consume us all.*"

For generations that had been the job of the reid. Now, I was the last.

"You don't have to do this," Dora finally spoke, sympathy in her expression. "You've done enough— given enough— Simon, it will be okay."

I closed my eyes. The sound of rain fielded my thoughts. The weight of Gen grounded me. *No,* I wanted to argue, *nothing will ever be alright ever again.*

I have nothing left.

Slowly, I opened my eyes. Decided.

"I will be anything Del Tor needs," I whispered, turning back to face my dead lover. I caressed his cheek, smearing more blood across his skin. To his slack form and unresponsive touch I said "Who else am I without him?"

Finally, agonizingly, Gen's chest rose and fell. That one breath was painfully shallow, and another did not come for minutes after. Blood began to flow from his mouth with each short, labored push of his lungs. Hen stayed kneeling beside me for those long minutes, letting me fall apart in silence. Dora said nothing.

"I know what you are hoping to accomplish," the merchant said, keeping his voice low and soft. "Even if *Haliz* can pull his body back to life, even if there is some part of him still remaining, do not hold on to the illusion he will return. He won't come through this as himself, if at all."

I looked at my lover, hollow and lost. I looked at myself, reflected in the water pooled around the roots of *Haliz*, much the same.

"I didn't."

Hen said nothing. He turned to Dora, touched her arm gently.

"Go to the others, tell them the news. A new reid rises tonight."

Gen's chest took in another shallow, wet breath.

Dora's eyes met mine again, struggling to find something, anything to say. She bowed her head, tears falling freely down her cheeks. Her breath came in a tremble.

"*Sanra, Reid Simon.*"

To be continued in Merged
https://linktr.ee/AuthorJennieElaine